New) WITHDRAWN

Y Lew Large Print
Lewis, C. S. 1898-1963.
The voyage of the Dawn
Treader

JAN 2011

THE VOYAGE
of the
DAWN TREADER

Also by C. S. Lewis
in Large Print:

The Magician's Nephew
The Lion, the Witch and the Wardrobe
The Horse and His Boy
Prince Caspian
Out of the Silent Planet
Till We Have Faces

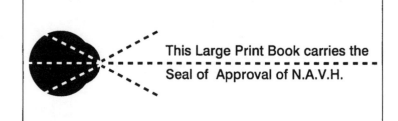

This Large Print Book carries the
Seal of Approval of N.A.V.H.

THE CHRONICLES *of* NARNIA

(BOOK FIVE)

C. S. LEWIS

THE VOYAGE of the *DAWN TREADER*

Illustrated by Pauline Baynes

Thorndike Press • Thorndike, Maine

Published in 2000 by arrangement with HarperCollins Publishers, Inc.

Thorndike Press Large Print Young Adult Series.

The tree indicium is a trademark of Thorndike Press.

The text of this Large Print edition is unabridged.
Other aspects of the book may vary from the original edition.

Set in 16 pt. Plantin by Christina S. Huff.

Printed in the United States on permanent paper.

Library of Congress Cataloging-in-Publication Data

Lewis, C. S. (Clive Staples), 1898–1963.
    The voyage of the Dawn Treader / C.S. Lewis ; illustrated by
    Pauline Baynes.
      p. cm.
    Originally published: New York : Macmillan, 1952. (Chronicles
of Narnia ; bk. 5)
    Summary: Lucy and Edmund, accompanied by their peevish
    cousin Eustace, sail to the land of Narnia where Eustace is
    temporarily transformed into a green dragon because of his
selfish behavior and skepticism.
    ISBN 0-7862-2235-2 (lg. print : hc : alk. paper)
  1. Large type books. [1.Fantasy. 2. Large type books.]
  I. Baynes, Pauline, ill. II. Title.
  PZ7.L58474 Vo   2001
  [Fic]—dc 21   99-057457

TO GEOFFREY BARFIELD

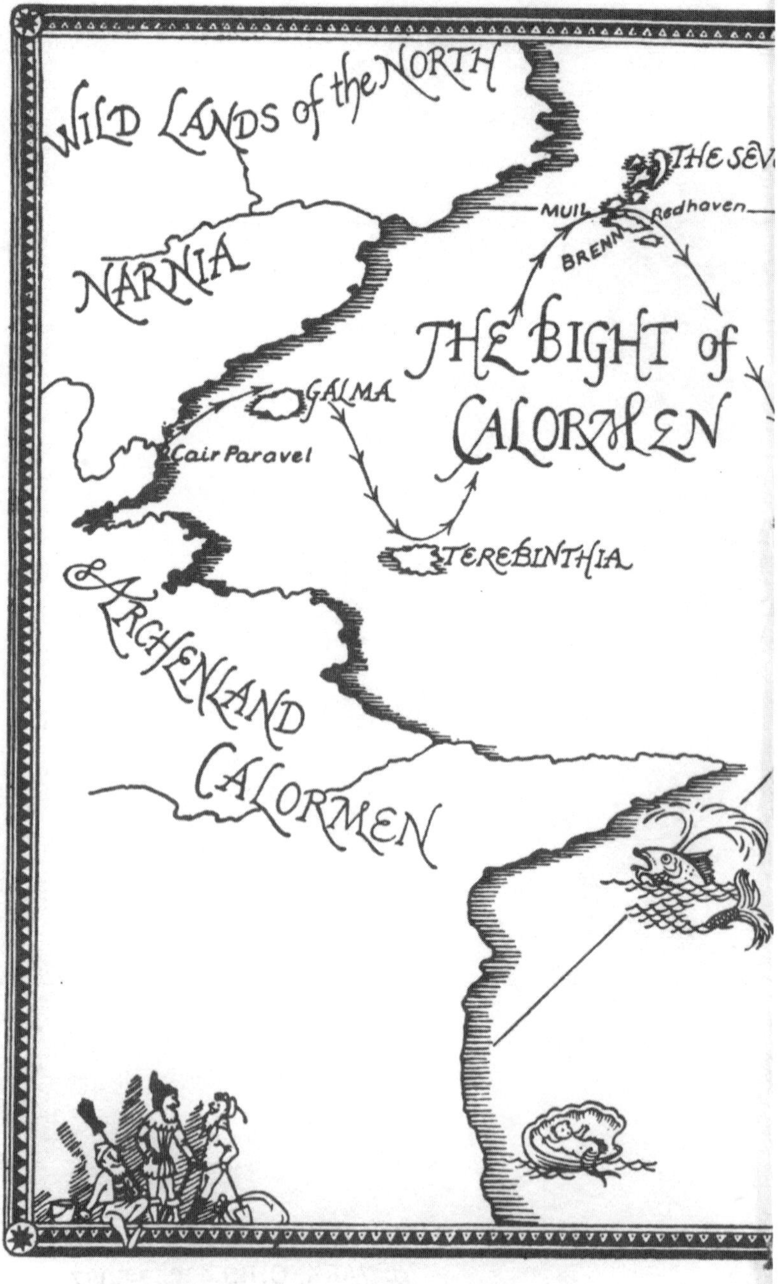

WILD LANDS of the NORTH

NARNIA

THE SEV

MUIL   Redhaven

BRENN

THE BIGHT of
CALORMEN

GALMA

Cair Paravel

TEREBINTHIA

ARCHENLAND
CALORMEN

KES

The first part of the VOYAGE

About here they joined the ship

FELIMATH THE LONE ISLANDS

DOORN CADRA

THE GREAT EASTERN OCEAN

CONTENTS

ONE
The Picture in the Bedroom 11

TWO
On Board the Dawn Treader 29

THREE
The Lone Islands 48

FOUR
What Caspian Did There 64

FIVE
The Storm and What Came of It 80

SIX
The Adventures of Eustace 97

SEVEN
How the Adventure Ended 115

EIGHT
Two Narrow Escapes 131

NINE
The Island of the Voices 149

TEN
The Magician's Book 165

ELEVEN
The Dufflepuds Made Happy   182

TWELVE
The Dark Island   198

THIRTEEN
The Three Sleepers   213

FOURTEEN
The Beginning of the End of the World   228

FIFTEEN
The Wonders of the Last Sea   243

SIXTEEN
The Very End of the World   259

ONE

THE PICTURE

IN THE BEDROOM

There was a boy called Eustace Clarence Scrubb, and he almost deserved it. His parents called him Eustace Clarence and masters called him Scrubb. I can't tell you how his friends spoke to him, for he had none. He didn't call his Father and Mother "Father" and "Mother," but Harold and Alberta. They were very up-to-date and advanced people. They were vegetarians, nonsmokers and teetotalers and wore a special kind of underclothes. In their house there was very little furniture and very few clothes on beds and the windows were always open.

Eustace Clarence liked animals, especially beetles, if they were dead and pinned on a card. He liked books if they were books of information and had pictures of grain elevators or of fat foreign children doing exercises in model schools.

Eustace Clarence disliked his cousins the four Pevensies, Peter, Susan, Edmund and

11

Lucy. But he was quite glad when he heard that Edmund and Lucy were coming to stay. For deep down inside him he liked bossing and bullying; and, though he was a puny little person who couldn't have stood up even to Lucy, let alone Edmund, in a fight, he knew that there are dozens of ways to give people a bad time if you are in your own home and they are only visitors.

Edmund and Lucy did not at all want to come and stay with Uncle Harold and Aunt Alberta. But it really couldn't be helped. Father had got a job lecturing in America for sixteen weeks that summer, and Mother was to go with him because she hadn't had a real holiday for ten years. Peter was working very hard for an exam and he was to spend the holidays being coached by old Professor Kirke in whose house these four children had had wonderful adventures long ago in the war years. If he had still been in that house he would have had them all to stay. But he had somehow become poor since the old days and was living in a small cottage with only one bedroom to spare. It would have cost too much money to take the other three all to America, and Susan had gone.

Grown-ups thought her the pretty one of the family and she was no good at school work (though otherwise very old for her age) and Mother said she "would get far more out of a trip to America than the youngsters." Edmund and Lucy tried not to grudge Susan her luck, but it was dreadful having to spend the summer holidays at their Aunt's. "But it's far worse for me," said Edmund, "because you'll at least have a room of your own and I shall have to share a bedroom with that record stinker, Eustace."

The story begins on an afternoon when Edmund and Lucy were stealing a few precious minutes alone together. And of course they were talking about Narnia, which was the name of their own private and secret country. Most of us, I suppose, have a secret country but for most of us it is only an imaginary country. Edmund and Lucy were luckier than other people in that respect. Their secret country was real. They had already visited it twice; not in a game or a dream but in reality. They had got there of course by Magic, which is the only way of getting to Narnia. And a promise, or very nearly a promise, had been made them in Narnia itself that they would some day get back. You may imagine that they talked about it a good deal, when they got the chance.

They were in Lucy's room, sitting on the edge of her bed and looking at a picture on the opposite wall. It was the only picture in the house that they liked. Aunt Alberta didn't like it at all (that was why it was put away in a little back room upstairs), but she couldn't get rid of it because it had been a wedding present from someone she did not want to offend.

It was a picture of a ship — a ship sailing straight toward you. Her prow was gilded and shaped like the head of a dragon with wide-open mouth. She had only one mast and one large, square sail which was a rich purple. The sides of the ship — what you could see of them where the gilded wings of the dragon ended — were green. She had just run up to the top of one glorious blue wave, and the nearer slope of that wave came down toward you, with streaks and bubbles on it. She was obviously running

14

fast before a gay wind, listing over a little on her port side. (By the way, if you are going to read this story at all, and if you don't know already, you had better get it into your head that the left of a ship when you are looking ahead, is *port,* and the right is *starboard.*) All the sunlight fell on her from that side, and the water on that side was full of greens and purples. On the other, it was darker blue from the shadow of the ship.

"The question is," said Edmund, "whether it doesn't make things worse, *looking* at a Narnian ship when you can't get there."

"Even looking is better than nothing," said Lucy. "And she is such a very Narnian ship."

"Still playing your old game?" said Eustace Clarence, who had been listening outside the door and now came grinning into the room. Last year, when he had been staying with the Pevensies, he had managed to hear them all talking of Narnia and he loved teasing them about it. He thought of course that they were making it all up; and as he was far too stupid to make anything up himself, he did not approve of that.

"You're not wanted here," said Edmund curtly.

"I'm trying to think of a limerick," said Eustace. "Something like this:

"Some kids who played games about
    Narnia
Got gradually balmier and balmier —"

"Well *Narnia* and *balmier* don't rhyme, to begin with," said Lucy.

"It's an assonance," said Eustace.

"Don't ask him what an assy-thingummy is," said Edmund. "He's only longing to be asked. Say nothing and perhaps he'll go away."

Most boys, on meeting a reception like this, would either have cleared out or flared up. Eustace did neither. He just hung about grinning, and presently began talking again.

"Do you like that picture?" he asked.

"For heaven's sake don't let him get started about Art and all that," said Edmund hurriedly, but Lucy, who was very truthful, had already said, "Yes, I do. I like it very much."

"It's a rotten picture," said Eustace.

"You won't see it if you step outside," said Edmund.

"Why do you like it?" said Eustace to Lucy.

"Well, for one thing," said Lucy, "I like it because the ship looks as if it was really moving. And the water looks as if it was really wet. And the waves look as if they were

16

really going up and down."

Of course Eustace knew lots of answers to this, but he didn't say anything. The reason was that at that very moment he looked at the waves and saw that they did look very much indeed as if they were going up and down. He had only once been in a ship (and then only as far as the Isle of Wight) and had been horribly seasick. The look of the waves in the picture made him feel sick again. He turned rather green and tried another look. And then all three children were staring with open mouths.

What they were seeing may be hard to believe when you read it in print, but it was almost as hard to believe when you saw it happening. The things in the picture were moving. It didn't look at all like a cinema either; the colors were too real and clean and out-of-doors for that. Down went the prow of the ship into the wave and up went a great shock of spray. And then up went the wave behind her, and her stern and her deck became visible for the first time, and then disappeared as the next wave came to meet her and her bows went up again. At the same moment an exercise book which had been lying beside Edmund on the bed flapped, rose and sailed through the air to the wall behind him, and Lucy felt all her hair whipping round her face as it does on a windy day. And this was a windy day; but the wind was blowing out of the picture toward them. And suddenly with the wind came the noises — the swishing of waves and the slap of water against the ship's sides and the creaking and the over-all high steady roar of air and water. But it was the smell, the wild, briny smell, which really convinced Lucy that she was not dreaming.

"Stop it," came Eustace's voice, squeaky with fright and bad temper. "It's some silly trick you two are playing. Stop it. I'll tell Alberta — Ow!"

The other two were much more accustomed to adventures, but, just exactly as Eustace Clarence said "Ow," they both said "Ow" too. The reason was that a great cold, salt splash had broken right out of the frame and they were breathless from the smack of it, besides being wet through.

"I'll smash the rotten thing," cried Eustace; and then several things happened at the same time. Eustace rushed toward the picture. Edmund, who knew something about magic, sprang after him, warning him to look out and not to be a fool. Lucy grabbed at him from the other side and was dragged forward. And by this time either they had grown much smaller or the picture

had grown bigger. Eustace jumped to try to pull it off the wall and found himself standing on the frame; in front of him was not glass but real sea, and wind and waves rushing up to the frame as they might to a rock. He lost his head and clutched at the other two who had jumped up beside him. There was a second of struggling and shouting, and just as they thought they had got their balance a great blue roller surged up round them, swept them off their feet, and drew them down into the sea. Eustace's despairing cry suddenly ended as the water got into his mouth.

Lucy thanked her stars that she had worked hard at her swimming last summer term. It is true that she would have got on much better if she had used a slower stroke, and also that the water felt a great deal colder than it had looked while it was only a picture. Still, she kept her head and kicked her shoes off, as everyone ought to do who falls into deep water in their clothes. She even kept her mouth shut and her eyes open. They were still quite near the ship; she saw its green side towering high above them, and people looking at her from the deck. Then, as one might have expected, Eustace clutched at her in a panic and down they both went.

When they came up again she saw a white figure diving off the ship's side. Edmund was close beside her now, treading water, and had caught the arms of the howling Eustace. Then someone else, whose face was vaguely familiar, slipped an arm under her from the other side. There was a lot of shouting going on from the ship, heads crowding together above the bulwarks, ropes being thrown. Edmund and the stranger were fastening ropes round her. After that followed what seemed a very long delay during which her face got blue and her teeth began chattering. In reality the delay was not very long; they were waiting till the moment when she could be got on board the ship without being dashed against its side. Even with all their best endeavors she had a bruised knee when she finally stood, dripping and shivering, on the deck. After her Edmund was heaved up, and then the miserable Eustace. Last of all came the stranger — a golden-headed boy some years older than herself.

"Ca— Ca— Caspian!" gasped Lucy as soon as she had breath enough. For Caspian it was; Caspian, the boy king of Narnia whom they had helped to set on the throne during their last visit. Immediately Edmund recognized him too. All three shook hands and clapped one another on the back with great delight.

"But who is your friend?" said Caspian almost at once, turning to Eustace with his cheerful smile. But Eustace was crying much harder than any boy of his age has a right to cry when nothing worse than a wetting has happened to him, and would only yell out, "Let me go. Let me go back. I don't *like* it."

"Let you go?" said Caspian. "But where?"

Eustace rushed to the ship's side, as if he expected to see the picture frame hanging above the sea, and perhaps a glimpse of Lucy's bedroom. What he saw was blue waves flecked with foam, and paler blue sky, both spreading without a break to the horizon. Perhaps we can hardly blame him if his heart sank. He was promptly sick.

"Hey! Rynelf," said Caspian to one of the sailors. "Bring spiced wine for their Majesties. You"ll need something to warm you after that dip." He called Edmund and Lucy their Majesties because they and Peter and Susan had all been Kings and Queens of Narnia long before his time. Narnian time flows differently from ours. If you spent a hundred years in Narnia, you would still come back to our world at the very same hour of the very same day on which you left. And then, if you went back to Narnia after spending a week here, you might find that a thousand Narnian years had passed, or only a day, or no time at all. You never know till you get there. Consequently, when the Pevensie children had returned to Narnia last time for their second visit, it was (for the Narnians) as if King Arthur came back to Britain, as some people say he will. And I say the sooner the better.

Rynelf returned with the spiced wine steaming in a flagon and four silver cups. It was just what one wanted, and as Lucy and Edmund sipped it they could feel the warmth going right down to their toes. But Eustace made faces and spluttered and spat it out and was sick again and began to cry again and asked if they hadn't any Plumptree's Vitaminized Nerve Food and could it be made with distilled water and anyway he insisted on being put ashore at the next station.

"This is a merry shipmate you've brought us, Brother," whispered Caspian to Edmund with a chuckle; but before he could say anything more Eustace burst out again.

"Oh! Ugh! What on earth's *that!* Take it away, the horrid thing."

He really had some excuse this time for feeling a little surprised. Something very curious indeed had come out of the cabin in the poop and was slowly approaching them. You might call it — and indeed it was — a Mouse. But then it was a Mouse on its hind legs and stood about two feet high. A thin band of gold passed round its head under one ear and over the other and in this was stuck a long crimson feather. (As the Mouse's fur was very dark, almost black, the effect was bold and striking.) Its left paw rested on the hilt of a sword very nearly as long as its tail. Its balance, as it paced gravely along the swaying deck, was perfect, and its manners courtly. Lucy and Edmund recognized it at once — Reepicheep, the most valiant of all the Talking Beasts of

Narnia, and the Chief Mouse. It had won undying glory in the second Battle of Beruna. Lucy longed, as she had always done, to take Reepicheep up in her arms and cuddle him. But this, as she well knew,

was a pleasure she could never have: it would have offended him deeply. Instead, she went down on one knee to talk to him.

Reepicheep put forward his left leg, drew back his right, bowed, kissed her hand, straightened himself, twirled his whiskers, and said in his shrill, piping voice:

"My humble duty to your Majesty. And to King Edmund, too." (Here he bowed again.) "Nothing except your Majesties' presence was lacking to this glorious venture."

"Ugh, take it away," wailed Eustace. "I hate mice. And I never could bear performing animals. They're silly and vulgar and — and sentimental."

"Am I to understand," said Reepicheep to Lucy after a long stare at Eustace, "that this singularly discourteous person is under your Majesty's protection? Because, if not —"

At this moment Lucy and Edmund both sneezed.

"What a fool I am to keep you all standing here in your wet things," said Caspian. "Come on below and get changed. I'll give you my cabin of course, Lucy, but I'm afraid we have no women's clothes on board. You'll have to make do with some of mine. Lead the way, Reepicheep, like a good fellow."

"To the convenience of a lady," said Reepicheep, "even a question of honor must give way — at least for the moment —" and here he looked very hard at Eustace. But Caspian hustled them on and in a few minutes Lucy found herself passing through the door into the stern cabin. She fell in love with it at once — the three square windows that looked out on the blue, swirling water astern, the low cushioned benches round three sides of the table, the swinging silver lamp overhead (Dwarfs' work, she knew at once by its exquisite delicacy) and the flat gold image of Aslan the Lion on the forward wall above the door. All this she took in a flash, for Caspian immediately opened a door on the starboard side, and said, "This'll be your room, Lucy. I'll just get some dry things for myself" — he was rummaging in one of the lockers while he spoke — "and then leave you to change. If you'll fling your wet things outside the door I'll get them taken to the galley to be dried."

Lucy found herself as much at home as if

she had been in Caspian's cabin for weeks, and the motion of the ship did not worry her, for in the old days when she had been a queen in Narnia she had done a good deal of voyaging. The cabin was very tiny but bright with painted panels (all birds and beasts and crimson dragons and vines) and spotlessly clean. Caspian's clothes were too big for her, but she could manage. His shoes, sandals and seaboots were hopelessly big but she did not mind going barefoot on board ship. When she had finished dressing she looked out of her window at the water rushing past and took a long deep breath. She felt quite sure they were in for a lovely time.

TWO

ON BOARD

THE DAWN TREADER

"Ah, there you are, Lucy," said Caspian. "We were just waiting for you. This is my captain, the Lord Drinian."

A dark-haired man went down on one knee and kissed her hand. The only others present were Reepicheep and Edmund.

"Where is Eustace?" asked Lucy.

"In bed," said Edmund, "and I don't think we can do anything for him. It only makes him worse if you try to be nice to him."

"Meanwhile," said Caspian, "we want to talk."

"By Jove, we do," said Edmund. "And first, about time. It's a year ago by our time since we left you just before your coronation. How long has it been in Narnia?"

"Exactly three years," said Caspian.

"All going well?" asked Edmund.

"You don't suppose I'd have left my kingdom and put to sea unless all was well,"

29

answered the King. "It couldn't be better. There's no trouble at all now between Telmarines, Dwarfs, Talking Beasts, Fauns and the rest. And we gave those troublesome giants on the frontier such a good beating last summer that they pay us tribute now. And I had an excellent person to leave as Regent while I'm away — Trumpkin, the Dwarf. You remember him?"

"Dear Trumpkin," said Lucy, "of course I do. You couldn't have made a better choice."

"Loyal as a badger, Ma'am, and valiant as — as a Mouse," said Drinian. He had been going to say "as a lion" but had noticed Reepicheep's eyes fixed on him.

"And where are we heading for?" asked Edmund.

"Well," said Caspian, "that's rather a long story. Perhaps you remember that when I was a child my usurping uncle Miraz got rid of seven friends of my father's (who might have taken my part) by sending them off to explore the unknown Eastern Seas beyond."

"Yes," said Lucy, "and none of them ever came back."

"Right. Well, on my coronation day, with Aslan's approval, I swore an oath that, if once I established peace in Narnia, I would sail east myself for a year and a day to find my father's friends or to learn of their deaths and avenge them if I could. These were their names: the Lord Revilian, the Lord Bern, the Lord Argoz, the Lord Mavramorn, the Lord Octesian, the Lord Restimar, and — oh, that other one who's so hard to remember."

"The Lord Rhoop, Sire," said Drinian.

"Rhoop, Rhoop, of course," said Caspian. "That is my main intention. But Reepicheep here has an even higher hope." Everyone's eyes turned to the Mouse.

"As high as my spirit," it said. "Though perhaps as small as my stature. Why should we not come to the very eastern end of the world? And what might we find there? I expect to find Aslan's own country. It is always from the east, across the sea, that the great Lion comes to us."

"I say, that *is* an idea," said Edmund in an awed voice.

"But do you think," said Lucy, "Aslan's country would be that sort of country — I mean, the sort you could ever *sail* to?"

"I do not know, Madam," said Reepicheep. "But there is this. When I was in my cradle a wood woman, a Dryad, spoke this verse over me:

"Where sky and water meet,
Where the waves grow sweet,

31

Doubt not, Reepicheep,
To find all you seek,
There is the utter East.

"I do not know what it means. But the spell of it has been on me all my life."

After a short silence Lucy asked, "And where are we now, Caspian?"

"The Captain can tell you better than I," said Caspian, so Drinian got out his chart and spread it on the table.

"That's our position," he said, laying his finger on it. "Or was at noon today. We had a fair wind from Cair Paravel and stood a little north for Galma, which we made on the next day. We were in port for a week, for the Duke of Galma made a great tournament for His Majesty and there he unhorsed many knights —"

"And got a few nasty falls myself, Drinian. Some of the bruises are there still," put in Caspian.

"— And unhorsed many knights," repeated Drinian with a grin. "We thought the Duke would have been pleased if the King's Majesty would have married his daughter, but nothing came of that —"

"Squints, and has freckles," said Caspian.

"Oh, poor girl," said Lucy.

"And we sailed from Galma," continued

Drinian, "and ran into a calm for the best part of two days and had to row, and then had wind again and did not make Terebinthia till the fourth day from Galma. And there their King sent out a warning not to land for there was sickness in Terebinthia, but we doubled the cape and put in at a little creek far from the city and watered. Then we had to lie off for three days before we got a southeast wind and stood out for Seven Isles. The third day out a pirate (Terebinthian by her rig) overhauled us, but when she saw us well armed she stood off after some shooting of arrows on either part —"

"And we ought to have given her chase and boarded her and hanged every mother's son of them," said Reepicheep.

"— And in five days more we were in sight of Muil, which, as you know, is the western-most of the Seven Isles. Then we rowed through the straits and came about sun-down into Redhaven on the isle of Brenn, where we were very lovingly feasted and had victuals and water at will. We left Redhaven six days ago and have made marvelously good speed, so that I hope to see the Lone Islands the day after tomorrow. The sum is, we are now nearly thirty days at sea and have sailed more than four hundred leagues from Narnia."

"And after the Lone Islands?" said Lucy.

"No one knows, your Majesty," answered Drinian. "Unless the Lone Islanders themselves can tell us."

"They couldn't in our days," said Edmund.

"Then," said Reepicheep, "it is after the Lone Islands that the adventure really begins."

Caspian now suggested that they might like to be shown over the ship before supper, but Lucy's conscience smote her and she said, "I think I really must go and see Eustace. Seasickness is horrid, you know. If I had my old cordial with me I could cure him."

"But you have," said Caspian. "I'd quite forgotten about it. As you left it behind I thought it might be regarded as one of the royal treasures and so I brought it — if you think it ought to be wasted on a thing like seasickness."

"It'll only take a drop," said Lucy.

Caspian opened one of the lockers beneath the bench and brought out the beautiful little diamond flask which Lucy remembered so well. "Take back your own, Queen," he said. They then left the cabin and went out into the sunshine.

In the deck there were two large, long hatches, fore and aft of the mast, and both open, as they always were in fair weather, to let light and air into the belly of the ship. Caspian led them down a ladder into the after hatch. Here they found themselves in a place where benches for rowing ran from side to side and the light came in through the oarholes and danced on the roof. Of course Caspian's ship was not that horrible thing, a galley rowed by slaves. Oars were used only when wind failed or for getting in and out of harbor and everyone (except Reepicheep whose legs were too short) had often taken a turn. At each side of the ship the space under the benches was left clear for the rowers' feet, but all down the center there was a kind of pit which went down to the very keel and this was filled with all kinds of things — sacks of flour, casks of water and beer, barrels of pork, jars of honey, skin bottles of wine, apples, nuts, cheeses, biscuits, turnips, sides of bacon. From the roof — that is, from the under side of the deck — hung hams and strings of on-ions, and also the men of the watch off-duty in their hammocks. Caspian led them aft, stepping from bench to bench; at least, it was stepping for him, and something between a step and a jump for Lucy, and a real long jump for Reepicheep. In this way they came to a partition with a door in it. Caspian opened the door and led them into a cabin which filled the stern underneath the deck cabins in the poop. It was of course not so nice. It was very low and the sides sloped together as they went down so that there was hardly any floor; and though it had windows of thick glass, they were not made to open because they were under water. In fact at this very moment, as the ship pitched they were alternately golden with sunlight and dim green with the sea.

"You and I must lodge here, Edmund," said Caspian. "We'll leave your kinsman the bunk and sling hammocks for ourselves."

"I beseech your Majesty —" said Drinian.

"No, no shipmate," said Caspian, "we have argued all that out already. You and Rhince" (Rhince was the mate) "are sailing the ship and will have cares and labors many a night when we are singing catches or telling stories, so you and he must have the port cabin above. King Edmund and I can lie very snug here below. But how is the stranger?"

Eustace, very green in the face, scowled and asked whether there was any sign of the storm getting less. But Caspian said, "What storm?" and Drinian burst out laughing.

"Storm, young master!" he roared. "This is as fair weather as a man could ask for."

"Who's that?" said Eustace irritably. "Send him away. His voice goes through my head."

"I've brought you something that will make you feel better, Eustace," said Lucy.

"Oh, go away and leave me alone," growled Eustace. But he took a drop from her flask, and though he said it was beastly stuff (the smell in the cabin when she opened it was delicious) it is certain that his face came the right color a few moments after he had swallowed it, and he must have felt better because, instead of wailing about the storm and his head, he began demanding to be put ashore and said that at the first port he would "lodge a disposition" against them all with the British Consul. But when Reepicheep asked what a disposition was and how you lodged it (Reepicheep thought it was some new way of arranging a single combat) Eustace could only reply, "Fancy not knowing that." In the end they succeeded in convincing Eustace that they were already sailing as fast as they could toward the nearest land they knew, and that they had no more power of sending him back to Cambridge — which was where Uncle Harold lived — than of sending him to the moon. After that he sulkily agreed to put on the fresh clothes which had been put out for him and come on deck.

Caspian now showed them over the ship, though indeed they had seen most of it already. They went up on the forecastle and saw the lookout man standing on a little shelf inside the gilded dragon's neck and peering through its open mouth. Inside the forecastle was the galley (or ship's kitchen) and quarters for such people as the boatswain, the carpenter, the cook and the master-archer. If you think it odd to have the galley in the bows and imagine the smoke from its chimney streaming back over the ship, that is because you are thinking of steamships where there is always a headwind. On a sailing ship the wind is coming from behind, and anything smelly is put as far forward as possible. They were taken up to the fighting-top, and at first it was rather alarming to rock to and fro there and see the deck looking small and far away beneath. You realized that if you fell there was no particular reason why you should fall on board rather than in the sea. Then they were taken to the poop, where Rhince was on duty with another man at the great tiller, and behind that the dragon's tail rose up, covered with gilding, and round inside it ran a little bench. The

name of the ship was *Dawn Treader*. She was only a little bit of a thing compared with one of our ships, or even with the cogs, dromonds, carracks and galleons which Narnia had owned when Lucy and Edmund had reigned there under Peter as the High King, for nearly all navigation had died out in the reigns of Caspian's ancestors. When his uncle, Miraz the usurper, had sent the seven lords to sea, they had had to buy a Galmian ship and man it with hired Galmian sailors. But now Caspian had begun to teach the Narnians to be sea-faring folk once more, and the *Dawn Treader* was the finest ship he had built yet. She was so small that, forward of the mast, there was hardly any deck room between the central hatch and the ship's boat on one side and the hen-coop (Lucy fed the hens) on the other. But she was a beauty of her kind, a "lady" as sailors say, her lines perfect, her colors pure, and every spar and rope and pin lovingly made. Eustace of course would be pleased with nothing, and kept on boasting about liners and motorboats and aeroplanes and submarines ("As if *he* knew anything about them," muttered Edmund), but the other two were delighted with the *Dawn Treader*, and when they returned aft to the cabin and supper, and saw the whole western sky lit up with an immense crimson sunset, and felt the quiver of the ship, and tasted the salt on their lips, and thought of unknown lands on the Eastern rim of the world, Lucy felt that she was almost too happy to speak.

What Eustace thought had best be told in his own words, for when they all got their clothes back, dried, next morning, he at once got out a little black notebook and a pencil and started to keep a diary. He always had this notebook with him and kept a record of his marks in it, for though he didn't care much about any subject for its own sake, he cared a great deal about marks and would even go to people and say, "I got so much. What did you get?" But as he didn't seem likely to get many marks on the *Dawn Treader* he now started a diary. This was the first entry.

"*August 7th*. Have now been twenty-four hours on this ghastly boat if it isn't a dream. All the time a frightful storm has been raging (it's a good thing I'm not seasick). Huge waves keep coming in over the front and I have seen the boat nearly go under any number of times. All the others pretend to take no notice of this, either from swank or because Harold says one of the most cowardly things ordinary people do is to shut their eyes to Facts. It's madness to come out into the sea in a rotten little thing like this. Not much bigger than a lifeboat. And, of course, absolutely primitive indoors. No proper saloon, no radio, no bathrooms, no deck-chairs. I was dragged all over it yesterday evening and it would make anyone sick to hear Caspian showing off his funny little toy boat as if it was the *Queen Mary*. I tried to tell him what real ships are like, but he's too dense. E. and L., *of course*, didn't back me up. I suppose a kid like L. doesn't realize the danger and E. is buttering up C.

as everyone does here. They call him a King. I said I was a Republican but he had to ask me what that meant! He doesn't seem to know anything at all. *Needless to say* I've been put in the worst cabin of the boat, a perfect dungeon, and Lucy has been given a whole room on deck to herself, almost a nice room compared with the rest of this place. C. says that's because she's a girl. I tried to make him see what Alberta says, that all that sort of thing is really lowering girls but he was too dense. Still, he might see that I shall be ill if I'm kept in that *hole* any longer. E. says we mustn't grumble because C. is sharing it with us himself to make room for L. As if that didn't make it more crowded and far worse. Nearly forgot to say that there is also a kind of Mouse thing that gives everyone the most frightful cheek. The others can put up with it if they like but I shall twist his tail pretty soon if he tries it on me. The food is frightful too."

The trouble between Eustace and Reepicheep arrived even sooner than might have been expected. Before dinner next day, when the others were sitting round the table waiting (being at sea gives one a magnificent appetite), Eustace came rushing in, wringing his hand and shouting out:

"That little brute has half killed me. I insist on it being kept under control. I could bring an action against you, Caspian. I could order you to have it destroyed."

At the same moment Reepicheep appeared. His sword was drawn and his whiskers looked very fierce but he was as polite as ever.

"I ask your pardons all," he said, "and especially her Majesty's. If I had known that he would take refuge here I would have awaited a more reasonable time for his correction."

"What on earth's up?" asked Edmund.

What had really happened was this. Reepicheep, who never felt that the ship was getting on fast enough, loved to sit on the bulwarks far forward just beside the dragon's head, gazing out at the eastern horizon and singing softly in his little chirruping voice the song the Dryad had made

43

for him. He never held on to anything, however the ship pitched, and kept his balance with perfect ease; perhaps his long tail, hanging down to the deck inside the bulwarks, made this easier. Everyone on board was familiar with this habit, and the sailors liked it because when one was on look-out duty it gave one somebody to talk to. Why exactly Eustace had slipped and reeled and stumbled all the way forward to the forecastle (he had not yet got his sea-legs) I never heard. Perhaps he hoped he would see land, or perhaps he wanted to hang about the galley and scrounge something. Anyway, as soon as he saw that long tail hanging down — and perhaps it was rather tempting — he thought it would be delightful to catch hold of it, swing Reepicheep round by it once or twice upside-down, then run away and laugh. At first the plan seemed to work beautifully. The Mouse was not much

heavier than a very large cat. Eustace had him off the rail in a trice and very silly he looked (thought Eustace) with his little limbs all splayed out and his mouth open. But unfortunately Reepicheep, who had fought for his life many a time, never lost his head even for a moment. Nor his skill. It is not very easy to draw one's sword when one is swinging round in the air by one's tail, but he did. And the next thing Eustace knew was two agonizing jabs in his hand which made him let go of the tail; and the next thing after that was that the Mouse had picked itself up again as if it were a ball bouncing off the deck, and there it was facing him, and a horrid long, bright, sharp thing like a skewer was waving to and fro within an inch of his stomach. (This doesn't count as below the belt for mice in Narnia because they can hardly be expected to reach higher.)

"Stop it," spluttered Eustace, "go away. Put that thing away. It's not safe. Stop it, I say. I'll tell Caspian. I'll have you muzzled and tied up."

"Why do you not draw your own sword, poltroon!" cheeped the Mouse. "Draw and fight or I'll beat you black and blue with the flat."

"I haven't got one," said Eustace. "I'm a

pacifist. I don't believe in fighting."

"Do I understand," said Reepicheep, withdrawing his sword for a moment and speaking very sternly, "that you do not intend to give me satisfaction?"

"I don't know what you mean," said Eustace, nursing his hand. "If you don't know how to take a joke I shan't bother my head about you."

"Then take that," said Reepicheep, "and that — to teach you manners — and the respect due to a knight — and a Mouse — and a Mouse's tail —" and at each word he gave Eustace a blow with the side of his rapier, which was thin, fine, dwarf-tempered steel and as supple and effective as a birch rod. Eustace (of course) was at a school where they didn't have corporal punishment, so the sensation was quite new to him. That was why, in spite of having no sea-legs, it took him less than a minute to get off that forecastle and cover the whole length of the deck and burst in at the cabin door — still hotly pursued by Reepicheep. Indeed it seemed to Eustace that the rapier as well as the pursuit was hot. It might have been red-hot by the feel.

There was not much difficulty in settling the matter once Eustace realized that everyone took the idea of a duel seriously and heard Caspian offering to lend him a sword, and Drinian and Edmund discussing whether he ought to be handicapped in some way to make up for his being so much bigger than Reepicheep. He apologized sulkily and went off with Lucy to have his hand bathed and bandaged and then went to his bunk. He was careful to lie on his side.

THREE

THE LONE ISLANDS

"Land in sight," shouted the man in the bows.

Lucy, who had been talking to Rhince on the poop, came pattering down the ladder and raced forward. As she went she was joined by Edmund, and they found Caspian, Drinian and Reepicheep already on the forecastle. It was a coldish morning, the sky very pale and the sea very dark blue with little white caps of foam, and there, a little way off on the starboard bow, was the nearest of the Lone Islands, Felimath, like a low green hill in the sea, and behind it, further off, the gray slopes of its sister Doorn.

"Same old Felimath! Same old Doorn," said Lucy, clapping her hands. "Oh — Edmund, how long it is since you and I saw them last!"

"I've never understood why they belong to Narnia," said Caspian. "Did Peter the High King conquer them?"

"Oh no," said Edmund. "They were Narnian before our time — in the days of

the White Witch."

(By the way, I have never yet heard how these remote islands became attached to the crown of Narnia; if I ever do, and if the story is at all interesting, I may put it in some other book.)

"Are we to put in here, Sire?" asked Drinian.

"I shouldn't think it would be much good landing on Felimath," said Edmund. "It was almost uninhabited in our days and it looks as if it was the same still. The people lived mostly on Doorn and a little on Avra — that's the third one; you can't see it yet. They only kept sheep on Felimath."

"Then we'll have to double that cape, I suppose," said Drinian, "and land on Doorn. That'll mean rowing."

"I'm sorry we're not landing on Felimath," said Lucy. "I'd like to walk there again. It was so lonely — a nice kind of loneliness, and all grass and clover and soft sea air."

"I'd love to stretch my legs too," said Caspian. "I tell you what. Why shouldn't we go ashore in the boat and send it back, and then we could walk across Felimath and let the *Dawn Treader* pick us up on the other side?"

If Caspian had been as experienced then as he became later on in this voyage he would not have made this suggestion; but at the moment it seemed an excellent one. "Oh do let's," said Lucy.

"You'll come, will you?" said Caspian to Eustace, who had come on deck with his hand bandaged.

"Anything to get off this blasted ship!" said Eustace.

"Blasted?" said Drinian. "How do you mean?"

"In a civilized country like where I come from," said Eustace, "the ships are so big that when you're inside you wouldn't know you were at sea at all."

"In that case you might just as well stay ashore," said Caspian. "Will you tell them to lower the boat, Drinian?"

The King, the Mouse, the two Pevensies, and Eustace all got into the boat and were pulled to the beach of Felimath. When the boat had left them and was being rowed back they all turned and looked round. They were surprised at how small the *Dawn Treader* looked.

Lucy was of course barefoot, having kicked off her shoes while swimming, but that is no hardship if one is going to walk on downy turf. It was delightful to be ashore again and to smell the earth and grass, even if at first the ground seemed to be pitching up and down like a ship, as it usually does for a while if one has been at sea. It was much warmer here than it had been on board and Lucy found the sand pleasant to her feet as they crossed it. There was a lark singing.

They struck inland and up a fairly steep, though low, hill. At the top of course they looked back, and there was the *Dawn Treader* shining like a great bright insect and crawling slowly northwestward with her oars. Then they went over the ridge and could see her no longer.

Doorn now lay before them, divided from Felimath by a channel about a mile wide; behind it and to the left lay Avra. The little white town of Narrowhaven on Doorn was easily seen.

"Hullo! What's this?" said Edmund suddenly.

In the green valley to which they were descending six or seven rough-looking men, all armed, were sitting by a tree.

"Don't tell them who we are," said Caspian.

"And pray, your Majesty, why not?" said Reepicheep who had consented to ride on Lucy's shoulder.

"It just occurred to me," replied Caspian, "that no one here can have heard from Narnia for a long time. It's just possible they may not still acknowledge our over-lordship. In which case it might not be quite safe to be known as the King."

"We have our swords, Sire," said Reepicheep.

"Yes, Reep, I know we have," said Caspian. "But if it is a question of re-conquering the three islands, I'd prefer to come back with a rather larger army."

By this time they were quite close to the strangers, one of whom — a big black-haired fellow — shouted out, "A good morning to you."

"And a good morning to you," said Caspian. "Is there still a Governor of the Lone Islands?"

"To be sure there is," said the man, "Governor Gumpas. His Sufficiency is at Narrowhaven. But you'll stay and drink with us."

Caspian thanked him, though neither he

nor the others much liked the look of their new acquaintance, and all of them sat down. But hardly had they raised their cups to their lips when the black-haired man nodded to his companions and, as quick as lightning, all the five visitors found themselves wrapped in strong arms. There was a moment's struggle but all the advantages were on one side, and soon everyone was disarmed and had their hands tied behind their backs — except Reepicheep, writhing in his captor's grip and biting furiously.

"Careful with that beast, Tacks," said the Leader. "Don't damage him. He'll fetch the best price of the lot, I shouldn't wonder."

"Coward! Poltroon!" squeaked Reepicheep. "Give me my sword and free my paws if you dare."

"Whew!" whistled the slave merchant (for that is what he was). "It can talk! Well I never did. Blowed if I take less than two hundred crescents for him." The Calormen crescent, which is the chief coin in those parts, is worth about a third of a pound.

"So that's what you are," said Caspian. "A kidnapper and slaver. I hope you're proud of it."

"Now, now, now, now," said the slaver. "Don't you start any jaw. The easier you take it, the pleasanter all round, see? I don't do this for fun. I've got my living to make same as anyone else."

"Where will you take us?" asked Lucy, getting the words out with some difficulty.

"Over to Narrowhaven," said the slaver. "For market day tomorrow."

"Is there a British Consul there?" asked Eustace.

"Is there a which?" said the man.

But long before Eustace was tired of trying to explain, the slaver simply said, "Well, I've had enough of this jabber. The Mouse is a fair treat but this one would talk the hind leg off a donkey. Off we go, mates."

Then the four human prisoners were roped together, not cruelly but securely, and made to march down to the shore. Reepicheep was carried. He had stopped biting on a threat of having his mouth tied up, but he had a great deal to say, and Lucy really won-

dered how any man could bear to have the things said to him which were said to the slave dealer by the Mouse. But the slave dealer, far from objecting, only said "Go on" whenever Reepicheep paused for breath, occasionally adding, "It's as good as a play," or, "Blimey, you can't help almost thinking it knows what it's saying!" or "Was it one of you what trained it?" This so infuriated Reepicheep that in the end the number of things he thought of saying all at once nearly suffocated him and he became silent.

When they got down to the shore that looked toward Doorn they found a little village and a long-boat on the beach and, lying a little further out, a dirty bedraggled looking ship.

"Now, youngsters," said the slave dealer, "let's have no fuss and then you'll have nothing to cry about. All aboard."

At that moment a fine-looking bearded man came out of one of the houses (an inn, I think) and said:

"Well, Pug. More of your usual wares?"

The slaver, whose name seemed to be Pug, bowed very low, and said in a wheedling kind of voice, "Yes, please your Lordship."

"How much do you want for that boy?" asked the other, pointing to Caspian.

"Ah," said Pug, "I knew your Lordship would pick on the best. No deceiving your Lordship with anything second rate. That boy, now, I've taken a fancy to him myself. Got kind of fond of him, I have. I'm that tender-hearted I didn't ever ought to have taken up this job. Still, to a customer like your Lordship —"

"Tell me your price, carrion," said the Lord sternly. "Do you think I want to listen to the rigmarole of your filthy trade?"

"Three hundred crescents, my Lord, to your honorable Lordship, but to anyone else —"

"I'll give you a hundred and fifty."

"Oh please, please," broke in Lucy. "Don't separate us, whatever you do. You don't know —" But then she stopped for she saw that Caspian didn't even now want to be known.

"A hundred and fifty, then," said the Lord. "As for you, little maiden, I am sorry I cannot buy you all. Unrope my boy, Pug. And look — treat these others well while they are in your hands or it'll be the worse for you."

"Well!" said Pug. "Now who ever heard of a gentleman in my way of business who treated his stock better than what I do? Well? Why, I treat 'em like my own children."

"That's likely enough to be true," said the other grimly.

The dreadful moment had now come. Caspian was untied and his new master said, "This way, lad," and Lucy burst into tears and Edmund looked very blank. But Caspian looked over his shoulder and said, "Cheer up. I'm sure it will come all right in the end. So long."

"Now, missie," said Pug. "Don't you start taking on and spoiling your looks for the market tomorrow. You be a good girl and then you won't have nothing to cry *about,* see?"

Then they were rowed out to the slave-ship and taken below into a long, rather dark place, none too clean, where they found many other unfortunate prisoners; for Pug was of course a pirate and had just returned from cruising among the islands and capturing what he could. The children didn't meet anyone whom they knew; the prisoners were mostly Galmians and Terebinthians. And there they sat in the straw and wondered what was happening to Caspian and tried to stop Eustace talking as if everyone except himself was to blame.

Meanwhile Caspian was having a much more interesting time. The man who had bought him led him down a little lane between two of the village houses and so out into an open place behind the village. Then he turned and faced him.

"You needn't be afraid of me, boy," he said. "I'll treat you well. I bought you for your face. You reminded me of someone."

"May I ask of whom, my Lord?" said Caspian.

"You remind me of my master, King Caspian of Narnia."

Then Caspian decided to risk everything on one stroke.

"My Lord," he said, "I *am* your master. I am Caspian, King of Narnia."

"You make very free," said the other. "How shall I know this is true?"

"Firstly by my face," said Caspian. "Secondly because I know within six guesses who you are. You are one of those seven lords of Narnia whom my Uncle Miraz sent to sea and whom I have come out to look for — Argoz, Bern, Octesian, Restimar, Mavramorn, or — or — I have forgotten the others. And finally, if your Lordship will give me a sword I will prove on any man's body in clean battle that I am Caspian the son of Caspian, lawful King of Narnia, Lord of Cair Paravel, and Emperor of the Lone Islands."

"By heaven," exclaimed the man, "it is his

father's very voice and trick of speech. My liege — your Majesty —" And there in the field he knelt and kissed the King's hand.

"The moneys your Lordship disbursed for our person will be made good from our own treasury," said Caspian.

"They're not in Pug's purse yet, Sire," said the Lord Bern, for he it was. "And never will be, I trust. I have moved His Sufficiency the Governor a hundred times to crush this vile traffic in man's flesh."

"My Lord Bern," said Caspian, "we must talk of the state of these Islands. But first what is your Lordship's own story?"

"Short enough, Sire," said Bern. "I came thus far with my six fellows, loved a girl of the islands, and felt I had had enough of the sea. And there was no purpose in returning to Narnia while your Majesty's uncle held the reins. So I married and have lived here ever since."

"And what is this governor, this Gumpas, like? Does he still acknowledge the King of Narnia for his lord?"

"In words, yes. All is done in the King's name. But he would not be best pleased to find a real, live King of Narnia coming in upon him. And if your Majesty came before him alone and unarmed — well he would not deny his allegiance, but he would pretend to disbelieve you. Your Grace's life would be in danger. What following has your Majesty in these waters?"

"There is my ship just rounding the point," said Caspian. "We are about thirty swords if it came to fighting. Shall we not have my ship in and fall upon Pug and free my friends whom he holds captive?"

"Not by my counsel," said Bern. "As soon as there was a fight two or three ships would put out from Narrowhaven to rescue Pug. Your Majesty must work by a show of more power than you really have, and by the terror of the King's name. It must not come to plain battle. Gumpas is a chicken-hearted man and can be over-awed."

After a little more conversation Caspian and Bern walked down to the coast a little west of the village and there Caspian winded his horn. (This was not the great magic horn of Narnia, Queen Susan's Horn: he had left that at home for his regent Trumpkin to use if any great need fell upon the land in the King's absence.) Drinian, who was on the lookout for a signal, recognized the royal horn at once and the *Dawn Treader* began standing in to shore. Then the boat put off again and in a few moments Caspian and the Lord Bern were on deck explaining the situation to Drinian. He, just like Caspian, wanted to lay the *Dawn Treader* alongside the slave-ship at once and board her, but Bern made the same objection.

"Steer straight down this channel, captain," said Bern, "and then round to Avra where my own estates are. But first run up the King's banner, hang out all the shields, and send as many men to the fighting-top as you can. And about five bowshots hence, when you get open sea on your port bow, run up a few signals."

"Signals? To whom?" said Drinian.

"Why, to all the other ships we haven't got but which it might be well that Gumpas thinks we have."

"Oh, I see," said Drinian, rubbing his hands. "And they'll read our signals. What shall I say? *Whole fleet round the South of Avra and assemble at — ?*"

"Bernstead," said the Lord Bern. "That'll do excellently. Their whole journey — if there *were* any ships — would be out of sight from Narrowhaven."

Caspian was sorry for the others languishing in the hold of Pug's slave-ship, but he could not help finding the rest of that day enjoyable. Late in the afternoon (for they had to do all by oar), having turned to starboard round the northeast end of Doorn and port again round the point of Avra, they entered into a good harbor on Avra's southern shore where Bern's pleasant lands sloped down to the water's edge. Bern's people, many of whom they saw working in the fields, were all freemen and it was a happy and prosperous fief. Here they all went ashore and were royally feasted in a low, pillared house overlooking the bay. Bern and his gracious wife and merry daughters made them good cheer. But after dark Bern sent a messenger over by boat to Doorn to order some preparations (he did not say exactly what) for the following day.

FOUR

WHAT CASPIAN

DID THERE

Next morning the Lord Bern called his
guests early, and after breakfast he asked
Caspian to order every man he had into full
armor. "And above all," he added, "let everything be as trim and scoured as if it were the
morning of the first battle in a great war between noble kings with all the world looking
on." This was done; and then in three
boatloads Caspian and his people, and Bern
with a few of his, put out for Narrowhaven.
The King's flag flew in the stern of his boat
and his trumpeter was with him.

When they reached the jetty at Narrowhaven, Caspian found a considerable crowd
assembled to meet them. "This is what I
sent word about last night," said Bern.
"They are all friends of mine and honest
people." And as soon as Caspian stepped
ashore the crowd broke out into hurrahs
and shouts of, "Narnia! Narnia! Long live
the King." At the same moment — and this

was also due to Bern's messengers — bells began ringing from many parts of the town. Then Caspian caused his banner to be advanced and his trumpet to be blown and every man drew his sword and set his face into a joyful sternness, and they marched up the street so that the street shook, and their armor shone (for it was a sunny morning) so that one could hardly look at it steadily.

At first the only people who cheered were those who had been warned by Bern's messenger and knew what was happening and wanted it to happen. But then all the children joined in because they liked a procession and had seen very few. And then all the schoolboys joined in because they also liked processions and felt that the more noise and disturbance there was the less likely they would be to have any school that morning. And then all the old women put their heads out of doors and windows and began chattering and cheering because it was a king, and what is a governor compared with that? And all the young women joined in for the same reason and also because Caspian and Drinian and the rest were so handsome. And then all the young men came to see what the young women were looking at, so that by the time Caspian reached the castle gates, nearly the whole town was shouting;

and where Gumpas sat in the castle, muddling and messing about with accounts and forms and rules and regulations, he heard the noise.

At the castle gate Caspian's trumpeter blew a blast and cried, "Open for the King of Narnia, come to visit his trusty and well-beloved servant the governor of Lone Islands." In those days everything in the islands was done in a slovenly, slouching manner. Only the little postern opened, and out came a tousled fellow with a dirty old hat on his head instead of a helmet, and a rusty old pike in his hand. He blinked at the flashing figures before him. "Carn—seez—fishansy," he mumbled (which was his way of saying, "You can't see His Sufficiency"). "No interviews without 'pointments 'cept 'tween nine 'n' ten p.m. second Saturday every month."

"Uncover before Narnia, you dog," thundered the Lord Bern, and dealt him a rap with his gauntleted hand which sent his hat flying from his head.

"Ere? Wot's it all about?" began the doorkeeper, but no one took any notice of him. Two of Caspian's men stepped through the postern and after some struggling with bars and bolts (for everything was rusty) flung both wings of the gate wide open. Then the

King and his followers strode into the court-yard. Here a number of the governor's guards were lounging about and several more (they were mostly wiping their mouths) came tumbling out of various doorways. Though their armor was in a disgraceful condition, these were fellows who might have fought if they had been led or had known what was happening; so this was the dangerous moment. Caspian gave them no time to think.

"Where is the captain?" he asked.

"I am, more or less, if you know what I mean," said a languid and rather dandified young person without any armor at all.

"It is our wish," said Caspian, "that our royal visitation to our realm of the Lone Islands should, if possible, be an occasion of joy and not of terror to our loyal subjects. If it were not for that, I should have something to say about the state of your men's armor and weapons. As it is, you are pardoned. Command a cask of wine to be opened that your men may drink our health. But at noon tomorrow I wish to see them here in this courtyard looking like men-at-arms and not like vagabonds. See to it on pain of our extreme displeasure."

The captain gaped but Bern immediately cried, "Three cheers for the King," and the soldiers, who had understood about the cask of wine even if they understood nothing else, joined in. Caspian then ordered most of his own men to remain in the courtyard. He, with Bern and Drinian and four others, went into the hall.

Behind a table at the far end with various secretaries about him sat his Sufficiency, the Governor of Lone Islands. Gumpas was a bilious-looking man with hair that had once been red and was now mostly gray. He glanced up as the strangers entered and then looked down at his papers saying automatically, "No interviews without appointments except between nine and ten p.m. on second Saturdays."

Caspian nodded to Bern and then stood aside. Bern and Drinian took a step forward and each seized one end of the table. They lifted it, and flung it on one side of the hall where it rolled over, scattering a cascade of letters, dossiers, ink-pots, pens, sealing-wax and documents. Then, not roughly but as firmly as if their hands were pincers of steel, they plucked Gumpas out of his chair and deposited him, facing it, about four feet away. Caspian at once sat down in the chair and laid his naked sword across his knees.

"My Lord," said he, fixing his eyes on Gumpas, "you have not given us quite the welcome we expected. We are the King of Narnia."

"Nothing about it in the correspondence," said the governor. "Nothing in the minutes. We have not been notified of any such thing. All irregular. Happy to consider any applications —"

"And we are come to inquire into your Sufficiency's conduct of your office," continued Caspian. "There are two points especially on which I require an explanation. Firstly I find no record that the tribute due from these Islands to the crown of Narnia has been received for about a hundred and fifty years."

"That would be a question to raise at the Council next month," said Gumpas. "If anyone moves that a commission of inquiry be set up to report on the financial history of the islands at the first meeting next year, why then . . ."

"I also find it very clearly written in our laws," Caspian went on, "that if the tribute is not delivered the whole debt has to be paid by the Governor of Lone Islands out of his private purse."

At this Gumpas began to pay real attention. "Oh, that's quite out of the question," he said. "It is an economic impossibility — er — your Majesty must be joking."

Inside, he was wondering if there were any way of getting rid of these unwelcome visitors. Had he known that Caspian had only one ship and one ship's company with him, he would have spoken soft words for the moment, and hoped to have them all surrounded and killed during the night. But he had seen a ship of war sail down the straits yesterday and seen it signaling, as he supposed, to its consorts. He had not then known it was the King's ship for there was not wind enough to spread the flag out and make the golden lion visible, so he had waited further developments. Now he imagined that Caspian had a whole fleet at Bernstead. It would never have occurred to Gumpas that anyone would walk into Narrowhaven to take the islands with less than fifty men; it was certainly not at all the kind of thing he could imagine doing himself.

"Secondly," said Caspian, "I want to know why you have permitted this abominable and unnatural traffic in slaves to grow up here, contrary to the ancient custom and usage of our dominions."

"Necessary, unavoidable," said his Sufficiency. "An essential part of the economic development of the islands, I assure you. Our present burst of prosperity depends on it."

"What need have you of slaves?"

"For export, your Majesty. Sell 'em to Calormen mostly; and we have other markets. We are a great center of the trade."

"In other words," said Caspian, "you don't need them. Tell me what purpose they serve except to put money into the pockets of such as Pug?"

"Your Majesty's tender years," said Gumpas, with what was meant to be a fatherly smile, "hardly make it possible that you should understand the economic problem involved. I have statistics, I have graphs, I have —"

"Tender as my years may be," said Caspian, "I believe I understand the slave trade from within quite as well as your Sufficiency. And I do not see that it brings into the islands meat or bread or beer or wine or timber or cabbages or books or instruments of music or horses or armor or anything else worth having. But whether it does or not, it must be stopped."

"But that would be putting the clock back," gasped the governor. "Have you no idea of progress, of development?"

"I have seen them both in an egg," said Caspian. "We call it 'Going Bad' in Narnia. This trade must stop."

"I can take no responsibility for any such measure," said Gumpas.

"Very well, then," answered Caspian, "we relieve you of your office. My Lord Bern, come here." And before Gumpas quite realized what was happening, Bern was kneeling with his hands between the King's hands and taking the oath to govern the Lone Islands in accordance with the old customs, rights, usages and laws of Narnia. And Caspian said, "I think we have had enough of governors," and made Bern a Duke, the Duke of Lone Islands.

"As for you, my Lord," he said to Gumpas, "I forgive you your debt for the tribute. But before noon tomorrow you and yours must be out of the castle, which is now the Duke's residence."

"Look here, this is all very well," said one

of Gumpas's secretaries, "but suppose all you gentlemen stop play-acting and we do a little business. The question before us really is —"

"The question is," said the Duke, "whether you and the rest of the rabble will leave without a flogging or with one. You may choose which you prefer."

When all this had been pleasantly settled, Caspian ordered horses, of which there were a few in the castle, though very ill-groomed, and he, with Bern and Drinian and a few others, rode out into the town and made for the slave market. It was a long low building near the harbor and the scene which they found going on inside was very much like any other auction; that is to say, there was a great crowd and Pug, on a platform, was roaring out in a raucous voice:

"Now, gentlemen, lot twenty-three. Fine Terebinthian agricultural laborer, suitable for the mines or the galleys. Under twenty-five years of age. Not a bad tooth in his head. Good, brawny fellow. Take off his shirt, Tacks, and let the gentlemen see. There's muscle for you! Look at the chest on him. Ten crescents from the gentleman in the corner. You must be joking, sir. Fifteen! Eighteen! Eighteen is bidden for lot twenty-three. Any advance on eighteen?

Twenty-one. Thank you, sir. Twenty-one is bidden —"

But Pug stopped and gaped when he saw the mail-clad figures who had clanked up to the platform.

"On your knees, every man of you, to the King of Narnia," said the Duke. Everyone heard the horses jingling and stamping outside and many had heard some rumor of the landing and the events at the castle. Most obeyed. Those who did not were pulled down by their neighbors. Some cheered.

"Your life is forfeit, Pug, for laying hands on our royal person yesterday," said Caspian. "But your ignorance is pardoned. The slave trade was forbidden in all our dominions quarter of an hour ago. I declare every slave in this market free."

He held up his hand to check the cheering of the slaves and went on, "Where are my friends?"

"That dear little gel and the nice young gentleman?" said Pug with an ingratiating smile. "Why, they were snapped up at once —"

"We're here, we're here, Caspian," cried Lucy and Edmund together and, "At your service, Sire," piped Reepicheep from another corner. They had all been sold but the men who had bought them were staying to bid for other slaves and so they had not yet been taken away. The crowd parted to let the three of them out and there was great hand-clasping and greeting between them and Caspian. Two merchants of Calormen at once approached. The Calormen have dark faces and long beards. They wear flowing robes and orange-colored turbans, and they are a wise, wealthy, courteous, cruel and ancient people. They bowed most politely to Caspian and paid him long compliments, all about the fountains of prosperity irrigating the gardens of prudence and virtue — and things like that — but of course what they wanted was the money they had paid.

"That is only fair, sirs," said Caspian. "Every man who has bought a slave today must have his money back. Pug, bring out your takings to the last minim." (A minim is the fortieth part of a crescent.)

"Does your good Majesty mean to beggar me?" whined Pug.

"You have lived on broken hearts all your life," said Caspian, "and if you *are* beggared, it is better to be a beggar than a slave. But where is my other friend?"

"Oh *him?*" said Pug. "Oh take *him* and welcome. Glad to have him off my hands. I've never seen such a drug in the market in all my born days. Priced him at five crescents in the end and even so nobody'd have him. Threw him in free with other lots and still no one would have him. Wouldn't touch him. Wouldn't look at him. Tacks, bring out Sulky."

Thus Eustace was produced, and sulky he certainly looked; for though no one would want to be sold as a slave, it is perhaps even more galling to be a sort of utility slave whom no one will buy. He walked up to Caspian and said, "I see. As usual. Been enjoying yourself somewhere while the rest of us were prisoners. I suppose you haven't even found out about the British Consul. Of course not."

That night they had a great feast in the castle of Narrowhaven and then, "Tomorrow for the beginning of our real adventures!" said Reepicheep when he had made his bows to everyone and went to bed. But it could not really be tomorrow or anything like it. For now they were preparing to leave all known lands and seas behind them and the fullest preparations had to be made. The *Dawn Treader* was emptied and drawn on land by eight horses over rollers and every bit of her was gone over by the most skilled shipwrights. Then she was launched again and victualed and watered as full as she could hold — that is to say for twenty-eight days. Even this, as Edmund noticed with disappointment, only gave them a fortnight's eastward sailing before they had to abandon their quest.

While all this was being done Caspian

missed no chance of questioning all the oldest sea captains whom he could find in Narrowhaven to learn if they had any knowledge or even any rumors of land further to the east. He poured out many a flagon of the castle ale to weather-beaten men with short gray beards and clear blue eyes, and many a tall yarn he heard in return. But those who seemed the most truthful could tell of no lands beyond the Lone Islands, and many thought that if you sailed too far east you would come into the surges of a sea without lands that swirled perpetually round the rim of the world — "And that, I reckon, is where your Majesty's friends went to the bottom."

The rest had only wild stories of islands inhabited by headless men, floating islands, waterspouts, and a fire that burned along the water. Only one, to Reepicheep's delight, said, "And beyond that, Aslan's country. But that's beyond the end of the world and you can't get there." But when they questioned him he could only say that he'd heard it from his father.

Bern could only tell them that he had seen his six companions sail away eastward and that nothing had ever been heard of them again. He said this when he and Caspian were standing on the highest point of Avra looking down on the eastern ocean. "I've often been up here of a morning," said the Duke, "and seen the sun come up out of the sea, and sometimes it looked as if it were only a couple of miles away. And I've wondered about my friends and wondered what there really is behind that horizon. Nothing, most likely, yet I am always half ashamed that I stayed behind. But I wish your Majesty wouldn't go. We may need your help here. This closing the slave market might make a new world; war with Calormen is what I foresee. My liege, think again."

"I have an oath, my lord Duke," said Caspian. "And anyway, what *could* I say to Reepicheep?"

FIVE

THE STORM

AND WHAT CAME OF IT

It was nearly three weeks after their landing that the *Dawn Treader* was towed out of Narrowhaven harbor. Very solemn farewells had been spoken and a great crowd had assembled to see her departure. There had been cheers, and tears too, when Caspian made his last speech to the Lone Islanders and parted from the Duke and his family, but as the ship, her purple sail still flapping idly, drew further from the shore, and the sound of Caspian's trumpet from the poop came fainter across the water, everyone became silent. Then she came into the wind. The sail swelled out, the tug cast off and began rowing back, the first real wave ran up under the *Dawn Treader*'s prow, and she was a live ship again. The men off duty went below, Drinian took the first watch on the poop, and she turned her head eastward round the south of Avra.

The next few days were delightful. Lucy

thought she was the most fortunate girl in the world, as she woke each morning to see the reflections of the sunlit water dancing on the ceiling of her cabin and looked round on all the nice new things she had got in the Lone Islands — seaboots and buskins and cloaks and jerkins and scarves. And then she would go on deck and take a look from the forecastle at a sea which was a brighter blue each morning and drink in an air that was a little warmer day by day. After that came breakfast and such an appetite as one only has at sea.

She spent a good deal of time sitting on the little bench in the stern playing chess with Reepicheep. It was amusing to see him lifting the pieces, which were far too big for him, with both paws and standing on tiptoes if he made a move near the center of the board. He was a good player and when he remembered what he was doing he usually won. But every now and then Lucy won because the Mouse did something quite ridiculous like sending a knight into the danger of a queen and castle combined. This happened because he had momentarily forgotten it was a game of chess and was thinking of a real battle and making the knight do what he would certainly have done in its place. For his mind was full of forlorn hopes, death-or-glory charges, and last stands.

But this pleasant time did not last. There came an evening when Lucy, gazing idly astern at the long furrow or wake they were leaving behind them, saw a great rack of clouds building itself up in the west with amazing speed. Then a gap was torn in it and a yellow sunset poured through the gap. All the waves behind them seemed to take on unusual shapes and the sea was a drab or yellowish color like dirty canvas. The air grew cold. The ship seemed to move uneasily as if she felt danger behind her. The sail would be flat and limp one minute and wildly full the next. While she was noting these things and wondering at a sinister change which had come over the very noise of the wind, Drinian cried, "All hands on deck." In a moment everyone became frantically busy. The hatches were battened down, the galley fire was put out, men went aloft to reef the sail. Before they had finished the storm struck them. It seemed to Lucy that a great valley in the sea opened just before their bows, and they rushed down into it, deeper down than she would have believed possible. A great gray hill of water, far higher than the mast, rushed to meet them; it looked certain death but they were tossed to the top of it. Then the ship seemed to spin round. A cataract of water poured over the deck; the poop and forecastle were like two islands with a fierce sea between them. Up aloft the sailors were lying out along the yard desperately trying to get control of the sail. A broken rope stood out sideways in the wind as straight and stiff as if it was a poker.

"Get below, Ma'am," bawled Drinian. And Lucy, knowing that landsmen — and landswomen — are a nuisance to the crew, began to obey. It was not easy. The *Dawn Treader* was listing terribly to starboard and the deck sloped like the roof of a house. She had to clamber round to the top of the ladder, holding on to the rail, and then stand by while two men climbed up it, and then get down it as best she could. It was well she was already holding on tight for at the foot of the ladder another wave roared across the deck, up to her shoulders. She was already almost wet through with spray and rain but this was colder. Then she made a dash for the cabin door and got in and shut out for a moment the appalling sight of the speed with which they were rushing into the dark, but not of course the horrible confusion of creakings, groanings, snappings, clatterings, roarings and boomings which

only sounded more alarming below than they had done on the poop.

And all next day and all the next it went on. It went on till one could hardly even remember a time before it had begun. And there always had to be three men at the tiller and it was as much as three could do to keep any kind of a course. And there always had to be men at the pump. And there was hardly any rest for anyone, and nothing could be cooked and nothing could be dried, and one man was lost overboard, and they never saw the sun.

When it was over Eustace made the following entry in his diary:

"*September 3.* The first day for ages when I have been able to write. We had been driven before a hurricane for thirteen days and nights. I know that because I kept a careful count, though the others all say it was only twelve. *Pleasant* to be embarked on a dangerous voyage with people who can't even count right! I have had a ghastly time, up and down enormous waves hour after hour, usually wet to the skin, and not even an *attempt* at giving us proper meals. Needless to say there's no wireless or even a rocket, so no chance of signaling anyone for help. It all proves what I keep on telling them, the madness of setting out in a rotten little tub like this. It would be bad enough even if one was with decent people instead of fiends in human form. Caspian and Edmund are simply brutal to me. The night we lost our mast (there's only a stump left now), though I was *not at all* well, they forced me to come on deck and work like a slave. Lucy shoved her oar in by saying that Reepicheep was longing to go only he was too small. I wonder she doesn't see that everything that little beast does is all for the sake of *showing off.* Even at her age she ought to have that amount of sense. Today the beastly boat is level at last and the sun's out and we have all been jawing about what to do. We have food enough, pretty beastly stuff most of it, to last for sixteen days. (The poultry were all washed overboard. Even if they hadn't been, the storm would have stopped them laying.) The real trouble is water. Two casks seem to have got a leak knocked in them and are empty. (Narnian efficiency again.) On short rations, half a pint a day each, we've got enough for twelve days. (There's still lots of rum and wine but even *they* realize that would only make them thirstier.)

"If we could, of course, the sensible thing would be to turn west at once and make for the Lone Islands. But it took us eighteen days to get where we are, running like mad with a gale behind us. Even if we got an east wind it might take us far longer to get back. And at present there's no sign of an east wind — in fact there's no wind at all. As for rowing back, it would take far too long and Caspian says the men couldn't row on half a pint of water a day. I'm pretty sure this is wrong. I tried to explain that perspiration really cools people down, so the men would need less water if they were working. He didn't take any notice of this, which is always his way when he can't think of an answer. The others all voted for going *on* in the hope of finding land. I felt it my duty to point out that we didn't know there *was* any land ahead and tried to get them to see the dangers of *wishful thinking*. Instead of producing a better plan they had the cheek to ask me what I proposed. So I just explained coolly and quietly that I had been kidnapped and brought away on this *idiotic* voyage without my consent, and it was hardly *my* business to get *them* out of their scrape.

"*September 4*. Still becalmed. Very short rations for dinner and I got less than anyone. Caspian is very clever at helping and thinks I don't see! Lucy for some reason tried to make up to me by offering me some of hers but that *interfering prig* Edmund wouldn't let her. Pretty hot sun. Terribly thirsty all evening.

"*September 5*. Still becalmed and very hot. Feeling rotten all day and am sure I've got a temperature. Of course they haven't the sense to keep a thermometer on board.

"*September 6*. A horrible day. Woke up in the night *knowing* I was feverish and *must* have a drink of water. Any doctor would have said so. Heaven knows I'm the last person to try to get any unfair advantage but I never *dreamed* that this water-rationing would be meant to apply to a sick man. In fact I would have woken the others up and asked for some only I thought it would be selfish to wake them. So I just got up and took my cup and tiptoed out of the Black Hole we slept in, taking great care not to disturb Caspian and Edmund, for they've been sleeping badly since the heat and the short water began. I always try to consider others whether they are nice to me or not. I got out all right into the big room, if you can call it a room, where the rowing benches and the luggage are. The thing of water is at this end. All was going beautifully, but before I'd drawn a cupful who should catch me but that *little spy* Reep. I tried to explain that I was going on deck for a breath of air (the business about the water had nothing to do with him) and he asked me why I had a cup. He made such a noise that the whole ship was roused. They treated me scandalously. I asked, as I think anyone would have, why Reepicheep was sneaking about the water cask in the middle of the night. He said that as he was too small to be any use on deck, he did sentry over the water every night so that one more man could go to sleep. Now comes their rotten unfairness: they all believed *him*. Can you beat it?

"I had to apologize or the dangerous little brute would have been at me with his sword. And then Caspian showed up in his true colors as a brutal tyrant and said out loud for everyone to hear that anyone found 'stealing' water in future would 'get two dozen.' I didn't know what this meant till Edmund explained to me. It comes in the sort of books those Pevensie kids read.

"After this cowardly threat Caspian changed his tune and started being *patronizing*. Said he was sorry for me and that everyone felt just as feverish as I did and we must all make the best of it, etc., etc. Odious stuck-up prig. Stayed in bed all day today.

"*September 7*. A little wind today but still from the west. Made a few miles eastward with part of the sail, set on what Drinian calls the jury-mast — that means the bowsprit set upright and tied (they call it 'lashed') to the stump of the real mast. Still terribly thirsty.

"*September 8*. Still sailing east. I stay in my bunk all day now and see no one except Lucy till the two *friends* come to bed. Lucy gives me a little of her water ration. She says girls don't get as thirsty as boys. I had often thought this but it ought to be more generally known at sea.

"*September 9*. Land in sight; a very high mountain a long way off to the southeast.

"*September 10*. The mountain is bigger and clearer but still a long way off. Gulls again today for the first time since I don't know how long.

"*September 11.* Caught some fish and had them for dinner. Dropped asnchor at about 7 p.m. in three fathoms of water in a bay of this mountainous island. That idiot Caspian wouldn't let us go ashore because it was getting dark and he was afraid of savages and wild beasts. Extra water ration tonight."

What awaited them on this island was going to concern Eustace more than anyone else, but it cannot be told in his words because after September 11 he forgot about keeping his diary for a long time.

When morning came, with a low, gray sky but very hot, the adventurers found they were in a bay encircled by such cliffs and crags that it was like a Norwegian fjord. In front of them, at the head of the bay, there was some level land heavily overgrown with trees that appeared to be cedars, through which a rapid stream came out. Beyond that was a steep ascent ending in a jagged ridge and behind that a vague darkness of mountains which ran into dull-colored clouds so that you could not see their tops. The nearer cliffs, at each side of the bay, were streaked here and there with lines of white which everyone knew to be waterfalls, though at that

distance they did not show any movement or make any noise. Indeed the whole place was very silent and the water of the bay as smooth as glass. It reflected every detail of the cliffs. The scene would have been pretty in a picture but was rather oppressive in real life. It was not a country that welcomed visitors.

The whole ship's company went ashore in two boatloads and everyone drank and washed deliciously in the river and had a meal and a rest before Caspian sent four men back to keep the ship, and the day's work began. There was everything to be done. The casks must be brought ashore and the faulty ones mended if possible and all refilled; a tree — a pine if they could get it — must be felled and made into a new mast; sails must be repaired; a hunting party organized to shoot any game the land might yield; clothes to be washed and mended; and countless small breakages on board to be set right. For the *Dawn Treader* herself — and this was more obvious now that they saw her at a distance — could hardly be recognized as the same gallant ship which had left Narrowhaven. She looked a crippled, discolored hulk which anyone might have taken for a wreck. And her officers and crew were no better — lean, pale, red-eyed from lack of sleep, and dressed in rags.

As Eustace lay under a tree and heard all these plans being discussed his heart sank. Was there going to be no rest? It looked as if their first day on the longed-for land was going to be quite as hard work as a day at sea. Then a delightful idea occurred to him. Nobody was looking — they were all chattering about their ship as if they actually liked the beastly thing. Why shouldn't he simply slip away? He would take a stroll inland, find a cool, airy place up in the mountains, have a good long sleep, and not rejoin the others till the day's work was over. He felt it would do him good. But he would take great care to keep the bay and the ship in sight so as to be sure of his way back. He wouldn't like to be left behind in this country.

He at once put his plan into action. He rose quietly from his place and walked away among the trees, taking care to go slowly and in an aimless manner so that anyone who saw him would think he was merely stretching his legs. He was surprised to find how quickly the noise of conversation died away behind him and how very silent and warm and dark green the wood became. Soon he felt he could venture on a quicker and more determined stride.

This soon brought him out of the wood. The ground began sloping steeply up in front of him. The grass was dry and slippery but manageable if he used his hands as well as his feet, and though he panted and mopped his forehead a good deal, he plugged away steadily. This showed, by the way, that his new life, little as he suspected it, had already done him some good; the old Eustace, Harold and Alberta's Eustace, would have given up the climb after about ten minutes.

Slowly, and with several rests, he reached the ridge. Here he had expected to have a view into the heart of the island, but the clouds had now come lower and nearer and a sea of fog was rolling to meet him. He sat down and looked back. He was now so high that the bay looked small beneath him and miles of sea were visible. Then the fog from the mountains closed in all round him, thick but not cold, and he lay down and turned this way and that to find the most comfortable position to enjoy himself.

But he didn't enjoy himself, or not for very long. He began, almost for the first time in his life, to feel lonely. At first this feeling grew very gradually. And then he began to worry about the time. There was not the slightest sound. Suddenly it occurred to him that he might have been lying there for hours. Perhaps the others had gone! Perhaps they had let him wander away on purpose simply in order to leave him behind! He leaped up in a panic and began the descent.

At first he tried to do it too quickly, slipped on the steep grass, and slid for sev-eral feet. Then he thought this had carried him too far to the left — and as he came up he had seen precipices on that side. So he clambered up again, as near as he could guess to the place he had started from, and began the descent afresh, bearing to his right. After that things seemed to be going better. He went very cautiously, for he could not see more than a yard ahead, and there was still perfect silence all around him. It is very unpleasant to have to go cautiously when there is a voice inside you saying all the time, "Hurry, hurry, hurry." For every moment the terrible idea of being left behind grew stronger. If he had understood Caspian and the Pevensies at all he would have known, of course, that there was not the least chance of their doing any such thing. But he had persuaded himself that they were all fiends in human form.

"At last!" said Eustace, as he came slithering down a slide of loose stones (*scree,* they call it) and found himself on the level. "And now, where are those trees? There *is* something dark ahead. Why, I do believe the fog is clearing."

It was. The light increased every moment and made him blink. The fog lifted. He was in an utterly unknown valley and the sea was nowhere in sight.

SIX

THE ADVENTURES

OF EUSTACE

At that very moment the others were washing hands and faces in the river and generally getting ready for dinner and a rest. The three best archers had gone up into the hills north of the bay and returned laden with a pair of wild goats which were now roasting over a fire. Caspian had ordered a cask of wine ashore, strong wine of Archenland which had to be mixed with water before you drank it, so there would be plenty for all. The work had gone well so far and it was a merry meal. Only after the second helping of goat did Edmund say, "Where's that blighter Eustace?"

Meanwhile Eustace stared round the unknown valley. It was so narrow and deep, and the precipices which surrounded it so sheer, that it was like a huge pit or trench. The floor was grassy though strewn with rocks, and here and there Eustace saw black burnt patches like those you see on the sides of a railway embankment in a dry summer.

About fifteen yards away from him was a pool of clear, smooth water. There was, at first, nothing else at all in the valley; not an animal, not a bird, not an insect. The sun beat down and grim peaks and horns of mountains peered over the valley's edge.

Eustace realized of course that in the fog he had come down the wrong side of the ridge, so he turned at once to see about getting back. But as soon as he had looked he shuddered. Apparently he had by amazing luck found the only possible way down — a long green spit of land, horribly steep and narrow, with precipices on either side. There was no other possible way of getting back. But could he do it, now that he saw what it was really like? His head swam at the very thought of it.

He turned round again, thinking that at any rate he'd better have a good drink from the pool first. But as soon as he had turned and before he had taken a step forward into the valley he heard a noise behind him. It was only a small noise but it sounded loud in that immense silence. It froze him dead-still where he stood for a second. Then he slewed round his neck and looked.

At the bottom of the cliff a little on his left hand was a low, dark hole — the entrance to a cave perhaps. And out of this two thin wisps of smoke were coming. And the loose stones just beneath the dark hollow were moving (that was the noise he had heard)

just as if something were crawling in the dark behind them.

Something *was* crawling. Worse still, something was coming out. Edmund or Lucy or you would have recognized it at once, but Eustace had read none of the right books. The thing that came out of the cave was something he had never even imagined — a long lead-colored snout, dull red eyes, no feathers or fur, a long lithe body that trailed on the ground, legs whose elbows went up higher than its back like a spider's, cruel claws, bat's wings that made a rasping noise on the stones, yards of tail. And the lines of smoke were coming from its two nostrils. He never said the word *Dragon* to himself. Nor would it have made things any better if he had.

But perhaps if he had known something about dragons he would have been a little surprised at this dragon's behavior. It did not sit up and clap its wings, nor did it shoot out a stream of flame from its mouth. The smoke from its nostrils was like the smoke of a fire that will not last much longer. Nor did it seem to have noticed Eustace. It moved very slowly toward the pool — slowly and with many pauses. Even in his fear Eustace

felt that it was an old, sad creature. He wondered if he dared make a dash for the ascent. But it might look round if he made any noise. It might come more to life. Perhaps it was only shamming. Anyway, what was the use of trying to escape by climbing from a creature that could fly?

It reached the pool and slid its horrible

scaly chin down over the gravel to drink: but before it had drunk there came from it a great croaking or clanging cry and after a few twitches and convulsions it rolled round on its side and lay perfectly still with one claw in the air. A little dark blood gushed from its wide-opened mouth. The smoke from its nostrils turned black for a moment and then floated away. No more came.

For a long time Eustace did not dare to move. Perhaps this was the brute's trick, the way it lured travelers to their doom. But one couldn't wait forever. He took a step nearer, then two steps, and halted again. The dragon remained motionless; he noticed too that the red fire had gone out of its eyes. At last he came up to it. He was quite sure now that it was dead. With a shudder he touched it; nothing happened.

The relief was so great that Eustace almost laughed out loud. He began to feel as if he had fought and killed the dragon instead of merely seeing it die. He stepped over it and went to the pool for his drink, for the heat was getting unbearable. He was not surprised when he heard a peal of thunder. Almost immediately afterward the sun disappeared and before he had finished his drink big drops of rain were falling.

The climate of this island was a very unpleasant one. In less than a minute Eustace was wet to the skin and half blinded with such rain as one never sees in Europe. There was no use trying to climb out of the valley as long as this lasted. He bolted for the only shelter in sight — the dragon's cave. There he lay down and tried to get his breath.

Most of us know what we should expect to find in a dragon's lair, but, as I said before, Eustace had read only the wrong books. They had a lot to say about exports and imports and governments and drains, but they were weak on dragons. That is why he was so puzzled at the surface on which he was lying. Parts of it were too prickly to be stones and too hard to be thorns, and there seemed to be a great many round, flat things, and it all clinked when he moved. There was light enough at the cave's mouth to examine it by. And of course Eustace found it to be what any of us could have told him in advance — treasure. There were crowns (those were the prickly things), coins, rings, bracelets, ingots, cups, plates and gems.

Eustace (unlike most boys) had never thought much of treasure but he saw at once the use it would be in this new world which he had so foolishly stumbled into through the picture in Lucy's bedroom at home. "They don't have any tax here," he said, "and you don't have to give treasure to the government. With some of this stuff I could have quite a decent time here — perhaps in Calormen. It sounds the least phony of these countries. I wonder how much I can carry? That bracelet now — those things in it are probably diamonds — I'll slip that on my own wrist. Too big, but not if I push it right up here above my elbow. Then fill my pockets with diamonds — that's easier than gold. I wonder when this infernal rain's going to let up?" He got into a less uncomfortable part of the pile, where it was mostly coins, and settled down to wait. But a bad fright, when once it is over, and especially a bad fright following a mountain walk, leaves you very tired. Eustace fell asleep.

By the time he was sound asleep and snoring the others had finished dinner and become seriously alarmed about him. They shouted, "Eustace! Eustace! Coo-ee!" till they were hoarse and Caspian blew his horn.

"He's nowhere near or he'd have heard that," said Lucy with a white face.

"Confound the fellow," said Edmund. "What on earth did he want to slink away like this for?"

"But we must do something," said Lucy.

"He may have got lost, or fallen into a hole, or been captured by savages."

"Or killed by wild beasts," said Drinian.

"And a good riddance if he has, *I* say," muttered Rhince.

"Master Rhince," said Reepicheep, "you never spoke a word that became you less. The creature is no friend of mine but he is of the Queen's blood, and while he is one of our fellowship it concerns our honor to find him and to avenge him if he is dead."

"Of course we've got to find him (if we *can*)," said Caspian wearily. "That's the nuisance of it. It means a search party and endless trouble. Bother Eustace."

Meanwhile Eustace slept and slept — and slept. What woke him was a pain in his arm. The moon was shining in at the mouth of the cave, and the bed of treasures seemed to have grown much more comfortable: in fact he could hardly feel it at all. He was puzzled by the pain in his arm at first, but presently it occurred to him that the bracelet which he had shoved up above his elbow had become strangely tight. His arm must have swollen while he was asleep (it was his left arm).

He moved his right arm in order to feel his left, but stopped before he had moved it an inch and bit his lip in terror. For just in front of him, and a little on his right, where the moonlight fell clear on the floor of the cave, he saw a hideous shape moving. He knew that shape: it was a dragon's claw. It had moved as he moved his hand and became still when he stopped moving his hand.

"Oh, what a fool I've been," thought Eustace. "Of course, the brute had a mate and it's lying beside me."

For several minutes he did not dare to move a muscle. He saw two thin columns of smoke going up before his eyes, black against the moonlight; just as there had been smoke coming from the other dragon's nose before it died. This was so alarming that he held his breath. The two columns of smoke vanished. When he could hold his breath no longer he let it out stealthily; instantly two jets of smoke appeared again. But even yet he had no idea of the truth.

Presently he decided that he would edge very cautiously to his left and try to creep out of the cave. Perhaps the creature was asleep — and anyway it was his only chance. But of course before he edged to the left he looked to the left. Oh horror! There was a dragon's claw on that side too.

No one will blame Eustace if at this moment he shed tears. He was surprised at the size of his own tears as he saw them splashing on to the treasure in front of him.

They also seemed strangely hot; steam went up from them.

But there was no good crying. He must try to crawl out from between the two dragons. He began extending his right arm. The dragon's fore-leg and claw on his right went through exactly the same motion. Then he thought he would try his left. The dragon limb on that side moved too.

Two dragons, one on each side, mimicking whatever he did! His nerve broke and he simply made a bolt for it.

There was such a clatter and rasping, and clinking of gold, and grinding of stones, as he rushed out of the cave that he thought they were both following him. He daren't look back. He rushed to the pool. The twisted shape of the dead dragon lying in the moonlight would have been enough to frighten anyone but now he hardly noticed it. His idea was to get into the water.

But just as he reached the edge of the pool two things happened. First of all, it came over him like a thunder-clap that he had been running on all fours — and why on earth had he been doing that? And secondly, as he bent toward the water, he thought for a second that yet another dragon was staring up at him out of the pool. But in an instant he realized the truth. The dragon face in the pool was his own reflection. There was no doubt of it. It moved as he moved: it opened and shut its mouth as he opened and shut his.

He had turned into a dragon while he was asleep. Sleeping on a dragon's hoard with greedy, dragonish thoughts in his heart, he had become a dragon himself.

That explained everything. There had been no two dragons beside him in the cave. The claws to right and left had been his own right and left claws. The two columns of smoke had been coming from his own nostrils. As for the pain in his left arm (or what had been his left arm) he could now see what had happened by squinting with his left eye. The bracelet which had fitted very nicely on the upper arm of a boy was far too small for the thick, stumpy foreleg of a dragon. It had sunk deeply into his scaly flesh and there was a throbbing bulge on each side of it. He tore at the place with his dragon's teeth but could not get it off.

In spite of the pain, his first feeling was one of relief. There was nothing to be afraid of any more. He was a terror himself now and nothing in the world but a knight (and not all of those) would dare to attack him. He could get even with Caspian and Edmund now —

But the moment he thought this he realized that he didn't want to. He wanted to be friends. He wanted to get back among humans and talk and laugh and share things. He realized that he was a monster cut off from the whole human race. An appalling loneliness came over him. He began to see that the others had not really been fiends at all. He began to wonder if he himself had been such a nice person as he had always supposed. He longed for their voices. He would have been grateful for a kind word even from Reepicheep.

When he thought of this the poor dragon that had been Eustace lifted up its voice and wept. A powerful dragon crying its eyes out under the moon in a deserted valley is a

sight and a sound hardly to be imagined.

At last he decided he would try to find his way back to the shore. He realized now that Caspian would never have sailed away and left him. And he felt sure that somehow or other he would be able to make people understand who he was.

He took a long drink and then (I know this sounds shocking, but it isn't if you think it over) he ate nearly all the dead dragon. He was half-way through it before he realized what he was doing; for, you see, though his mind was the mind of Eustace, his tastes and his digestion were dragonish. And there is nothing a dragon likes so well as fresh dragon. That is why you so seldom find more than one dragon in the same country.

Then he turned to climb out of the valley. He began the climb with a jump and as soon as he jumped he found that he was flying. He had quite forgotten about his wings and it was a great surprise to him — the first pleasant surprise he had had for a long time. He rose high into the air and saw innumerable mountain-tops spread out beneath him in the moonlight. He could see the bay like a silver slab and the *Dawn Treader* lying at anchor and camp fires twinkling in the woods beside the beach. From a great height he launched himself down toward them in a single glide.

Lucy was sleeping very soundly for she had sat up till the return of the search party in hope of good news about Eustace. It had been led by Caspian and had come back late and weary. Their news was disquieting. They had found no trace of Eustace but had seen a dead dragon in a valley. They tried to make the best of it and everyone assured everyone else that there were not likely to be more dragons about, and that one which was dead at about three o'clock that afternoon (which was when they had seen it) would hardly have been killing people a very few hours before.

"Unless it ate the little brat and died of him: he'd poison anything," said Rhince. But he said this under his breath and no one heard it.

But later in the night Lucy was wakened, very softly, and found the whole company gathered close together and talking in whispers.

"What is it?" said Lucy.

"We must all show great constancy," Caspian was saying. "A dragon has just flown over the tree-tops and lighted on the beach. Yes, I am afraid it is between us and the ship. And arrows are no use against dragons. And they're not at all afraid of fire."

"With your Majesty's leave —" began Reepicheep.

"No, Reepicheep," said the King very firmly, "you are *not* to attempt a single combat with it. And unless you promise to obey me in this matter I'll have you tied up. We must just keep close watch and, as soon as it is light, go down to the beach and give it battle. I will lead. King Edmund will be on my right and the Lord Drinian on my left. There are no other arrangements to be made. It will be light in a couple of hours. In an hour's time let a meal be served out and what is left of the wine. And let everything be done silently."

"Perhaps it will go away," said Lucy.

"It'll be worse if it does," said Edmund, "because then we shan't know where it is. If there's a wasp in the room I like to be able to see it."

The rest of the night was dreadful, and when the meal came, though they knew they ought to eat, many found that they had very poor appetites. And endless hours seemed to pass before the darkness thinned and birds began chirping here and there and the world got colder and wetter than it had been all night and Caspian said, "Now for it, friends."

They got up, all with swords drawn, and

formed themselves into a solid mass with Lucy in the middle and Reepicheep on her shoulder. It was nicer than the waiting about and everyone felt fonder of everyone else than at ordinary times. A moment later they were marching. It grew lighter as they came to the edge of the wood. And there on the sand, like a giant lizard, or a flexible crocodile, or a serpent with legs, huge and horrible and humpy, lay the dragon.

But when it saw them, instead of rising up and blowing fire and smoke, the dragon retreated — you could almost say it waddled — back into the shallows of the bay.

"What's it wagging its head like that for?" said Edmund.

"And now it's nodding," said Caspian.

"And there's something coming from its eyes," said Drinian.

"Oh, can't you see," said Lucy. "It's crying. Those are tears."

"I shouldn't trust to that, Ma'am," said Drinian. "That's what crocodiles do, to put you off your guard."

"It wagged its head when you said that," remarked Edmund. "Just as if it meant No. Look, there it goes again."

"Do you think it understands what we're saying?" asked Lucy.

The dragon nodded its head violently.

Reepicheep slipped off Lucy's shoulder and stepped to the front.

"Dragon," came his shrill voice, "can you understand speech?"

The dragon nodded.

"Can you speak?"

It shook its head.

"Then," said Reepicheep, "it is idle to ask you your business. But if you will swear friendship with us raise your left foreleg above your head."

It did so, but clumsily because that leg was sore and swollen with the golden bracelet.

"Oh look," said Lucy, "there's something wrong with its leg. The poor thing — that's probably what it was crying about. Perhaps it came to us to be cured like in Androcles and the lion."

"Be careful, Lucy," said Caspian. "It's a very clever dragon but it may be a liar."

Lucy had, however, already run forward, followed by Reepicheep, as fast as his short legs could carry him, and then of course the boys and Drinian came too.

"Show me your poor paw," said Lucy. "I might be able to cure it."

The dragon-that-had-been-Eustace held out its sore leg gladly enough, remembering how Lucy's cordial had cured him of seasickness before he became a dragon. But he was disappointed. The magic fluid reduced the swelling and eased the pain a little but it could not dissolve the gold.

Everyone had now crowded round to watch the treatment, and Caspian suddenly exclaimed, "Look!" He was staring at the bracelet.

SEVEN

HOW THE

ADVENTURE ENDED

"Look at what?" said Edmund.

"Look at the device on the gold," said Caspian.

"A little hammer with a diamond above it like a star," said Drinian. "Why, I've seen that before."

"Seen it!" said Caspian. "Why, of course you have. It is the sign of a great Narnian house. This is the Lord Octesian's arm-ring."

"Villain," said Reepicheep to the dragon, "have you devoured a Narnian lord?" But the dragon shook his head violently.

"Or perhaps," said Lucy, "this *is* the Lord Octesian, turned into a dragon — under an enchantment, you know."

"It needn't be either," said Edmund. "All dragons collect gold. But I think it's a safe guess that Octesian got no further than this island."

"Are you the Lord Octesian?" said Lucy

to the dragon, and then, when it sadly shook its head, "Are you someone enchanted — someone human, I mean?"

It nodded violently.

And then someone said — people disputed afterward whether Lucy or Edmund said it first — "You're not — not Eustace by any chance?"

And Eustace nodded his terrible dragon head and thumped his tail in the sea and everyone skipped back (some of the sailors with ejaculations I will not put down in writing) to avoid the enormous and boiling tears which flowed from his eyes.

Lucy tried hard to console him and even screwed up her courage to kiss the scaly face, and nearly everyone said "Hard luck" and several assured Eustace that they would all stand by him and many said there was sure to be some way of disenchanting him and they'd have him as right as rain in a day or two. And of course they were all very anxious to hear his story, but he couldn't speak. More than once in the days that followed he attempted to write it for them on the sand. But this never succeeded. In the first place Eustace (never having read the right books) had no idea how to tell a story straight. And for another thing, the muscles and nerves of the dragon-claws that he had to use had never learned to write and were not built for writing anyway. As a result he never got nearly to the end before the tide came in and washed away all the writing except the bits he had already trodden on or accidentally swished out with his tail. And all that anyone had seen would be something like this — the dots are for the bits he had smudged out —

I WNET TO SLEE . . . RGOS AGRONS I MEAN DRANGONS CAVE CAUSE ITWAS DEAD AND AINING SO HAR . . . WOKE UP AND COU . . . . GET OFFF MI ARM OH BOTHER . . .

It was, however, clear to everyone that Eustace's character had been rather improved by becoming a dragon. He was anxious to help. He flew over the whole island and found that it was all mountainous and inhabited only by wild goats and droves of wild swine. Of these he brought back many carcasses as provisions for the ship. He was a very humane killer too, for he could dispatch a beast with one blow of his tail so that it didn't know (and presumably still doesn't know) it had been killed. He ate a few himself, of course, but always alone, for now that he was a dragon he liked his food raw but he could never bear to let others see him at his messy meals. And one day, flying slowly and wearily but in great triumph, he bore back to camp a great tall pine tree which he had torn up by the roots in a distant valley and which could be made into a capital mast. And in the evening if it turned chilly, as it sometimes did after the heavy rains, he was a comfort to everyone, for the whole party would come and sit with their backs against his hot sides and get well warmed and dried; and one puff of his fiery breath would light the most obstinate fire. Sometimes he would take a select party for a fly on his back, so that they could see wheeling below them the green slopes, the rocky heights, the narrow pit-like valleys and far out over the sea to the eastward a spot of darker blue on the blue horizon which might be land.

The pleasure (quite new to him) of being liked and, still more, of liking other people, was what kept Eustace from despair. For it was very dreary being a dragon. He shuddered whenever he caught sight of his own reflection as he flew over a mountain lake. He hated the huge bat-like wings, the saw-edged ridge on his back, and the cruel, curved claws. He was almost afraid to be alone with himself and yet he was ashamed to be with the others. On the evenings when

he was not being used as a hot-water bottle he would slink away from the camp and lie curled up like a snake between the wood and the water. On such occasions, greatly to his surprise, Reepicheep was his most constant comforter. The noble Mouse would creep away from the merry circle at the camp fire and sit down by the dragon's head, well to the windward to be out of the way of his smoky breath. There he would explain that what had happened to Eustace was a striking illustration of the turn of Fortune's wheel, and that if he had Eustace at his own house in Narnia (it was really a hole not a house and the dragon's head, let alone his body, would not have fitted in) he could show him more than a hundred examples of emperors, kings, dukes, knights, poets, lovers, astrono-mers, philosophers, and magicians, who had fallen from prosperity into the most dis-tressing circumstances, and of whom many

had recovered and lived happily ever afterward. It did not, perhaps, seem so very comforting at the time, but it was kindly meant
and Eustace never forgot it.

But of course what hung over everyone
like a cloud was the problem of what to do
with their dragon when they were ready to
sail. They tried not to talk of it when he was
there, but he couldn't help overhearing
things like, "Would he fit all along one side
of the deck? And we'd have to shift all the
stores to the other side down below so as to
balance," or, "Would towing him be any
good?" or "Would he be able to keep up by
flying?" and (most often of all), "But how
are we to feed him?" And poor Eustace realized more and more that since the first day
he came on board he had been an unmiti-
gated nuisance and that he was now a
greater nuisance still. And this ate into his
mind, just as that bracelet ate into his
foreleg. He knew that it only made it worse
to tear at it with his great teeth, but he
couldn't help tearing now and then, especially on hot nights.

About six days after they had landed on
Dragon Island, Edmund happened to wake
up very early one morning. It was just getting gray so that you could see the tree-

trunks if they were between you and the bay but not in the other direction. As he woke he thought he heard something moving, so he raised himself on one elbow and looked about him: and presently he thought he saw a dark figure moving on the seaward side of the wood. The idea that at once occurred to his mind was, "Are we so sure there are no natives on this island after all?" Then he thought it was Caspian — it was about the right size — but he knew that Caspian had been sleeping next to him and could see that he hadn't moved. Edmund made sure that his sword was in its place and then rose to investigate.

He came down softly to the edge of the wood and the dark figure was still there. He saw now that it was too small for Caspian and too big for Lucy. It did not run away. Edmund drew his sword and was about to challenge the stranger when the stranger said in a low voice, "Is that you, Edmund?"

"Yes. Who are you?" said he.

"Don't you know me?" said the other. "It's me — Eustace."

"By jove," said Edmund, "so it is. My dear chap —"

"Hush," said Eustace and lurched as if he were going to fall.

"Hello!" said Edmund, steadying him.

"What's up? Are you ill?"

Eustace was silent for so long that Edmund thought he was fainting; but at last he said, "It's been ghastly. You don't know . . . but it's all right now. Could we go and talk somewhere? I don't want to meet the others just yet."

"Yes, rather, anywhere you like," said Edmund. "We can go and sit on the rocks over there. I say, I *am* glad to see you — er — looking yourself again. You must have had a pretty beastly time."

They went to the rocks and sat down looking out across the bay while the sky got paler and paler and the stars disappeared except for one very bright one low down and near the horizon.

"I won't tell you how I became a — a dragon till I can tell the others and get it all over," said Eustace. "By the way, I didn't even know it *was* a dragon till I heard you all using the word when I turned up here the other morning. I want to tell you how I stopped being one."

"Fire ahead," said Edmund.

"Well, last night I was more miserable than ever. And that beastly arm-ring was hurting like anything —"

"Is that all right now?"

Eustace laughed — a different laugh from

any Edmund had heard him give before — and slipped the bracelet easily off his arm. "There it is," he said, "and anyone who likes can have it as far as I'm concerned. Well, as I say, I was lying awake and wondering what on earth would become of me. And then — but, mind you, it may have been all a dream. I don't know."

"Go on," said Edmund, with considerable patience.

"Well, anyway, I looked up and saw the very last thing I expected: a huge lion coming slowly toward me. And one queer thing was that there was no moon last night, but there was moonlight where the lion was. So it came nearer and nearer. I was terribly afraid of it. You may think that, being a dragon, I could have knocked any lion out easily enough. But it wasn't that kind of fear. I wasn't afraid of it eating me, I was just afraid of *it* — if you can understand. Well, it came close up to me and looked straight into my eyes. And I shut my eyes tight. But that wasn't any good because it told me to follow it."

"You mean it spoke?"

"I don't know. Now that you mention it, I don't think it did. But it told me all the same. And I knew I'd have to do what it told me, so I got up and followed it. And it led

123

me a long way into the mountains. And there was always this moonlight over and round the lion wherever we went. So at last we came to the top of a mountain I'd never seen before and on the top of this mountain there was a garden — trees and fruit and everything. In the middle of it there was a well.

"I knew it was a well because you could see the water bubbling up from the bottom of it: but it was a lot bigger than most wells — like a very big, round bath with marble steps going down into it. The water was as clear as anything and I thought if I could get in there and bathe it would ease the pain in my leg. But the lion told me I must undress first. Mind you, I don't know if he said any words out loud or not.

"I was just going to say that I couldn't undress because I hadn't any clothes on when I suddenly thought that dragons are snaky sort of things and snakes can cast their skins. Oh, of course, thought I, that's what the lion means. So I started scratching myself and my scales began coming off all over the place. And then I scratched a little deeper and, instead of just scales coming off here and there, my whole skin started peeling off beautifully, like it does after an illness, or as if I was a banana. In a minute or two I just stepped out of it. I could see it lying there beside me, looking rather nasty. It was a most lovely feeling. So I started to go down into the well for my bathe.

"But just as I was going to put my feet into the water I looked down and saw that they were all hard and rough and wrinkled and scaly just as they had been before. Oh, that's all right, said I, it only means I had another smaller suit on underneath the first one, and I'll have to get out of it too. So I scratched and tore again and this under-skin peeled off beautifully and out I stepped and left it lying beside the other one and went down to the well for my bathe.

"Well, exactly the same thing happened again. And I thought to myself, oh dear, however many skins have I got to take off? For I was longing to bathe my leg. So I scratched away for the third time and got off a third skin, just like the two others, and stepped out of it. But as soon as I looked at myself in the water I knew it had been no good.

"Then the lion said — but I don't know if it spoke — 'You will have to let me undress you.' I was afraid of his claws, I can tell you, but I was pretty nearly desperate now. So I just lay flat down on my back to let him do it.

"The very first tear he made was so deep

that I thought it had gone right into my heart. And when he began pulling the skin off, it hurt worse than anything I've ever felt. The only thing that made me able to bear it was just the pleasure of feeling the stuff peel off. You know — if you've ever picked the scab of a sore place. It hurts like billy — oh but it *is* such fun to see it coming away."

"I know exactly what you mean," said Edmund.

"Well, he peeled the beastly stuff right off — just as I thought I'd done it myself the other three times, only they hadn't hurt — and there it was lying on the grass: only ever so much thicker, and darker, and more knobbly-looking than the others had been. And there was I as smooth and soft as a peeled switch and smaller than I had been. Then he caught hold of me — I didn't like that much for I was very tender underneath now that I'd no skin on — and threw me into the water. It smarted like anything but only for a moment. After that it became perfectly delicious and as soon as I started swimming and splashing I found that all the pain had gone from my arm. And then I saw why. I'd turned into a boy again. You'd think me simply phony if I told you how I felt about my own arms. I know they've no

126

muscle and are pretty mouldy compared with Caspian's, but I was so glad to see them.

"After a bit the lion took me out and dressed me —"

"Dressed you. With his paws?"

"Well, I don't exactly remember that bit. But he did somehow or other: in new clothes — the same I've got on now, as a matter of fact. And then suddenly I was back here. Which is what makes me think it must have been a dream."

"No. It wasn't a dream," said Edmund.

"Why not?"

"Well, there are the clothes, for one thing. And you have been — well, un-dragoned, for another."

"What do you think it was, then?" asked Eustace.

"I think you've seen Aslan," said Edmund.

"Aslan!" said Eustace. "I've heard that name mentioned several times since we joined the *Dawn Treader*. And I felt — I don't know what — I hated it. But I was hating everything then. And by the way, I'd like to apologize. I'm afraid I've been pretty beastly."

"That's all right," said Edmund. "Between ourselves, you haven't been as bad as I was on my first trip to Narnia. You were

127

only an ass, but I was a traitor."

"Well, don't tell me about it, then," said Eustace. "But who is Aslan? Do you know him?"

"Well — he knows me," said Edmund. "He is the great Lion, the son of the Emperor-beyond-the-Sea, who saved me and saved Narnia. We've all seen him. Lucy sees him most often. And it may be Aslan's country we are sailing to."

Neither said anything for a while. The last bright star had vanished and though they could not see the sunrise because of the mountains on their right, they knew it was going on because the sky above them and the bay before them turned the color of roses. Then some bird of the parrot kind screamed in the wood behind them, they heard movements among the trees, and finally a blast on Caspian's horn. The camp was astir.

Great was the rejoicing when Edmund and the restored Eustace walked into the breakfast circle round the campfire. And now of course everyone heard the earlier part of his story. People wondered whether the other dragon had killed the Lord Octesian several years ago or whether Octesian himself had been the old dragon. The jewels with which Eustace had crammed his pockets in the cave had disappeared along with the clothes he had then been wearing: but no one, least of all Eustace himself, felt any desire to go back to that valley for more treasure.

In a few days now the *Dawn Treader*, remasted, repainted, and well stored, was ready to sail. Before they embarked Caspian caused to be cut on a smooth cliff facing the bay the words:

DRAGON ISLAND
DISCOVERED BY CASPIAN X,
KING OF NARNIA, ETC.
IN THE FOURTH
YEAR OF HIS REIGN.
HERE, AS WE SUPPOSE,
THE LORD OCTESIAN HAD HIS DEATH

It would be nice, and fairly nearly true, to say that "from that time forth Eustace was a different boy." To be strictly accurate, he began to be a different boy. He had relapses. There were still many days when he could be very tiresome. But most of those I shall not notice. The cure had begun.

The Lord Octesian's arm ring had a curious fate. Eustace did not want it and offered it to Caspian and Caspian offered it to Lucy. She did not care about having it. "Very well, then, catch as catch can," said

Caspian and flung it up in the air. This was when they were all standing looking at the inscription. Up went the ring, flashing in the sunlight, and caught, and hung, as neatly as

a well-thrown quoit, on a little projection on the rock. No one could climb up to get it from below and no one could climb down to get it from above. And there, for all I know, it is hanging still and may hang till that world ends.

EIGHT

TWO NARROW ESCAPES

Everyone was cheerful as the _Dawn Treader_ sailed from Dragon Island. They had fair winds as soon as they were out of the bay and came early next morning to the unknown land which some of them had seen when flying over the mountains while Eustace was still a dragon. It was a low green island inhabited by nothing but rabbits and a few goats, but from the ruins of stone huts, and from blackened places where fires had been, they judged that it had been peopled not long before. There were also some bones and broken weapons.

"Pirates' work," said Caspian.

"Or the dragon's," said Edmund.

The only other thing they found here was a little skin boat, or coracle, on the sands. It was made of hide stretched over a wicker framework. It was a tiny boat, barely four feet long, and the paddle which still lay in it was in proportion. They thought that either it had been made for a child or else that the people of that country had been Dwarfs.

Reepicheep decided to keep it, as it was just the right size for him; so it was taken on board. They called that land Burnt Island, and sailed away before noon.

For some five days they ran before a south-southeast wind, out of sight of all lands and seeing neither fish nor gull. Then they had a day that rained hard till the afternoon. Eustace lost two games of chess to Reepicheep and began to get like his old and disagreeable self again, and Edmund said he wished they could have gone to America with Susan. Then Lucy looked out of the stern windows and said:

"Hello! I do believe it's stopping. And what's *that?*"

They all tumbled up to the poop at this and found that the rain had stopped and that Drinian, who was on watch, was also staring hard at something astern. Or rather, at several things. They looked a little like smooth rounded rocks, a whole line of them with intervals of about forty feet in between.

"But they can't be rocks," Drinian was saying, "because they weren't there five minutes ago."

"And one's just disappeared," said Lucy.

"Yes, and there's another one coming up," said Edmund.

"And nearer," said Eustace.

"Hang it!" said Caspian. "The whole thing is moving this way."

"And moving a great deal quicker than we can sail, Sire," said Drinian. "It'll be up with us in a minute."

They all held their breath, for it is not at all nice to be pursued by an unknown something either on land or sea. But what it turned out to be was far worse than anyone had suspected. Suddenly, only about the length of a cricket pitch from their port side, an appalling head reared itself out of the sea. It was all greens and vermilions with purple blotches — except where shellfish clung to it — and shaped rather like a horse's, though without ears. It had enormous eyes, eyes made for staring through the dark depths of the ocean, and a gaping mouth filled with double rows of sharp fish-like teeth. It came up on what they first took to be a huge neck, but as more and more of it emerged everyone knew that this was not its neck but its body and that at last they were seeing what so many people have foolishly wanted to see — the great Sea Serpent. The folds of its gigantic tail could be seen far away, rising at intervals from the surface. And now its head was towering up higher than the mast.

Every man rushed to his weapon, but there was nothing to be done, the monster was out of reach. "Shoot! Shoot!" cried the Master Bowman, and several obeyed, but the arrows glanced off the Sea Serpent's hide as if it was iron-plated. Then, for a dreadful minute, everyone was still, staring up at its eyes and mouth and wondering where it would pounce.

But it didn't pounce. It shot its head forward across the ship on a level with the yard of the mast. Now its head was just beside the fighting-top. Still it stretched and stretched till its head was over the starboard bulwark. Then down it began to come — not onto the crowded deck but into the water, so that the whole ship was under an arch of serpent. And almost at once that arch began to get smaller: indeed on the starboard the Sea Serpent was now almost touching the *Dawn Treader*'s side.

Eustace (who had really been trying very hard to behave well, till the rain and the chess put him back) now did the first brave thing he had ever done. He was wearing a sword that Caspian had lent him. As soon as the serpent's body was near enough on the starboard side he jumped on to the bulwark and began hacking at it with all his might. It is true that he accomplished nothing beyond breaking Caspian's second-best sword into bits, but it was a fine thing for a beginner to have done.

Others would have joined him if at that moment Reepicheep had not called out, "Don't fight! Push!" It was so unusual for the Mouse to advise anyone not to fight that, even in that terrible moment, every eye turned to him. And when he jumped up on to the bulwark, forward of the snake, and set his little furry back against its huge scaly, slimy back, and began pushing as hard as he could, quite a number of people saw what he meant and rushed to both sides of the ship to do the same. And when, a moment later, the Sea Serpent's head appeared again, this time on the port side, and this time with its back to them, then everyone understood.

The brute had made a loop of itself round the *Dawn Treader* and was beginning to draw the loop tight. When it got quite tight — snap! — there would be floating matchwood where the ship had been and it could pick them out of the water one by one. Their only chance was to push the loop backward till it slid over the stern; or else (to put the same thing another way) to push the ship forward out of the loop.

Reepicheep alone had, of course, no more chance of doing this than of lifting up a cathedral, but he had nearly killed himself with trying before others shoved him aside.

Very soon the whole ship's company except Lucy and the Mouse (which was fainting) was in two long lines along the two bulwarks, each man's chest to the back of the man in front, so that the weight of the whole line was in the last man, pushing for their lives. For a few sickening seconds (which seemed like hours) nothing appeared to happen. Joints cracked, sweat dropped, breath came in grunts and gasps. Then they felt that the ship was moving. They saw that the snake-loop was further from the mast than it had been. But they also saw that it was smaller. And now the real danger was at hand. Could they get it over the poop, or was it already too tight? Yes. It would just fit. It was resting on the poop rails. A dozen or more sprang up on the poop. This was far better. The Sea Serpent's body was so low now that they could make a line across the poop and push side by side. Hope rose high till everyone remembered the high carved stern, the dragon tail, of the *Dawn Treader*. It would be quite impossible to get the brute over that.

"An axe," cried Caspian hoarsely, "and still shove." Lucy, who knew where everything was, heard him where she was standing on the main deck staring up at the poop. In a few seconds she had been below, got the axe, and was rushing up the ladder to the poop. But just as she reached the top there came a great crashing noise like a tree coming down and the ship rocked and darted forward. For at that very moment, whether because the Sea Serpent was being pushed so hard, or because it foolishly decided to draw the noose tight, the whole of the carved stern broke off and the ship was free.

The others were too exhausted to see what Lucy saw. There, a few yards behind them, the loop of Sea Serpent's body got rapidly smaller and disappeared into a splash. Lucy always said (but of course she was very excited at the moment, and it may have been only imagination) that she saw a look of idiotic satisfaction on the creature's face. What is certain is that it was a very stupid animal, for instead of pursuing the ship it turned its head round and began nosing all along its own body as if it expected to find the wreckage of the *Dawn Treader* there. But the *Dawn Treader* was already well away, running before a fresh breeze, and the men lay and sat panting and groaning all about the deck, till presently they were able to talk about it, and then to laugh about it. And when some rum had been served out they even raised a cheer;

and everyone praised the valor of Eustace (though it hadn't done any good) and of Reepicheep.

After this they sailed for three days more and saw nothing but sea and sky. On the fourth day the wind changed to the north and the seas began to rise; by the afternoon it had nearly become a gale. But at the same time they sighted land on their port bow.

"By your leave, Sire," said Drinian, "we will try to get under the lee of that country by rowing and lie in harbor, maybe till this is over." Caspian agreed, but a long row against the gale did not bring them to the land before evening. By the last light of that day they steered into a natural harbor and anchored, but no one went ashore that night. In the morning they found themselves in the green bay of a rugged, lonely-looking country which sloped up to a rocky summit. From the windy north beyond that summit clouds came streaming rapidly. They lowered the boat and loaded her with any of the water casks which were now empty.

"Which stream shall we water at, Drinian?" said Caspian as he took his seat in the stern-sheets of the boat. "There seem to be two coming down into the bay."

"It makes little odds, Sire," said Drinian. "But I think it's a shorter pull to that on the starboard — the eastern one."

"Here comes the rain," said Lucy.

"I should think it does!" said Edmund, for it was already pelting hard. "I say, let's go to the other stream. There are trees there and we'll have some shelter."

"Yes, let's," said Eustace. "No point in getting wetter than we need."

But all the time Drinian was steadily steering to the starboard, like tiresome people in cars who continue at forty miles an hour while you are explaining to them that they are on the wrong road.

"They're right, Drinian," said Caspian. "Why don't you bring her head round and make for the western stream?"

"As your Majesty pleases," said Drinian a little shortly. He had had an anxious day with the weather yesterday, and he didn't like advice from landsmen. But he altered course; and it turned out afterward that it was a good thing he did.

By the time they had finished watering, the rain was over and Caspian, with Eustace, the Pevensies, and Reepicheep, decided to walk up to the top of the hill and see what could be seen. It was a stiffish climb through coarse grass and heather and they saw neither man nor beast, except seagulls. When they reached the top they saw that it was a very small island, not more than twenty acres; and from this height the sea looked larger and more desolate than it did from the deck, or even the fighting-top, of the *Dawn Treader*.

"Crazy, you know," said Eustace to Lucy in a low voice, looking at the eastern horizon. "Sailing on and on into *that* with no idea what we may get to." But he only said it out of habit, not really nastily as he would have done at one time.

It was too cold to stay long on the ridge for the wind still blew freshly from the north.

"Don't let's go back the same way," said Lucy as they turned; "let's go along a bit and come down by the other stream, the one Drinian wanted to go to."

Everyone agreed to this and after about fifteen minutes they were at the source of the second river. It was a more interesting place than they had expected; a deep little mountain lake, surrounded by cliffs except for a narrow channel on the seaward side out of which the water flowed. Here at last they were out of the wind, and all sat down in the heather above the cliff for a rest.

All sat down, but one (it was Edmund) jumped up again very quickly.

"They go in for sharp stones on this island," he said, groping about in the heather. "Where is the wretched thing? . . . Ah, now I've got it . . . Hullo! It wasn't a stone at all, it's a sword-hilt. No, by jove, it's a whole sword; what the rust has left of it. It must have lain here for ages."

"Narnian, too, by the look of it," said Caspian, as they all crowded round.

"I'm sitting on something too," said Lucy. "Something hard." It turned out to be the remains of a mail shirt. By this time everyone was on hands and knees, feeling in the thick heather in every direction. Their search revealed, one by one, a helmet, a dagger, and a few coins; not Calormen crescents but genuine Narnian "Lions" and "Trees" such as you might see any day in the market-place of Beaversdam or Beruna.

"Looks as if this might be all that's left of one of our seven lords," said Edmund.

"Just what I was thinking," said Caspian. "I wonder which it was. There's nothing on the dagger to show. And I wonder how he died."

"And how we are to avenge him," added Reepicheep.

Edmund, the only one of the party who had read several detective stories, had meanwhile been thinking.

"Look here," he said, "there's something

very fishy about this. He can't have been killed in a fight."

"Why not?" asked Caspian.

"No bones," said Edmund. "An enemy might take the armor and leave the body. But who ever heard of a chap who'd won a fight carrying away the body and leaving the armor?"

"Perhaps he was killed by a wild animal," Lucy suggested.

"It'd be a clever animal," said Edmund, "that would take a man's mail shirt off."

"Perhaps a dragon?" said Caspian.

"Nothing doing," said Eustace. "A dragon couldn't do it. I ought to know."

"Well, let's get away from the place, anyway," said Lucy. She had not felt like sitting down again since Edmund had raised the question of bones.

"If you like," said Caspian, getting up. "I don't think any of this stuff is worth taking away."

They came down and round to the little opening where the stream came out of the lake, and stood looking at the deep water within the circle of cliffs. If it had been a hot day, no doubt some would have been tempted to bathe and everyone would have had a drink. Indeed, even as it was, Eustace was on the very point of stooping down and scooping up some water in his hands when Reepicheep and Lucy both at the same moment cried, "Look," so he forgot about his drink and looked into the water.

The bottom of the pool was made of large grayish-blue stones and the water was perfectly clear, and on the bottom lay a life-size figure of a man, made apparently of gold. It lay face downward with its arms stretched out above its head. And it so happened that as they looked at it, the clouds parted and the sun shone out. The golden shape was lit up from end to end. Lucy thought it was the most beautiful statue she had ever seen.

"Well!" whistled Caspian. "That was worth coming to see! I wonder, can we get it out?"

"We can dive for it, Sire," said Reepicheep.

"No good at all," said Edmund. "At least, if it's really gold — solid gold — it'll be far too heavy to bring up. And that pool's twelve or fifteen feet deep if it's an inch. Half a moment, though. It's a good thing I've brought a hunting spear with me. Let's see what the depth *is* like. Hold on to my hand, Caspian, while I lean out over the water a bit." Caspian took his hand and Edmund, leaning forward, began to lower his spear into the water.

Before it was half-way in Lucy said, "I

don't believe the statue is gold at all. It's only the light. Your spear looks just the same color."

"What's wrong?" asked several voices at once; for Edmund had suddenly let go of the spear.

"I couldn't hold it," gasped Edmund. "It seemed so *heavy.*"

"And there it is on the bottom now," said Caspian, "and Lucy is right. It looks just the same color as the statue."

But Edmund, who appeared to be having some trouble with his boots — at least he was bending down and looking at them — straightened himself all at once and shouted out in the sharp voice which people hardly ever disobey:

"Get back! Back from the water. All of you. At once!!"

They all did and stared at him.

"Look," said Edmund, "look at the toes of my boots."

"They look a bit yellow," began Eustace.

"They're gold, solid gold," interrupted Edmund. "Look at them. Feel them. The leather's pulled away from it already. And they're as heavy as lead."

"By Aslan!" said Caspian. "You don't mean to say — ?"

"Yes, I do," said Edmund. "That water turns things into gold. It turned the spear into gold, that's why it got so heavy. And it was just lapping against my feet (it's a good thing I wasn't barefoot) and it turned the toe-caps into gold. And that poor fellow on the bottom — well, you see."

"So it isn't a statue at all," said Lucy in a low voice.

"No. The whole thing is plain now. He was here on a hot day. He undressed on top of the cliff — where we were sitting. The clothes have rotted away or been taken by birds to line nests with; the armor's still there. Then he dived and —"

"Don't," said Lucy. "What a horrible thing."

"And what a narrow shave *we've* had," said Edmund.

"Narrow indeed," said Reepicheep. "Anyone's finger, anyone's foot, anyone's whisker, or anyone's tail, might have slipped into the water at any moment."

"All the same," said Caspian, "we may as well test it." He stooped down and wrenched up a spray of heather. Then, very cautiously, he knelt beside the pool and dipped it in. It was heather that he dipped; what he drew out was a perfect model of heather made of the purest gold, heavy and soft as lead.

"The King who owned this island," said Caspian slowly, and his face flushed as he spoke, "would soon be the richest of all Kings of the world. I claim this land forever as a Narnian possession. It shall be called Goldwater Island. And I bind all of you to secrecy. No one must know of this. Not even Drinian — on pain of death, do you hear?"

"Who are you talking to?" said Edmund. "I'm no subject of yours. If anything it's the other way round. I am one of the four ancient sovereigns of Narnia and you are under allegiance to the High King my brother."

"So it has come to that, King Edmund, has it?" said Caspian, laying his hand on his sword-hilt.

"Oh, stop it, both of you," said Lucy. "That's the worst of doing anything with boys. You're all such swaggering, bullying idiots — oooh! —" Her voice died away into a gasp. And everyone else saw what she had seen.

Across the gray hillside above them —
gray, for the heather was not yet in bloom —
without noise, and without looking at them,
and shining as if he were in bright sunlight
though the sun had in fact gone in, passed
with slow pace the hugest lion that human
eyes have ever seen. In describing the scene
Lucy said afterward, "He was the size of an
elephant," though at another time she only
said, "The size of a cart-horse." But it was
not the size that mattered. Nobody dared to
ask what it was. They knew it was Aslan.

And nobody ever saw how or where he
went. They looked at one another like
people waking from sleep.

"What were we talking about?" said Caspian. "Have I been making rather an ass of
myself?"

"Sire," said Reepicheep, "this is a place
with a curse on it. Let us get back on board
at once. And if I might have the honor of
naming this island, I should call it Deathwater."

"That strikes me as a very good name,
Reep," said Caspian, "though now that I
come to think of it, I don't know why. But
the weather seems to be settling and I dare
say Drinian would like to be off. What a lot
we shall have to tell him."

But in fact they had not much to tell for

the memory of the last hour had all become confused.

"Their Majesties all seemed a bit bewitched when they came aboard," said Drinian to Rhince some hours later when the *Dawn Treader* was once more under sail and Deathwater Island already below the horizon. "Something happened to them in that place. The only thing I could get clear was that they think they've found the body of one of these lords we're looking for."

"You don't say so, Captain," answered Rhince. "Well, that's three. Only four more. At this rate we might be home soon after the New Year. And a good thing too. My baccy's running a bit low. Good night, Sir."

NINE

THE ISLAND

OF THE VOICES

And now the winds which had so long been from the northwest began to blow from the west itself and every morning when the sun rose out of the sea the curved prow of the *Dawn Treader* stood up right across the middle of the sun. Some thought that the sun looked larger than it looked from Narnia, but others disagreed. And they sailed and sailed before a gentle yet steady breeze and saw neither fish nor gull nor ship nor shore. And stores began to get low again, and it crept into their hearts that perhaps they might have come to a sea which went on forever. But when the very last day on which they thought they could risk continuing their eastward voyage dawned, it revealed, right ahead between them and the sunrise, a low land lying like a cloud.

They made harbor in a wide bay about the middle of the afternoon and landed. It was a very different country from any they had yet seen. For when they had crossed the sandy beach they found all silent and empty as if it were an uninhabited land, but before them there were level lawns in which the grass was as smooth and short as it used to be in the grounds of a great English house where ten gardeners were kept. The trees, of which there were many, all stood well apart from one another, and there were no broken branches and no leaves lying on the ground. Pigeons sometimes cooed but there was no other noise.

Presently they came to a long, straight, sanded path with not a weed growing on it and trees on either hand. Far off at the other end of this avenue they now caught sight of a house — very long and gray and quiet-looking in the afternoon sun.

Almost as soon as they entered this path Lucy noticed that she had a little stone in her shoe. In that unknown place it might have been wiser for her to ask the others to wait while she took it out. But she didn't; she just dropped quietly behind and sat down to take off her shoe. Her lace had got into a knot.

Before she had undone the knot the others were a fair distance ahead. By the time she had got the stone out and was putting the shoe on again she could no longer hear them. But almost at once she heard something else. It was not coming from the direction of the house.

What she heard was a thumping. It sounded as if dozens of strong workmen were hitting the ground as hard as they could with great wooden mallets. And it was very quickly coming nearer. She was already sitting with her back to a tree, and as the tree was not one she could climb, there was really nothing to do but to sit dead still and press herself against the tree and hope she wouldn't be seen.

Thump, thump, thump . . . and whatever it was must be very close now for she could feel the ground shaking. But she could see nothing. She thought the thing — or things — must be just behind her. But then there came a thump on the path right in front of her. She knew it was on the path not only by the sound but because she saw the sand scatter as if it had been struck a heavy blow. But she could see nothing that had struck it. Then all the thumping noises drew together about twenty feet away from her and suddenly ceased. Then came the Voice.

It was really very dreadful because she could still see nobody at all. The whole of that park-like country still looked as quiet and empty as it had looked when they first landed. Nevertheless, only a few feet away from her, a voice spoke. And what it said was:

"Mates, now's our chance."

Instantly a whole chorus of other voices replied, "Hear him. Hear him. 'Now's our chance,' he said. Well done, Chief. You never said a truer word."

"What I say," continued the first voice, "is, get down to the shore between them and their boat, and let every mother's son look to his weapons. Catch 'em when they try to put to sea."

"Eh, that's the way," shouted all the other voices. "You never made a better plan, Chief. Keep it up, Chief. You couldn't have a better plan than that."

"Lively, then, mates, lively," said the first voice. "Off we go."

"Right again, Chief," said the others. "Couldn't have a better order. Just what we were going to say ourselves. Off we go."

Immediately the thumping began again — very loud at first but soon fainter and fainter, till it died out in the direction of the sea.

Lucy knew there was no time to sit puzzling as to what these invisible creatures might be. As soon as the thumping noise had died away she got up and ran along the path after the others as quickly as her legs would carry her. They must at all costs be warned.

While this had been happening the others had reached the house. It was a low building — only two stories high — made of a beautiful mellow stone, many-windowed, and partially covered with ivy. Everything was so still that Eustace said, "I think it's empty," but Caspian silently pointed to the column of smoke which rose from one chimney.

They found a wide gateway open and passed through it into a paved courtyard. And it was here that they had their first indication that there was something odd about this island. In the middle of the courtyard stood a pump, and beneath the pump a bucket. There was nothing odd about that. But the pump handle was moving up and down, though there seemed to be no one moving it.

"There's some magic at work here," said Caspian.

"Machinery!" said Eustace. "I do believe we've come to a civilized country at last."

At that moment Lucy, hot and breathless, rushed into the courtyard behind them. In a low voice she tried to make them understand what she had overheard. And when they had partly understood it even the bravest of them did not look very happy.

"Invisible enemies," muttered Caspian. "And cutting us off from the boat. This is an ugly furrow to plow."

"You've no idea what *sort* of creatures they are, Lu?" asked Edmund.

"How can I, Ed, when I couldn't see them?"

"Did they sound like humans from their footsteps?"

"I didn't hear any noise of feet — only voices and this frightful thudding and thumping — like a mallet."

"I wonder," said Reepicheep, "do they become visible when you drive a sword into them?"

"It looks as if we shall find out," said Caspian. "But let's get out of this gateway. There's one of these gentry at that pump listening to all we say."

They came out and went back on to the path where the trees might possibly make them less conspicuous. "Not that it's any good *really*," said Eustace, "trying to hide from people you can't see. They may be all round us."

"Now, Drinian," said Caspian. "How would it be if we gave up the boat for lost, went down to another part of the bay, and signaled to the *Dawn Treader* to stand in and take us aboard?"

"Not depth for her, Sire," said Drinian.

"We could swim," said Lucy.

"Your Majesties all," said Reepicheep, "hear me. It is folly to think of avoiding an invisible enemy by any amount of creeping and skulking. If these creatures mean to bring us to battle, be sure they will succeed. And whatever comes of it I'd sooner meet them face to face than be caught by the tail."

"I really think Reep is in the right this time," said Edmund.

"Surely," said Lucy, "if Rhince and the others on the *Dawn Treader* see us fighting on the shore they'll be able to do *something*."

"But they won't see us fighting if they can't see any enemy," said Eustace miserably. "They'll think we're just swinging our swords in the air for fun."

There was an uncomfortable pause.

"Well," said Caspian at last, "let's get on with it. We must go and face them. Shake hands all round — arrow on the string, Lucy — swords out, everyone else — and now for it. Perhaps they'll parley."

It was strange to see the lawns and the great trees looking so peaceful as they marched back to the beach. And when they arrived there, and saw the boat lying where they had left her, and the smooth sand with no one to be seen on it, more than one doubted whether Lucy had not merely imagined all she had told them. But before they reached the sand, a voice spoke out of the air.

"No further, masters, no further now," it

said. "We've got to talk with you first. There's fifty of us and more here with weapons in our fists."

"Hear him, hear him," came the chorus. "That's our Chief. You can depend on what he says. He's telling you the truth, he is."

"I do not see these fifty warriors," observed Reepicheep.

"That's right, that's right," said the Chief Voice. "You don't see us. And why not? Because we're invisible."

"Keep it up, Chief, keep it up," said the Other Voices. "You're talking like a book. They couldn't ask for a better answer than that."

"Be quiet, Reep," said Caspian, and then added in a louder voice, "You invisible people, what do you want with us? And what have we done to earn your enmity?"

"We want something that little girl can do for us," said the Chief Voice. (The others explained that this was just what they would have said themselves.)

"Little girl!" said Reepicheep. "The lady is a queen."

"We don't know about queens," said the Chief Voice. ("No more we do, no more we do," chimed in the others.) "But we want something she can do."

"What is it?" said Lucy.

"And if it is anything against her Majesty's honor or safety," added Reepicheep, "you will wonder to see how many we can kill before we die."

"Well," said the Chief Voice. "It's a long story. Suppose we all sit down?"

The proposal was warmly approved by the other voices but the Narnians remained standing.

"Well," said the Chief Voice. "It's like this. This island has been the property of a great magician time out of mind. And we all are — or perhaps in a manner of speaking, I might say, we were — his servants. Well, to cut a long story short, this magician that I was speaking about, he told us to do something we didn't like. And why not? Because we didn't want to. Well, then, this same magician he fell into a great rage; for I ought to tell you he owned the island and he wasn't used to being crossed. He was terribly downright, you know. But let me see, where am I? Oh yes, this magician then, he goes upstairs (for you must know he kept all his magic things up there and we all lived down below), I say he goes upstairs and puts a spell on us. An uglifying spell. If you saw us now, which in my opinion you may thank your stars you can't, you wouldn't believe what we looked like before we were uglified.

You wouldn't really. So there we all were so ugly we couldn't bear to look at one another. So then what did we do? Well, I'll tell you what we did. We waited till we thought this same magician would be asleep in the afternoon and we creep upstairs and go to his magic book, as bold as brass, to see if we can do anything about this uglification. But we were all of a sweat and a tremble, so I won't deceive you. But, believe me or believe me not, I do assure you that we couldn't find anything in the way of a spell for taking off the ugliness. And what with time getting on and being afraid that the old gentleman might wake up any minute — I was all of a muck sweat, so I won't deceive you — well, to cut a long story short, whether we did right or whether we did wrong, in the end we see a spell for making people invisible. And we thought we'd rather be invisible than go on being as ugly as all that. And why? Because we'd like it better. So my little girl, who's just about your little girl's age, and a sweet child she was before she was uglified, though now — but least said soonest mended — I say, my little girl she says the spell, for it's got to be a little girl or else the magician himself, if you see my meaning, for otherwise it won't work. And why not? Because nothing happens. So my Clipsie says the spell, for I ought to have told you she reads beautifully, and there we all were as invisible as you could wish to see. And I do assure you it was a relief not to see one another's faces. At first, anyway. But the long and the short of it is we're mortal tired of being invisible. And there's another thing. We never reckoned on this magician (the one I was telling you about before) going invisible too. But we haven't ever seen him since. So we don't know if he's dead, or gone away, or whether he's just sitting upstairs being invisible, and perhaps coming down and being invisible there. And, believe me, it's no manner of use listening because he always did go about with his bare feet on, making no more noise than a great big cat. And I'll tell all you gentlemen straight, it's getting more than what our nerves can stand."

Such was the Chief Voice's story, but very much shortened, because I have left out what the Other Voices said. Actually he never got out more than six or seven words without being interrupted by their agreements and encouragements, which drove the Narnians nearly out of their minds with impatience. When it was over there was a very long silence.

"But," said Lucy at last, "what's all this

got to do with us? I don't understand."

"Why, bless me, if I haven't gone and left out the whole point," said the Chief Voice.

"That you have, that you have," roared the Other Voices with great enthusiasm. "No one couldn't have left it out cleaner and better. Keep it up, Chief, keep it up."

"Well, I needn't go over the whole story again," began the Chief Voice.

"No. Certainly not," said Caspian and Edmund.

"Well, then, to put it in a nutshell," said the Chief Voice, "we've been waiting for ever so long for a nice little girl from foreign parts, like it might be you, Missie — that would go upstairs and go to the magic book and find the spell that takes off the invisibleness, and say it. And we all swore that the first strangers as landed on this island (having a nice little girl with them, I mean, for if they hadn't it'd be another matter) we wouldn't let them go away alive unless they'd done the needful for us. And that's why, gentlemen, if your little girl doesn't come up to scratch, it will be our painful duty to cut all your throats. Merely in the way of business, as you might say, and no offense, I hope."

"I don't see all your weapons," said Reepicheep. "Are they invisible too?" The words were scarcely out of his mouth before they heard a whizzing sound and next moment a spear had stuck, quivering, in one of the trees behind them.

"That's a spear, that is," said the Chief Voice.

"That it is, Chief, that it is," said the others. "You couldn't have put it better."

"And it came from my hand," the Chief Voice continued. "They get visible when they leave us."

"But why do you want *me* to do this?" asked Lucy. "Why can't one of your own people? Haven't you got any girls?"

"We dursen't, we dursen't," said all the Voices. "We're not going upstairs again."

"In other words," said Caspian, "you are asking this lady to face some danger which you daren't ask your own sisters and daughters to face!"

"That's right, that's right," said all the Voices cheerfully. "You couldn't have said it better. Eh, you've had some education, you have. Anyone can see that."

"Well, of all the outrageous —" began Edmund, but Lucy interrupted.

"Would I have to go upstairs at night, or would it do in daylight?"

"Oh, daylight, daylight, to be sure," said the Chief Voice. "Not at night. No one's

162

asking you to do that. Go upstairs in the dark? Ugh."

"All right, then, I'll do it," said Lucy. "No," she said, turning to the others, "don't try to stop me. Can't you see it's no use? There are dozens of them there. We can't fight them. And the other way there *is* a chance."

"But a magician!" said Caspian.

"I know," said Lucy. "But he mayn't be as bad as they make out. Don't you get the idea that these people are not very brave?"

"They're certainly not very clever," said Eustace.

"Look here, Lu," said Edmund. "We really can't let you do a thing like this. Ask Reep, I'm sure he'll say just the same."

"But it's to save my own life as well as yours," said Lucy. "I don't want to be cut to bits with invisible swords any more than anyone else."

"Her Majesty is in the right," said Reepicheep. "If we had any assurance of saving *her* by battle, our duty would be very plain. It appears to me that we have none. And the service they ask of her is in no way contrary to her Majesty's honor, but a noble and heroical act. If the Queen's heart moves her to risk the magician, I will not speak against it."

As no one had ever known Reepicheep to be afraid of anything, he could say this without feeling at all awkward. But the boys, who had all been afraid quite often, grew very red. None the less, it was such obvious sense that they had to give in. Loud cheers broke from the invisible people when their decision was announced, and the Chief Voice (warmly supported by all the others) invited the Narnians to come to supper and spend the night. Eustace didn't want to accept, but Lucy said, "I'm sure they're not treacherous. They're not like that at all," and the others agreed. And so, accompanied by an enormous noise of thumpings (which became louder when they reached the flagged and echoing courtyard) they all went back to the house.

TEN

THE MAGICIAN'S BOOK

The invisible people feasted their guests royally. It was very funny to see the plates and dishes coming to the table and not to see anyone carrying them. It would have been funny even if they had moved along level with the floor, as you would expect things to do in invisible hands. But they didn't. They progressed up the long dining-hall in a series of bounds or jumps. At the highest point of each jump a dish would be about fifteen feet up in the air; then it would come down and stop quite suddenly about three feet from the floor. When the dish contained anything like soup or stew the result was rather disastrous.

"I'm beginning to feel very inquisitive about these people," whispered Eustace to Edmund. "Do you think they're human at all? More like huge grasshoppers or giant frogs, I should say."

"It does look like it," said Edmund. "But don't put the idea of the grasshoppers into Lucy's head. She's not too keen on insects; especially big ones."

The meal would have been pleasanter if it had not been so exceedingly messy, and also if the conversation had not consisted entirely of agreements. The invisible people agreed about everything. Indeed most of their remarks were the sort it would not be easy to disagree with: "What I always say is, when a chap's hungry, he likes some victuals," or "Getting dark now; always does at night," or even "Ah, you've come over the water. Powerful wet stuff, ain't it?" And Lucy could not help looking at the dark yawning entrance to the foot of the staircase — she could see it from where she sat — and wondering what she would find when she went up those stairs next morning. But it was a good meal otherwise, with mushroom soup and boiled chickens and hot boiled ham and gooseberries, redcurrants, curds, cream, milk, and mead. The others liked the mead but Eustace was sorry afterward that he had drunk any.

When Lucy woke up next morning it was like waking up on the day of an examination or a day when you are going to the dentist. It was a lovely morning with bees buzzing in and out of her open window and the lawn outside looking very like somewhere in England. She got up and dressed and tried to talk and eat ordinarily at breakfast. Then, after being instructed by the Chief Voice about what she was to do upstairs, she bid goodbye to the others, said nothing, walked to the bottom of the stairs, and began going up them without once looking back.

It was quite light, that was one good thing. There was, indeed, a window straight ahead of her at the top of the first flight. As long as she was on that flight she could hear the *tick-tock-tick-tock* of a grandfather clock in the hall below. Then she came to the landing and had to turn to her left up the next flight; after that she couldn't hear the clock any more.

Now she had come to the top of the stairs. Lucy looked and saw a long, wide passage with a large window at the far end. Apparently the passage ran the whole length of the house. It was carved and paneled and carpeted and very many doors opened off it on each side. She stood still and couldn't hear the squeak of a mouse, or the buzzing of a fly, or the swaying of a curtain, or anything — except the beating of her own heart.

"The last doorway on the left," she said to herself. It did seem a bit hard that it should be the last. To reach it she would have to walk past room after room. And in any room there might be the magician — asleep, or awake, or invisible, or even dead. But it wouldn't do to think about that. She set out on her journey. The carpet was so thick that her feet made no noise.

"There's nothing whatever to be afraid of yet," Lucy told herself. And certainly it was a quiet, sunlit passage; perhaps a bit too quiet. It would have been nicer if there had not been strange signs painted in scarlet on the doors — twisty, complicated things which obviously had a meaning and it mightn't be a very nice meaning either. It would have been nicer still if there weren't those masks hanging on the wall. Not that they were exactly ugly — or not so very ugly — but the empty eye-holes did look queer, and if you let yourself you would soon start imagining that the masks were doing things as soon as your back was turned to them.

After about the sixth door she got her first real fright. For one second she felt almost certain that a wicked little bearded face had popped out of the wall and made a grimace at her. She forced herself to stop and look at it. And it was not a face at all. It was a little mirror just the size and shape of her own face, with hair on the top of it and a beard hanging down from it, so that when you looked in the mirror your own face fitted into the hair and beard and it looked as if they belonged to you. "I just caught my own

reflection with the tail of my eye as I went past," said Lucy to herself. "That was all it was. It's quite harmless." But she didn't like the look of her own face with that hair and beard, and went on. (I don't know what the Bearded Glass was for because I am not a magician.)

Before she reached the last door on the left, Lucy was beginning to wonder whether the corridor had grown longer since she began her journey and whether this was part of the magic of the house. But she got to it at last. And the door was open.

It was a large room with three big windows and it was lined from floor to ceiling with books; more books than Lucy had ever seen before, tiny little books, fat and dumpy books, and books bigger than any church Bible you have ever seen, all bound in leather and smelling old and learned and magical. But she knew from her instructions that she need not bother about any of these. For *the* Book, the Magic Book, was lying on a reading-desk in the very middle of the room. She saw she would have to read it standing (and anyway there were no chairs) and also that she would have to stand with her back to the door while she read it. So at once she turned to shut the door.

It wouldn't shut.

Some people may disagree with Lucy about this, but I think she was quite right. She said she wouldn't have minded if she could have shut the door, but that it was unpleasant to have to stand in a place like that with an open doorway right behind your back. I should have felt just the same. But there was nothing else to be done.

One thing that worried her a good deal was the size of the Book. The Chief Voice had not been able to give her any idea whereabouts in the Book the spell for making things visible came. He even seemed rather surprised at her asking. He expected her to begin at the beginning and go on till she came to it; obviously he had never thought that there was any other way of finding a place in a book. "But it might take me days and weeks!" said Lucy, looking at the huge volume, "and I feel already as if I'd been in this place for hours."

She went up to the desk and laid her hand on the book; her fingers tingled when she touched it as if it were full of electricity. She tried to open it but couldn't at first; this, however, was only because it was fastened by two leaden clasps, and when she had undone these it opened easily enough. And what a book it was!

It was written, not printed; written in a clear, even hand, with thick downstrokes and thin up-strokes, very large, easier than print, and so beautiful that Lucy stared at it for a whole minute and forgot about reading it. The paper was crisp and smooth and a nice smell came from it; and in the margins, and round the big colored capital letters at the beginning of each spell, there were pictures.

There was no title page or title; the spells began straight away, and at first there was nothing very important in them. They were cures for warts (by washing your hands in moonlight in a silver basin) and toothache and cramp, and a spell for taking a swarm of bees. The picture of the man with toothache was so lifelike that it would have set your

own teeth aching if you looked at it too long, and the golden bees which were dotted all round the fourth spell looked for a moment as if they were really flying.

Lucy could hardly tear herself away from that first page, but when she turned over, the next was just as interesting. "But I must get on," she told herself. And on she went for about thirty pages which, if she could have remembered them, would have taught her how to find buried treasure, how to remember things forgotten, how to forget things you wanted to forget, how to tell whether anyone was speaking the truth, how to call up (or prevent) wind, fog, snow, sleet or rain, how to produce enchanted sleeps and how to give a man an ass's head (as they did to poor Bottom). And the longer she read the more wonderful and more real the pictures became.

Then she came to a page which was such a blaze of pictures that one hardly noticed the writing. Hardly — but she *did* notice the first words. They were, *An infallible spell to make beautiful her that uttereth it beyond the lot of mortals.* Lucy peered at the pictures with her face close to the page, and though they had seemed crowded and muddlesome before, she found she could now see them quite clearly. The first was a picture of a girl standing at a reading-desk reading in a huge book. And the girl was dressed exactly like Lucy. In the next picture Lucy (for the girl in the picture was Lucy herself) was standing up with her mouth open and a rather terrible expression on her face, chanting or reciting something. In the third picture the beauty beyond the lot of mortals had come to her. It was strange, considering how small the pictures had looked at first, that the Lucy in the picture now seemed quite as big as the real Lucy; and they looked into each other's eyes and the real Lucy looked away after a few minutes because she was dazzled by the beauty of the other Lucy; though she could still see a sort of likeness to herself in that beautiful face. And now the pictures came crowding on her thick and fast. She saw herself throned on high at a great tournament in Calormen and all the Kings of the world fought because of her beauty. After that it turned from tournaments to real wars, and all Narnia and Archenland, Telmar and Calormen, Galma and Terebinthia, were laid waste with the fury of the kings and dukes and great lords who fought for her favor. Then it changed and Lucy, still beautiful beyond the lot of mortals, was back in England. And Susan (who had always been the beauty of the family) came home from America. The Susan in the picture looked exactly like the real Susan only plainer and with a nasty expression. And Susan was jealous of the dazzling beauty of Lucy, but that didn't matter a bit because no one cared anything about Susan now.

"I *will* say the spell," said Lucy. "I don't care. I will." She said *I don't care* because she had a strong feeling that she mustn't.

But when she looked back at the opening words of the spell, there in the middle of the writing, where she felt quite sure there had been no picture before, she found the great face of a lion, of The Lion, Aslan himself, staring into hers. It was painted such a bright gold that it seemed to be coming toward her out of the page; and indeed she never was quite sure afterward that it hadn't really moved a little. At any rate she knew the expression on his face quite well. He was growling and you could see most of his teeth. She became horribly afraid and turned over the page at once.

A little later she came to a spell which would let you know what your friends thought about you. Now Lucy had wanted very badly to try the other spell, the one that made you beautiful beyond the lot of mortals. So she felt that to make up for not having said it, she really would say this one. And all in a hurry, for fear her mind would change, she said the words (nothing will induce me to tell you what they were). Then she waited for something to happen.

As nothing happened she began looking at the pictures. And all at once she saw the very last thing she expected — a picture of a third-class carriage in a train, with two schoolgirls sitting in it. She knew them at once. They were Marjorie Preston and Anne Featherstone. Only now it was much more than a picture. It was alive. She could see the telegraph posts flicking past outside the window. Then gradually (like when the radio is "coming on") she could hear what they were saying.

"Shall I see anything of you this term?" said Anne, "or are you still going to be all taken up with Lucy Pevensie."

"Don't know what you mean by *taken up*," said Marjorie.

"Oh yes, you do," said Anne. "You were crazy about her last term."

"No, I wasn't," said Marjorie. "I've got more sense than that. Not a bad little kid in her way. But I was getting pretty tired of her before the end of term."

"Well, you jolly well won't have the chance any other term!" shouted Lucy.

"Two-faced little beast." But the sound of her own voice at once reminded her that she was talking to a picture and that the real Marjorie was far away in another world.

"Well," said Lucy to herself, "I did think better of her than that. And I did all sorts of things for her last term, and I stuck to her when not many other girls would. And she knows it too. And to Anne Featherstone, of all people! I wonder are all my friends the same? There are lots of other pictures. No. I won't look at any more. I won't, I won't" — and with a great effort she turned over the page, but not before a large, angry tear had splashed on it.

On the next page she came to a spell "for the refreshment of the spirit." The pictures were fewer here but very beautiful. And what Lucy found herself reading was more like a story than a spell. It went on for three pages and before she had read to the bottom of the page she had forgotten that she was reading at all. She was living in the story as if it were real, and all the pictures were real too. When she had got to the third page and come to the end, she said, "That is the loveliest story I've ever read or ever shall read in my whole life. Oh, I wish I could have gone on reading it for ten years. At least I'll read it over again."

But here part of the magic of the Book came into play. You couldn't turn back. The right-hand pages, the ones ahead, could be turned; the left-hand pages could not.

"Oh, what a shame!" said Lucy. "I did so want to read it again. Well, at least I must remember it. Let's see . . . it was about . . . about . . . oh dear, it's all fading away again. And even this last page is going blank. This is a very queer book. How can I have forgotten? It was about a cup and a sword and a tree and a green hill, I know that much. But I can't remember and what *shall* I do?"

And she never could remember; and ever since that day what Lucy means by a good story is a story which reminds her of the forgotten story in the Magician's Book.

She turned on and found to her surprise a page with no pictures at all; but the first words were *A Spell to make hidden things visible*. She read it through to make sure of all the hard words and then said it out loud. And she knew at once that it was working because as she spoke the colors came into the capital letters at the top of the page and the pictures began appearing in the margins. It was like when you hold to the fire something written in Invisible Ink and the writing gradually shows up; only instead of the dingy color of lemon juice (which is the easiest Invisible Ink) this was all gold and blue and scarlet. They were odd pictures and contained many figures that Lucy did not much like the look of. And then she thought, "I suppose I've made everything visible, and not only the Thumpers. There might be lots of other invisible things hanging about a place like this. I'm not sure that I want to see them all."

At that moment she heard soft, heavy footfalls coming along the corridor behind her; and of course she remembered what she had been told about the Magician walking in his bare feet and making no more noise than a cat. It is always better to turn round than to have anything creeping up behind your back. Lucy did so.

Then her face lit up till, for a moment (but of course she didn't know it), she looked almost as beautiful as that other Lucy in the picture, and she ran forward with a little cry of delight and with her arms stretched out. For what stood in the doorway was Aslan himself, The Lion, the highest of all High Kings. And he was solid and real and warm and he let her kiss him and bury herself in his shining mane. And from the low, earthquakelike sound that came from inside him, Lucy even dared to think that he was purring.

"Oh, Aslan," said she, "it was kind of you to come."

"I have been here all the time," said he, "but you have just made me visible."

"Aslan!" said Lucy almost a little reproachfully. "Don't make fun of me. As if anything *I* could do would make *you* visible!"

"It did," said Aslan. "Do you think I wouldn't obey my own rules?"

After a little pause he spoke again.

"Child," he said, "I think you have been eavesdropping."

"Eavesdropping?"

"You listened to what your two schoolfellows were saying about you."

"Oh that? I never thought that was eavesdropping, Aslan. Wasn't it magic?"

"Spying on people by magic is the same as spying on them in any other way. And you have misjudged your friend. She is weak, but she loves you. She was afraid of the older girl and said what she does not mean."

"I don't think I'd ever be able to forget what I heard her say."

"No, you won't."

"Oh dear," said Lucy. "Have I spoiled everything? Do you mean we would have gone on being friends if it hadn't been for this — and been really great friends — all our lives perhaps — and now we never shall."

"Child," said Aslan, "did I not explain to you once before that no one is ever told what *would have happened?*"

"Yes, Aslan, you did," said Lucy. "I'm sorry. But please —"

"Speak on, dear heart."

"Shall I ever be able to read that story again; the one I couldn't remember? Will you tell it to me, Aslan? Oh do, do, do."

"Indeed, yes, I will tell it to you for years and years. But now, come. We must meet the master of this house."

ELEVEN

THE DUFFLEPUDS
MADE HAPPY

Lucy followed the great lion out into the passage and at once she saw coming toward them an old man, barefoot, dressed in a red robe. His white hair was crowned with a chaplet of oak leaves, his beard fell to his girdle, and he supported himself with a curiously carved staff. When he saw Aslan he bowed low and said, "Welcome, Sir, to the least of your houses."

"Do you grow weary, Coriakin, of ruling such foolish subjects as I have given you here?"

"No," said the Magician, "they are very stupid but there is no real harm in them. I begin to grow rather fond of the creatures. Sometimes, perhaps, I am a little impatient, waiting for the day when they can be governed by wisdom instead of this rough magic."

"All in good time, Coriakin," said Aslan.

"Yes, all in very good time, Sir," was the

answer. "Do you intend to show yourself to them?"

"Nay," said the Lion, with a little half-growl that meant (Lucy thought) the same as a laugh. "I should frighten them out of their senses. Many stars will grow old and come to take their rest in islands before your people are ripe for that. And today before sunset I must visit Trumpkin the Dwarf where he sits in the castle of Cair Paravel counting the days till his master Caspian comes home. I will tell him all your story, Lucy. Do not look so sad. We shall meet soon again."

"Please, Aslan," said Lucy, "what do you call *soon?*"

"I call all times soon," said Aslan; and instantly he was vanished away and Lucy was alone with the Magician.

"Gone!" said he, "and you and I quite crestfallen. It's always like that, you can't keep him; it's not as if he were a *tame* lion. And how did you enjoy my book?"

"Parts of it very much indeed," said Lucy. "Did you know I was there all the time?"

"Well, of course I knew when I let the Duffers make themselves invisible that you would be coming along presently to take the spell off. I wasn't quite sure of the exact day. And I wasn't especially on the watch this morning. You see they had made me invisible too and being invisible always makes me so sleepy. Heigh-ho — there I'm yawning again. Are you hungry?"

"Well, perhaps I am a little," said Lucy. "I've no idea what the time is."

"Come," said the Magician. "All times may be soon to Aslan; but in my home all hungry times are one o'clock."

He led her a little way down the passage and opened a door. Passing in, Lucy found herself in a pleasant room full of sunlight and flowers. The table was bare when they entered, but it was of course a magic table, and at a word from the old man the table-cloth, silver, plates, glasses and food appeared.

"I hope that is what you would like," said he. "I have tried to give you food more like the food of your own land than perhaps you have had lately."

"It's lovely," said Lucy, and so it was; an omelette, piping hot, cold lamb and green peas, a strawberry ice, lemon-squash to drink with the meal and a cup of chocolate to follow. But the magician himself drank only wine and ate only bread. There was nothing alarming about him, and Lucy and he were soon chatting away like old friends.

"When will the spell work?" asked Lucy.

"Will the Duffers be visible again at once?"

"Oh yes, they're visible now. But they're probably all asleep still; they always take a rest in the middle of the day."

"And now that they're visible, are you going to let them off being ugly? Will you make them as they were before?"

"Well, that's rather a delicate question," said the Magician. "You see, it's only *they* who think they were so nice to look at before. They say they've been uglified, but that isn't what I called it. Many people might say the change was for the better."

"Are they awfully conceited?"

"They are. Or at least the Chief Duffer is, and he's taught all the rest to be. They always believe every word he says."

"We'd noticed that," said Lucy.

"Yes — we'd get on better without him, in a way. Of course I could turn him into something else, or even put a spell on him which would make them not believe a word he said. But I don't like to do that. It's better for them to admire him than to admire nobody."

"Don't they admire *you?*" asked Lucy.

"Oh, not *me,*" said the Magician. "They wouldn't admire *me.*"

"What was it you uglified them for — I mean, what they call *uglified?*"

185

"Well, they wouldn't do what they were told. Their work is to mind the garden and raise food — not for me, as they imagine, but for themselves. They wouldn't do it at all if I didn't make them. And of course for a garden you want water. There is a beautiful spring about half a mile away up the hill. And from that spring there flows a stream which comes right past the garden. All I asked them to do was to take their water from the stream instead of trudging up to the spring with their buckets two or three times a day and tiring themselves out besides spilling half of it on the way back. But they wouldn't see it. In the end they refused point blank."

"Are they as stupid as all that?" asked Lucy.

The Magician sighed. "You wouldn't believe the troubles I've had with them. A few months ago they were all for washing up the plates and knives before dinner: they said it saved time afterward. I've caught them planting boiled potatoes to save cooking them when they were dug up. One day the cat got into the dairy and twenty of them were at work moving all the milk out; no one thought of moving the cat. But I see you've finished. Let's go and look at the Duffers now they can be looked at."

They went into another room which was full of polished instruments hard to understand — such as Astrolabes, Orreries, Chronoscopes, Poesimeters, Choriambuses and Theodolinds — and here, when they had come to the window, the Magician said, "There. There are your Duffers."

"I don't see anybody," said Lucy. "And what are those mushroom things?"

The things she pointed at were dotted all over the level grass. They were certainly very like mushrooms, but far too big — the stalks about three feet high and the umbrellas about the same length from edge to edge. When she looked carefully she noticed too that the stalks joined the umbrellas not in the middle but at one side which gave an unbalanced look to them. And there was something — a sort of little bundle — lying on the grass at the foot of each stalk. In fact the longer she gazed at them the less like mushrooms they appeared. The umbrella part was not really round as she had thought at first. It was longer than it was broad, and it widened at one end. There were a great many of them, fifty or more.

The clock struck three.

Instantly a most extraordinary thing happened. Each of the "mushrooms" suddenly turned upside-down. The little bundles which had lain at the bottom of the stalks were heads and bodies. The stalks themselves were legs. But not two legs to each body. Each body had a single thick leg right under it (not to one side like the leg of a onelegged man) and at the end of it, a single enormous foot — a broad-toed foot with the toes curling up a little so that it looked rather like a small canoe. She saw in a moment why they had looked like mushrooms. They had been lying flat on their backs each with its single leg straight up in the air and its enormous foot spread out above it. She learned afterward that this was their ordinary way of resting; for the foot kept off both rain and sun and for a Monopod to lie under its own foot is almost as good as being in a tent.

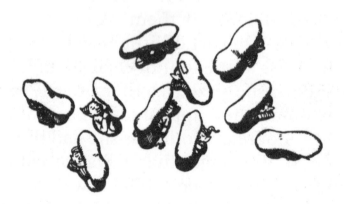

"Oh, the funnies, the funnies," cried Lucy, bursting into laughter. "Did *you* make them like that?"

"Yes, yes. I made the Duffers into Monopods," said the Magician. He too was laughing till the tears ran down his cheeks. "But watch," he added.

It was worth watching. Of course these little one-footed men couldn't walk or run as we do. They got about by jumping, like fleas or frogs. And what jumps they made! — as if each big foot were a mass of springs. And with what a bounce they came down; that was what made the thumping noise which had so puzzled Lucy yesterday. For now they were jumping in all directions and calling out to one another, "Hey, lads! We're visible again."

"Visible we are," said one in a tasseled red cap who was obviously the Chief Monopod. "And what I say is, when chaps are visible, why, they can see one another."

"Ah, there it is, there it is, Chief," cried all the others. "There's the point. No one's got a clearer head than you. You couldn't have made it plainer."

"She caught the old man napping, that little girl did," said the Chief Monopod. "We've beaten him this time."

"Just what we were going to say ourselves," chimed the chorus. "You're going stronger than ever today, Chief. Keep it up, keep it up."

"But do they dare to talk about you like

that?" said Lucy. "They seemed to be so afraid of you yesterday. Don't they know you might be listening?"

"That's one of the funny things about the Duffers," said the Magician. "One minute they talk as if I ran everything and overheard everything and was extremely dangerous. The next moment they think they can take me in by tricks that a baby would see through — bless them!"

"Will they have to be turned back into their proper shapes?" asked Lucy. "Oh, I do hope it wouldn't be unkind to leave them as they are. Do they really mind very much? They seem pretty happy. I say — look at that jump. What were they like before?"

"Common little dwarfs," said he. "Nothing like so nice as the sort you have in Narnia."

"It *would* be a pity to change them back," said Lucy. "They're so funny: and they're rather nice. Do you think it would make any difference if I told them that?"

"I'm sure it would — if you could get it into their heads."

"Will you come with me and try?"

"No, no. You'll get on far better without me."

"Thanks awfully for the lunch," said Lucy and turned quickly away. She ran down the stairs which she had come up so nervously that morning and cannoned into Edmund at the bottom. All the others were there with him waiting, and Lucy's conscience smote her when she saw their anxious faces and realized how long she had forgotten them.

"It's all right," she shouted. "Everything's all right. The Magician's a brick — and I've seen *Him* — Aslan."

After that she went from them like the wind and out into the garden. Here the earth was shaking with the jumps and the air ringing with the shouts of the Monopods. Both were redoubled when they caught sight of her.

"Here she comes, here she comes," they cried. "Three cheers for the little girl. Ah! She put it across the old gentleman properly, she did."

"And we're extremely regrettable," said the Chief Monopod, "that we can't give you the pleasure of seeing us as we were before we were uglified, for you wouldn't believe the difference, and that's the truth, for there's no denying we're mortal ugly now, so we won't deceive you."

"Eh, that we are, Chief, that we are," echoed the others, bouncing like so many toy balloons. "You've said it, you've said it."

"But I don't think you are at all," said Lucy, shouting to make herself heard. "I think you look very nice."

"Hear her, hear her," said the Monopods. "True for you, Missie. Very nice we look. You couldn't find a handsomer lot." They said this without any surprise and did not seem to notice that they had changed their minds.

"She's a-saying," remarked the Chief Monopod, "as how we looked very nice before we were uglified."

"True for you, Chief, true for you," chanted the others. "That's what she says. We heard her ourselves."

"I did *not*," bawled Lucy. "I said you're very nice *now*."

"So she did, so she did," said the Chief Monopod, "said we were very nice then."

"Hear 'em both, hear 'em both," said the

Monopods. "There's a pair for you. Always right. They couldn't have put it better."

"But we're saying just the opposite," said Lucy, stamping her foot with impatience.

"So you are, to be sure, so you are," said the Monopods. "Nothing like an opposite. Keep it up, both of you."

"You're enough to drive anyone mad," said Lucy, and gave it up. But the Monopods seemed perfectly contented, and she decided that on the whole the conversation had been a success.

And before everyone went to bed that evening something else happened which made them even more satisfied with their one-legged condition. Caspian and all the Narnians went back as soon as possible to the shore to give their news to Rhince and the others on board the *Dawn Treader*, who were by now very anxious. And, of course, the Monopods went with them, bouncing like footballs and agreeing with one another in loud voices till Eustace said, "I wish the Magician would make them inaudible instead of invisible." (He was soon sorry he had spoken because then he had to explain that an inaudible thing is something you can't hear, and though he took a lot of trouble he never felt sure that the Monopods had really understood, and what especially annoyed him was that they said in the end, "Eh, he can't put things the way our Chief does. But you'll learn, young man. Hark to *him*. He'll show you how to say things. There's a speaker for you!") When they reached the bay, Reepicheep had a brilliant idea. He had his little coracle lowered and paddled himself about in it till the Monopods were thoroughly interested. He then stood up in it and said, "Worthy and intelligent Monopods, you do not need boats. Each of you has a foot that will do instead. Just jump as lightly as you can on the water and see what happens."

The Chief Monopod hung back and warned the others that they'd find the water powerful wet, but one or two of the younger ones tried it almost at once; and then a few others followed their example, and at last the whole lot did the same. It worked perfectly. The huge single foot of a Monopod acted as a natural raft or boat, and when Reepicheep had taught them how to cut rude paddles for themselves, they all paddled about the bay and round the *Dawn Treader*, looking for all the world like a fleet of little canoes with a fat dwarf standing up in the extreme stern of each. And they had races, and bottles of wine were lowered down to them from the ship as prizes, and the sailors stood leaning over the ship's sides and laughed till their own sides ached.

The Duffers were also very pleased with their new name of Monopods, which seemed to them a magnificent name though they never got it right. "That's what we are," they bellowed. "Moneypuds, Pomonods, Poddymons. Just what it was on the tips of our tongue to call ourselves." But they soon got it mixed up with their old name of Duffers and finally settled down to calling themselves the Dufflepuds; and that is what they will probably be called for centuries.

That evening all the Narnians dined upstairs with the Magician, and Lucy noticed how different the whole top floor looked now that she was no longer afraid of it. The mysterious signs on the doors were still mysterious but now looked as if they had kind and cheerful meanings, and even the bearded mirror now seemed funny rather than frightening. At dinner everyone had by magic what everyone liked best to eat and drink, and after dinner the Magician did a very useful and beautiful piece of magic. He laid two blank sheets of parchment on the table and asked Drinian to give him an exact account of their voyage up to date: and as Drinian spoke, everything he described came out on the parchment in fine clear lines till at last each sheet was a splendid map of the Eastern Ocean, showing Galma, Terebinthia, the Seven Isles, Dragon Island, Burnt Island, Deathwater, and the land of the Duffers itself, all exactly the right sizes and in the right positions. They were the first maps ever made of those seas and better than any that have been made since without magic. For on these, though the towns and mountains looked at first just as they would on an ordinary map, when the Magician lent them a magnifying glass you saw that they were perfect little pictures of the real things, so that you could see the very castle and slave market and streets in Narrowhaven, all very clear though very distant, like things seen through the wrong end of a telescope. The only drawback was that the coastline of most of the islands was incomplete, for the map showed only what Drinian had seen with his own eyes. When they were finished the Magician kept one himself and presented the other to Caspian: it still hangs in his Chamber of Instruments at Cair Paravel. But the Magician could tell them nothing about seas or lands further east. He did, however, tell them that about seven years before a Narnian ship had put in at his waters and that she had on board the Lords Revilian, Argoz, Mavramorn and Rhoop: so they judged that the golden man they had seen lying in Deathwater must be the Lord Restimar.

Next day, the Magician magically mended the stern of the *Dawn Treader* where it had been damaged by the Sea Serpent and loaded her with useful gifts. There was a most friendly parting, and when she sailed, two hours after noon, all the Dufflepuds paddled out with her to the harbor mouth, and cheered until she was out of sound of their cheering.

TWELVE

THE DARK ISLAND

After this adventure they sailed on south and a little east for twelve days with a gentle wind, the skies being mostly clear and the air warm, and saw no bird or fish, except that once there were whales spouting a long way to starboard. Lucy and Reepicheep played a good deal of chess at this time. Then on the thirteenth day, Edmund, from the fighting-top, sighted what looked like a great dark mountain rising out of the sea on their port bow.

They altered course and made for this land, mostly by oar, for the wind would not serve them to sail northeast. When evening fell they were still a long way from it and rowed all night. Next morning the weather was fair but a flat calm. The dark mass lay ahead, much nearer and larger, but still very dim, so that some thought it was still a long way off and others thought they were running into a mist.

About nine that morning, very suddenly, it was so close that they could see that it was not land at all, nor even, in an ordinary sense, a mist. It was a Darkness. It is rather hard to describe, but you will see what it was like if you imagine yourself looking into the mouth of a railway tunnel — a tunnel either so long or so twisty that you cannot see the light at the far end. And you know what it would be like. For a few feet you would see the rails and sleepers and gravel in broad daylight; then there would come a place where they were in twilight; and then, pretty suddenly, but of course without a sharp dividing line, they would vanish altogether into smooth, solid blackness. It was just so here. For a few feet in front of their bows they could see the swell of the bright greenish-blue water. Beyond that, they could see the water looking pale and gray as it would look late in the evening. But beyond that again, utter blackness as if they had come to the edge of moonless and starless night.

Caspian shouted to the boatswain to keep her back, and all except the rowers rushed forward and gazed from the bows. But there was nothing to be seen by gazing. Behind them was the sea and the sun, before them the Darkness.

"Do we go into this?" asked Caspian at length.

"Not by my advice," said Drinian.

"The Captain's right," said several sailors.

"I almost think he is," said Edmund.

Lucy and Eustace didn't speak but they felt very glad inside at the turn things seemed to be taking. But all at once the clear voice of Reepicheep broke in upon the silence.

"And why not?" he said. "Will someone explain to me why not."

No one was anxious to explain, so Reepicheep continued:

"If I were addressing peasants or slaves," he said, "I might suppose that this suggestion proceeded from cowardice. But I hope it will never be told in Narnia that a company of noble and royal persons in the flower of their age turned tail because they were afraid of the dark."

"But what manner of use would it be plowing through that blackness?" asked Drinian.

"Use?" replied Reepicheep. "Use, Captain? If by use you mean filling our bellies or our purses, I confess it will be no use at all. So far as I know we did not set sail to look for things useful but to seek honor and adventure. And here is as great an adventure as ever I heard of, and here, if we turn back, no little impeachment of all our honors."

Several of the sailors said things under their breath that sounded like "Honor be

blowed," but Caspian said:

"Oh, *bother* you, Reepicheep. I almost wish we'd left you at home. All right! If you put it that way, I suppose we shall have to go on. Unless Lucy would rather not?"

Lucy felt that she would very much rather not, but what she said out loud was, "I'm game."

"Your Majesty will at least order lights?" said Drinian.

"By all means," said Caspian. "See to it, Captain."

So the three lanterns, at the stern, and the prow and the masthead, were all lit, and Drinian ordered two torches amidships. Pale and feeble they looked in the sunshine. Then all the men except some who were left below at the oars were ordered on deck and fully armed and posted in their battle stations with swords drawn. Lucy and two archers were posted on the fighting-top with bows bent and arrows on the string. Rynelf was in the bows with his line ready to take soundings. Reepicheep, Edmund, Eustace and Caspian, glittering in mail, were with him. Drinian took the tiller.

"And now, in Aslan's name, forward!" cried Caspian. "A slow, steady stroke. And let every man be silent and keep his ears open for orders."

With a creak and a groan the *Dawn Treader* started to creep forward as the men began to row. Lucy, up in the fighting-top, had a wonderful view of the exact moment at which they entered the darkness. The bows had already disappeared before the sunlight had left the stern. She saw it go. At one minute the gilded stern, the blue sea, and the sky, were all in broad daylight: next minute the sea and sky had vanished, the stern lantern — which had been hardly noticeable before — was the only thing to show where the ship ended. In front of the lantern she could see the black shape of Drinian crouching at the tiller. Down below her the two torches made visible two small patches of deck and gleamed on swords and helmets, and forward there was another island of light on the forecastle. Apart from that, the fighting-top, lit by the masthead light which was only just above her, seemed to be a little lighted world of its own floating in lonely darkness. And the lights themselves, as always happens with lights when you have to have them at the wrong time of day, looked lurid and unnatural. She also noticed that she was very cold.

How long this voyage into the darkness lasted, nobody knew. Except for the creak of the rowlocks and the splash of the oars there was nothing to show that they were moving at all. Edmund, peering from the bows, could see nothing except the reflection of the lantern in the water before him. It looked a greasy sort of reflection, and the ripple made by their advancing prow appeared to be heavy, small, and lifeless. As time went on everyone except the rowers began to shiver with cold.

Suddenly, from somewhere — no one's sense of direction was very clear by now — there came a cry, either of some inhuman voice or else a voice of one in such extremity of terror that he had almost lost his humanity.

Caspian was still trying to speak — his mouth was too dry — when the shrill voice of Reepicheep, which sounded louder than usual in that silence, was heard.

"Who calls?" it piped. "If you are a foe we do not fear you, and if you are a friend your enemies shall be taught the fear of us."

"Mercy!" cried the voice. "Mercy! Even if you are only one more dream, have mercy. Take me on board. Take me, even if you strike me dead. But in the name of all mercies do not fade away and leave me in this horrible land."

"Where are you?" shouted Caspian. "Come aboard and welcome."

There came another cry, whether of joy or terror, and then they knew that someone was swimming toward them.

"Stand by to heave him up, men," said Caspian. "Aye, aye, your Majesty," said the sailors. Several crowded to the port bulwark with ropes and one, leaning far out over the side, held the torch. A wild, white face appeared in the blackness of the water, and then, after some scrambling and pulling, a dozen friendly hands had heaved the stranger on board.

Edmund thought he had never seen a wilder-looking man. Though he did not otherwise look very old, his hair was an untidy mop of white, his face was thin and drawn, and, for clothing, only a few wet rags hung about him. But what one mainly noticed were his eyes, which were so widely opened that he seemed to have no eyelids at all, and stared as if in an agony of pure fear. The moment his feet reached the deck he said:

"Fly! Fly! About with your ship and fly! Row, row, row for your lives away from this accursed shore."

"Compose yourself," said Reepicheep, "and tell us what the danger is. We are not used to flying."

The stranger started horribly at the voice

of the Mouse, which he had not noticed be-fore.

"Nevertheless you will fly from here," he gasped. "This is the Island where Dreams come true."

"That's the island I've been looking for this long time," said one of the sailors. "I reckon I'd find I was married to Nancy if we landed here."

"And I'd find Tom alive again," said an-other.

"Fools!" said the man, stamping his foot with rage. "That is the sort of talk that brought me here, and I'd better have been drowned or never born. Do you hear what I say? This is where dreams — dreams, do you understand — come to life, come real. Not daydreams: dreams."

There was about half a minute's silence and then, with a great clatter of armor, the whole crew were tumbling down the main hatch as quick as they could and flinging themselves on the oars to row as they had never rowed be-fore; and Drinian was swinging round the tiller, and the boatswain was giving out the quickest stroke that had ever been heard at sea. For it had taken everyone just that half-minute to remember certain dreams they had had — dreams that make you afraid of going to sleep again — and to realize what it would mean to land on a country where dreams come true.

Only Reepicheep remained unmoved.

"Your Majesty, your Majesty," he said, "are you going to tolerate this mutiny, this poltroonery? This is a panic, this is a rout."

"Row, row," bellowed Caspian. "Pull for all our lives. Is her head right, Drinian? You can say what you like, Reepicheep. There are some things no man can face."

"It is, then, my good fortune not to be a man," replied Reepicheep with a very stiff bow.

Lucy from up aloft had heard it all. In an instant that one of her own dreams which she had tried hardest to forget came back to her as vividly as if she had only just woken from it. So *that* was what was behind them, on the island, in the darkness! For a second she wanted to go down to the deck and be with Edmund and Caspian. But what was the use? If dreams began coming true, Edmund and Caspian themselves might turn into something horrible just as she reached them. She gripped the rail of the fighting-top and tried to steady herself. They were rowing back to the light as hard as they could: it would be all right in a few seconds. But oh, if only it could be all right now!

Though the rowing made a good deal of noise it did not quite conceal the total silence which surrounded the ship. Everyone knew it would be better not to listen, not to strain his ears for any sound from the darkness. But no one could help listening. And soon everyone was hearing things. Each one heard something different.

"Do you hear a noise like . . . like a huge pair of scissors opening and shutting . . . over there?" Eustace asked Rynelf.

"Hush!" said Rynelf. "I can hear *them* crawling up the sides of the ship."

"*It's* just going to settle on the mast," said Caspian.

"Ugh!" said a sailor. "There are the gongs beginning. I knew they would."

Caspian, trying not to look at anything (especially not to keep looking behind him), went aft to Drinian.

"Drinian," he said in a very low voice. "How long did we take rowing in? — I mean rowing to where we picked up the stranger."

"Five minutes, perhaps," whispered Drinian. "Why?"

"Because we've been more than that already trying to get out."

Drinian's hand shook on the tiller and a line of cold sweat ran down his face. The same idea was occurring to everyone on board. "We shall never get out, never get out," moaned the rowers. "He's steering us wrong. We're going round and round in circles. We shall never get out." The stranger, who had been lying in a huddled heap on the deck, sat up and burst out into a horrible screaming laugh.

"Never get out!" he yelled. "That's it. Of course. We shall never get out. What a fool I was to have thought they would let me go as easily as that. No, no, we shall never get out."

Lucy leant her head on the edge of the fighting-top and whispered, "Aslan, Aslan, if ever you loved us at all, send us help now." The darkness did not grow any less, but she began to feel a little — a very, very little — better. "After all, nothing has really happened to us yet," she thought.

"Look!" cried Rynelf's voice hoarsely from the bows. There was a tiny speck of light ahead, and while they watched a broad beam of light fell from it upon the ship. It did not alter the surrounding darkness, but the whole ship was lit up as if by searchlight. Caspian blinked, stared round, saw the faces of his companions all with wild, fixed expressions. Everyone was staring in the same direction: behind everyone lay his black, sharply edged shadow.

Lucy looked along the beam and presently saw something in it. At first it looked like a cross, then it looked like an aeroplane, then it looked like a kite, and at last with a whirring of wings it was right overhead and was an albatross. It circled three times round the mast and then perched for an instant on the crest of the gilded dragon at the prow. It called out in a strong sweet voice what seemed to be words though no one understood them. After that it spread its wings, rose, and began to fly slowly ahead, bearing a little to starboard. Drinian steered after it not doubting that it offered good guidance. But no one except Lucy knew that as it circled the mast it had whispered to her, "Courage, dear heart," and the voice, she felt sure, was Aslan's, and with the voice a delicious smell breathed in her face.

In a few moments the darkness turned into a grayness ahead, and then, almost before they dared to begin hoping, they had shot out into the sunlight and were in the warm, blue world again. And all at once everybody realized that there was nothing to be afraid of and never had been. They blinked their eyes and looked about them. The brightness of the ship herself astonished them: they had half expected to find that the darkness would cling to the white and the green and the gold in the form of some grime or scum. And then first one, and then another, began laughing.

"I reckon we've made pretty good fools of ourselves," said Rynelf.

Lucy lost no time in coming down to the deck, where she found the others all gathered round the newcomer. For a long time he was too happy to speak, and could only gaze at the sea and the sun and feel the bulwarks and the ropes, as if to make sure he was really awake, while tears rolled down his cheeks.

"Thank you," he said at last. "You have saved me from . . . but I won't talk of that. And now let me know who you are. I am a Telmarine of Narnia, and when I was worth anything men called me the Lord Rhoop."

"And I," said Caspian, "am Caspian, King of Narnia, and I sail to find you and your companions who were my father's friends."

Lord Rhoop fell on his knees and kissed the King's hand. "Sire," he said, "you are the man in all the world I most wished to see. Grant me a boon."

"What is it?" asked Caspian.

"Never to bring me back there," he said. He pointed astern. They all looked. But they saw only bright blue sea and bright blue sky. The Dark Island and the darkness had vanished for ever.

"Why!" cried Lord Rhoop. "You have destroyed it!"

"I don't think it was us," said Lucy.

"Sire," said Drinian, "this wind is fair for the southeast. Shall I have our poor fellows up and set sail? And after that, every man who can be spared, to his hammock."

"Yes," said Caspian, "and let there be grog all round. Heigh-ho, I feel I could sleep the clock round myself."

So all afternoon with great joy they sailed southeast with a fair wind. But nobody noticed when the albatross had disappeared.

THIRTEEN

THE THREE SLEEPERS

The wind never failed but it grew gentler every day till at length the waves were little more than ripples, and the ship glided on hour after hour almost as if they were sailing on a lake. And every night they saw that there rose in the east new constellations which no one had ever seen in Narnia and perhaps, as Lucy thought with a mixture of joy and fear, no living eye had seen at all. Those new stars were big and bright and the nights were warm. Most of them slept on deck and talked far into the night or hung over the ship's side watching the luminous dance of the foam thrown up by their bows.

On an evening of startling beauty, when the sunset behind them was so crimson and purple and widely spread that the very sky itself seemed to have grown larger, they came in sight of land on their starboard bow. It came slowly nearer and the light behind them made it look as if the capes and headlands of this new country were all on fire. But presently they were sailing along its coast and its western cape now rose up astern of them, black against the red sky and sharp as if it was cut out of cardboard, and then they could see better what this country was like. It had no mountains but many gentle hills with slopes like pillows. An attractive smell came from it — what Lucy called "a dim, purple kind of smell," which Edmund said (and Rhince thought) was rot, but Caspian said, "I know what you mean."

They sailed on a good way, past point after point, hoping to find a nice deep harbor, but had to content themselves in the end with a wide and shallow bay. Though it had seemed calm out at sea there was of course surf breaking on the sand and they could not bring the *Dawn Treader* as far in as they would have liked. They dropped anchor a good way from the beach and had a wet and tumbling landing in the boat. The Lord Rhoop remained. He wished to see no more islands. All the time that they remained in this country the sound of the long breakers was in their ears.

Two men were left to guard the boat and Caspian led the others inland, but not far because it was too late for exploring and the light would soon go. But there was no need to go far to find an adventure. The level valley which lay at the head of the bay showed no road or track or other sign of habitation. Underfoot was fine springy turf dotted here and there with a low bushy growth which Edmund and Lucy took for heather. Eustace, who was really rather good at botany, said it wasn't, and he was probably right; but it was something of very much the same kind.

When they had gone less than a bowshot from the shore, Drinian said, "Look! What's that?" and everyone stopped.

"Are they great trees?" said Caspian.

"Towers, I think," said Eustace.

"It might be giants," said Edmund in a lower voice.

"The way to find out is to go right in among them," said Reepicheep, drawing his sword and pattering off ahead of everyone else.

"I think it's a ruin," said Lucy when they had got a good deal nearer, and her guess was the best so far. What they now saw was a wide oblong space flagged with smooth stones and surrounded by gray pillars but unroofed. And from end to end of it ran a long table laid with a rich crimson cloth that came down nearly to the pavement. At either side of it were many chairs of stone richly carved and with silken cushions upon the seats. But on the table itself there was set out such a banquet as had never been seen, not even when Peter the High King kept his court at Cair Paravel. There were turkeys and geese and peacocks, there were boars' heads and sides of venison, there were pies shaped like ships under full sail or like dragons and elephants, there were ice puddings and bright lobsters and gleaming salmon, there were nuts and grapes, pineapples and peaches, pomegranates and melons and tomatoes. There were flagons of gold and silver and curiously — wrought glass; and the smell of the fruit and the wine blew toward them like a promise of all happiness.

"I *say!*" said Lucy.

They came nearer and nearer, all very quietly.

"But where are the guests?" asked Eustace.

"We can provide that, Sir," said Rhince.

"Look!" said Edmund sharply. They were actually within the pillars now and standing on the pavement. Everyone looked where Edmund had pointed. The chairs were not all empty. At the head of the table and in the two places beside it there was something — or possibly three somethings.

"What are *those?*" asked Lucy in a whisper. "It looks like three beavers sitting on the table."

"Or a huge bird's nest," said Edmund.

"It looks more like a haystack to me," said Caspian.

Reepicheep ran forward, jumped on a chair and thence on to the table, and ran along it, threading his way as nimbly as a dancer between jeweled cups and pyramids of fruit and ivory salt-cellars.

He ran right up to the mysterious gray mass at the end: peered, touched, and then called out:

"These will not fight, I think."

Everyone now came close and saw that what sat in those three chairs was three men, though hard to recognize as men till you looked closely. Their hair, which was gray, had grown over their eyes till it almost concealed their faces, and their beards had grown over the table, climbing round and entwining plates and goblets as brambles entwine a fence, until, all mixed in one great mat of hair, they flowed over the edge and down to the floor. And from their heads the hair hung over the backs of their chairs so that they were wholly hidden. In fact the three men were nearly all hair.

"Dead?" said Caspian.

"I think not, Sire," said Reepicheep, lifting one of their hands out of its tangle of hair in his two paws. "This one is warm and his pulse beats."

"This one, too, and this," said Drinian.

"Why, they're only asleep," said Eustace.

"It's been a long sleep, though," said Edmund, "to let their hair grow like this."

"It must be an enchanted sleep," said Lucy. "I felt the moment we landed on this island that it was full of magic. Oh! do you think we have perhaps come here to break it?"

"We can try," said Caspian, and began shaking the nearest of the three sleepers. For a moment everyone thought he was going to be successful, for the man breathed hard and muttered, "I'll go eastward no more. Out oars for Narnia." But he sank back almost at once into a yet deeper sleep than before: that is, his heavy head sagged a few inches lower toward the table and all efforts to rouse him again were useless. With the second it was much the same. "Weren't born to live like animals. Get to the east while you've a chance — lands behind the sun," and sank down. And the third only said, "Mustard, please," and slept hard.

"*Out oars for Narnia,* eh?" said Drinian.

"Yes," said Caspian, "you are right, Drinian. I think our quest is at an end. Let's look at their rings. Yes, these are their devices. This is the Lord Revilian. This is the Lord Argoz: and this, the Lord Mavramorn."

"But we can't wake them," said Lucy. "What are we to do?"

"Begging your Majesties' pardons all," said Rhince, "but why not fall to while you're discussing it? We don't see a dinner like this every day."

"Not for your life!" said Caspian.

"That's right, that's right," said several of the sailors. "Too much magic about here. The sooner we're back on board the better."

"Depend upon it," said Reepicheep, "it was from eating this food that these three lords came by a seven years' sleep."

"I wouldn't touch it to save my life," said Drinian.

"The light's going uncommon quick," said Rynelf.

"Back to ship, back to ship," muttered the men.

"I really think," said Edmund, "they're right. We can decide what to do with the three sleepers tomorrow. We daren't eat the food and there's no point in staying here for the night. The whole place smells of magic — and danger."

"I am entirely of King Edmund's opinion," said Reepicheep, "as far as concerns the ship's company in general. But I myself will sit at this table till sunrise."

"Why on earth?" said Eustace.

"Because," said the Mouse, "this is a very great adventure, and no danger seems to me so great as that of knowing when I get back to Narnia that I left a mystery behind me through fear."

"I'll stay with you, Reep," said Edmund.

"And I too," said Caspian.

"And me," said Lucy. And then Eustace volunteered also. This was very brave of him because never having read of such things or even heard of them till he joined the *Dawn Treader* made it worse for him than for the others.

"I beseech your Majesty —" began Drinian.

"No, my Lord," said Caspian. "Your place is with the ship, and you have had a day's work while we five have idled." There was a lot of argument about this but in the end Caspian had his way. As the crew marched off to the shore in the gathering dusk none of the five watchers, except perhaps Reepicheep, could avoid a cold feeling in the stomach.

They took some time choosing their seats at the perilous table. Probably everyone had the same reason but no one said it out loud. For it was really a rather nasty choice. One could hardly bear to sit all night next to those three terrible hairy objects which, if not dead, were certainly not alive in the ordinary sense. On the other hand, to sit at the far end, so that you would see them less and less as the night grew darker, and wouldn't know if they were moving, and perhaps wouldn't see them at all by about two o'clock — no, it was not to be thought of. So they sauntered round and round the table saying, "What about here?" and "Or perhaps a bit further on," or, "Why not on this side?" till at last they settled down somewhere about the middle but nearer to the sleepers than to the other end. It was about ten by now and almost dark. Those strange new constellations burned in the east. Lucy would have liked it better if they had been the Leopard and the Ship and other old friends of the Narnian sky.

They wrapped themselves in their sea cloaks and sat still and waited. At first there was some attempt at talk but it didn't come to much. And they sat and sat. And all the time they heard the waves breaking on the beach.

After hours that seemed like ages there came a moment when they all knew they had been dozing a moment before but were all suddenly wide awake. The stars were all in quite different positions from those they had last noticed. The sky was very black except for the faintest possible grayness in the east. They were cold, though thirsty, and stiff. And none of them spoke because now at last something was happening.

Before them, beyond the pillars, there was the slope of a low hill. And now a door opened in the hillside, and light appeared in the doorway, and a figure came out, and the door shut behind it. The figure carried a light, and this light was really all that they could see distinctly. It came slowly nearer and nearer till at last it stood right at the table opposite to them. Now they could see that it was a tall girl, dressed in a single long garment of clear blue which left her arms bare. She was bareheaded and her yellow hair hung down her back. And when they looked at her they thought they had never before known what beauty meant.

The light which she had been carrying was a tall candle in a silver candlestick which she now set upon the table. If there had been any wind off the sea earlier in the night it must have died down by now, for the flame of the candle burned as straight and still as if it were in a room with the windows shut and the curtains drawn. Gold and silver on the table shone in its light.

Lucy now noticed something lying lengthwise on the table which had escaped her attention before. It was a knife of stone, sharp as steel, a cruel-looking, ancient-looking thing.

No one had yet spoken a word. Then — Reepicheep first, and Caspian next — they all rose to their feet, because they felt that she was a great lady.

"Travelers who have come from far to Aslan's table," said the girl. "Why do you not eat and drink?"

"Madam," said Caspian, "we feared the food because we thought it had cast our friends into an enchanted sleep."

"They have never tasted it," she said.

"Please," said Lucy, "what happened to them?"

"Seven years ago," said the girl, "they came here in a ship whose sails were rags and her timbers ready to fall apart. There were a few others with them, sailors, and when they came to this table one said, 'Here is the good place. Let us set sail and reef sail and row no longer but sit down and end our days in peace!' And the second said, 'No, let us re-embark and sail for Narnia and the west; it may be that Miraz is dead.' But the third, who was a very masterful man, leaped up and said, 'No, by heaven. We are men and Telmarines, not brutes. What should we do but seek adventure after adventure? We have not long to live in any event. Let us spend what is left in seeking the unpeopled world behind the sunrise.' And as they quarreled he caught up the Knife of Stone which lies there on the table and would have fought with his comrades. But it is a thing not right for him to touch. And as his fingers closed upon the hilt, deep sleep fell upon all the three. And till the enchantment is undone they will never wake."

"What is this Knife of Stone?" asked Eustace.

"Do none of you know it?" said the girl.

"I — I think," said Lucy, "I've seen something like it before. It was a knife like it that the White Witch used when she killed Aslan at the Stone Table long ago."

"It was the same," said the girl, "and it was brought here to be kept in honor while the world lasts."

Edmund, who had been looking more and more uncomfortable for the last few minutes, now spoke.

"Look here," he said, "I hope I'm not a coward — about eating this food, I mean — and I'm sure I don't mean to be rude. But we have had a lot of queer adventures on this voyage of ours and things aren't always what they seem. When I look in your face I can't help believing all you say: but then that's just what might happen with a witch too. How are we to know you're a friend?"

"You can't know," said the girl. "You can only believe — or not."

After a moment's pause Reepicheep's small voice was heard.

"Sire," he said to Caspian, "of your courtesy fill my cup with wine from that flagon: it is too big for me to lift. I will drink to the lady."

Caspian obeyed and the Mouse, standing on the table, held up a golden cup between its tiny paws and said, "Lady, I pledge you." Then it fell to on cold peacock, and in a short while everyone else followed his example. All were very hungry and the meal, if

not quite what you wanted for a very early breakfast, was excellent as a very late supper.

"Why is it called Aslan's table?" asked Lucy presently.

"It is set here by his bidding," said the girl, "for those who come so far. Some call this island the World's End, for though you can sail further, this is the beginning of the end."

"But how does the food *keep?*" asked the practical Eustace.

"It is eaten, and renewed every day," said the girl. "This you will see."

"And what are we to do about the Sleepers?" asked Caspian. "In the world from which my friends come" (here he nodded at Eustace and the Pevensies) "they have a story of a prince or a king coming to a castle where all the people lay in an enchanted sleep. In that story he could not dissolve the enchantment until he had kissed the Princess."

"But here," said the girl, "it is different. Here he cannot kiss the Princess till he has dissolved the enchantment."

"Then," said Caspian, "in the name of Aslan, show me how to set about that work at once."

"My father will teach you that," said the girl.

"Your father!" said everyone. "Who is he? And where?"

"Look," said the girl, turning round and pointing at the door in the hillside. They could see it more easily now, for while they had been talking the stars had grown fainter and great gaps of white light were appearing in the grayness of the eastern sky.

FOURTEEN

THE BEGINNING OF THE END

OF THE WORLD

Slowly the door opened again and out there came a figure as tall and straight as the girl's but not so slender. It carried no light but light seemed to come from it. As it came nearer, Lucy saw that it was like an old man. His silver beard came down to his bare feet in front and his silver hair hung down to his heels behind and his robe appeared to be made from the fleece of silver sheep. He looked so mild and grave that once more all the travelers rose to their feet and stood in silence.

But the old man came on without speaking to the travelers and stood on the other side of the table opposite to his daughter. Then both of them held up their arms before them and turned to face the east. In that position they began to sing. I wish I could write down the song, but no one who was present could remember it. Lucy said afterward that it was high, almost shrill, but very beautiful, "A cold kind of song, an early morning kind of song." And as they sang, the gray clouds lifted from the eastern sky and the white patches grew bigger and bigger till it was all white, and the sea began to shine like silver. And long afterward (but those two sang all the time) the east began to turn red and at last, unclouded, the sun came up out of the sea and its long level ray shot down the length of the table on the gold and silver and on the Stone Knife.

Once or twice before, the Narnians had wondered whether the sun at its rising did not look bigger in these seas than it had looked at home. This time they were certain. There was no mistaking it. And the brightness of its ray on the dew and on the table was far beyond any morning brightness they had ever seen. And as Edmund said afterward, "Though lots of things happened on that trip which *sound* more exciting, that moment was really the most exciting." For now they knew that they had truly come to the beginning of the End of the World.

Then something seemed to be flying at them out of the very center of the rising sun: but of course one couldn't look steadily in that direction to make sure. But presently the air became full of voices — voices which took up the same song that the Lady and her Father were singing, but in far wilder tones and in a language which no one knew. And soon after that the owners of these voices could be seen. They were birds, large and white, and they came by hundreds and thousands and alighted on everything; on the grass, and the pavement, on the table, on your shoulders, your hands, and your head, till it looked as if heavy snow had fallen. For, like snow, they not only made everything white but blurred and blunted all shapes. But Lucy, looking out from between

the wings of the birds that covered her, saw one bird fly to the Old Man with something in its beak that looked like a little fruit, unless it was a little live coal, which it might have been, for it was too bright to look at. And the bird laid it in the Old Man's mouth.

Then the birds stopped their singing and appeared to be very busy about the table. When they rose from it again everything on the table that could be eaten or drunk had disappeared. These birds rose from their meal in their thousands and hundreds and carried away all the things that could not be eaten or drunk, such as bones, rinds, and shells, and took their flight back to the rising sun. But now, because they were not singing, the whir of their wings seemed to set the whole air a-tremble. And there was the table pecked clean and empty, and the three old Lords of Narnia still fast asleep.

Now at last the Old Man turned to the travelers and bade them welcome.

"Sir," said Caspian, "will you tell us how to undo the enchantment which holds these three Narnian Lords asleep."

"I will gladly tell you that, my son," said the Old Man. "To break this enchantment you must sail to the World's End, or as near as you can come to it, and you must come back having left at least one of your company behind."

"And what must happen to that one?" asked Reepicheep.

"He must go on into the utter east and never return into the world."

"That is my heart's desire," said Reepicheep.

"And are we near the World's End now, Sir?" asked Caspian. "Have you any knowledge of the seas and lands further east than this?"

"I saw them long ago," said the Old Man, "but it was from a great height. I cannot tell you such things as sailors need to know."

"Do you mean you were flying in the air?" Eustace blurted out.

"I was a long way above the air, my son," replied the Old Man. "I am Ramandu. But I see that you stare at one another and have not heard this name. And no wonder, for the days when I was a star had ceased long before any of you knew this world, and all the constellations have changed."

"Golly," said Edmund under his breath. "He's a *retired* star."

"Aren't you a star any longer?" asked Lucy.

"I am a star at rest, my daughter," answered Ramandu. "When I set for the last time, decrepit and old beyond all that you can reckon, I was carried to this island. I am not so old now as I was then. Every morning a bird brings me a fire-berry from the valleys in the Sun, and each fire-berry takes away a little of my age. And when I have become as young as the child that was born yesterday, then I shall take my rising again (for we are at earth's eastern rim) and once more tread the great dance."

"In our world," said Eustace, "a star is a huge ball of flaming gas."

"Even in your world, my son, that is not what a star is but only what it is made of. And in this world you have already met a star: for I think you have been with Coriakin."

"Is he a retired star, too?" said Lucy.

"Well, not quite the same," said Ramandu. "It was not quite as a rest that he was set to govern the Duffers. You might call it a punishment. He might have shone for thousands of years more in the southern winter sky if all had gone well."

"What did he do, Sir?" asked Caspian.

"My son," said Ramandu, "it is not for you, a son of Adam, to know what faults a star can commit. But come, we waste time in such talk. Are you yet resolved? Will you sail further east and come again, leaving one to return no more, and so break the enchantment? Or will you sail westward?"

"Surely, Sire," said Reepicheep, "there is no question about that? It is very plainly part of our quest to rescue these three lords from enchantment."

"I think the same, Reepicheep," replied Caspian. "And even if it were not so, it would break my heart not to go as near the World's End as the *Dawn Treader* will take us. But I am thinking of the crew. They signed on to seek the seven lords, not to reach the rim of the Earth. If we sail east from here we sail to find the edge, the utter east. And no one knows how far it is. They're brave fellows, but I see signs that some of them are weary of the voyage and long to have our prow pointing to Narnia again. I don't think I should take them further without their knowledge and consent. And then there's the poor Lord Rhoop. He's a broken man."

"My son," said the star, "it would be no use, even though you wished it, to sail for the World's End with men unwilling or men deceived. That is not how great unenchantments are achieved. They must know where they go and why. But who is this broken man you speak of?"

Caspian told Ramandu the story of Rhoop.

"I can give him what he needs most," said Ramandu. "In this island there is sleep without stint or measure, and sleep in which no faintest footfall of a dream was ever heard. Let him sit beside these other three and drink oblivion till your return."

"Oh, do let's do that, Caspian," said Lucy. "I'm sure it's just what he would love."

At that moment they were interrupted by

the sound of many feet and voices: Drinian and the rest of the ship's company were approaching. They halted in surprise when they saw Ramandu and his daughter; and then, because these were obviously great people, every man uncovered his head. Some sailors eyed the empty dishes and flagons on the table with eyes filled with regret.

"My lord," said the King to Drinian, "pray send two men back to the *Dawn Treader* with a message to the Lord Rhoop. Tell him that the last of his old shipmates are here asleep — a sleep without dreams — and that he can share it." When this had been done, Caspian told the rest to sit down and laid the whole situation before them. When he had finished there was a long silence and some whispering until presently the Master Bowman got to his feet, and said:

"What some of us have been wanting to ask for a long time, your Majesty, is how we're ever to get home when we do turn, whether we turn here or somewhere else. It's been west and northwest winds all the way, barring an occasional calm. And if that doesn't change, I'd like to know what hopes we have of seeing Narnia again. There's not much chance of supplies lasting while we *row* all that way."

"That's landsman's talk," said Drinian. "There's always a prevailing west wind in these seas all through the late summer, and it always changes after the New Year. We'll have plenty of wind for sailing westward; more than we shall like from all accounts."

"That's true, Master," said an old sailor who was a Galmian by birth. "You get some ugly weather rolling up from the east in January and February. And by your leave, Sire, if I was in command of this ship, I'd say to winter here and begin the voyage home in March."

"What'd you eat while you were wintering here?" asked Eustace.

"This table," said Ramandu, "will be filled with a king's feast every day at sunset."

"Now you're talking!" said several sailors.

"Your Majesties and gentlemen and ladies all," said Rynelf, "there's just one thing I want to say. There's not one of us chaps as was pressed on this journey. We're volunteers. And there's some here that are looking very hard at that table and thinking about king's feasts who were talking very loud about adventures on the day we sailed from Cair Paravel, and swearing they wouldn't come home till we'd found the end of the world. And there were some standing on the quay who would have given all they had to come with us. It was thought a finer thing then to have a cabin-boy's berth on the *Dawn Treader* than to wear a knight's belt. I don't know if you get the hang of what I'm saying. But what I mean is that I think chaps who set out like us will look as silly as — as those Dufflepuds — if we come home and say we got to the beginning of the world's end and hadn't the heart to go further."

Some of the sailors cheered at this but some said that that was all very well.

"This isn't going to be much fun," whispered Edmund to Caspian. "What are we to do if half those fellows hang back?"

"Wait," Caspian whispered back. "I've still a card to play."

"Aren't you going to say anything, Reep?" whispered Lucy.

"No. Why should your Majesty expect it?" answered Reepicheep in a voice that most people heard. "My own plans are made. While I can, I sail east in the *Dawn Treader*. When she fails me, I paddle east in my coracle. When she sinks, I shall swim east with my four paws. And when I can swim no longer, if I have not reached Aslan's country, or shot over the edge of the world in some vast cataract, I shall sink with my nose to the sunrise and Peepiceep will be head of the talking mice in Narnia."

"Hear, hear," said a sailor. "I'll say the same, barring the bit about the coracle, which wouldn't bear me." He added in a lower voice, "I'm not going to be outdone by a mouse."

At this point Caspian jumped to his feet. "Friends," he said, "I think you have not quite understood our purpose. You talk as if we had come to you with our hat in our hand, begging for shipmates. It isn't like that at all. We and our royal brother and sister and their kinsman and Sir Reepicheep, the good knight, and the Lord Drinian have an errand to the world's edge. It is our pleasure to choose from among such of you as are willing those whom we deem worthy of so high an enterprise. We have not said that any can come for the asking. That is why we shall now command the Lord Drinian and Master Rhince to consider carefully what men among you are the hardest in battle, the most skilled seamen, the purest in blood, the most loyal to our person, and the cleanest of life and manners; and to give their names to us in a schedule." He paused and went on in a quicker voice, "Aslan's mane!" he exclaimed. "Do you think that the privilege of seeing the last things is to be bought for a song? Why, every man that comes with us shall bequeath the title of Dawn Treader to all his descendants, and when we land at Cair Paravel on the homeward voyage he shall have either gold or land enough to make him rich all his life. Now — scatter over the island, all of you. In half an hour's time I shall receive the names that Lord Drinian brings me."

There was rather a sheepish silence and then the crew made their bows and moved away, one in this direction and one in that, but mostly in little knots or bunches, talking.

"And now for the Lord Rhoop," said Caspian.

But turning to the head of the table he saw that Rhoop was already there. He had arrived, silent and unnoticed, while the discussion was going on, and was seated beside the Lord Argoz. The daughter of Ramandu stood beside him as if she had just helped him into his chair; Ramandu stood behind him and laid both his hands on Rhoop's gray head. Even in daylight a faint silver light came from the hands of the star. There was a smile on Rhoop's haggard face. He held out one of his hands to Lucy and the other to Caspian. For a moment it looked as if he were going to say something. Then his smile brightened as if he were feeling some

delicious sensation, a long sigh of content-
ment came from his lips, his head fell forward, and he slept.

"Poor Rhoop," said Lucy. "I *am* glad. He
must have had terrible times."

"Don't let's even think of it," said
Eustace.

Meanwhile Caspian's speech, helped perhaps by some magic of the island, was
having just the effect he intended. A good
many who had been anxious enough to *get*
out of the voyage felt quite differently about
being *left* out of it. And of course whenever
any one sailor announced that he had made
up his mind to ask for permission to sail, the
ones who hadn't said this felt that they were
getting fewer and more uncomfortable. So
that before the half-hour was nearly over
several people were positively "sucking up"
to Drinian and Rhince (at least that was
what they called it at my school) to get a
good report. And soon there were only three
left who didn't want to go, and those three
were trying very hard to persuade others to
stay with them. And very shortly after that
there was only one left. And in the end he
began to be afraid of being left behind all on
his own and changed his mind.

At the end of the half-hour they all came
trooping back to Aslan's Table and stood at

one end while Drinian and Rhince went and sat down with Caspian and made their report; and Caspian accepted all the men but that one who had changed his mind at the last moment. His name was Pittencream and he stayed on the Island of the Star all the time the others were away looking for the World's End, and he very much wished he had gone with them. He wasn't the sort of man who could enjoy talking to Ramandu and Ramandu's daughter (nor they to him), and it rained a good deal, and though there was a wonderful feast on the Table every night, he didn't very much enjoy it. He said it gave him the creeps sitting there alone (and in the rain as likely as not) with those four Lords asleep at the end of the Table. And when the others returned he felt so out of things that he deserted on the voyage home at the Lone Islands, and went and lived in Calormen, where he told wonderful stories about his adventures at the End of the World, until at last he came to believe them himself. So you may say, in a sense, that he lived happily ever after. But he could never bear mice.

That night they all ate and drank together at the great Table between the pillars where the feast was magically renewed: and next morning the *Dawn Treader* set sail once more just when the great birds had come and gone again.

"Lady," said Caspian, "I hope to speak with you again when I have broken the enchantments." And Ramandu's daughter looked at him and smiled.

FIFTEEN

THE WONDERS OF THE LAST SEA

Very soon after they had left Ramandu's country they began to feel that they had already sailed beyond the world. All was different. For one thing they all found that they were needing less sleep. One did not want to go to bed nor to eat much, nor even to talk except in low voices. Another thing was the light. There was too much of it. The sun when it came up each morning looked twice, if not three times, its usual size. And every morning (which gave Lucy the strangest feeling of all) the huge white birds, singing their song with human voices in a language no one knew, streamed overhead and vanished astern on their way to their breakfast at Aslan's Table. A little later they came flying back and vanished into the east.

"How beautifully clear the water is!" said Lucy to herself, as she leaned over the port side early in the afternoon of the second day. And it was. The first thing that she noticed was a little black object, about the size of a shoe, traveling along at the same speed as the ship. For a moment she thought it was something floating on the surface. But then there came floating past a bit of stale bread which the cook had just thrown out of the galley. And the bit of bread looked as if it were going to collide with the black thing, but it didn't. It passed above it, and Lucy now saw that the black thing could not be on the surface. Then the black thing suddenly got very much bigger and flicked back to normal size a moment later.

Now Lucy knew she had seen something just like that happen somewhere else — if only she could remember where. She held her hand to her head and screwed up her face and put out her tongue in the effort to remember. At last she did. Of course! It was like what you saw from a train on a bright sunny day. You saw the black shadow of your own coach running along the fields at the same pace as the train. Then you went into a cutting; and immediately the same shadow flicked close up to you and got big, racing along the grass of the cuttingbank. Then you came out of the cutting and — flick! — once more the black shadow had gone back to its normal size and was running along the fields.

"It's our shadow! — the shadow of the *Dawn Treader*," said Lucy. "Our shadow running along on the bottom of the sea. That time when it got bigger it went over a hill. But in that case the water must be clearer than I thought! Good gracious, I must be seeing the bottom of the sea; fathoms and fathoms down."

As soon as she had said this she realized that the great silvery expanse which she had been seeing (without noticing) for some time was really the sand on the sea-bed and that all sorts of darker or brighter patches were not lights and shadows on the surface but real things on the bottom. At present, for instance, they were passing over a mass of soft purply green with a broad, winding strip of pale gray in the middle of it. But now that she knew it was on the bottom she saw it much better. She could see that bits of the dark stuff were much higher than other bits and were waving gently. "Just like trees in a wind," said Lucy. "And I do believe that's what they are. It's a submarine forest."

They passed on above it and presently the pale streak was joined by another pale streak. "If I was down there," thought Lucy, "that streak would be just like a road through the wood. And that place where it joins the other would be a crossroads. Oh, I do wish I was. Hallo! the forest is coming to an end. And I do believe the streak really was a road! I can still see it going on across the open sand. It's a different color. And it's marked out with something at the edges — dotted lines. Perhaps they are stones. And now it's getting wider."

But it was not really getting wider, it was getting nearer. She realized this because of the way in which the shadow of the ship came rushing up toward her. And the road — she felt sure it was a road now — began to go in zigzags. Obviously it was climbing up a steep hill. And when she held her head sideways and looked back, what she saw was very like what you see when you look down a winding road from the top of a hill. She could even see the shafts of sunlight falling through the deep water onto the wooded valley — and, in the extreme distance, everything melting away into a dim greenness. But some places — the sunny ones, she thought — were ultramarine blue.

She could not, however, spend much time looking back; what was coming into view in the forward direction was too exciting. The road had apparently now reached the top of the hill and ran straight forward. Little specks were moving to and fro on it. And now something most wonderful, fortunately in full sunlight — or as full as it can be when it falls through fathoms of water — flashed into sight. It was knobbly and jagged and of a pearly, or perhaps an ivory, color. She was so nearly straight above it that at first she could hardly make out what it was. But everything became plain when she noticed its shadow. The sunlight was falling across Lucy's shoulders, so the shadow of the thing lay stretched out on the sand behind it. And by its shape she saw clearly that it was a shadow of towers and pinnacles, minarets and domes.

"Why! — it's a city or a huge castle," said Lucy to herself. "But I wonder why they've built it on top of a high mountain?"

Long afterward when she was back in England and talked all these adventures over with Edmund, they thought of a reason and I am pretty sure it is the true one. In the sea, the deeper you go, the darker and colder it gets, and it is down there, in the dark and cold, that dangerous things live — the squid and the Sea Serpent and the Kraken. The valleys are the wild, unfriendly places. The sea-people feel about their valleys as we do about mountains, and feel about their mountains as we feel about valleys. It is on the heights (or, as we would say, "in the shallows") that there is warmth and peace. The reckless hunters and brave knights of the sea go down into the depths on quests and adventures, but return home to the heights for rest and peace, courtesy and council, the sports, the dances and the songs.

They had passed the city and the sea-bed was still rising. It was only a few hundred feet below the ship now. The road had disappeared. They were sailing above an open park-like country, dotted with little groves of brightly-colored vegetation. And then — Lucy nearly squealed aloud with excitement — she had seen People.

There were between fifteen and twenty of them, and all mounted on sea-horses — not the tiny little sea-horses which you may have seen in museums but horses rather bigger than themselves. They must be noble and lordly people, Lucy thought, for she could catch the gleam of gold on some of their foreheads and streamers of emerald- or orange-colored stuff fluttered from their shoulders in the current. Then:

"Oh, bother these fish!" said Lucy, for a whole shoal of small fat fish, swimming quite close to the surface, had come between her and the Sea People. But though this spoiled her view it led to the most interesting thing of all. Suddenly a fierce little fish of a kind she had never seen before came darting up from below, snapped, grabbed, and sank rapidly with one of the fat fish in its mouth. And all the Sea People were sitting on their horses staring up at what had happened. They seemed to be talking and laughing. And before the hunting fish had got back to them with its prey, another of the same kind came up from the Sea People. And Lucy was almost certain that one big Sea Man who sat on his sea-horse in the middle of the party had sent it or released it; as if he had been holding it back till then in his hand or on his wrist.

"Why, I do declare," said Lucy, "it's a hunting party. Or more like a hawking party. Yes, that's it. They ride out with these little fierce fish on their wrists just as we used to ride out with falcons on our wrists when we were Kings and Queens at Cair Paravel long ago. And then they fly them — or I suppose I should say *swim* them — at the others. How —"

She stopped suddenly because the scene was changing. The Sea People had noticed the Dawn Treader. The shoal of fish had scattered in every direction: the People themselves were coming up to find out the meaning of this big, black thing which had come between them and the sun. And now they were so close to the surface that if they had been in air, instead of water, Lucy could have spoken to them. There were men and women both. All wore coronets of some kind and many had chains of pearls.

They wore no other clothes. Their bodies were the color of old ivory, their hair dark purple. The King in the center (no one could mistake him for anything but the King) looked proudly and fiercely into Lucy's face and shook a spear in his hand. His knights did the same. The faces of the ladies were filled with astonishment. Lucy felt sure they had never seen a ship or a human before — and how should they, in seas beyond the world's end where no ship ever came?

"What are you staring at, Lu?" said a voice close beside her.

Lucy had been so absorbed in what she was seeing that she started at the sound, and when she turned she found that her arm had gone "dead" from leaning so long on the rail in one position. Drinian and Edmund were beside her.

"Look," she said.

They both looked, but almost at once Drinian said in a low voice:

"Turn round at once, your Majesties — that's right, with our backs to the sea. And don't look as if we were talking about anything important."

"Why, what's the matter?" said Lucy as she obeyed.

"It'll never do for the sailors to see *all that*," said Drinian. "We'll have men falling in love with a sea-woman, or falling in love with the under-sea country itself, and jumping overboard. I've heard of that kind of thing happening before in strange seas. It's always unlucky to see *these* people."

"But we used to know them," said Lucy. "In the old days at Cair Paravel when my brother Peter was High King. They came to the surface and sang at our coronation."

"I think that must have been a different kind, Lu," said Edmund. "They could live in the air as well as under water. I rather think these can't. By the look of them they'd have surfaced and started attacking us long ago if they could. They seem very fierce."

"At any rate," began Drinian, but at that moment two sounds were heard. One was a plop. The other was a voice from the fighting-top shouting, "Man overboard!" Then everyone was busy. Some of the sailors hurried aloft to take in the sail; others hurried below to get to the oars; and Rhince, who was on duty on the poop, began to put the helm hard over so as to come round and back to the man who had gone overboard. But by now everyone knew that it wasn't strictly a man. It was Reepicheep.

"Drat that mouse!" said Drinian. "It's more trouble than all the rest of the ship's company put together. If there is any scrape to be got into, in it will get! It ought to be put in irons — keelhauled — marooned — have its whiskers cut off. Can anyone see the little blighter?"

All this didn't mean that Drinian really disliked Reepicheep. On the contrary he liked him very much and was therefore frightened about him, and being frightened put him in a bad temper — just as your mother is much angrier with you for running out into the road in front of a car than a stranger would be. No one, of course, was afraid of Reepicheep's drowning, for he was an excellent swimmer; but the three who knew what was going on below the water were afraid of those long, cruel spears in the hands of the Sea People.

In a few minutes the *Dawn Treader* had come round and everyone could see the black blob in the water which was Reepicheep. He was chattering with the greatest excitement but as his mouth kept on getting filled with water nobody could understand what he was saying.

"He'll blurt the whole thing out if we don't shut him up," cried Drinian. To prevent this he rushed to the side and lowered a rope himself, shouting to the sailors, "All right, all right. Back to your places. I hope I can heave a *mouse* up without help." And as Reepicheep began climbing up the rope — not very nimbly because his wet fur made him heavy — Drinian leaned over and whispered to him, "Don't tell. Not a word."

But when the dripping Mouse had reached the deck it turned out not to be at all interested in the Sea People.

"Sweet!" he cheeped. "Sweet, sweet!"

"What are you talking about?" asked Drinian crossly. "And you needn't shake yourself all over *me*, either."

"I tell you the water's sweet," said the Mouse. "Sweet, fresh. It isn't salt."

For a moment no one quite took in the importance of this. But then Reepicheep once more repeated the old prophecy:

"Where the waves grow sweet,
Doubt not, Reepicheep,
There is the utter East."

Then at last everyone understood.

"Let me have a bucket, Rynelf," said Drinian.

It was handed him and he lowered it and up it came again. The water shone in it like glass.

"Perhaps your Majesty would like to taste it first," said Drinian to Caspian.

The King took the bucket in both hands, raised it to his lips, sipped, then drank deeply and raised his head. His face was changed. Not only his eyes but everything about him seemed to be brighter.

"Yes," he said, "it is sweet. That's real water, that. I'm not sure that it isn't going to kill me. But it is the death I would have chosen — if I'd known about it till now."

"What do you mean?" asked Edmund.

"It — it's like light more than anything else," said Caspian.

"That is what it is," said Reepicheep. "Drinkable light. We must be very near the end of the world now."

There was a moment's silence and then Lucy knelt down on the deck and drank from the bucket.

"It's the loveliest thing I have ever tasted," she said with a kind of gasp. "But oh — it's strong. We shan't need to *eat* anything now."

And one by one everybody on board drank. And for a long time they were all silent. They felt almost too well and strong to bear it; and presently they began to notice another result. As I have said before, there had been too much light ever since they left the island of Ramandu — the sun too large (though not too hot), the sea too bright, the air too shining. Now, the light grew no less — if anything, it increased — but they could bear it. They could look straight up at the sun without blinking. They could see more light than they had ever seen before. And the deck and the sail and their own faces and bodies became brighter and brighter and every rope shone. And next morning, when the sun rose, now five or six times its old size, they stared hard into it and could see the very feathers of the birds that came flying from it.

Hardly a word was spoken on board all that day, till about dinner-time (no one wanted any dinner, the water was enough for them) Drinian said:

"I can't understand this. There is not a breath of wind. The sail hangs dead. The sea is as flat as a pond. And yet we drive on as fast as if there were a gale behind us."

"I've been thinking that, too," said Caspian. "We must be caught in some strong current."

"H'm," said Edmund. "That's not so nice if the World really has an edge and we're getting near it."

"You mean," said Caspian, "that we might be just — well, poured over it?"

"Yes, yes," cried Reepicheep, clapping his paws together. "That's how I've always imagined it — the World like a great round table and the waters of all the oceans endlessly pouring over the edge. The ship will tip up — stand on her head — for one moment we shall see over the edge — and then, down, down, the rush, the speed —"

"And what do you think will be waiting for us at the bottom, eh?" said Drinian.

"Aslan's country, perhaps," said the Mouse, its eyes shining. "Or perhaps there isn't any bottom. Perhaps it goes down for ever and ever. But whatever it is, won't it be worth anything just to have looked for one moment beyond the edge of the world."

"But look here," said Eustace, "this is all rot. The world's round — I mean, round like a ball, not like a table."

"*Our* world is," said Edmund. "But is this?"

"Do you mean to say," asked Caspian, "that you three come from a round world (round like a ball) and you've never told me! It's really too bad of you. Because we have fairy-tales in which there are round worlds and I always loved them. I never believed there were any real ones. But I've always wished there were and I've always longed to live in one. Oh, I'd give anything — I wonder why you can get into our world and we never get into yours? If only I had the chance! It must be exciting to live on a thing like a ball. Have you ever been to the parts where people walk about upside-down?"

Edmund shook his head. "And it isn't like that," he added. "There's nothing particularly exciting about a round world when you're there."

SIXTEEN

THE VERY END

OF THE WORLD

Reepicheep was the only person on board besides Drinian and the two Pevensies who had noticed the Sea People. He had dived in at once when he saw the Sea King shaking his spear, for he regarded this as a sort of threat or challenge and wanted to have the matter out there and then. The excitement of discovering that the water was now fresh had distracted his attention, and before he remembered the Sea People again Lucy and Drinian had taken him aside and warned him not to mention what he had seen.

As things turned out they need hardly have bothered, for by this time the *Dawn Treader* was gliding over a part of the sea which seemed to be uninhabited. No one except Lucy saw anything more of the People, and even she had only one short glimpse. All morning on the following day they sailed in fairly shallow water and the bottom was weedy. Just before midday Lucy saw a large shoal of fishes grazing on the weed. They were all eating steadily and all moving in the same direction. "Just like a flock of sheep," thought Lucy. Suddenly she saw a little Sea Girl of about her own age in the middle of them — a quiet, lonely-looking girl with a sort of crook in her hand. Lucy felt sure that this girl must be a shepherdess — or perhaps a fish-herdess — and that the shoal was really a flock at pasture. Both the fishes and the girl were quite close to the surface. And just as the girl, gliding in the shallow water, and Lucy, leaning over the bulwark, came opposite to one another, the girl looked up and stared straight into Lucy's face. Neither could speak to the other and in a moment the Sea Girl dropped astern. But Lucy will never forget her face. It did not look frightened or angry like those of the other Sea People. Lucy had liked that girl and she felt certain the girl had liked her. In that one moment they had somehow become friends. There does not seem to be much chance of their meeting again in that world or any other. But if ever they do they will rush together with their hands held out.

After that for many days, without wind in her shrouds or foam at her bows, across a waveless sea, the *Dawn Treader* glided smoothly east. Every day and every hour the light became more brilliant and still they could bear it. No one ate or slept and no one wanted to, but they drew buckets of dazzling water from the sea, stronger than wine and somehow wetter, more liquid, than ordinary water, and pledged one another silently in deep drafts of it. And one or two of the sailors who had been oldish men when the voyage began now grew younger every day. Everyone on board was filled with joy and excitement, but not an excitement that made one talk. The further they sailed the less they spoke, and then almost in a whisper. The stillness of that last sea laid hold on them.

"My Lord," said Caspian to Drinian one day, "what do you see ahead?"

"Sire," said Drinian, "I see whiteness. All along the horizon from north to south, as far as my eyes can reach."

"That is what I see too," said Caspian, "and I cannot imagine what it is."

"If we were in higher latitudes, your Majesty," said Drinian, "I would say it was ice. But it can't be that; not here. All the same, we'd better get men to the oars and hold the ship back against the current. Whatever the stuff is, we don't want to crash into it at this speed!"

They did as Drinian said, and so con-

tinued to go slower and slower. The whiteness did not get any less mysterious as they
approached it. If it was land it must be a
very strange land, for it seemed just as
smooth as the water and on the same level
with it. When they got very close to it
Drinian put the helm hard over and turned
the *Dawn Treader* south so that she was
broadside on to the current and rowed a
little way southward along the edge of the
whiteness. In so doing they accidentally
made the important discovery that the current was only about forty feet wide and the
rest of the sea as still as a pond. This was
good news for the crew, who had already
begun to think that the return journey to
Ramandu's land, rowing against stream all
the way, would be pretty poor sport. (It also
explained why the shepherd girl had
dropped so quickly astern. She was not in
the current. If she had been she would have
been moving east at the same speed as the
ship.)

And still no one could make out what the
white stuff was. Then the boat was lowered
and it put off to investigate. Those who remained on the *Dawn Treader* could see that
the boat pushed right in amidst the whiteness. Then they could hear the voices of the
party in the boat (clear across the still water)

talking in a shrill and surprised way. Then there was a pause while Rynelf in the bows of the boat took a sounding; and when, after that, the boat came rowing back there seemed to be plenty of the white stuff inside her. Everyone crowded to the side to hear the news.

"Lilies, your Majesty!" shouted Rynelf, standing up in the bows.

"*What* did you say?" asked Caspian.

"Blooming lilies, your Majesty," said Rynelf. "Same as in a pool or in a garden at home."

"Look!" said Lucy, who was in the stern of the boat. She held up her wet arms full of white petals and broad flat leaves.

"What's the depth, Rynelf?" asked Drinian.

"That's the funny thing, Captain," said Rynelf. "It's still deep. Three and a half fathoms clear."

"They can't be real lilies — not what we call lilies," said Eustace.

Probably they were not, but they were very like them. And when, after some consultation, the *Dawn Treader* turned back into the current and began to glide eastward through the Lily Lake or the Silver Sea (they tried both these names but it was the Silver Sea that stuck and is now on Caspian's map) the strangest part of their travels began. Very soon the open sea which they were leaving was only a thin rim of blue on the western horizon. Whiteness, shot with faintest color of gold, spread round them on every side, except just astern where their passage had thrust the lilies apart and left an open lane of water that shone like dark green glass. To look at, this last sea was very like the Arctic; and if their eyes had not by now grown as strong as eagles' the sun on all that whiteness — especially at early morning when the sun was hugest — would have been unbearable. And every evening the same whiteness made the daylight last longer. There seemed no end to the lilies. Day after day from all those miles and leagues of flowers there rose a smell which Lucy found it very hard to describe; sweet-yes, but not at all sleepy or overpowering, a fresh, wild, lonely smell that seemed to get into your brain and make you feel that you could go up mountains at a run or wrestle with an elephant. She and Caspian said to one another, "I feel that I can't stand much more of this, yet I don't want it to stop."

They took soundings very often but it was only several days later that the water became shallower. After that it went on getting shallower. There came a day when they had to row out of the current and feel their way forward at a snail's pace, rowing. And soon it was clear that the *Dawn Treader* could sail no further east. Indeed it was only by very clever handling that they saved her from grounding.

"Lower the boat," cried Caspian, "and then call the men aft. I must speak to them."

"What's he going to do?" whispered Eustace to Edmund. "There's a queer look in his eyes."

"I think we probably all look the same," said Edmund.

They joined Caspian on the poop and soon all the men were crowded together at the foot of the ladder to hear the King's speech.

"Friends," said Caspian, "we have now fulfilled the quest on which you embarked. The seven lords are all accounted for and as Sir Reepicheep has sworn never to return, when you reach Ramandu's Land you will doubtless find the Lords Revilian and Argoz and Mavramorn awake. To you, my Lord Drinian, I entrust this ship, bidding you sail to Narnia with all the speed you may, and above all not to land on the Island of Deathwater. And instruct my regent, the Dwarf Trumpkin, to give to all these, my shipmates, the rewards I promised them.

They have been earned well. And if I come not again it is my will that the Regent, and Master Cornelius, and Trufflehunter the Badger, and the Lord Drinian choose a King of Narnia with the consent —"

"But, Sire," interrupted Drinian, "are you abdicating?"

"I am going with Reepicheep to see the World's End," said Caspian.

A low murmur of dismay ran through the sailors.

"We will take the boat," said Caspian. "You will have no need of it in these gentle seas and you must build a new one on Ramandu's island. And now —"

"Caspian," said Edmund suddenly and sternly, "you can't do this."

"Most certainly," said Reepicheep, "his Majesty cannot."

"No indeed," said Drinian.

"Can't?" said Caspian sharply, looking for a moment not unlike his uncle Miraz.

"Begging your Majesty's pardon," said Rynelf from the deck below, "but if one of us did the same it would be called deserting."

"You presume too much on your long service, Rynelf," said Caspian.

"No, Sire! He's perfectly right," said Drinian.

"By the Mane of Aslan," said Caspian, "I

had thought you were all my subjects here, not my schoolmasters."

"I'm not," said Edmund, "and I say you can *not* do this."

"Can't again," said Caspian. "What do you mean?"

"If it please your Majesty, we mean *shall not*," said Reepicheep with a very low bow. "You are the King of Narnia. You break faith with all your subjects, and especially with Trumpkin, if you do not return. You shall not please yourself with adventures as if you were a private person. And if your Majesty will not hear reason it will be the truest loyalty of every man on board to follow me in disarming and binding you till you come to your senses."

"Quite right," said Edmund. "Like they did with Ulysses when he wanted to go near the Sirens."

Caspian's hand had gone to his sword hilt, when Lucy said, "And you've almost promised Ramandu's daughter to go back."

Caspian paused. "Well, yes. There is that," he said. He stood irresolute for a moment and then shouted out to the ship in general.

"Well, have your way. The quest is ended. We all return. Get the boat up again."

"Sire," said Reepicheep, "we do not *all* return. I, as I explained before —"

"Silence!" thundered Caspian. "I've been lessoned but I'll not be baited. Will no one silence that Mouse?"

"Your Majesty promised," said Reepicheep, "to be good lord to the Talking Beasts of Narnia."

"Talking beasts, yes," said Caspian. "I said nothing about beasts that never stop talking." And he flung down the ladder in a temper and went into the cabin, slamming the door.

But when the others rejoined him a little later they found him changed; he was white and there were tears in his eyes.

"It's no good," he said. "I might as well have behaved decently for all the good I did with my temper and swagger. Aslan has spoken to me. No — I don't mean he was actually here. He wouldn't fit into the cabin, for one thing. But that gold lion's head on the wall came to life and spoke to me. It was terrible — his eyes. Not that he was at all rough with me — only a bit stern at first. But it was terrible all the same. And he said — he said — oh, I can't bear it. The worst thing he could have said. You're to go on — Reep and Edmund, and Lucy, and Eustace; and I'm to go back. Alone. And at once. And what *is* the good of anything?"

"Caspian, dear," said Lucy. "You knew we'd have to go back to our own world sooner or later."

"Yes," said Caspian with a sob, "but this is sooner."

"You'll feel better when you get back to Ramandu's Island," said Lucy.

He cheered up a little later on, but it was a grievous parting on both sides and I will not dwell on it. About two o'clock in the afternoon, well victualed and watered (though they thought they would need neither food nor drink) and with Reepicheep's coracle on board, the boat pulled away from the *Dawn Treader* to row through the endless carpet of lilies. The *Dawn Treader* flew all her flags and hung out her shields to honor their departure. Tall and big and homelike she looked from their low position with the lilies all round them. And even before she was out of sight they saw her turn and begin rowing slowly westward. Yet though Lucy shed a few tears, she could not feel it as much as you might have expected. The light, the silence, the tingling smell of the Silver Sea, even (in some odd way) the loneliness itself, were too exciting.

There was no need to row, for the current drifted them steadily to the east. None of them slept or ate. All that night and all next

day they glided eastward, and when the third day dawned — with a brightness you or I could not bear even if we had dark glasses on — they saw a wonder ahead. It was as if a wall stood up between them and the sky, a greenish-gray, trembling, shimmering wall. Then up came the sun, and at its first rising they saw it through the wall and it turned into wonderful rainbow colors. Then they knew that the wall was really a long, tall wave — a wave endlessly fixed in one place as you may often see at the edge of a waterfall. It seemed to be about thirty feet high, and the current was gliding them swiftly toward it. You might have supposed they would have thought of their danger. They didn't. I don't think anyone could have in their position. For now they saw something not only behind the wave but behind the sun. They could not have seen even the sun if their eyes had not been strengthened by the water of the Last Sea. But now they could look at the rising sun and see it clearly and see things beyond it. What they saw — eastward, beyond the sun — was a range of mountains. It was so high that either they never saw the top of it or they forgot it. None of them remembers seeing any sky in that direction. And the mountains must really have been outside the world. For any mountains even a quarter of a twentieth of that height ought to have had ice and snow on them. But these were warm and green and full of forests and waterfalls however high you looked. And suddenly there came a breeze from the east, tossing the top of the wave into foamy shapes and ruffling the smooth water all round them. It lasted only a second or so but what it brought them in that second none of those three children will ever forget. It brought both a smell and a sound, a musical sound. Edmund and Eustace would never talk about it afterward. Lucy could only say, "It would break your heart." "Why," said I, "was it so sad?" "Sad!! No," said Lucy.

No one in that boat doubted that they were seeing beyond the End of the World into Aslan's country.

At that moment, with a crunch, the boat ran aground. The water was too shallow now for it. "This," said Reepicheep, "is where I go on alone."

They did not even try to stop him, for everything now felt as if it had been fated or had happened before. They helped him to lower his little coracle. Then he took off his sword ("I shall need it no more," he said) and flung it far away across the lilied sea. Where it fell it stood upright with the hilt above the surface. Then he bade them good-bye, trying to be sad for their sakes; but he was quivering with happiness. Lucy, for the first and last time, did what she had always wanted to do, taking him in her arms and caressing him. Then hastily he got into his coracle and took his paddle, and the current caught it and away he went, very black against the lilies. But no lilies grew on the wave; it was a smooth green slope. The coracle went more and more quickly, and beautifully it rushed up the wave's side. For one split second they saw its shape and Reepicheep's on the very top. Then it vanished, and since that moment no one can truly claim to have seen Reepicheep the Mouse. But my belief is that he came safe to Aslan's country and is alive there to this day.

As the sun rose the sight of those mountains outside the world faded away. The wave remained but there was only blue sky behind it.

The children got out of the boat and waded — not toward the wave but southward with the wall of water on their left. They could not have told you why they did this; it was their fate. And though they had felt — and been — very grown-up on the *Dawn Treader*, they now felt just the opposite and held hands as they waded through the lilies. They never felt tired. The water was warm and all the time it got shallower. At last they were on dry sand, and then on grass — a huge plain of very fine short grass, almost level with the Silver Sea and spreading in every direction without so much as a mole-hill.

And of course, as it always does in a perfectly flat place without trees, it looked as if the sky came down to meet the grass in front of them. But as they went on they got the strangest impression that here at last the sky did really come down and join the earth — a blue wall, very bright, but real and solid: more like glass than anything else. And soon they were quite sure of it. It was very near now.

But between them and the foot of the sky there was something so white on the green grass that even with their eagles' eyes they could hardly look at it. They came on and saw that it was a Lamb.

"Come and have breakfast," said the Lamb in its sweet milky voice.

Then they noticed for the first time that there was a fire lit on the grass and fish roasting on it. They sat down and ate the

fish, hungry now for the first time for many days. And it was the most delicious food they had ever tasted.

"Please, Lamb," said Lucy, "is this the way to Aslan's country?"

"Not for you," said the Lamb. "For you the door into Aslan's country is from your own world."

"What!" said Edmund. "Is there a way into Aslan's country from our world too?"

"There is a way into my country from all

the worlds," said the Lamb; but as he spoke his snowy white flushed into tawny gold and his size changed and he was Aslan himself, towering above them and scattering light from his mane.

"Oh, Aslan," said Lucy. "Will you tell us how to get into your country from our world?"

"I shall be telling you all the time," said Aslan. "But I will not tell you how long or short the way will be; only that it lies across a river. But do not fear that, for I am the great Bridge Builder. And now come; I will open the door in the sky and send you to your own land."

"Please, Aslan," said Lucy. "Before we go, will you tell us when we can come back to Narnia again? Please. And oh, do, do, do make it soon."

"Dearest," said Aslan very gently, "you and your brother will never come back to Narnia."

"Oh, *Aslan!!*" said Edmund and Lucy both together in despairing voices.

"You are too old, children," said Aslan, "and you must begin to come close to your own world now."

"It isn't Narnia, you know," sobbed Lucy. "It's *you*. We shan't meet *you* there. And how can we live, never meeting you?"

"But you shall meet me, dear one," said Aslan.

"Are — are you there too, Sir?" said Edmund.

"I am," said Aslan. "But there I have another name. You must learn to know me by that name. This was the very reason why you were brought to Narnia, that by knowing me here for a little, you may know me better there."

"And is Eustace never to come back here either?" said Lucy.

"Child," said Aslan, "do you really need to know that? Come, I am opening the door in the sky." Then all in one moment there was a rending of the blue wall (like a curtain being torn) and a terrible white light from beyond the sky, and the feel of Aslan's mane and a Lion's kiss on their foreheads and then — the back bedroom in Aunt Alberta's home at Cambridge.

Only two more things need to be told. One is that Caspian and his men all came safely back to Ramandu's Island. And the three lords woke from their sleep. Caspian married Ramandu's daughter and they all reached Narnia in the end, and she became a great queen and the mother and grandmother of great kings. The other is that back in our own world everyone soon started saying how Eustace had improved, and how "You'd never know him for the same boy": everyone except Aunt Alberta, who said he had become very commonplace and tiresome and it must have been the influence of those Pevensie children.

The employees of Thorndike Press hope you have enjoyed this Large Print book. All our Large Print titles are designed for easy reading, and all our books are made to last. Other Thorndike Press Large Print books are available at your library, through selected bookstores, or directly from us.

For information about titles, please call:

(800) 223-1244
(800) 223-6121

To share your comments, please write:

Publisher
Thorndike Press
P.O. Box 159
Thorndike, Maine 04986

THE SECOND MRS ADAMS

THE SECOND
MRS ADAMS

BY

SANDRA MARTON

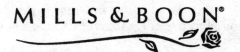

MILLS & BOON®

MILLS & BOON and
MILLS & BOON with the Rose Device
are registered trademarks of the publisher.

First published in Great Britain 1996
Large Print edition 1997
Harlequin Mills & Boon Limited,
Eton House, 18-24 Paradise Road,
Richmond, Surrey TW9 1SR

© Sandra Myles 1996

ISBN 0 263 15045 3

Set in Times Roman
16-9705-61500 C15½-16½

Printed and bound in Great Britain
by Mackays of Chatham PLC, Chatham

CHAPTER ONE

THE siren was loud.

Painfully, agonizingly loud.

The sound was a live thing, burrowing deep into her skull, tunneling into the marrow of her bones.

Make it stop, she thought, oh please, make it stop.

But even when it did, the silence didn't take the pain away.

"My head," she whispered. "My head."

No one was listening. Or perhaps no one could hear her. Was she really saying anything or was she only thinking the words?

People were crowded around, faces looking down at her, some white with concern, others sweaty with curiosity. Hands were moving over her now, very gently, and then they were lifting her; oh, God, it hurt!

"Easy," somebody said, and then she was inside a . . . a what? A truck? No. It was an ambulance. And now the doors closed and the ambulance began to move and the sound, that

5

awful sound, began again and they were flying through the streets.

Terror constricted her throat.

What's happened to me? she thought desperately.

She tried to gasp out the words but she couldn't form them. She was trapped in silence and in pain as they raced through the city.

Had there been an accident? A picture formed in her mind of wet, glistening pavement, a curb, a taxi hurtling toward her. She heard again the bleat of a horn and the squeal of tires seeking a purchase that was not to be found...

No. No! she thought, and then she screamed her denial but the scream rose to mingle with the wail of the siren as she tumbled down into velvet darkness.

She lay on her back and drifted in the blue waters of a dream. There was a bright yellow light overhead.

Was it the sun?

There were voices... Disembodied voices, floating on the air. Sentence fragments that made no sense, falling around her with the coldness of snow.

"...five more CC's..."

"...blood pressure not stabilized yet..."

"...wait for a CAT scan before..."

The voices droned on. It wasn't anything to do with her, she decided drowsily, and fell back into the darkness.

The next time she awoke, the voices were still talking.

"...no prognosis, at this stage..."

"...touch and go for a while, but..."

They *were* talking about her. But why? What was wrong with her? She wanted to ask, she wanted to tell them to stop discussing her as if she weren't there because she *was* there, it was just that she couldn't get her eyes to open because the lids were so heavy.

She groaned and a hand closed over hers, the fingers gripping hers reassuringly.

"Joanna?"

Who?

"Joanna, can you hear me?"

Joanna? Was that who she was? Was that her name?

"...head injuries are often unpredictable..."

The hand tightened on hers. "Dammit, stop talking about her as if she weren't here!"

The voice was as masculine as the touch, blunt with anger and command. Blessedly, the buzz of words ceased. Joanna tried to move her fingers, to press them against the ones that clasped hers and let the man know she was grateful for what he'd done, but she couldn't. Though her mind willed it, her hand wouldn't respond. It felt like the rest of her, as lifeless as a lump of lead. She could only lie there un-moving, her fingers caught within those of the stranger's.

"It's all right, Joanna," he murmured. "I'm here."

His voice soothed her but his words sent fear coursing through her blood. Who? she thought wildly, who was here?

Without warning, the blackness opened be-neath her and sucked her down.

When she awoke next, it was to silence.

She knew at once that she was alone. There were no voices, no hand holding hers. And though she felt as if she were floating, her mind felt clear.

Would she be able to open her eyes this time? The possibility that she couldn't terrified her. Was she paralyzed? No. Her toes moved, and her fingers. Her hands, her legs . . .

All right, then.

Joanna took a breath, held it, then slowly let it out. Then she raised eyelids that felt as if they had been coated with cement.

The sudden rush of light was almost blinding. She blinked against it and looked around her.

She was in a hospital room. There was no mistaking it for anything else. The high ceiling and the bottle suspended beside the bed, dripping something pale and colorless into her vein, confirmed it.

The room was not unpleasant. It was large, drenched in bright sunlight and filled with baskets of fruit and vases of flowers.

Was all that for her? It had to be; hers was the only bed in the room.

What had happened to her? She had seen no cast on her legs or her arms; nothing ached in her body or her limbs. Except for the slender plastic tubing snaking into her arm, she might have awakened from a nap.

Was there a bell to ring? She lifted her head from the pillow. Surely there was a way to call some...

"Ahh!"

Pain lanced through her skull with the keenness of a knife. She fell back and shut her eyes against it.

"Mrs. Adams?"

Joanna's breath hissed from between her teeth.

"Mrs. Adams, do you hear me? Open your eyes, please, Mrs. Adams, and look at me."

It hurt, God, it hurt, but she managed to look up into a stern female face that was instantly softened by a smile.

"That's the way, Mrs. Adams. Good girl. How do you feel?"

Joanna opened her mouth but nothing came out. The nurse nodded sympathetically.

"Wait a moment. Let me moisten your lips with some ice chips. There, how's that?"

"My head hurts," Joanna said in a cracked whisper.

The nurse's smile broadened, as if something wonderful had happened.

"Of course it does, dear. I'm sure the doctor will give you something for it as soon as he's seen you. I'll just go and get him . . ."

Joanna's hand shot out. She caught the edge of the woman's crisp white sleeve.

"Please," she said, "what happened to me?"

"Doctor Corbett will explain everything, Mrs. Adams."

"Was I in an accident? I don't remember. A car. A taxi . . ."

"Hush now, dear." The woman extricated herself gently from Joanna's grasp and made her way toward the door. "Just lie back and relax, Mrs. Adams. I'll only be a moment."

"Wait!"

The single word stopped the nurse with its urgency. She paused in the doorway and swung around.

"What is it, Mrs. Adams?"

Joanna stared at the round, kindly face. She felt the seconds flying away from her with every pounding beat of her heart.

"You keep calling me...you keep saying, 'Mrs. Adams...'"

She saw the sudden twist in the nurse's mouth, the dawning of sympathetic realization in the woman's eyes.

"Can you tell me," Joanna said in a broken whisper, "can you tell me who... What I mean is, could you tell me, please, who I am?"

The doctor came. Two doctors, actually, one a pleasant young man with a gentle touch and another, an older man with a patrician air and a way of looking at her as if she weren't really there while he poked and prodded but that was OK because Joanna felt as if she wasn't really there, surely not here in this bed, in this room, without any idea in the world of who she was.

"Mrs. Adams" they all called her, and like some well-trained dog, she learned within moments to answer to the name, to extend her arm and let them take out the tubing, to say "Yes?"

when one of them addressed her by the name, but who was Mrs. Adams?

Joanna only knew that she was here, in this room, and that to all intents and purposes, her life had begun an hour before.

She asked questions, the kind she'd never heard anywhere but in a bad movie and even when she thought that, it amazed her that she'd know there was such a thing as a bad movie.

But the doctor, the young one, said that was what amnesia was like, that you remembered some things and not others, that it wasn't as if your brain had been wiped clean of everything, and Joanna thought thank goodness for that or she would lie here like a giant turnip. She said as much to the young doctor and he laughed and she laughed, even though it hurt her head when she did, and then, without any warning, she wasn't laughing at all, she was sobbing as if her heart were going to break, and a needle slid into her arm and she fell into oblivion.

It was nighttime when she woke next.

The room was dark, except for the light seeping in from the hushed silence of the corridor just outside the partly open door. The blackness beyond the windowpane was broken by the glow of lights from what surely had to be a city.

Joanna stirred restlessly. "Nurse?" she whispered.

"Joanna."

She knew the voice. It was the same masculine one that she'd heard an eternity ago when she'd surfaced from unconsciousness.

"Yes," she said.

She heard the soft creak of leather and a shape rose from the chair beside her bed. Slowly, carefully, she turned her head on the pillow.

His figure was shrouded in shadow, his face indistinct. She could see only that he was big and broad of shoulder, that he seemed powerful, almost mystical in the darkness.

"Joanna," he said again, his voice gruff as she'd remembered it yet tinged now with a husky softness. His hand closed over hers and this time she had no difficulty flexing her fingers and threading them through his, clasping his hand and holding on as if to a lifeline. "Welcome back," he said, and she could hear the smile and the relief in the words.

Joanna swallowed hard. There was so much she wanted to ask, but it seemed so stupid to say, "who am I?" or "who are you?" or "where am I?" or "how did I get here?"

"You probably have a lot of questions," he said, and she almost sobbed with relief.

"Yes," she murmured.

He nodded. "Ask them, then—or shall I get the nurse first? Do you need anything? Want anything? Water, or some cracked ice, or perhaps you need to go to the bathroom?"

"Answers," Joanna said urgently, her hand tightening on his, "I need answers."

"Of course. Shall I turn up the light?"

"No," she said quickly. If he turned up the light, this would all become real. And it wasn't real. It couldn't be. "No, it's fine this way, thank you."

"Very well, then." The bed sighed as he sat down beside her. His hip brushed against hers, and she could feel the heat of him, the strength and the power. "Ask away, and I'll do my best to answer."

Joanna licked her lips. "What—what happened? I mean, how did I get here? Was there an accident?"

He sighed. "Yes."

"I seem to remember... I don't know. It was raining, I think."

"Yes," he said again. His hand tightened on hers. "It was."

"I stepped off the curb. The light was with me, I'd checked because... because..." She frowned. There was a reason, she knew there was, and it had something to do with him, but how could it when she didn't...when she had no idea who he...

Joanna whimpered, and the man bent down and clasped her shoulders.

"It's all right," he said, "it's all right, Joanna."

It wasn't, though. The touch of his hands on her was gentle but she could feel the tightly leashed rage in him, smell its hot, masculine scent on the carefully filtered hospital air.

"The taxi..."

"Yes."

"It—it came flying through the intersection..."

"Hush."

"I saw it, but by the time I did it was too late..."

Her voice quavered, then broke. The man cursed softly and his hands slid beneath her back and he lifted her toward him, cradling her against his chest.

Pain bloomed like an evil, white-hot flower behind her eyes. A cry rose in her throat and burst from her lips. Instantly, he lay her back against the pillows.

"Hell," he said. "I'm sorry, Joanna. I shouldn't have moved you."

Strangely, the instant of pain had been a small price to pay for the comfort she'd felt in his arms. His strength had seemed to flow into her body; his heartbeat had seemed to give determination to hers.

She wanted to tell him that, but how did you say such things to a stranger?

"Joanna? Are you all right?"

She nodded. "I'm fine. I just—I have so many questions..."

He brushed the back of his hand along her cheek in a wordless gesture.

"I need to know." She took a breath. "Tell me the rest, please. The taxi hit me, didn't it?"

"Yes."

"And an ambulance brought me to... What is this place?"

"You're in Manhattan Hospital."

"Am I... am I badly hurt?" He hesitated, and she swallowed hard. "Please, tell me the truth. What kind of injuries do I have?"

"Some bruises. A cut above your eye...they had to put in stitches—"

"Why can't I remember anything? Do I have amnesia?"

She asked it matter-of-factly, as if she'd been inquiring about nothing more devastating than a common cold, but he wasn't a fool, she knew he could sense the panic that she fought to keep from her voice because the hands that still clasped her shoulders tightened again.

"The taxi only brushed you," he said. "But when you fell, you hit your head against the curb."

"My mind is like a—a blackboard that's been wiped clean. You keep calling me 'Joanna' but the name has no meaning to me. I don't know who 'Joanna' is."

Her eyes had grown accustomed to the shadowy darkness; she could almost see him clearly now. He had a hard face with strong features: a straight blade of a nose, a slash of a mouth, hair that looked to be thick and dark and perhaps a bit overlong.

"And me?" His voice had fallen to a whisper; she had to strain to hear it. "Do you know who I am, Joanna?"

She took a deep, shuddering breath. Should she remember him? Should she at least know his name?

"No," she said. "No. I don't."

There was a long, almost palpable silence. She felt the quick bite of his fingers into her flesh and then he lifted his hands away, carefully, slowly, as if she were a delicate glass figurine he'd just returned to its cabinet for fear a swift movement would make it shatter.

He rose slowly to his feet and now she could see that he was tall, that the broad shoulders were matched by a powerful chest that tapered to a narrow waist, slim hips and long, well-proportioned legs. He stood beside the bed looking down at her, and then he nodded and thrust his fingers through his hair in a gesture instinct told her was as familiar to her as it was habitual to him.

"The doctors told me to expect this," he said, "but..."

He shrugged so helplessly, despite the obvious power of his silhouette, that Joanna's heart felt his frustration.

"I'm sorry," she murmured. "I'm terribly, terribly sorry."

His smile was bittersweet. He sat down beside her again and took her hand in his. She had a fleeting memory, one that was gone before she could make sense of it. She saw his dark head bent over a woman's hand, saw his lips pressed to the palm...

Was the woman her? Was he going to bring her hand to his mouth and kiss it?

Anticipation, bright as the promise of a new day and sweet as the nectar of a flower, made her pulse-beat quicken. But all he did was lay her hand down again and pat it lightly with his.

"It isn't your fault, Joanna. There's nothing to apologize for."

She had the feeling that there was, that she owed him many apologies for many things, but that was silly. How could she owe anything to a man she didn't know?

"Please," she said softly, "tell me your name."

His mouth twisted. Then he rose to his feet, walked to the window and stared out into the night. An eternity seemed to pass before he turned and looked at her again.

"Of course." There was a difference in him now, in his tone and in the way he held himself, and it frightened her. "My name is David. David Adams."

Joanna hesitated. The black pit that had swallowed her so many times since the accident seemed to loom at her feet.

"David Adams," she murmured, turning the name over in her mind, trying—failing—to find in it some hint of familiarity. "We—we have the same last name."

He laughed, though there was no levity to it.

"I can see you haven't lost your talent for understatement, Joanna. Yes, we have the same last name."

"Are we related, then?"

His mouth twisted again, this time with a wry smile. "Indeed, we are, my love. You see, Joanna, I'm your husband."

CHAPTER TWO

THE nurses all knew him by name, but after ten days there was nothing surprising in that.

What was surprising, David thought as his driver competently snaked the Bentley through the crowded streets of midtown Manhattan, was that he'd become something of a celebrity in the hospital.

Morgana, his P.A., had laughed when he'd first expressed amazement and then annoyance at his star status.

"I'm not Richard Gere, for heaven's sake," he'd told her irritably after he'd been stopped half a dozen times for his autograph en route to Joanna's room. "What in hell do they want with the signature of a stodgy Wall Street banker?"

Morgana had pointed out that he wasn't just a Wall Street banker, he was the man both the President of the World Bank and the President of the United States turned to for financial advice, even though his politics were not known by either.

As for stodgy... Morgana reminded him that *CityLife* magazine had only last month named him to its list of New York's Ten Sexiest Men.

David, who'd been embarrassed enough by the designation so he'd done an admirable job of all but forgetting it, had flushed.

"Absurd of them to even have mentioned my name in that stupid article," he'd muttered, and Morgana, honest as always, had agreed.

The media thought otherwise. In a rare week of no news, an accident involving the beautiful young wife of New York's Sexiest Stockbroker was a four-star event.

The ghouls had arrived at the Emergency Room damned near as fast as he had so that when he'd jumped from his taxi he'd found himself in a sea of microphones and cameras and shouted questions, some so personal he wouldn't have asked them of a close friend. David had clenched his jaw, ignored them all and shoved his way through the avaricious mob without pausing.

That first encounter had taught him a lesson. Now, he came and went by limousine even though he hated the formality and pretentiousness of the oversize car he never used but for the most formal business occasions. Joanna had liked it, though. She loved the luxury of the plush passenger compartment with its built-in bar, TV and stereo.

David's mouth twisted. What irony, that the car he disliked and his wife loved should have become his vehicle of choice, since the accident.

It had nothing to do with the bar or the TV. It was just that he'd quickly learned that the reporters who still hung around outside the hospital pounced on taxis like hyenas on wounded wildebeests. Arriving by limo avoided the problem. The car simply pulled up at the physicians' entrance, David stepped out, waved to the security man as if he'd been doing it every day of his life and walked straight in. The reporters had yet to catch on, though it wouldn't matter, after tonight. This would be his last visit to the hospital.

By this time tomorrow, Joanna would be installed in a comfortable suite at Bright Meadows Rehabilitation Center. The place had an excellent reputation, both for helping its patients recover and for keeping them safe from unwelcome visitors. Bright Meadows was accustomed to catering to high-profile guests. No one whose name hadn't been placed on an approved list would get past the high stone walls and there was even a helicopter pad on the grounds, if a phalanx of reporters decided to gather at the gates.

Hollister pulled up to the private entrance as usual and David waved to the guard as he walked briskly through the door and into a waiting elevator. He was on the verge of breathing a sigh of relief when a bottle blonde with a triumphant smile on her face and a microphone clutched in her hand sprang out of the shadows and into the elevator. She jammed her finger on the Stop button and turned up the wattage on her smile.

"Mr. Adams," she said, "millions of interested *Sun* readers want to know how Mrs. Adams is doing."

"She's doing very well, thank you," David said politely.

"Is she really?" Her voice dropped to a whisper that oozed compassion the same way a crocodile shed tears. "You can tell *Sun* readers the truth, David. What's the real extent of your wife's injuries?"

"Would you take your finger off that button, please, miss?"

The blonde edged nearer. "Is it true she's in a coma?"

"Step back, please, and let go of that button."

"David." The blond leaned forward, her heavily kohled eyes, her cleavage and her microphone all aimed straight at him. "We heard that your wife's accident occurred while she was en route to the airport for your second honeymoon in the Caribbean. Can you confirm that for our readers?''

David's jaw tightened. He could sure as hell wipe that look of phony sympathy from the blonde's face, he thought grimly. All he had to do was tell her the truth, that Joanna had been on her way to the airport, all right, and then to the Caribbean—and to the swift, civilized divorce they had agreed upon.

But the last thing he'd ever do was feed tabloid gossip. His life was private. Besides, ending the marriage was out of the question now. He and Joanna were husband and wife, by license if not by choice. He would stand by her, provide the best care possible until she was well again...

''Mr. Adams?''

The blonde wasn't going to give up easily. She had rearranged her face so that her expression had gone from compassion to sincere inquiry. He thought of telling her that the last time he'd seen that look it had been on the face of a shark that had a sincere interest in one or more of his limbs while he'd been diving off the Mexican coast.

"I only want to help you share your problems with our readers," she said. "Sharing makes grief so much easier to bear, don't you agree?"

David smiled. "Well, Miss..."

"Washbourne." She smiled back, triumphant. "Mona Washbourne, but you can call me Mona."

"Well, Mona, I'll be happy to share this much." David's smile vanished as quickly as it had appeared. He raised his arm, shot back the cuff of his dark blue suit jacket, and looked at his watch. "Get that mike out of my face and your finger off that button in the next ten seconds or you're going to regret it."

"Is that a threat, Mr. Adams?"

"Your word, Mona, not mine."

"Because it certainly sounded like one. And I've got every word, right here, on my tape rec—"

"I never make threats, I only make promises. Anyone who's had any dealings with me can tell you that." His eyes met hers. "You're down to four seconds, and still counting."

Whatever Mona Washbourne saw in that cold, steady gaze made her jerk her finger from the Stop button and step out of the elevator.

"Didn't you ever hear of freedom of the press? You can't go around bullying reporters."

"Is that what you are?" David said politely. He punched the button for Joanna's floor and the doors began to shut. "A member of the press? Damn. And here I was, thinking you were a..."

The doors snapped closed. Just as well, he thought wearily, and leaned back against the wall. Insulting the Mona Washbournes of the world only made them more vicious, and what was the point? He was accustomed to pressure, it was part of the way he earned his living.

OK, so the last week and a half had been rough. Personally rough. He didn't love Joanna anymore, hell, he wasn't even sure if he had ever loved her to begin with, but that didn't mean he hadn't almost gone crazy with fear when the call had come, notifying him of the accident. He wasn't heartless. What man wouldn't react to the news that the woman he was married to had been hurt?

And, as it had turned out, "hurt" was a wild word to describe what had happened to Jo. David's mouth thinned. She'd lost her memory. She didn't remember anything. Not her name, not their marriage...

Not him.

The elevator doors opened. The nurse on duty looked up, frowning, an automatic reminder that it was past visiting hours on her lips, but then her stern features softened into a girlish smile.

"Oh, it's you, Mr. Adams. We thought you might not be stopping by this evening."

"I'm afraid I got tied up in a meeting, Miss Howell."

"Well, certainly, sir. That's what I told Mrs. Adams, that you were probably running late."

"How is my wife this evening?"

"Very well, sir." The nurse's smile broadened. "She's had her hair done. Her makeup, too. I suspect you'll find her looking more and more like her old self."

"Ah." David nodded. "Yes, well, that's good news."

He told himself that it was as he headed down the hall toward Joanna's room. She hadn't looked at all like herself since the accident.

"Why are you looking at me like that?" she'd asked him, just last evening, and when he hadn't answered, her hand had shot to her forehead, clamping over the livid, half-moon scar that marred her perfect skin. "It's ugly, isn't it?"

David had stood there, wanting to tell her that what he'd been staring at was the sight of a Joanna he'd all but forgotten, one who lent grace and beauty even to an undistinguished white hospital gown, who wore her dark hair loose in a curling, silken cloud, whose dark-lashed violet eyes were not just free of makeup but wide and vulnerable, whose full mouth was the pink of roses.

He hadn't said any of that, of course, partly because it was just sentimental slop and partly because he knew she wouldn't want to hear it. That Joanna had disappeared months after their wedding and the Joanna who'd replaced her was always careful about presenting an impeccably groomed self to him and to the world. So he'd muttered something about the scar being not at all bad and then he'd changed the subject, but he hadn't forgotten the moment.

It had left a funny feeling in his gut, seeing Joanna that way, as if a gust of wind had blown across a calendar and turned the pages backward. He'd mentioned it to Morgana in passing, not the clutch in his belly but how different Joanna looked and his Personal Assistant, with the clever, understanding instincts of one woman for another, had cluck-clucked.

"The poor girl," she'd said, "of course she looks different! Think what she's gone through, David. She probably dreads looking at herself in the mirror. Her cosmetic case and a visit from her hairdresser will go a long way toward cheering her spirits. Shall I make the arrangements?"

David had hesitated, though he couldn't imagine the reason. Then he'd said yes, of course, that he'd have done it himself, if he'd thought of it, and Morgana had smiled and said that the less men knew about women's desires to make themselves beautiful, the better.

So Morgana had made the necessary calls, and he'd seen to it that Joanna's own robes, nightgowns and slippers were packed by her maid and delivered to the hospital first thing this morning, and now, as he knocked and then opened the door of her room, he was not surprised to find the Joanna he knew waiting for him.

She was standing at the window, her back to him. She was dressed in a pale blue cashmere robe, her hair drawn back from her face and secured at the nape in an elegant knot. Her posture was straight and proud—or was there a curve to her shoulders and a tremble to them, as well?

He stepped inside the room and let the door swing shut behind him.

"Joanna?"

She turned at the sound of his voice and he saw that everything about her had gone back to normal. The vulnerability had left her eyes; they'd been done up in some way he didn't pretend to understand so that they were

somehow less huge and far more sophisticated.
The bright color had been toned down in her
cheeks and her mouth, while still full and
beautiful, was no longer the color of a rose but
of the artificial blossoms only found in a lipstick tube.

The girl he had once called his Gypsy was
gone. The stunning Manhattan sophisticate was
back and it was stupid to feel a twinge of loss
because he'd lost his Gypsy a long, long time
ago.

"David," Joanna said. "I didn't expect
you."

"I was stuck in a meeting . . . Joanna? Have
you been crying?"

"No," she said quickly, "no, of course not.
I just—I have a bit of a headache, that's all."
She swallowed; he could see the movement of
muscle in her long, pale throat. "Thank you
for the clothes you sent over."

"Don't be silly. I should have thought of
having your own things delivered to you days
ago."

The tip of her tongue snaked across her lips.
She looked down at her robe, then back at him.

"You mean . . . I selected these things
myself?"

He nodded. "Of course. Ellen packed them
straight from your closet."

"Ellen?"

"Your maid."

"My..." She gave a little laugh, walked to the bed and sat down on the edge of the mattress. "I have a maid?" David nodded. "Well, thank her for me, too, please. Oh, and thank you for arranging for me to have my hair and my makeup done."

"It isn't necessary to thank me, Joanna. But you're welcome."

He spoke as politely as she did, even though he had the sudden urge to tell her that he'd liked her better with her hair wild and free, with color in her cheeks that didn't come from a makeup box and her eyes dark and sparkling with laughter.

She was beautiful now but she'd been twice as beautiful before.

David frowned. The pressure of the past ten days was definitely getting to him. There was no point in remembering the past when the past had never been real.

"So," he said briskly, "are you looking forward to getting sprung from this place tomorrow?"

Joanna stared at him. She knew what she was supposed to say. And the prospect of getting out of the hospital had been exciting...until she'd begun to think about what awaited her outside these walls.

By now, she knew she and David lived in a town house near Central Park but she couldn't begin to imagine what sort of life they led. David was rich, that much was obvious, and yet she had the feeling she didn't know what it meant to lead the life of a wealthy woman.

Which was, of course, crazy, because she didn't know what it meant to lead any sort of life, especially one as this stranger's wife.

He was so handsome, this man she couldn't remember. So unabashedly male, and here she'd been lying around looking like something the cat had dragged in, dressed in a shapeless hospital gown with no makeup at all on her face and her hair wild as a whirlwind, and then her clothes and her hairdresser and her makeup had arrived and she'd realized that her husband preferred her to look chic and sophisticated.

No wonder he'd looked at her as if he'd never seen her before just last evening.

Maybe things would improve between them now. The nurses all talked about how lucky she was to be Mrs. David Adams. He was gorgeous, they giggled, so sexy...

So polite, and so cold.

The nurses didn't know that, but Joanna did. Was that how he'd always treated her? As if they were strangers who'd just met, always careful to do and say the right thing? Or was it the accident that had changed things between them? Was he so removed, so proper, because he knew she couldn't remember him or their marriage?

Joanna wanted to ask, but how could you ask such intimate things of a man you didn't know?

"Joanna, what's the matter?" She blinked and looked up at David. His green eyes were narrowed with concern as they met hers. "Have the doctors changed their minds about releasing you?"

Joanna forced a smile to her lips. "No, no, the cell door's still scheduled to open at ten in the morning. I was just thinking about...about how it's going to be to go...to go..." Home, she thought. She couldn't bring herself to say the word, but then, she didn't have to. She wasn't going home tomorrow, she was going to a rehab center. More white-tiled walls, more high ceilings, more brightly smiling nurses... "Where is Big Meadows, anyway?"

"Bright Meadows," David said, with a smile. "It's about an hour's drive from here. You'll like the place, Jo. Lots of trees, rolling hills, an Olympic-size swimming pool and there's even an exercise room. Nothing as high-tech as your club, I don't think, but even so—"

"My club?"

Damn, David thought, damn! The doctors had warned him against jogging her memory until she was ready, until she began asking questions on her own.

"Sorry. I didn't mean to—"

"Do I belong to an exercise club?"

"Well, yeah."

"You mean, one of those places where you dress up in a silly Spandex suit so you can climb on a treadmill to work up a sweat?"

David grinned. It was his unspoken description of the Power Place, to a tee.

"I think the Power Place would be offended to hear itself described in quite that way but I can't argue with it, either."

Joanna laughed. "I can't even imagine doing that. I had the TV on this morning and there was this roomful of people jumping up and down . . . they looked so silly, and now you're telling me that I do the same thing?"

"The Power Place," David said solemnly, "would definitely not like to hear you say that."

"Why don't I run outdoors? Or walk? Didn't you say I—we—live near Central Park?"

His smile tilted. It was as if she was talking about another person instead of herself.

"Yes. We live less than a block away. And I don't know why you didn't run there. I do, every morning."

"Without me?" she said.

"Yes. Without you."

"Didn't we ever run together?"

He stared at her. They had; he'd almost forgotten. She'd run right along with him the first few weeks after their marriage. They'd even gone running one warm, drizzly morning and had the path almost all to themselves. They'd been jogging along in silence when she'd suddenly yelled out a challenge and sped away from him. He'd let her think she was going to beat him for thirty or forty yards and then he'd put on some speed, come up behind her, snatched her into his arms and tumbled them both off the path and into the grass. He'd kissed her until she'd stopped laughing and gone soft with desire in his arms, and then they'd flagged a cab to take them the short block back home...

He frowned, turned away and strode to the closet. "You said you preferred to join the club," he said brusquely, "that it was where all your friends went and that it was a lot more pleasant and a lot safer to run on an indoor track than in the park. Have you decided what you're going to wear tomorrow?''

''But how could it be safer? If you and I ran together, I was safe enough, wasn't I?''

''It was better that way, Joanna. We both agreed that it was. My schedule's become more and more erratic. I have to devote a lot of hours to business. You know that. I mean, you don't know it, not anymore, but...''

''That's OK, you don't have to explain.'' Joanna smiled tightly. ''You're a very busy man. And a famous one. The nurses all keep telling me how lucky I am to be married to you.''

David's hand closed around the mauve silk suit hanging in the closet.

''They ought to mind their business,'' he said gruffly.

''Don't be angry with them, David. They mean well.''

''Everybody ought to mind their damned business,'' he said, fighting against the rage he felt suddenly, inexplicably, rising within him. ''The nurses, the reporters—''

''Reporters?''

For the second time that night, David cursed himself. He could hear the sudden panic in Joanna's voice and he turned and looked at her.

"Don't worry about them. I won't let them get near you."

"But why..." She stopped, then puffed out her breath. "Of course. They want to know about the accident, about me, because I'm Mrs. David Adams."

"They won't bother you, Joanna. Once I get you to Bright Meadows..."

"The doctors say I'll have therapy at Bright Meadows."

"Yes."

"What kind of therapy?"

"I don't know exactly. They have to evaluate you first."

"Evaluate me?" she said with a quick smile.

"Look, the place is known throughout the country. The staff, the facilities, are all highly rated."

Joanna ran the tip of her tongue across her lips. "I don't need therapy," she said brightly. "I just need to remember."

"The therapy will help you do that."

"How?" She tilted her head up. Her smile was brilliant, though he could see it wobble just a little. "There's nothing wrong with me physically, David. Or mentally. I don't need to go for walks on the arm of an aide or learn basketweaving or—or lie on a couch while some doctor asks me silly questions about a childhood I can't remember.''

David's frown deepened. She was saying the same things he'd said when Bright Meadows had been recommended to him.

''Joanna's not crazy,'' he'd said bluntly, ''and she's not crippled.''

The doctors had agreed, but they'd pointed out that there really wasn't anywhere else to send a woman with amnesia ... unless, of course, Mr. Adams wished to take his wife home? She needed peaceful, stress-free surroundings and, at least temporarily, someone to watch out for her. Could a man who put in twelve-hour days provide that?

No, David had said, he could not. He had to devote himself to his career. He had a high-powered Wall Street firm to run and clients to deal with. Besides, though he didn't say so to the doctors, he knew that he and Joanna could never endure too much time alone together.

There was no question but that Bright Meadows was the right place for Joanna. The doctors, and David, had agreed.

Had Joanna agreed, too? He was damned if he could remember.

''David?''

He looked at Joanna. She was smiling tremulously.

"Couldn't I just... isn't there someplace I could go that isn't a hospital? A place I could stay, I mean, where maybe the things around me would jog my memory?"

"You need peace and quiet, Joanna. Our town house isn't—"

She nodded and turned away, but not before he'd seen the glitter of tears in her eyes. She was crying. Quietly, with great dignity, but she was crying all the same.

"Joanna," he said gently, "don't."

"I'm sorry." She rose quickly and hurried to the window where she stood with her back to him. "Go on home, please, David. It's late, and you've had a long day. The last thing you need on your hands is a woman who's feeling sorry for herself."

Had she always been so slight? His mental image of his wife was of a slender, tall woman with a straight back and straight shoulders, but the woman he saw at the window seemed small and painfully defenseless.

"Jo," he said, and he started slowly toward her, "listen, everything's going to be OK. I promise."

She nodded. "Sure," she said in a choked whisper.

He was standing just behind her now, close enough so that he could see the reddish glints in her black hair, so that he could almost convince himself he smelled the delicate scent of gardenia that had always risen from her skin until she'd changed to some more sophisticated scent.

"Joanna, if you don't like Bright Meadows, we'll find another place and—"

She spun toward him, her eyes bright with tears and with something else. Anger?

"Dammit, don't talk to me as if I were a child!"

"I'm not. I'm just trying to reassure you. I'll see to it you have the best of care. You know that."

"I don't know anything," she said, her voice trembling not with self-pity but yes, definitely, with anger. "You just don't understand, do you? You think, if you have them fix my hair and my face, and ship me my clothes and make me look like Joanna Adams, I'll turn into Joanna Adams."

"No," David said quickly. "I mean, yes, in a way. I'm trying to help you be who you are."

Joanna lifted her clenched fist and slammed it against his chest. David stumbled back, not from the blow which he'd hardly felt, but from shock. He couldn't remember Joanna raising her voice, let alone her hand. Well, yes, there'd been that time after they were first married,

when he'd been caught late at a dinner meeting
and he hadn't telephoned and she'd been frantic
with worry by the time he came in at two in the
morning . . .

"Damn you, David! I don't know who I am!
I don't know this Joanna person." She raised
her hand again, this time to punctuate each of
her next words with a finger poked into his
chest. "And I certainly don't know you!"

"What do you want to know? Ask and I'll
tell you."

She took a deep, shuddering breath. "For
starters, I'd like to know why I'm expected to
believe I'm really your wife!"

David started to laugh, then stopped. She
wasn't joking. One look into her eyes was proof
of that. They had gone from violet to a color
that was almost black. Her hands were on her
hips, her posture hostile. She looked furious,
defiant . . . and incredibly beautiful.

"What are you talking about?"

"What do you mean, what am I talking
about? I said it clearly enough, didn't I? You
say I'm your wife, but I don't remember you.
So why should I let you run my life?"

"Joanna, for heaven's sake——"

"Can you *prove* that we're married?"

David threw up his hands. "I don't believe
this!"

"Can you prove it, David?"

"Of course I can prove it! What would you like to see? Our marriage license? The cards we both signed and mailed out last Christmas? Dammit, of course we're married. Why would I lie about such a thing?"

He wouldn't. She knew that, deep down inside, but that had nothing to do with this. She was angry. She was furious. Let *him* try waking up in a hospital bed without knowing who he was, let *him* try having a stranger walk in and announce that as of that moment, all the important decisions of your life were being taken out of your hands.

But most of all, let him deal with the uncomfortable feeling that the person you were married to had been a stranger for a long, long time, not just since you'd awakened with a lump on your head and a terrible blankness behind your eyes.

"Answer me, Joanna. Why in hell would I lie?"

"I don't know. I'm not even saying that you are. I'm just trying to point out that the only knowledge I have of my own identity is your word."

David caught hold of her shoulders. "My word is damned well all you need!"

It was, she knew it was. It wasn't just the things the nurses had said about how lucky she was to be the wife of such a wonderful man as David Adams. She'd managed to read a bit about him in a couple of old magazines she'd found in the lounge.

On the face of it, David Adams was Everywoman's Dream.

But she wasn't Everywoman. She was lost on a dark road without a light to guide her and the only thing she felt whenever she thought of herself as Mrs. David Adams was a dizzying sense of disaster mingled in with something else, something just as dizzying but also incredibly exciting.

It terrified her, almost as much as the lack of a past, yet instinct warned that she mustn't let him know that, that the best defense against whatever it was David made her feel when he got too close was a strong offense, and so instead of backing down under his furious glare, Joanna glared right back.

"No," she said, "your word isn't enough! I don't know anything about you. Not anything, what you eat for breakfast or——or what movies you like to see or who chooses those——those stodgy suits you wear or——"

"Stodgy?" he growled. "Stodgy?"

"You heard me."

David stared down at the stranger he held clasped by the shoulders. Stodgy? Hell, for Joanna to use that word to describe him was ludicrous. She was right, she didn't know the first thing about him; they were strangers.

What she couldn't know was that it had been that way for a long time.

But not always. No, not always, he thought while his anger grew, and before he could think too much about what he was about to do, he hauled Joanna into his arms and kissed her.

She gave a gasp of shock and struggled against the kiss. But he was remorseless, driven at first by pure male outrage and then by the taste of her, a taste he had not known in months. The feel of her in his arms, the softness of her breasts against his chest, the long length of her legs against his, made him hard with remembering.

He fisted one hand in her hair, holding her captive to his kiss, while the other swept down and cupped her bottom, lifting her into his embrace, bringing her so close to him that he felt the sudden quickened beat of her heart, heard the soft little moan that broke in her throat as his lips parted hers, and then her arms were around his neck and she was kissing him back as hungrily as he was kissing her...

"Oh, my, I'm terribly sorry. I'll come back a bit later, shall I?"

They sprang apart at the sound of the shocked female voice. Both of them looked at the door where the night nurse stood staring at them, her eyes wide.

"I thought Mrs. Adams might want some help getting ready for bed but I suppose...I mean, I can see..." The nurse blushed. "Has Mrs. Adams regained her memory?"

"Mrs. Adams is capable of being spoken to, not about," Joanna said sharply. Her cheeks colored but her gaze was steady. "And no, she has not regained her memory."

"No," David said grimly, "she has not." He stalked past the nurse and pushed open the door. "But she's going to," he said. "She can count on it."

CHAPTER THREE

ALL right. Ok. So he'd made an ass of himself last night.

David stood in his darkened kitchen at six o'clock in the morning and told himself it didn't take a genius to figure that much out.

Kissing Joanna, losing his temper...the whole thing had been stupid. It had been worse than stupid. Joanna wasn't supposed to get upset and he sure as hell had upset her.

So why hadn't he just gone home, phoned her room and apologized? Why couldn't he just mentally kick himself in the tail, then put what had happened out of his head?

They were all good questions. It was just too bad that he didn't have any good answers, and he'd already wasted half the night trying to come up with one.

He'd always prided himself on his ability to face a mistake squarely, learn from it, then put it behind him and move on.

That was the way he'd survived childhood in a series of foster homes, a double hitch in the Marines and then a four year scholarship at an

Ivy League university where he'd felt as out of place as a wolf at a sheep convention.

So, why was he standing here, drinking a cup of the worst coffee he'd ever tasted in his life, replaying that kiss as if it were a videotape caught in a loop?

He made a face, dumped the contents of the pot and the cup into the sink, then washed them both and put them into the drainer. Mrs. Timmons, his cook cum housekeeper, would be putting in an appearance in half an hour.

Why should she have to clean up a mess that he'd made?

David opened the refrigerator, took out a pitcher of orange juice and poured himself a glass. You made a mess, you cleaned it up...which brought him straight back to why he was standing around here in the first place.

The unvarnished truth was that if he'd divorced Joanna sooner, he wouldn't be in this situation. By the time she'd stepped off that curb, she'd have been out of his life.

He'd known almost two years ago that he wanted out of the marriage, that the woman he'd taken as his wife had been nothing but a figment of his imagination. Joanna hadn't been a sweet innocent whose heart he'd stolen. She'd been a cold-blooded schemer who'd set out to snare a rich husband, and she'd succeeded.

Because it had taken him so damned long to admit the truth, he was stuck in this sham of a marriage for God only knew how much longer.

David slammed the refrigerator door shut with far more force than the job needed, walked to the glass doors that opened onto the tiny patch of green that passed for a private garden in midtown Manhattan, and stared at the early morning sky.

Corbett and his team of white-coated witch doctors wouldn't say how long it would take her to recover. They wouldn't even guarantee there'd be a recovery. The only thing they'd say was that she needed time.

"These things can't be rushed," Corbett had said solemnly. "Your wife needs a lot of rest, Mr. Adams. No shocks. No unpleasant surprises. That's vital. You do understand that, don't you?"

David understood it, all right. There was no possibility of walking into Joanna's room and saying, "Good evening, Joanna, and by the way, did I mention that we were in the middle of a divorce when you got hit by that taxi?"

Not that he'd have done it anyway. He didn't feel anything for Joanna, one way or another. Emotionally, mentally, he'd put her out of his life. Still, he couldn't in good conscience turn his back on her when she didn't even remember her own name.

When she didn't even remember him, or that she was his wife.

It was crazy, but as the days passed, that had been the toughest thing to take. It was one thing to want a woman out of your life but quite another to have her look at you blankly, or speak to you as if you were a stranger, her tone proper and always polite.

Until last night, when she'd suddenly turned on him in anger. And then he'd felt an answering anger rise deep inside himself, one so intense it had blurred his brain. What in hell had possessed him to haul her into his arms and kiss her like that? He'd thought she was going to slug him. What he'd never expected was that she'd turn soft and warm in his arms and kiss him back.

For a minute he'd almost forgotten that he didn't love her anymore, that she had never loved him, that everything he'd thought lay between them had been built on the quicksand of lies and deceit.

He turned away from the garden.

Maybe he should have listened to his attorney instead of the doctors. Jack insisted it was stupid to let sentiment get in the way of reality.

"So she shouldn't have any shocks," he'd said, "so big deal, she shouldn't have played you for a sucker, either. You want to play the saint, David? OK, that's fine. Pay her medical bills. Put her into that fancy sanitarium and shell out the dough for however long it takes for her to remember who she is. Put a fancy settlement into her bank account—but before you do any of that, first do yourself a favor and divorce the broad."

David had puffed out his breath.

"I hear what you're saying, Jack. But her doctors say—"

"Forget her doctors. Listen, if you want I can come up with our own doctors who'll say she's *non compos mentis* or that she's faking it and you're more than entitled to divorce her, if that's what's worrying you."

"Nothing's worrying me," David had replied brusquely. "I just want to be able to look at myself in the mirror. I survived four years being married to Joanna. I'll survive another couple of months."

Brave words, and true ones. David put his empty glass into the dishwasher, switched off the kitchen light and headed through the silent house toward the staircase and his bedroom.

And survive he would. He understood Jack's concern but he wasn't letting Joanna back into his life, he was just doing what he could to ease her into a life of her own.

She didn't affect him anymore, not down deep where it mattered. The truth was that she never had. He'd tricked himself into thinking he'd loved her when actually the only part of his anatomy Joanna had ever reached was the part that had been getting men into trouble from the beginning of time . . . the part that had responded to her last night.

Well, there was no more danger of that. He wouldn't be seeing much of his wife after today. Once he'd driven her to Bright Meadows, that would be it. Except for paying the bills and a once-a-week visit, she'd be the problem of the Bright Meadows staff, not his.

Sooner or later, her memory would come back. And when it did, this pretense of a marriage would be over.

Joanna sat in the back of the chauffeured Bentley and wondered what Dr. Corbett would say if she told him she almost preferred being in the hospital to being in this car with her husband.

For that matter, what would her husband say?

She shot David a guarded look.

Not much, judging by his stony profile, folded arms and cold silence. From the looks of things, he wasn't any more pleased they were trapped inside this overstuffed living room on wheels than she was.

What a terrible marriage theirs must have been. Her throat constricted. Dr. Corbett had made a point of telling her that you didn't lose your intellect when you lost your memory. Well, you didn't lose your instincts, either, and every instinct she possessed told her that the marriage of Joanna and David Adams had not been a storybook love affair.

Was he like this with everyone, or only with her? He never seemed to smile, to laugh, to show affection.

Maybe that was why what had happened last night had been such a shock. That outburst of raw desire was the last thing she'd expected. Had it been a rarity or was that the way it had been between them before the accident, polite tolerance interrupted by moments of rage that ended with her clinging to David's shoulders, almost pleading for him to take her, while the world spun out from beneath her feet?

She'd hardly slept last night. Even after she'd rung for the nurse and asked for a sleeping pill, she'd lain staring into the darkness, trying to imagine what would have happened if that passionate, incredible kiss hadn't been interrupted.

She liked to think she'd have regained her senses, pulled out of David's arms and slapped him silly.

But a sly whisper inside her head said that maybe she wouldn't have, that maybe, instead, they'd have ended up on the bed and to hell with the fact that the man kissing her was an absolute stranger.

Eventually, she'd tumbled into exhausted sleep only to dream about David stripping away her robe and nightgown, kissing her breasts and her belly and then taking her right there, on that antiseptically white hospital bed with her legs wrapped around his waist and her head thrown back and her sobs of pleasure filling the room.

A flush rose into Joanna's cheeks.

Which only proved how little dreams had to do with reality. David had apologized for his behaviour and she'd accepted the apology, but if he so much as touched her again, she'd— she'd—

"What's the matter?"

She turned and looked at him. He was frowning, though that wasn't surprising. His face had been set in a scowl all morning.

"Nothing," she said brightly.

"I thought I heard you whimper."

"Whimper? Me?" She laughed, or hoped she did. "No, I didn't...well, maybe I did. I have a, ah, a bit of a headache."

"Well, why didn't you say so?" He leaned forward and opened the paneled bar that was built into the Bentley. "Corbett gave you some pills, didn't he?"

"Yes, but I don't need them."

"Dammit, must you argue with me about everything?"

"I don't argue about everything...do I?"

David looked at her. She didn't. Actually, she never had. It was just this mood he was in this morning.

He sighed and shook his head. "Sorry. I guess I'm just feeling irritable today. Look, it can't hurt to take a couple of whatever he gave you, can it?"

"No, I suppose not."

He smiled, a first for the day that she could recall, poured her a tumbler of iced Perrier and handed it to her.

"Here. Swallow them down with this."

Joanna shook two tablets out of the vial and did as he'd asked.

"There," she said politely. "Are you happy now?"

It was the wrong thing to say. His brow furrowed instantly and his mouth took on that narrowed look she was coming to recognize and dislike.

"Since when did worrying about what makes me happy ever convince you to do anything?"

The words were out before he could call them back. Damn, he thought, what was the matter with him? A couple of hours ago, he'd been congratulating himself on his decision to play the role of supportive husband. Now, with at least half an hour's drive time to go, he was close to blowing the whole thing.

And whose fault was that? He'd walked into Joanna's room this morning and she'd looked at him as if she expected him to turn into a monster.

"I'm sorry about last night," he'd said gruffly, and she'd made a gesture that made it clear that what had happened had no importance at all...but she'd jumped like a scared cat when he'd tried to help her into the back of the car and just a couple of minutes ago, after sitting like a marble statue for the past hour, he'd caught her shooting him the kind of nervous look he'd always figured people reserved for vicious dogs.

Oh, hell, he thought, and turned toward her.

"Listen," he said, "about what happened last night..."

"I don't want to talk about it."

"No, neither do I. I just want to assure you it won't happen again."

"No," she said. Her eyes met his. "It won't."

"We've both been under a lot of pressure. The accident, your loss of memory..."

"What about before the accident?"

"What do you mean?"

Joanna hesitated. "I get the feeling that we...that we didn't have a very happy marriage."

It was his turn to hesitate now, but he couldn't bring himself to lie.

"It was a marriage," he said finally. "I don't know how to quantify it."

Joanna nodded. What he meant was, no, they hadn't been happy. It wasn't a surprise. Her husband didn't like her very much and she...well, she didn't know him enough to like him or dislike him, but it was hard to imagine she could ever have been in love with a man like this.

"Did Dr. Corbett tell you not to discuss our relationship with me? Whether it was good or not, I mean?"

"No," he said, this time with all honesty. "I didn't discuss our marriage with Corbett. Why would I?"

"I don't know. I just thought…" She sighed and tugged at the hem of her skirt. Not that there was any reason to. The hem fell well below her knees. "I just thought he might have asked you questions about—about us."

"I wouldn't have answered them," David said bluntly. "Corbett's a neurosurgeon, not a shrink."

"I know. I guess I've just got psychiatry on the brain this morning, considering where we're going."

"Bright Meadows? But I told you, it's a rehab center."

"Oh, I know that. I just can't get this weird picture out of my head. I don't know where it comes from but I keep seeing a flight of steps leading up to an old mansion with a nurse standing on top of the steps. She's wearing a white uniform and a cape, and she has—I know it's silly, but she has a mustache and buck teeth and a hump on her back."

David burst out laughing. "Cloris Leachman!"

"Who?"

"An actress. What you're remembering is a scene from an old movie with Mel Brooks called... I think it was *High Anxiety*. He played a shrink and she played—give me a minute—she played evil Nurse Diesel.''

Joanna laughed. ''Evil Nurse Diesel?''

''Uh-huh. We found the movie playing on cable late one night, not long after we met. We both said we didn't like Mel Brooks' stuff, slapstick comedy, but we watched for a few minutes and we got hooked. After a while, we were both laughing so hard we couldn't stop.''

''Really?''

''Oh, yeah. We watched right to the end, and then I phoned around until I found an all-night place to order pizza and you popped a bottle of wine into the freezer to chill and then...''
And then I told you that I loved you and asked you to be my wife.

''And then?''

David shrugged. ''And then, we decided we'd give Mel Brooks' movies another chance.'' He cleared his throat. ''It's got to be a good sign, that you remembered a movie.''

She nodded. ''A snippet of a movie, at least.''

''Anyway, there's nothing to worry about.'' He reached out and patted her hand. ''Believe me, you're not going to find anything like that waiting for you at Bright Meadows.''

*   *   *

She didn't.

There was no nurse with a mustache and too many teeth waiting at the top of the steps. There were no dreary corridors or spaced-out patients wandering the grounds.

Instead, there was an air of almost manic cheer about the place. The receptionist smiled, the admitting nurse bubbled, the attendant who led them to a private, sun-drenched room beamed with goodwill.

"I just know you're going to enjoy your stay with us, Mrs. Adams," the girl said.

She sounds as if she's welcoming me to a hotel, Joanna thought. But this isn't a hotel, it's a hospital, even if nobody calls it that, and I'm not sick. I just can't remember anything...

No. She couldn't think about that or the terror of it would rise up and she'd scream.

And she couldn't do that. She'd kept the fear under control until now, she hadn't let anyone see the panic that woke her in the night, heart pounding and pillow soaked with sweat.

Joanna turned toward the window and forced herself to take a deep, deep breath.

"Joanna?" David looked at the straight, proud back. A few strands of dark hair had come loose; they hung down against his wife's neck. He knew Joanna would fix it if she knew, that she'd never tolerate such imperfection.

Despite the straightness of her spine, the severity of her suit, the tumble of curls lent her a vulnerability. He thought of how she'd once been . . . of how she'd once seemed.

All right, he knew that what she'd seemed had been a lie, that she wasn't the sweet, loving wife he'd wanted, but even so, she was in a tough spot now. It couldn't be easy, losing your memory.

He crossed the room silently, put his hands on her shoulders. He felt her jump beneath his touch and when he turned her gently toward him and she looked up at him, he even thought he saw her mouth tremble.

"Joanna," he said, his voice softening, "look, if you don't like this place, I'm sure there are others that—"

"This is fine," she said briskly.

He blinked, looked at her again, and knew he'd let his imagination work overtime. Her lips were curved in a cool smile and her eyes were clear.

David's hands fell to his sides. Whatever he'd thought he'd seen in her a moment ago had been just another example of how easily he could still be taken in, if not by his wife then by his own imagination.

"I'm sure I'm going to like it here," she said. "Now, if you don't mind terribly, I really would like to take a nap."

"Of course. I'd forgotten what an exhausting day this must have been for you." He started for the door. Halfway there, he paused and swung toward her. "I, uh, I'm not quite certain when I'll be able to get to see you again."

"Don't worry about it, David. This is a long way to come after a day's work and besides, I'm sure I'll be so busy I won't have time for visitors."

"That's exactly what I was thinking."

Joanna smiled. "Safe trip home," she said.

She held the smile until the door snicked shut after him. Then it dropped from her lips and she buried her face in her hands and wept.

Until today, she'd thought nothing could be as awful as waking up and remembering nothing about your life.

Now, she knew that it was even more horrible to realize that you were part of a loveless marriage.

"Mr. Adams?"

David looked up. He'd had his nose buried in a pile of reports he'd dredged out of the briefcase he always kept near at hand until the voice of his chauffeur intruded over the intercom.

"What is it, Hollister?"

"Sorry to bother you, sir, but I just caught a report on the radio about an overturned tractor trailer near the tunnel approach to the city."

David sighed and ran his hand through his hair. It wasn't any bother at all. The truth was, he didn't have the foggiest idea what was in the papers spread out on the seat beside him. He'd tried his damnedest to concentrate but that split instant when he'd seen those wispy curls lying against Joanna's pale skin kept intruding.

"Did they say anything about the traffic?"

"It's tied up for miles. Would you want me to take the long way? We could detour to the Palisades Parkway and take the bridge."

"Yes, that's a good idea, Hollister. Take the next turnoff and..." David frowned, then leaned forward. "No, the hell with that. Just pull over."

"Sir?"

"I said, pull over. Up ahead, where the shoulder of the road widens."

"Is there a problem, Mr. Adams?"

A taut smile twisted across David's mouth.

"No," he said, as the big car glided to a stop. "I just want to change seats with you."

"Sir?" Hollister said again. There was a world of meaning in the single word.

David laughed and jerked open the car door.

"I feel like driving, Hollister. You can stay up front, if you like. Just slide across the seat and put your belt on because I'm in the mood to see if this car can do anything besides look good."

For the first time in memory, Hollister smiled.

"She can do a lot besides look good, sir. She's not your Jaguar by a long shot but if you put your foot right to the floor, I think she'll surprise you."

David grinned. He waited until his chauffeur had fastened his seat belt and then he did as the man had suggested, put the car in gear and the pedal to the metal, and forgot everything but the road.

He called Joanna every evening, promptly at seven. Their conversations were always the same.

How was she? he asked.

Fine, she answered.

And how was she getting along at Bright Meadows?

She said "fine" to that one, too.

Friday evening, when he phoned, he told her he had some work to do Saturday but he'd see her on Sunday.

Only if he could fit it into his schedule, she said.

His teeth ground together at the polite distance in the words. Evidently, she didn't need to remember the past to know how she wanted to behave in the present.

"I'll be there," he said grimly, and hung up the phone.

Sunday morning, he went for his usual run. He showered, put on a pair of time-worn jeans, a pair of sneakers and—in deference to the warming Spring weather—a lightweight blue sweatshirt. Then he got behind the wheel of the Jaguar and drove upstate.

Halfway there, he realized that he was out of uniform. Joanna didn't care for the casual look. She didn't care for this car, either. She had, a long time ago. At least, she'd pretended she had.

The hell with it. It was too late to worry about and besides, it was one thing to pretend they hadn't been about to get divorced and quite another to redo his life. He'd done that for damned near four years and that had been three years and a handful of months too many.

The grounds of the rehab center were crowded with patients and visitors, but he spotted Joanna as soon as he drove through the gates. She was sitting on a stone bench beside a dogwood tree that was just coming into flower, the creamy blossoms a counterpoint to her dark hair. She was reading a book and oblivious to anything around her, which was typical of her. It was how she'd dealt with him during so much of the time they'd been married, as if she were living on a separate planet.

It made him furious, which was stupid, because he'd gotten over giving a damn about how she acted a long time ago. Still, after he'd parked the car and walked back to where she was sitting, he had to force himself to smile.

"Hi."

She looked up, her dark eyes wide with surprise.

"David!"

"Why so shocked?" He sat down beside her. "I told you I'd be here today."

"Well, I know what you said, but..."

But he hadn't cared enough to come up all week. Not that it mattered to her if she saw him or not...

"But?"

Joanna shut the book and put it on the bench beside her. "Nothing," she said. "I guess you just caught me by surprise."

He waited for her to say something more. When she didn't, he cleared his throat.

"So, how are things going? Have you settled in?"

"Oh, yes. Everyone's very nice."

"Good. And are they helping you?"

"Have I remembered, do you mean?" Joanna got to her feet and he rose, too. They began walking slowly along a path that wound behind the main building. "No, not a thing. Everyone tells me to be patient."

"But it's hard."

"Yes." She looked up at him. "For you, too."

He knew he was supposed to deny it, but he couldn't.

"Yes," he said quietly, "for me, too."

Joanna nodded. "I just can't help wondering..."

"What?"

She shook her head. She'd promised herself not to say anything; the words had just slipped out.

"Nothing."

"Come on, Joanna, you were going to ask me something. What is it?"

"Well, I know I'm not a doctor or anything, but—" She hesitated. "Wouldn't my memory come back faster if I were in familiar surroundings?" He looked at her, saying nothing, and she spoke more quickly. "You don't know what it's like, David, not to be able to picture your own house. The furniture, or the colors of the walls..."

"You want to come home," he said.

Joanna looked up at him. There was no mistaking the sudden flatness in his voice.

"I just want to get my memory back," she said softly. "It's what you want, too, isn't it?"

A muscle flickered in his jaw. "It wouldn't work," he said carefully. "You need peace and quiet, someone to look after you. I'm hardly ever home before ten at night and even when I am, the phone's forever ringing, and the fax is going..."

A cold hand seemed to clamp around her heart.

"I understand," she said.

"Who would take care of you? I could hire a nurse, yes, but—"

"I don't need anyone to take care of me." Her voice took on an edge. "I'm an amnesiac, not an invalid."

"Well, I know, but what about therapy?"

"What about it?" she said with sudden heat. "I don't see how learning to paint by numbers or weave baskets is going to help my memory."

David stopped and clasped her shoulders. He turned her toward him.

"You don't really weave baskets, do you?"

She sighed. "No, not really."

"Good." A grin twitched across his mouth. "For a minute there, I thought Nurse Diesel might be breathing down our necks."

Joanna's mouth curved. "Don't even mention that movie when you're here," she said in an exaggerated whisper. "They've got no sense of humor when it comes to things like that."

He laughed. "You said something?"

"Sure. The first day, an aide came to call for me. She said she was taking me to physical therapy and we got into this old, creaky elevator and headed for the basement. 'So,' I said, when the doors finally wheezed open, 'is this where you guys keep the chains and cattle prods?'" Joanna's eyes lit with laughter. "I thought she was going to go bonkers. I got a five minute lecture on the strides that have been made in mental health, blah, blah, blah..."

"Thanks for the warning."

"My pleasure."

√ They smiled at each other and then David cleared his throat, took Joanna's elbow politely, and they began walking again.

"What kind of therapy are you getting?"

"Oh, this and that. You can paint or sculpt in clay, and there's an hour of exercise in the pool and then a workout in the gym under the eye of a physical therapist—"

"Yeah, but there's nothing wrong with you physically."

"It's just the way things are done here. There's a routine and you follow it. Up at six, breakfast at six-thirty. An hour of painting or working with clay and then an hour in the pool before your morning appointment with your shrink."

"You see a psychiatrist, too?"

"Yes."

"Why?"

She made a face. "So far, to talk about how I'm going to adapt to my loss of memory. It didn't go over so well when I said I didn't want to adapt, that I wanted to get my memory back." She laughed. "Now I think the doctor's trying to figure why I'm always so hostile."

"That's ridiculous."

"Well, I said so, too, but she said—"

"I'll speak to the Director, Joanna. Someone must have forgotten to read your chart. You're not here for psychiatric counseling or for physical therapy, you're here to regain your memory."

"Don't waste your breath." Joanna stepped off the path. David watched her as she kicked off her shoes and sank down on the grass. "Mmm," she said, leaning back on her hands, tilting her face up and closing her eyes, "doesn't the sun feel wonderful?"

"Wonderful," he said, while he tried to figure out if he'd ever before seen her do anything so out of character. Did she know she was probably going to get grass stains on her yellow silk skirt? He kicked off his sneakers and sat down beside her. "What do you mean, don't waste my breath?"

"I already spoke to the Director. And he said since nobody knew much about amnesia and since I was here, the best thing I could do would be to put myself in their hands. I suppose it makes sense."

David nodded. "I suppose."

Joanna opened her eyes and smiled at him. "But I swear, if Nurse Diesel comes tripping into the room, I'll brain her with a raffia basket."

It stayed with him as he made the drive home. Nurse Diesel.

It was a joke. He knew that. Bright Meadows was state of the art. It was about as far from a snake pit as you could get. The staff was terrific, the food was good—Joanna had joked that she'd already gained a pound though he couldn't see where. And what was wrong with spending some quiet time talking to a psychiatrist? And for the pool and all the rest...for a woman who used to spend half her day sweating on the machines at a trendy east side gym, physical therapy was a cinch.

His hands tightened on the wheel of the Jag.

But what did any of that have to do with helping her recover from amnesia? And that was the bottom line because until Joanna got her memory back, his life was stuck on hold.

Wouldn't my memory come back faster in familiar surroundings?

Maybe. On the other hand, maybe not. The last thing he wanted was to move his wife back into his life again, even if it was only on a temporary basis.

Besides, what he'd said about the house in Manhattan was true. It was nothing like Bright Meadows, with its big lawn, its sun-dappled pond, its bright rooms...

The house in Connecticut had all that, the lawns, the pond, the big, bright rooms. It had peace and quiet, birds singing in the gardens, it had everything including things that might stimulate Joanna's memory. They'd spent the first months of their marriage there and the days had been filled with joy and laughter...

Forget that. It was a stupid thought. He couldn't commute to the office from there, it was too far, even if he'd wanted to give it a try, which he didn't. He hated that damned house.

Joanna was better off where she was.

David stepped down harder on the gas.

She was much better off, and if that last glimpse he'd had of her as he left stayed with him for a couple of hours, so what? It had just been a trick of the light that seemed to have put the glint of tears in her eyes as she'd waved goodbye.

Even if it wasn't the light, what did he care?

He drove faster.

What in bloody hell did he care?

He drove faster still, until the old Jag was damned near flying, and then he muttered a couple of words he hadn't used since his days in the Corps, swerved the car onto the grass, swung it into a hard U-turn and headed back to Bright Meadows to tell his wife to pack her things, dump them into the back of the car and climb into the seat next to him so he could take her home.

Home to New York, because there wasn't a way in the world he would ever again take the almost ex-Mrs. Adams to Connecticut.

Not in this lifetime.

CHAPTER FOUR

IT STARTED raining, not long after David drove away from Bright Meadows for the second time.

He turned on the windshield wipers and Joanna listened to them whisper into the silence. The sound of the rain on the canvas roof and the tires hissing on the wet roadway was almost enough to lull her into a false sense of security.

Home. David was taking her home.

It was the last thing she'd ever expected, considering his reaction each time she'd suggested it, but now it was happening.

She was going home.

It was hard to believe that she'd stood on the lawn at Bright Meadows only a couple of hours ago, staring after David's car as it sped out the gate, telling herself that it was stupid to cry and stupider still to think that it wasn't her recovery he'd been thinking about when he'd insisted she was better off at the rehab center as much as it was the desire to keep her out of his life.

Why would her husband want to do that?

Before she'd even thought of an answer, she'd seen his car coming back up the drive. He'd pulled over, told her in brusque tones that he'd reconsidered what she'd said and that he'd decided she was right, she might get her memory back a lot faster if she were in familiar surroundings.

Joanna had felt almost giddy with excitement, even though he'd made it sound as if the change in plans was little more than an updated medical prescription.

"You go and pack," he'd said briskly, "while I do whatever needs doing to check you out of this place."

Before she knew it, she was sitting beside him on the worn leather seat of the aged sports car as it flew along the highway toward home.

Whatever that might be like.

A shudder went through her. David looked at her. Actually, he wasn't so much looking at her as he was glowering. Her stomach clenched. Was he already regretting his decision?

"Are you cold, Joanna?"

"No," she said quickly, "not a bit." She tried hard to sound bright and perky. "I'm just excited."

"Well, don't get too excited. Corbett wouldn't approve if your blood pressure shot up."

He smiled, to make it clear he was only joking. Joanna smiled back but then she locked her hands together in her lap.

"You don't have to worry," she said quietly. "I'm not going to be a burden to you."

"I never suggested you would be."

"Well, no, but I want to be sure we have this straight. I'm not sick, David."

"I know that."

"And I'm not an invalid. I'm perfectly capable of taking care of myself."

He sighed and shifted his long legs beneath the dash.

"Did I ever say you weren't?"

"I just want to be sure you understand that you're not going to have to play nursemaid."

"I'm not concerned about it," he said patiently. "Besides, there'll be plenty of people to look after you."

"I don't need looking after." She heard the faint edge in her words and she took a deep breath and told herself to calm down. "You won't have to hire a nurse or a companion or whatever."

"Well, we'll try it and see how it goes."

"It'll go just fine. I'm looking forward to doing things for myself."

"As long as you don't push too hard," he said. "I want you to promise to take it easy for a week or two."

"I will." Joanna looked down at her folded hands. "Thank you," she said softly.

"For what?"

"For changing your mind and agreeing to take me ... to take me home."

He shrugged his shoulders. "There's no need to thank me. The more I thought about it, the more sensible it seemed. Anyway, I knew it was what you wanted."

But not what he wanted. The unspoken words hung in the air between them. After a moment, Joanna sighed.

"Is it much farther?"

"Only another half hour or so." He glanced over at her. "You look exhausted, Jo. Why don't you put your head back, close your eyes and rest for a while?"

"I'm not tired, I'm just..." She stopped in midsentence. How stupid she was. David's suggestion had been meant as much for himself as for her. He might be taking her home but he didn't have to spend an hour and a half trying to make polite conversation. "You're right," she said, and shot him a quick smile, "I think I will."

Joanna lay her head back and shut her eyes. This was better anyway, not just for him but for her. Let him think she was tired. Otherwise, she might just blurt out the truth.

The closer they got to their destination, the more nervous she felt.

Nervous? She almost laughed.

Be honest, she told herself. You're terrified.

All her babbling about wanting to go home was just that. What good could come of returning to a house she wouldn't recognize with a man she didn't know?

Mars might be a better place than "home."

She looked at David from beneath the sweep of her lashes. Oh, that rigid jaw. Those tightly clamped lips. The hands, white-knuckled on the steering wheel.

She wasn't the only one with second thoughts. It was clear that her husband regretted his spur-of-the-moment decision, too.

Why? Had their marriage really been so awful? It must have been. There was no other way to explain the way he treated her, the careful politeness, the distant, unemotional behavior.

The only real emotion he'd shown her had been the night in her hospital room, when he'd kissed her.

The memory made her tingle. That kiss...that passionate, angry kiss. It had left her shaken, torn between despising his touch and the almost uncontrollable desire to go into his arms and give herself up to the heat.

Joanna's breath hitched. What was the matter with her? She'd been so caught up in wanting to go home that she hadn't given a moment's thought to what it might really mean. She and David were husband and wife. Did he expect...would he expect her to...? He hadn't so much as touched her since that night in the hospital, not even to kiss her cheek. Surely, he didn't think...

She shivered.

"Jo? What is it?"

She sat up straight, looked at David, then fixed her eyes on the ribbon of road unwinding ahead.

"I...I think you're right. I am feeling a little cold."

"I'll turn on the heat." He reached for a knob on the dashboard. "You always said that the heating system in this old heap was better suited to polar bears than people."

"Did I?" She smiled and stroked her hand lightly over the seat. "Actually, I can't imagine I ever said an unkind word about this beautiful old car."

He looked over at her. "Beautiful?"

"Mmm. What kind is it, anyway? A Thunderbird? A Corvette?"

"It's a '60 Jaguar XK 150," he said quietly.

"Ah," she said, her smile broadening, "an antique. Have you had it long?"

"Not long." His tone was stilted. "Just a few years."

"It must take lots of work, keeping an old car like this."

"Yeah." His hands tightened on the steering wheel. "Yeah, it does."

Her fingers moved across the soft leather again. "I'll bet you don't trust anybody to work on it."

David shot her a sharp look. "What makes you say that?"

"I don't know. It just seems logical. Why? Am I wrong?"

"No." He stared out at the road, forcing himself to concentrate on the slick asphalt. "No, you hit it right on the head. I do whatever needs doing on this car myself."

"Untouched by human hands, huh?" she said with a quick smile.

A muscle knotted in his jaw. "Somebody else who worked on the car with me used to say that, a long time ago."

"A super-mechanic, I'll bet."

"Yeah," he said briskly, "something like that." There was a silence and then he shifted his weight in his seat. "Will you look at that rain? It's coming down in buckets."

Joanna sighed. For a minute or two, it had looked as if they were going to have a real conversation.

"Yes," she said, "it certainly is."

David nodded. "Looks like the weatherman was wrong, as usual."

Such banal chitchat, Joanna thought, but better by far than uncomfortable silence.

"Still," she said brightly, "that's good, isn't it? One of the nurses was saying that it had been a dry Spring."

David sprang on the conversational lifeline as eagerly as she had.

"Dry isn't the word for it. The tulips in the park barely bloomed. And you know those roses you planted three summers ago? The pink ones? They haven't even..."

"I planted roses? I thought you said we lived in New York."

"We do." His hands tightened on the wheel. "But we have another place in..." His words trailed off in midsentence. "Hell," he muttered, "I'm sorry, Jo. I keep putting my foot in it today. I shouldn't have mentioned the damned roses or the house."

"Why not?"

"What do you mean, why not?" He glared at her. "Because you can't possibly remember either one, that's why not."

"That doesn't mean you shouldn't talk about them. If we're going to avoid mention of anything I might not remember, what will there be left to talk about? Nothing but the weather," Joanna said, answering her own question, "and not even we can talk about the possibility of rain all the time."

"I suppose you're right."

"Of course I'm right! I don't expect you to censor everything you say. Besides, maybe it'll help if we—if you talk about the past."

"I just don't want to put any pressure on you, Joanna. You know what the doctors advised, that it was best to let your memory come back on its own."

"If it comes back at all." She flashed him a dazzling smile, one that couldn't quite mask the sudden tremor in her voice. "They also said there were no guarantees."

"You're going to be fine," he said with more conviction than he felt.

Joanna turned on him in sudden fury. "Don't placate me, David. Dropping platitudes all over the place isn't going to..." The rush of angry words stuttered to a halt. "Sorry," she whispered. "I didn't mean..."

A jagged streak of lightning lit the road ahead. The rain, which had been a steady gray curtain, suddenly roared against the old car. Fat drops, driven by the wind, flew through Joanna's window. She grabbed for the crank but it wouldn't turn. David made a face. He reached across her, grasped it and forced it to move.

"Got to fix that thing," he muttered. "Sorry."

Joanna nodded. She was sorry, he was sorry. They were so polite, like cautious acquaintances. But they weren't acquaintances, they were husband and wife.

Dear heaven, there was something terribly wrong in this relationship.

Her throat tightened. Whatever had possessed her to want to go home with this man?

She turned her face to the rain-blurred window and wished she had stayed at Bright Meadows. It hadn't been home, but at least it had been safe.

David looked at his wife, then at the road.

Well, he thought, his hand tightening on the steering wheel, wasn't that interesting?

His soft-spoken, demure wife had shown her temper again.

A faint smile touched his lips.

Four years ago, that quick, fiery display wouldn't have surprised him. Not that the Joanna he'd married had been bad-tempered. She just hadn't been afraid to let her emotions show. In his world, where people seemed to think that sort of thing wasn't proper, his wife's willingness to show her feelings had been refreshing and endearing.

Not that it had lasted. Not that it could. David's hands clamped more tightly on the steering wheel. It had been a pose. His beloved wife had worn a mask to win his heart and once she'd decided it was safe to let it slip, she had.

As Morgana had pointed out, no one could keep up the innocent act forever.

He just wished to hell he knew who this was, seated beside him. This Joanna wasn't the woman he'd married nor the one he was divorcing. Everything about her was so familiar... And so unfamiliar. He'd known it ever since she'd regained consciousness after the accident, but he was uncomfortably aware of it today, starting with the minute she'd walked to the Jag to start the trip home.

He'd waited for her to make a face and ask where the Bentley was but she hadn't. Well, why would she? he'd reminded himself; she didn't remember how she'd felt about either car.

What he hadn't expected was the way she'd smiled when she'd settled in beside him, how she'd asked if the car really could go as fast as it looked. And then all those musings about how he probably never let anyone but him work on it.

That had struck too close to home. The Jag had been their project. They'd bought it together, tackled its restoration together, Joanna learning as fast as he could teach her until she was damned near as good at puttering under the hood as he was.

A bittersweet memory sprang into his head. They'd spent the week in Connecticut. He'd been called back to the city on business that he'd disposed of in record time and he'd gotten back to the house early, to find Joanna bent over the Jag's engine with her coverall-clad bottom in the air.

"Oh, David," she'd said, laughing as he'd grabbed her and whirled her around, "I was going to surprise you with this new—"

He'd never let her finish the sentence. He'd kissed her instead, and swung her up into his arms and carried her to their bedroom where he'd stripped away the bulky coverall to find her wearing nothing underneath but a tiny pair of white lace panties that he'd eased down her long, lovely legs . . .

He glanced over at those legs now. Her skirt had climbed up during the drive so that it was mid-thigh. She hadn't thought to adjust it. She hadn't thought to adjust her hair, either; the wind had tugged several strands loose from their moorings of pins and lacquer so that dark wisps curled sexily against her throat. David's gaze drifted lower. The quick burst of raindrops had dampened her silk blouse, the chill kiss of it tightening her nipples so they thrust against the fabric.

The Joanna he knew would have surely been aware of that. She would have fixed her hair, tugged down her skirt, crossed her arms over her breasts if she'd had to, done whatever it took to keep him from noticing that she was female, that she had sexual reactions if not sexual instincts.

David forced all his powers of concentration back to the rain-slicked road.

He had to stop thinking of Joanna as if she weren't Joanna. She had lost her memory but he had not lost his. He knew her. He knew the real woman.

And he had the increasingly uncomfortable feeling that he should have left her back at Bright Meadows, where she belonged.

The city glittered beneath the rain. It was beautiful, Joanna thought, and there was a vague familiarity to it the way there is to a place you've never visited but only seen in photographs.

David gave her a comforting smile.

"Just another couple of blocks," he said.

She nodded. Her hands lay in her lap, so tightly clasped that she could feel her nails digging into her flesh.

Would she recognize something? Would there be a moment when her memory would come rushing back?

In a movie, perhaps. But this was the real world, not one played out on the silver screen. The car made its way through clots of heavy traffic, turned onto Fifth Avenue, then down a side street. It was quiet here, the curb lined with plane trees in leaf, the town houses shouldering against each other in a way that spoke of money, power and elegant antiquity.

David pulled the car to the curb and shut off the engine. Joanna stared blankly at a building she had never seen before.

She'd asked him to tell her about their house when they'd first set out from Bright Meadows. Now, she could see that he'd described the place right down to the last detail. There was the gray stone facade and the windows with their black shutters; there were the black wrought-iron banisters and the stone steps leading to the front door.

Her stomach knotted in panic. "David," she said, swinging toward him...

But he'd already opened the car door and stepped out into the pouring rain.

"Stay put," he said, raising his voice over the deluge. "I'll go inside and get an umbrella and then I'll put the car away."

She flung her door open and got out. "No. No, wait..."

Her voice died away and she stood staring at the house, oblivious to the cold beat of the rain.

This is our home, she thought, mine and David's.

Her stomach twisted tighter. I want to go back to Bright Meadows, she thought desperately, oh, please...

"Dammit, Jo, what are you doing?"

David's voice broke through her frantic thoughts. He put his arm around her waist and began urging her forward.

"Come inside," he growled, "before you're soaked to the skin!"

She shook her head and pulled back against the tug of his arm. She didn't want to go into that house. She hated this place, *hated* it!

"For god's sake," David muttered, and he swung her into his arms. Caught off balance, she had no choice but to fling her arms around his neck.

Time seemed to stand still. The wet street, the rain...everything faded to insignificance. She was aware only of the feel of her husband's hard shoulders as she clutched them, the warmth of his powerful body against hers.

His eyes met hers; his arms tightened around her...

The door to the house swung open. "Sir," a voice said, "we had no idea..."

The moment of awareness shattered. "No," David said coolly, as he strode up the steps, "neither did I."

A tall, spare man with thinning hair stood in the doorway. Joanna recognized him as the chauffeur who'd driven her to Bright Meadows. Now, seeing him at the entrance to the town house, her mouth fell open in surprise.

"That's the limousine driver," she whispered to David. "What's he doing here?"

"His name is Hollister, Joanna. He lives here."

"Lives here?" she repeated stupidly.

"Madam," Hollister said, inclining his head as David moved past him, "welcome home."

"Hollister," David said, "is our chauffeur."

"You mean...that huge car we took to Bright Meadows belongs to us?"

"It does. Hollister drives it." He shot the man a wry smile. "And when he's not driving the Bentley, he's our butler."

"Our butler?" Joanna said, even more stupidly, craning her neck for a last glimpse of Hollister's bony, expressionless face. "David." Her voice fell to a whisper. "David, please, put me—"

"How do you do, madam."

A stern-faced woman in a dark dress stepped out of the gloomy darkness of the oak-paneled foyer.

"And this," David said, "is Mrs. Timmons. Our housekeeper."

A housekeeper, too? Joanna forced a smile to her lips.

"Hello, Mrs. Timmons." She bent her head toward David and this time there was an urgency to her whispered words. "David, really, what will they think? If you'd just put me down—"

"And that," David said, as he started up a flight of long stairs, "is Ellen."

Joanna caught a flash of ruffled white apron, red hair and wide blue eyes.

"Madam," a girlish voice said shyly.

"Ellen," Joanna repeated numbly. She stared over David's shoulder as Ellen smiled and bobbed a curtsy. *A curtsy*? Did people really still do such things?

"A butler? A housekeeper? And a maid?" she whispered incredulously as they reached the second floor hall. "Do all those people really work for us?"

David smiled tightly. "You might say that."

"What do you mean, I might say..."

"Except for Mrs. Timmons, it's probably more accurate to say that the staff is yours." He shouldered open a door, stepped through it, and hit the light switch on the wall beside him with his elbow. "The staff," he said, lowering her to her feet, "and this bedroom."

Whatever questions Joanna had intended to ask flew out of her head as she stared in disbelief at her surroundings.

Last night she'd watched a program on television at Bright Meadows, something about Versailles or Fontainebleau; one of the glittering French palaces. Now, she wished she'd paid closer attention.

Whoever had designed this room must have taken their cue from a palace. The walls were covered with cream silk that matched the drapes at the windows and the coverings and hangings on the canopied bed. The floor was laid with richly patterned rugs. The furniture was white brushed with gold, except for a mirrored vanity table on the opposite wall. Its glass surface was covered with an assortment of stoppered bottles and jars, enough to stock a cosmetics shop.

The room was feminine and deeply sensual...and yet it wasn't. It was like a stage set; Joanna had the feeling that if she looked behind the walls and the furniture, she'd find out they were made of painted canvas.

She turned toward David in bewilderment. "This can't be my room."

He looked at her, his expression unreadable. "It is, I assure you. Now, get out of that wet dress while I go and get Ellen."

"No. I mean, I'd rather you didn't. I need a couple of minutes to...to..." She gave a hesitant laugh. "David, are you sure this room is...?"

He smiled sardonically. "It certainly isn't mine. I'm afraid vanities and frills aren't my style."

"You mean, we don't share a..."

She caught herself before the next word had tumbled out but it was too late. David's expression changed; she saw it before he turned away.

"No," he said. "We don't."

"Oh."

Oh? she thought, staring after him as he went into the adjoining bathroom. She'd just found out that she slept in a room only Marie Antoinette would have envied, that she and her husband didn't share a bedroom, and "Oh" was all she could manage?

Not that that part disappointed her. Sharing a room with a stranger wasn't what she wanted at all, it was only that the news had caught her by surprise...

"I've started the water in the tub."

She looked up. She could hear the water thundering in the bathroom as David came toward her. He'd pushed up the sleeves of his blue shirt; his forearms were muscled and tanned and dusted with dark hair.

"Joanna? I said—"

"I heard you." She cleared her throat. "Thank you."

"There's nothing to thank me for. Running a bath doesn't take any great effort."

"I meant...thank you for what you've done. For bringing me...home."

"Don't be silly," he said briskly. "You've every right to be here. Now, come on. Get out of those wet things and into a hot tub."

"David..." She reached out and put her hand lightly on his arm. "I know this isn't easy for either one of us. But I...I'm sure that my memory will come back soon."

His muscles tightened under her fingers. "Are you saying things seem familiar?"

"No," she admitted, "not yet. But they will. They have to," she said, with just a hint of desperation. "My memory will come back and then you and I can go back to living our normal lives."

David's eyes, as deep and as green as a winter sea, met hers.

"Our normal lives," he said.

"Yes." She gave a forced little laugh. "Whatever that may mean."

A muscle knotted in his jaw. For just a moment, she was certain he was going to say something, something she didn't think she wanted to hear, but the seconds ticked away and then he nodded.

"Of course," he said politely. "Now go on, take your bath. I'll tell Mrs. Timmons to make you a light supper and serve you here, on a tray."

"Alone, you mean?"

"I think it's best, don't you? I have some work to do and this way you can just get out of the tub, put on a robe and relax."

Joanna felt the sharp prick of tears behind her eyes, and felt immeasurably silly.

She was home, which was what she'd wanted, and her husband had shown nothing but kindness and consideration. He'd carried her up the stairs, drawn her bath and now he was offering her the chance to end the day quietly...

"Joanna?"

She looked up and smiled brightly. "That's very thoughtful of you, David. Yes, please, if you don't mind I think I'd like to have my supper alone. I'm...I'm awfully tired. You understand."

"Of course." He walked to the door and looked back at her, his hand on the knob. "I'll see you in the morning, then."

"In the morning," she said, "sure."

She held her bright smile until the door had shut after him. Then she walked slowly into the bathroom, sat down on the edge of the oversize circular tub and shut off the taps. The air was steamy, almost thick, and all at once the tears she'd fought against moments ago flooded her eyes and streamed down her face.

David was everything a woman could hope for.

But he wanted nothing to do with her. He didn't love her. He didn't even like her. She was not welcome in this house or in his life.

And she had absolutely no idea why.

CHAPTER FIVE

JOANNA had told David she'd see him the next morning, but he was gone by the time she came down the stairs at eight o'clock.

That was fine. The last thing she wanted to do was try and make small talk on her first day in this unfamiliar place that seemed more like a museum than a home.

She had breakfast under the cool, watchful eye of Mrs. Timmons, who seemed to offer silent disapproval of a meal made up of half a grapefruit and a cup of black coffee. Then she wandered from room to room, waiting for something to strike a familiar chord.

Nothing did.

At noon, as she was sitting in solitary splendor at a dining room table designed to seat twelve, David telephoned.

Hollister brought her the telephone.

How was she feeling? David asked politely. Did she need anything?

Joanna looked around her. A crown and a scepter, she thought, suppressing a rise of hysterical laughter.

"Don't worry about me," she said, very calmly, "I'm fine."

The conversation took no more than a minute. When it ended, Hollister gave a little bow and took the phone away. Mrs. Timmons marched in after him, bearing a huge lobster salad.

"You used to like this," she said in a crisp, no-nonsense voice, "or aren't I supposed to mention that kind of stuff?"

The frank, unsmiling face and blunt words were as out of place in this elegant setting as they were welcome. Joanna smiled.

"Mention whatever you wish," she said, "otherwise I'm liable to end up biting into cardboard, just to find out if it was ever to my taste."

The housekeeper almost smiled. "Fine," she said, and clomped out.

After lunch, Joanna went outside and sat in the pocket garden behind the house. It was a sad, forlorn little place with one scrawny maple doing its best to survive.

Just like me, she thought, and she shuddered and went back inside and up to her room. She napped, woke up and read a magazine, then wandered through the rooms some more.

Mrs. Timmons was in the kitchen, slicing vegetables at the sink.

"Anything I can do to help?" Joanna asked from the doorway.

The housekeeper looked at her as if she were suffering not just from amnesia but from insanity.

"No, thank you, madam," she said, and went back to her work.

At six, David phoned again, with apologies. He'd tried everything to get out of a sudden meeting but it was impossible. Would Joanna mind having dinner without him?

She bit her lip to keep from saying that she'd already had dinner without him last night; what would be the difficulty in doing it again?

"Of course not," she said briskly. "We'll have dessert and coffee together, when you get home."

But he didn't get home until almost ten, and by then she was in bed.

She heard his footsteps first on the stairs, then coming down the hall. They stopped just outside her closed door and her heart stopped, too.

Joanna held her breath, imagining her husband's hand on the knob, imagining the door slowly opening . . .

The footsteps moved on. Further down the hall, a door opened, then softly shut and she fell back against the pillows in relief.

It *was* relief she felt, wasn't it?

Of course it was. What else could it be?

He was waiting for her in the dining room when she came down the next morning.

"Good morning," he said. "Sorry about last night."

"No problem," she said with a shrug of her shoulders. "I needed an early night anyway. I'm not operating on all burners yet."

David nodded. His hair was damp, as if he'd just finished showering, and suddenly she remembered what he'd said about running in the park early each morning.

"Were you out running?"

"Yes. I didn't wake you, did I? Going out so early, I mean."

"No, no, I slept like a log. I was only going to say..."

"What?"

What, indeed? They'd already talked about running together and he'd made it crystal clear that he hadn't wanted her company in the past. Why on earth would he want it now?

"I was only going to say that...that I'll have to get out for a walk, considering we're so near the park."

"Next week."

"What?"

"I said—"

"I heard what you said, David, I just didn't believe it. Or am I in the habit of asking your permission before I do something?"

His mouth twisted. "I only meant that you should wait until you're stronger."

"I am not ill," she said, her eyes flashing. "I've told you, I'm not—"

"An invalid. Yes, so you have. But going out alone, in a neighborhood that's strange to you, might be daunting."

She smiled through stiff lips. "New York still has street signs, doesn't it? Believe me, I'll find my way home without sprinkling bread crumbs behind me."

To her surprise, he laughed. "I'll bet you will." His smile faded. They stood looking at each other in an increasingly uncomfortable silence and then he cleared his throat. "Well, it's getting late. You'll forgive me if I hurry off, Jo, won't you?"

"Of course."

She smiled brightly as he picked up a leather briefcase from a table near the door. After a barely perceptible hesitation, he bent and dropped a light kiss on her forehead.

"Have a good day," he said. And he was gone.

A good day, Joanna thought. Tears stung her eyes.

"Mrs. Adams?"

Joanna blinked hard, took a steadying breath and turned around to see the housekeeper standing in the doorway to the dining room.

"Yes, Mrs. Timmons?"

"Your breakfast is ready. Half a grapefruit and black coffee, as usual."

"Oh. Thank you. I'll be... Mrs. Timmons?"

"Madam?"

"Was that my usual? My breakfast, I mean. Grapefruit and black coffee?"

The housekeeper's lips thinned in disapproval. "For as long as it mattered, it was."

"Do you think we might try something different?"

Mrs. Timmons's brows lifted a little. "We could, if you wish. What would you like?"

Joanna blushed. "I don't really know. I mean... I'm open to suggestion."

"Cinnamon toast," the housekeeper said, her eyes on Joanna's face, "orange juice, and hot chocolate."

"Hot chocolate!" Joanna laughed. "No, I don't think so."

"Coffee, then, but with sugar and cream. How does that sound, madam?"

"It sounds lovely." Joanna took a breath. "Do you have a minute to talk, Mrs. Timmons?"

The housekeeper's eyes narrowed. "If you wish."

Joanna ran the tip of her tongue over her lips. "Well, to begin with, I'd be pleased if you called me 'Joanna.'"

Mrs. Timmons's face paled. "I couldn't possibly do that, madam."

"Then call me 'Mrs. Adams.' Just don't...don't keep calling me 'madam.'" Joanna gave a little laugh. "I have enough trouble thinking of myself as 'Joanna,' let alone as anybody called 'madam.'"

The older woman's mouth opened, then shut again. After a moment, she nodded.

"I'll try and remember that, ma...Mrs. Adams."

"And I was wondering... Do you know who...uh, who furnished this house?"

"Why, you did, of course."

Joanna sighed. The answer was unpleasant, but not exactly a surprise.

"There's just one last thing..." She hesitated. "What did I usually do with my days?"

"Breakfast at eight, your health club at ten, and then, of course, your afternoons were quite full."

"Full? Do you mean . . . do I have some kind of part-time job?"

Joanna had the uneasy feeling that it was all Mrs. Timmons could do to keep from laughing.

"Certainly not, Mrs. Adams. You had your lunches, your charity commitments, your board meetings."

"Oh. I see."

"And then there were your three times a week hairdresser's appointments—"

"I had my hair done three times a week?" Joanna said, her voice rising in disbelief.

"You have a standing appointment on Friday at the nail salon, and, of course, there are your massages . . ."

"My massages," Joanna echoed faintly. She wanted to laugh. Or maybe she wanted to cry. It was hard to know which.

"You might wish to check your appointment book. Perhaps it's in the library. Or in your desk, in your bedroom."

"That's all right," Joanna said quickly, "I'll, ah, I'll forego all that for a while, until I'm feeling more like my old self . . ."

Her old self, who was beginning to sound more and more like one absolutely, monumentally pretentious bore.

The day was a duplicate of the one before.

She wandered through the house. She read.

She sat in the garden. She had lunch, took a nap, and woke as restless as a tiger.

In midafternoon, she took a light jacket and headed for the door. Hollister, appearing from out of nowhere, reached it the same instant.

"If madam wishes to go anywhere," he said, "I am at her disposal."

"Thank you," Joanna said politely, "but I'm going for a walk."

"A walk, madam?"

"Yes," she said. "You know, left foot, right foot...a walk. In the park."

"Madam might wish to reconsider..."

Joanna yanked open the door. "Madam is out of here," she said, and slammed the door behind her.

The walk cleared her head.

She'd snapped at David this morning, and then at Hollister. There was no reason for it; everyone meant well, and she knew it.

It was she who was being difficult, not the staff or her husband.

It was just that it all seemed so strange...a wry smile curved over her lips as she made her way up the stairs to her room. This was the life she'd led, but was this the life she'd wanted?

It didn't seem possible.

Ellen was in the bathroom, pouring perfumed oil into the tub.

"There you are, ma'am. I'm just running your bath."

Joanna sighed and sat down on the edge of the bed.

"Ellen, do you think you could stop calling me 'ma'am'? I keep expecting to turn around and find the Queen of England hovering just over my shoulder."

Ellen giggled. "As you wish, madam."

"What I wish," Joanna said, "is that you'd call me Mrs. Adams."

"Oh, but, madam... You were very specific when you hired me, you said I was to address you as 'ma'am' or 'madam.'"

"Just forget whatever I said," Joanna said, more sharply than she'd intended. "I mean... things have changed. Besides, if you call me 'Mrs. Adams' it will help me get used to the sound of my own name."

"Yes, Mrs. Adams."

Joanna smiled. "Thank you. Now, what's this about running a bath?"

"Well, you bathe every day at this time, ma... Mrs. Adams. Then you dress for dinner."

"Dress?" Joanna looked down at herself. She was wearing a navy dress and matching kidskin pumps. Dreary, she thought, and frowned.

"Yes, Mrs. Adams."

"As in, long gown, white gloves and tiara?"

"Not quite so formal," Ellen said seriously. "A short dress, no gloves, and I suppose I could find a comb for your chignon, if you like."

"Do I do this every night? Dress for dinner, I mean?"

"Oh, yes, Mrs. Adams, you do."

Joanna's smile faded. A morning spent doing a lot of nothing, then an afternoon doing more of the same, followed by a soak in a perfumed bath while she considered what dress to wear for dinner.

What a useless existence.

Was this what it meant to be David Adams's wife? She thought of how he'd looked on Sunday, when he'd taken her away from Bright Meadows. The faded jeans, so worn and snug they'd outlined his body, the sweatshirt, straining over his broad shoulders. She thought of his admission that he never let anyone work on his car except him.

Why would a man like that marry a woman who made an art of doing nothing?

"My—my husband dresses for dinner, too?"

"Oh, yes. Mr. Adams showers and changes to a dark suit." Ellen sighed. "I think it's just so old-fashioned and romantic."

Old-fashioned. Romantic. Joanna's pulse quickened. Perhaps she was getting the wrong picture. Dressing for dinner didn't have to be stuffy, it could be everything Ellen had just called it.

"All right," she said, "I'll tell you what. I'll shower, and you pick a dress for me to wear tonight."

"Shower? But—"

"Trust me, Ellen. Unless I'm shivering cold or dying of the flu, I'm not a bath person."

The maid looked at her, her face puzzled. Two out of two, Joanna thought, remembering the way Mrs. Timmons had looked at her this morning. Neither her maid nor her house-keeper could fit the present Joanna Adams inside the skin of the old, and if you added Joanna Adams herself, the score went to a perfect three out of three.

It was a sobering, even frightening, thought.

At seven, dressed in black *peau de soie*, Joanna started down the stairs.

The dress wasn't much to her liking—it was blousey, almost shapeless, not short enough to be sexy or long enough to be fashionable, and it made her feel twice her age. But then, that description pretty much fit everything in her closet.

Why on earth had she bought all that clothing?

She'd as much as asked the question of Ellen, who'd shrugged.

"You shopped at all the best stores, Mrs. Adams."

"Did I?" Joanna had said softly, staring into the mirror.

Maybe she'd forgotten more than the details of her own life, she thought as she reached the bottom of the staircase; maybe she'd forgotten the tenets of high fashion.

She hung on to that thought as she paused in the doorway to the library. She could see David waiting for her before the fireplace, his back to her, one foot up on the edge of the stone hearth, his hands tucked into the pockets of his trousers.

What a handsome man he was, even from this angle. Those incredible shoulders. Those long legs and that tight bottom...

Her taste in furniture, clothes and hairstyles might be in doubt. But her taste in men seemed to have been impeccable.

David turned around.

"Joanna," he said.

Color flew into her cheeks.

"David." She swallowed dryly. "Hello."

His gaze swept over her. She waited for him to say something complimentary about her appearance but he didn't. She studied his face, trying to read his expression, but it was like trying to read the face of a statue.

"Well," she said brightly, "how was your day?"

"It was fine," he said evenly. "How was yours?"

Her heart sank. They were going to have another one of their standard, oh-so-polite conversations. How was your day? he'd asked and she was supposed to say it was fine, it was pleasant, it was...

"Dull."

David's eyebrows lifted. "Dull?"

"Well, yes. I didn't do anything."

His eyes narrowed. "You did something. You went for a walk."

Her head came up. "Ah, I see Hollister reported in, did he?"

"Hollister was only following orders."

"You mean, you told him to spy on me?"

David ran his hand through his hair. "It's been a long day, Jo. Let's not quarrel."

"Do we?" Joanna said quickly. "Quarrel, I mean?"

"No," he said, after a pause, "not really." It was true. Even their decision to divorce had been reached in a civilized way. No raised voices, no anger...no regrets. "Why do you ask?"

Because at least, if we quarreled, there was something more than this terrible nothingness between us...

She sighed. "No reason. I just wondered."

"Look, I'm only trying to make sure you don't overdo."

She sighed again. "I know."

"Before you know it, you'll be phoning up old friends, going to lunch, maybe even attending one or two of those meetings of yours."

"Yuck."

"Yuck?" David laughed. "Did you say 'yuck'?"

She blushed. "I meant to say that, uh, that doesn't sound very exciting, either."

Why had she let the conversation take this turn? David was watching her with a sudden intensity that made her feel like a mouse under the eye of a hungry cat. There was no way she could explain what she felt to him when she couldn't even explain it to herself.

"Don't pay any attention to me," she said with a little laugh. "I've probably been lying around feeling sorry for myself for too long."

She turned away from him, searching desperately for a diversion. Her gaze fell on the built-in bar across the room. "What great-looking hors d'oeuvres," she said, hurrying toward them. "Cheese, and olives...what's this?"

"*Chèvre*," David said as she picked up a tiny cracker spread with a grainy white substance and popped it into her mouth.

"*Chèvre*?"

"Goat cheese."

Joanna stared at him. "Goat cheese?" Her nose wrinkled.

"Yeah. You love the stuff."

She shuddered, snatched up a cocktail napkin, and wiped her mouth.

"Not anymore."

He grinned. "It's even worse than it sounds. That's not just goat cheese, it's goat cheese rolled in ash."

"Ash?" she repeated in amazement. "As in, what's on the end of a cigarette?"

His grin widened. "I don't think so, but does it really matter?"

"You're right, it doesn't. Ash. And goat cheese." She laughed. "What will they think of next?"

"Chocolate-dipped tofu," he said solemnly. Her eyes widened and he held up his hand. "Scout's honor. It was part of the buffet at a business dinner last week. The Halloran merger. You remem... A deal I've been working on."

Her smile slipped, but only a little. "And how was the chocolate-dipped tofu?"

"I didn't touch the stuff. Morgana tried it and said it was great, but you know..." He frowned. "Sorry, Jo. I keep forgetting. Morgana is my P.A."

"Your...?"

"Personal Assistant."

Joanna nodded. "Oh. And she—she went to this dinner with you?"

"Of course." He hesitated. "She'd like to stop by and see you. She's wanted to, ever since the accident, but I told her I wasn't sure if you were up to seeing visitors, even when they're old friends."

Old friends? A woman named Morgana, who spent more time with her husband than she did? His assistant? His personal assistant?

"That was thoughtful of you, David. Please tell—Morgana—that I need just a little more time, would you?"

"Of course."

Joanna smiled at him, her lips curving up softly, and he realized that she'd inadvertently wiped away all that bright red lipstick she favored and he despised. Her mouth was full, pink and softly inviting, and he suddenly wondered what she'd do if leaned down and kissed it. He wouldn't touch her; he'd just kiss her, stroke the tip of his tongue across that sweet, lush flesh . . .

Hell!

"Well," he said briskly, "how about a drink?"

He didn't wait for an answer. Instead, he poured some bourbon for himself and sherry for Joanna. Her fingers closed around the delicate stem of the glass as he handed it to her.

"To your recovery," he said, raising his glass.

She echoed the sentiment, then took a sip of her drink. The pale gold liquid slipped down her throat and she grimaced.

"What's wrong?" David said. "Has the sherry gone bad?"

"It's probably just me. This is just a little bit dry for my taste, that's all."

He looked at her. "Is it?"

"But it's good," she said quickly. "Really."

"Come on, Jo. I can see that you don't like it."

She hesitated. "But . . . but I used to," she said in a suddenly small voice, "didn't I?"

"Tastes change," he said with studied casualness. "I'll pour you something else. What would you prefer?"

A picture popped instantly into her head. A bottle, dark amber in color, with a red and white label...

"Jo?"

She smiled uneasily. "I know this is going to sound ridiculous, but...I just thought of something called Pete's Wicked Ale."

David went very still. "Did you?"

"Isn't that crazy? Who'd name something... What's the matter?"

"You used to drink Pete's." His voice was low, almost a whisper. "A long time ago, before you decided that sherry was...that you preferred sherry to ale."

Joanna began to tremble. "Oh, God!"

"Easy." David took the glass from her hand. He led her to the sofa and helped her sit. "Put your head down and take a deep breath."

"I'm...I'm OK."

"You're not OK, you're as white as a sheet."

"I just...what's happening to me, David?" She lifted her face to his and stared at him through eyes that had gone from violet to black.

"You're remembering things, that's all."

"It's more than that." Her voice shook. "I feel as if I'm trapped inside a black tunnel and—and every now and then I look up and I see a flash of light, but it never lasts long enough for me to really see anything."

"Dammit, Joanna, put your head down!" David put his hand on her hair and forced her face toward her knees. "I knew this would happen if you went sailing off as if nothing had happened to you."

"I'm not sick!" She shoved at his hand and leaped to her feet. "Didn't you listen to anything I said? I'm—I'm lost, David, lost, and I can't . . . I can't . . ."

Her eyes rolled up into her head and she began to slump to the floor. David cursed, caught her in his arms, and strode from the dining room.

"Ellen," he bellowed. "Mrs. Timmons!"

The housekeeper and the maid came running. When Mrs. Timmons saw David hurrying up the stairs with Joanna in his arms, her hands flew to her mouth.

"Oh, my Lord, Mr. David, what happened?"

"Ellen, you get some ice. Mrs. Timmons, you call the doctor. Tell him my wife's fainted and I want him here now."

"Yes, sir. I'll do my best but it's after hours and—"

"Just get him, dammit!" David shouldered open the door to Joanna's room. Her eyes fluttered open as he lay her down gently on the bed.

"David?" she whispered. "What...what happened?"

"You're all right," he said gently. "You fainted, that's all."

"Fainted." She made a sound he supposed was a laugh. God, her face was as pale as the pillow sham. "I couldn't have fainted. It's—it's so Victorian."

"Sir?" David looked around. Ellen was standing in the doorway, her eyes wide, with a basin of ice and a towel.

"That's fine, Ellen. Just bring that to me—thank you. And shut the door after you when you leave."

Joanna stared up at him, her face still pale. "I can't believe I fainted."

"Well, you did. You overdid," he said grimly. "Too much, too soon, that's all. Can you turn your head a bit? That's the way."

"My head hurts," she said, and winced. "What are you doing?"

"What does it look like I'm doing? I'm getting you out of this dress."

She caught his hand but he shrugged her off and went on opening the tiny jet buttons that ran down the front of the black silk dress.

"David, don't. I'm OK. I can—"

"You can't," he said, even more grimly, "and you won't. Dammit, woman, how can a dress be tight enough at the throat to cut off your air and so loose everyplace else that it turns you into a sack of potatoes?"

"A sack of..." Joanna flushed. "You don't like this dress?"

"I don't like flour sacks. What man does? And what the hell does what I like or not like have to do with what you wear? Sit up a little. That's it. Now lift your arm...the other one. Good girl."

She stared at him as he tossed the dress aside. "But I thought...I assumed..." She thought of the closetful of ugly clothes, of the awful furniture in the room, of the servants David had so pointedly said were hers, and her mouth began to tremble.

"I don't understand," she whispered.

"Turn on your side."

She obeyed without thinking. His voice was toneless, his touch as impersonal as a physician's. She felt his hands at the nape of her neck, and then her hair came tumbling down over her shoulders.

"There," he said, "that's better. No wonder your head hurts. You've got enough pins stuck into your scalp to...to..."

His angry, rushed words ground to a halt. He had turned her toward him again and as he looked down at her, his heart seemed to constrict within his chest.

She was so beautiful. So much the woman he still remembered, the woman he'd never been able to get out of his mind. Stripped of the ugly dress, her hair flowing down over her creamy shoulders, her eyes wide and fixed on his, she was everything he remembered, everything he'd ever wanted, and the name he'd once called her whispered from his lips.

"Gypsy," he said huskily.

Who? Joanna thought, who? It wasn't her name, surely...and yet, as she looked up in David's eyes and saw the way he was looking at her, she felt as if she were falling back to another time and place.

Gypsy, she thought, oh, yes, she would be his Gypsy, if that was what he wanted, she would dance for him by firelight, she would whirl around him in an ever-tightening circle until she fell into his waiting arms. She would do whatever he asked of her, she would love him forever...

"Joanna," he whispered.

He bent toward her, then hesitated. Joanna didn't think, she simply reached up, clasped his face and brought him to her.

His mouth closed over hers.

His kiss was gentle, soft and sweet. But she could feel him trembling and she knew what was happening, that he was fighting to control what was raging through him, the need to plunder her mouth, to ravage her until she cried out with need. She knew, because it was raging through her, too.

"David," she sighed.

He groaned and his arms swept around her as he came down on the bed beside her. Her body was soft as silk and hot as the sun against his; his hand swept up and cupped her breast; she moaned and he felt her nipple spring to life beneath the silk of her slip and press against his palm...

"Mr. Adams?"

He raised his head and stared blindly at the closed door. Someone was knocking on it and calling his name.

"Mr. Adams? It's Ellen, sir. Dr. Corbett's arrived. Shall I send him up?"

David looked down at Joanna. Her face was flushed with color, her eyes were dark as the night. Her mouth was softly swollen and pink from his kisses....

But it meant nothing. Nothing. If he valued his own sanity, he had to keep remembering that.

His wife, his beautiful, lying wife, was unexcelled at this game. Her body still remembered how to play, even if her mind did not.

"David?"

Her voice was as soft as it always was. It was her heart that was hard.

"David," she said again, and he stood up, took her robe from where it lay at the foot of the bed, and tossed it to her.

"Cover yourself," he said coldly, and then he turned his back on his wife and on temptation.

CHAPTER SIX

JOANNA was stunned by the tone of cold command in her husband's voice.

"What?"

"You heard me," he growled. "Cover yourself—unless you don't object to Corbett knowing what you were up to a minute ago."

She felt the blood drain from her face. "What *I* was up to?"

"All right. What we were up to. Does that make you feel better?"

She grabbed the robe he'd tossed to her and shoved her arms through the sleeves. She was trembling, not with the aftermath of desire but with the fury of humiliation.

"Nothing could make me feel better," she said shakily, "except being able to start my life beginning the day before I met you."

"My sentiments exactly. The sooner you get your memory back, the better it will be for the both of us."

Joanna swung her legs to the floor and stood up, stumbling a little as she did. David reached out to help her but she swatted his hands away.

123

"Don't touch me. Don't you ever touch me again. Do you understand?"

David stared at his wife. Her eyes blazed black in her face. Suddenly, he was overcome with guilt. What had just happened was as much his fault as hers. Hell, who was he kidding? It was all his fault. She had no memory but he—he remembered everything. And she was right. She hadn't started this ugly scene, he had.

"Joanna," he said, "listen—"

"Get out of my room."

"Jo, please, I'm trying to apolo—"

She snatched a perfume bottle from the vanity and hurled it at him. He ducked and it whizzed by his head and shattered against the wall just as the door banged open.

Doctor Corbett paused in the doorway. He looked at the shards of glass that glittered against the carpet, then cleared his throat and raised a politely inquisitive face to David and Joanna.

"Excuse me," he said, "is there a problem here?"

"Yes!" Joanna glared at David. "I want this man out of my room!"

Corbett turned to David. "Mr. Adams," he said gently, "perhaps you'll give me a few moments alone with your...."

"Be my guest, Doctor. Take a few years, if you like," David snarled.

The door slammed shut after him. The doctor waited and then cleared his throat again.

"Well, Mrs. Adams," he said briskly, "why don't you tell me what's going on here?"

Joanna swung toward him. "I'll tell you what's going on," she said furiously. "I'll tell you what's...what's..." Her shoulders slumped. She felt the rage that had been driving her draining from her system. "Oh, hell," she muttered, "hell!" She sank down on the edge of her bed and wiped her sleeve across suddenly damp eyes. "I want my memory back," she said in a choked whisper. "Is that asking so much?"

"My dear Mrs. Adams—"

"Don't call me that!" Joanna's head snapped up, her eyes gleaming once again with anger. "It's bad enough I'm married to that— that cold-blooded Neanderthal! I certainly don't need to be reminded of it all the time."

Corbett sighed. Then he pulled a Kleenex from a box on the table beside Joanna's bed and handed it to her.

"Suppose you tell me what happened tonight," he said quietly. "All I really know is that your housekeeper phoned my service and said you'd collapsed."

"I didn't collapse!" Joanna dabbed at her eyes, wiped her nose, then balled up the tissue and threw it into a wicker wastebasket. "David blew what happened out of all proportion. I just felt woozy for a minute, that's all."

"Woozy," Corbett repeated.

"Yes. I know it's not the sort of fancy medical term you use, but..." She stopped, bit her lip, and looked at him. "I'm sorry, Doctor. I don't know why I'm letting my anger out on you."

"That's all right."

"No, it isn't. It's myself I'm angry at."

"For what?"

"What do you mean, for what?" She threw her arms wide. "For everything! For having something as stupid as amnesia, that's for what!"

"There's nothing 'stupid' about amnesia," Corbett said gently. "And you didn't have a choice in acquiring it. You suffered a head injury, and it's going to take time to heal."

"It will heal though, won't it? You said—"

"There are no guarantees but, as I've told you, I've every reason to believe your memory will return." Corbett drew out the bench from the vanity table and sat down facing her. "Right now, I'm more concerned about what you call this 'wooziness' you felt tonight. Did it come on suddenly? Or was it precipitated by some event?''

She sighed. "It didn't happen out of the blue, if that's what you're asking. I . . . I remembered something. Not much, there was just a momentary flash . . . but it startled me.''

"So, it was the shock of remembering that made you feel . . . what? Dizzy? Weak?''

She nodded. "Yes.''

"And then?'' Corbett prompted.

"And then, David told Mrs. Timmons to phone you and he brought me up here and . . . and . . .'' Her voice trailed off.

"And you quarreled?''

She thought of how David had undressed her, of how he'd let down her hair. Of how he'd kissed her and how she'd responded with heated, almost unbearable passion . . . and of how he'd reacted then, with an anger that had bordered on disgust.

"Joanna?''

Color washed over her skin. "You could say that,'' she murmured, and looked down at her lap.

Corbett reached for his leather medical bag. "Very well. Let's just check a few things, shall we?''

"Check whatever you like. There's nothing wrong with me. Not physically, anyway.''

She was right. The doctor's examination was thorough and when it was over, he pronounced her in excellent health.

"In excellent health," Joanna said with a bitter smile. "It's like that awful old joke, the one about the operation being a success but the patient dying."

"You're making fine progress. You've started to remember things."

"A picture of a bottle of beer flashing through my head isn't exactly the same as getting my memory back, Doctor."

"Joanna." Corbett took her hand in his. "You must have patience. I know this is difficult for you and for your husband, but—"

"Oh, please!" Joanna snatched back her hand. "Don't waste your sympathy on David!"

"Surely, you realize your condition is affecting him as well as you?"

"Look," she said, after a brief hesitation, "I know I must sound like a shrew. But you can't imagine what David's like."

"No," Corbett said mildly, "I can't. I only know what I've observed, that he came to the hospital every evening of your stay, that he agreed to bring you home when you seemed unhappy at Bright Meadows, that he's stood by you during a most difficult period."

Joanna stared at the doctor. Then she gave a deep, deep sigh.

"You're right, I suppose. And I have tried to keep in mind that this can't be easy for him."

"Joanna, the worst thing about loss of memory is the pressure it brings to bear on a relationship. That's why you both need to be patient as you restructure yours."

"Yes, but..." She hesitated. "But it's hard," she said softly, "when you don't know what things were like between you in the first place. I mean, what if...what if things had been shaky for a couple—a hypothetical couple—in the past? How could they possibly restructure a relationship successfully? One of them would know the truth and the other—the other would be working in the dark."

Corbett smiled. "There are those who would say the one working in the dark was fortunate."

"Fortunate?" Joanna's head came up. "That I don't know—that this hypothetical person doesn't know what sort of marriage she had?"

"Without a past, there can be no regrets. No anger, no recriminations... It's like starting over again with a clean slate."

Joanna laughed softly. "I didn't know they taught Optimism in med school."

"Philosophy was my love before I decided on medicine." Corbett chuckled. "Sometimes, it still comes in handy." He patted her hand, then stood up. "I'm going to give you something to help you sleep. And I'm going to leave you a prescription you must promise to follow."

"What kind of prescription? You said I was healthy."

"I want you to stop worrying about the past. *Carpe diem*, Joanna. Seize the day. The past is lost to *all* of us, not just to you. It's today and tomorrow that matter."

A slight smile curved across Joanna's lips. "More leftover class notes from Philosophy, Doctor?"

"Just an old-fashioned mother who loved quoting the classics." Corbett took a vial of tablets from his bag, shook two into her palm and poured her a glass of water from the thermos jug on the night table. "It's time you started living your life again."

"That sounds terrific, Doctor Corbett, but I don't know what 'my life' is."

"Then find out," he said briskly, snapping shut his bag. "Surely you had friends, interests, things you enjoyed doing...?"

"From what I can gather, I seem to have made an art of doing as little as possible," she said with a faintly bitter smile.

"Then try something new. Something you can share with David, perhaps. But don't go on moping and feeling sorry for yourself."

"Me?" Joanna handed him the glass. Her voice rose in indignation. "But I haven't..." Her gaze met Corbett's. She laughed and fell back against the pillows. "That's some combination," she said wryly, "philosophy and medicine."

Corbett grinned. "Just think of me as Ann Landers, M.D." He waved a hand in salute and shut the bedroom door.

The doctor's advice made sense.

She couldn't recall the past. Much as it upset Joanna to admit it, she didn't even have any guarantee that she ever would.

So whatever condition her marriage had been in didn't matter. It was what she made of it now that counted.

David didn't seem to like her very much. Well, she thought early the next morning as she pulled on a pair of cotton shorts and a tank top, maybe she hadn't been a very likeable person.

No. That couldn't be, she thought with a smile...

But it was possible, wasn't it?

Or maybe they'd hit a rough patch in their marriage. Maybe they'd begun to drift apart.

Not that it mattered. The doctor was right. *Carpe diem*. The past was gone and only the present mattered, and when you came down to it, she didn't know all that much about the present, either, especially as it related to her husband.

Share something with David, Corbett had advised.

But what? What did her husband do with his spare time? What were his interests? Who were his friends?

Joanna glanced at her watch as she pulled her hair back into a ponytail and secured it with a coated rubber band. She had lots of questions and hardly any answers. Well, starting today, she was going to go after those answers.

Quietly, she opened the door to her bedroom and stepped out into the corridor.

David was in for a surprise.

"Surprise" wasn't the right word.

"Shocked" came closer to the truth, judging by the look on his face when he came trotting down the steps ten minutes later and saw her.

"Joanna?" He stared at her as if she might be an hallucination. "What are you doing up at this hour?"

She smiled at him over her shoulder. She'd been doing stretching exercises while she waited, using one of the marquetry benches that flanked the foyer door for support.

"Good morning," she said, as she finished her last stretch. "And it's not really so early, is it?"

He tore his astonished gaze from her and glanced at his watch.

"Are you kidding? It's just after six."

"Well, I was awake so I figured, instead of just lying in bed vegetating, I might as well get up and do something useful." She jerked her head in the direction of the kitchen. "I made a pot of coffee."

"Yes. Yes, I thought I smelled coffee."

"Would you like some?"

"No. Ah, no, thank you." He edged past her, as if she might vaporize if touched. "I prefer to wait until after my run but you go ahead and, ah, and have a cup."

"I already did." She followed after him, to the front door. "You don't mind, do you?"

"That you made coffee? No, of course not."

"That I've decided to run with you."

He swung toward her. "That you've...?" His gaze flew over her again, taking in her gray sweat shorts, her tank top, her ponytail, her running shoes. She'd decided to run with him?

His brain couldn't seem to process the information. She hadn't run with him in months. In years. She hadn't done any of this in years, gotten up at this hour, put up the morning coffee, worn this tattered outfit that had once made his pulse beat quicken...hell, that *still* made his pulse beat quicken because she was the only woman he'd ever known who could fill out a shirt that way, or pair of shorts, the only one whose early morning, unmade-up face was a face that would have put Helen of Troy to shame...

Dammit, Adams, are you nuts?

"David? Do you mind?"

He frowned, shook his head. "No," he said coldly, "I suppose not."

She smiled. "Thanks. I was hoping you wouldn't mi—"

"It's a free country," he said as he swung the door open and started down toward the street. "And a big park. Just do your best to keep up, Joanna, because I don't feel much like tailoring my pace to suit yours."

Gracious. That was the word to describe her husband's acceptance of her presence, Joanna thought sarcastically as she panted after him half an hour later, gracious and charming and oh-so-welcoming.

But she was matching the pace he'd set, even if her legs were screaming and her breath was wheezing in lungs that felt as if they were on fire.

It had occurred to her, one or two times, that David was deliberately trying to exhaust her but why would he do that?

No. She was just out of shape, that was all.

But she'd be damned if she'd admit it.

Stupid. That was the word to describe his acceptance of his wife's presence, David thought grimly as he pounded through the park, stupid and pointless and all-around dumb.

Why hadn't he just told her he didn't want any part of her? That he was perfectly happy with the way things had been for the past few years, thank you very much, with him running alone and her doing her la-di-da exercises at her fancy health club.

She'd caught him off guard, that was why. Well, it wouldn't happen again. He couldn't imagine what insanity had gotten into her today, especially after what had happened between them last night. Corbett had come down from her bedroom looking smug and mysterious; he'd said she was in excellent health and that he'd advised her to get on with the business of living.

Was this Joanna's idea of how to do that?

David didn't think so. The real Joanna hadn't thought so, either, and if he was playing his cards right, this new one would soon come to the same conclusion.

He was running harder and faster than he'd run in years, running in a way that would exhaust anybody, especially a devotee of glitter Spandex, odor-free sweat and fancy treadmills.

By the time they got back to the house, she'd be finished with early morning runs and whatever foolishness had sent her along on this one.

Still, he had to admit, she was keeping up.

He frowned, put his head down, and ran harder.

But she wasn't finished with early morning runs, not by a long shot.

She was waiting for him the next morning, and the morning after that. By the third day, he adjusted his pace back to where it had been before Joanna had intruded.

He did it for her sake. Hell, it wasn't fair to tax her so, even if Corbett said she was fine.

He certainly didn't do it for his. And he certainly didn't enjoy having her tag along.

But when she wasn't bent over the bench in the foyer Friday morning, doing those stretching exercises that tilted her sexy little bottom into the air, David paused on the steps while he tried to figure out what the strange emotion stealing over him might be.

Disappointment?

No. Hell, no, why would he—

"Hi."

Joanna was standing in the door to the library, clutching a cup of coffee in her hands, smiling at him over the rim.

His heart did something absolutely stupid, as if it were on a string, yo-yoing in his chest.

"Hi," he said, and managed not to smile back.

"You're early."

"Am I? Well, that's OK, if you're not ready to—"

"I'm ready. Just let me put this cup in the sink and I'll be—"

"Jo?" He shoved his hand into his hair and scraped it back from his forehead.

"Yes?"

"I was going to say... I was going to say..."

He knew what he'd been going to say, that they might skip this morning's run, take their coffee out into the little garden, drink it together at the minuscule wrought-iron table under the tree and talk about nothing in particular and everything under the sun, just the way they used to, a million years ago.

"Yes, David?"

He looked at her. Was he crazy? He had to be. It was bad enough they'd started running together but they'd also started spending the evening together, too. Joanna waited for him to get home, no matter how late, before sitting down to dinner. He'd even begun to look forward to it, just sharing their mealtime, talking, telling her about the inconsequential bits and pieces of his day...

Why was he letting these things happen? Nothing, *nothing*, had changed. Joanna had lost her memory but sooner or later she'd get it back. She'd remember who she was and what she wanted. She'd turn into the real Joanna Adams again, the one that lay hidden beneath that mask of sexy innocence, and when she did...when she did, he had no intention of watching it happen again.

Feeling disappointment turn to despair once in a lifetime was more than enough.

He stood straighter and, with a cool smile, pulled the door open.

"I'd rather not wait, if it's all the same to you," he said politely. "I'd prefer running by myself today." The sudden hurt in her eyes knotted in his gut and his irritation with himself only made him twist the knot tighter. "Oh, by the way, Joanna...don't expect me for dinner tonight. There's a fund-raiser at the Gallery of Alternative Arts and I've agreed to attend."

Joanna stared at her husband. It had taken him no time at all to undo the progress of the past days. She wanted to weep; she wanted to slug him. Instead, she did the only thing she knew she ought to do, which was to smile brightly.

"How nice for you," she said.

"Yes, isn't it?" he answered, blithely ignoring the fact that tonight's event was just the kind of thing he hated, a bunch of fat cats standing around stroking each other's fur, telling themselves they were helping the world when all they were really doing was making asses of themselves. He hadn't even intended to go to the damned gala until desperation had forced his hand a couple of seconds ago. "Morgana reminded me of it yesterday."

"Morgana," Joanna repeated, even more brightly.

"My Personal—"

"—Assistant." She nodded. "Yes, I know."

"Anyhow, don't wait up. These things usually run late."

"Oh, of course. Well, have a good run. And a good day. And a good..."

He was gone.

Joanna stood in the open doorway, watching her husband. His stride was long and loose as he ran toward Fifth Avenue without so much as a backward glance.

Her bottom lip trembled.

So much for sharing.

So much for getting back into life.

So much for letting herself think there might be a human being lurking inside the man she was married to.

She slammed the door, made her way back to the kitchen, rinsed out her cup and put it away.

"*Carpe diem*, my foot," she muttered.

Dr. Corbett's advice had been useless. Useless. She'd wasted her time, wasted her hopes.

That's right, Joanna. You might as well go back to sitting around and feeling sorry for yourself.

Her head jerked up.

"I'm not feeling sorry for myself!"

Sure you are. You're thinking that he could have waited while you rinsed your coffee cup, that he could have asked you to go with him tonight.

Unless, of course, he was taking the ever-present, ever-helpful Morgana.

A muscle ticked in Joanna's cheek. She put her cup down, trotted up the stairs to her room and to the Queen Anne secretary that stood on one wall. There was a white-leather appointment book in the top drawer; she'd flipped through it a couple of times, shuddering at the stuff she saw scrawled over the weekly calendar pages, nonsense about hairdresser's appointments and dress fittings and luncheons and meetings that sounded senseless and silly...

There it was, under today's date, in her handwriting.

Eight p.m., Gal. of Alt. Arts, benefit for Tico the Chimp.

Her eyes widened. Tico the Chimp?

She closed the book, lay it aside, and stared into space. Tico the Chimp. The elusive Morgana. And David, all under one roof.

Joanna shucked off her running clothes and headed for the shower.

CHAPTER SEVEN

AMNESIA, as Joanna was quickly learning, was a strangely elective ailment.

She didn't remember any of the details of her own life. But when she thought back to what Ellen had said—that she shopped in only the best stores—a list came quickly to mind.

And though she'd apparently bought only dark, conservative clothing in those fashionable shops, surely they also carried other things. They had to sell dresses that were bright in color and didn't have sleeves to the wrist and hems to mid-calf, that didn't make a woman look as if she were... what had David said? As if she were a sack of potatoes?

There was only one way to find out.

Joanna dressed quickly, without giving much thought to her selections. What was there to think about, when all her clothing had a grim sameness? Even her underwear was dowdy and utilitarian.

She paid even less attention to her hair. She hadn't yet grasped the knack of neatly knotting it low on her neck. Ellen had been fixing it, most mornings, but today was her maid's day off and even if it hadn't been, Joanna was too impatient to wait while her curls were brushed and sprayed into submission. So she simply caught her hair in one hand, gave it a twist, then pinned it into place.

Ugh, she thought, grimacing as she caught a glimpse of herself in the mirror, she looked even more funereal than usual.

Not that it would matter, after this jaunt...

My God, Joanna, are you sure you know what you're doing?

"No," she said, into the silence, "I don't."

She thought of her husband's biting comments about her dress, about the way she wore her hair. She thought of her doctor's admonition that she give up searching for the past and instead concentrate on the present and the future.

She thought of Morgana, and tonight's party.

And then she took one last deep breath and set out to face New York.

She let Hollister drive her to the first store on her list, then told him not to wait.

It was not an order that pleased him.

"But, madam..."

"Go on, Hollister. Go to the park or something. Take your girl out for a spin." Joanna laughed at the look on his face. "You do have a girl, don't you?"

"Madam, really—"

"Hollister, really," she said gently, "I much prefer to do my shopping on my own."

Once inside the store, the giddiness that had been bubbling inside her since she'd read the entry in her appointment book was all but swept away by a sense of near panic.

The store was so big... Why had she come? Nothing about it was familiar; she had no idea where to start or even what to start looking for.

"Madam? May I help you?"

Joanna turned toward the smartly dressed young saleswoman who'd materialized at her elbow.

"Yes," she said gratefully. "I'd like to buy a dress. Something—something special, to wear to a party tonight."

The girl's eyes moved quickly and professionally over her.

"Certainly, madam," she replied, "if you'll just come with me...?"

Within moments, Joanna found herself in a sea of dresses.

"Here we are, madam. Did you have a preference as to color?"

"Does it matter?" Joanna said with a little laugh. She turned in a slow circle. "The only color I see is black."

The salesgirl smiled coolly. "Black is always fashionable, as madam can attest."

Joanna looked down at herself. She was wearing the first thing that had come to hand in her closet, a long-sleeved, long-skirted, incredibly expensive and incredibly unattractive two-piece dress and yes, indeed, it was black.

"Always," she said, and smiled politely at the salesgirl, "but not always interesting. Haven't you got other colors? Something in yellow, perhaps, or pale blue?" Her gaze lit on a mannequin in the next department. "Something like that, for instance."

"That?" the clerk said, her voice losing its cultured purr and rising in dismay. "But that dress is . . . it's heliotrope!"

"I'd have called it violet," Joanna said. The girl trailed behind as she walked toward the mannequin. "But perhaps you're right. It's lighter than a true violet."

"I don't think this is quite what madam is looking for," the clerk said with a quick, artificial smile. "The neckline is rather low."

"Shockingly low."

"The skirt is very short."

Joanna nodded. "It seems to be."

"This dress is definitely not madam's style."

"How do you know that, Miss..." Joanna peered at the salesgirl's identification tag. "How do you know that, Miss Simpson?"

"Why, from looking at...I mean, it's my job to listen to what a customer tells me and then determine what will best meet her needs."

"Then do it, please," Joanna said with a pleasant smile. "I've told you I need a special dress for this evening, and that I particularly like this one. Please show me to the fitting room and bring me this dress in a—what would you think? A ten?"

The baffled clerk stared at her. "I don't know, not for certain. It's difficult to assess madam's proper weight and shape in the dress she's wearing."

Joanna smiled wistfully. "So I've been told."

Size ten was too big.

Eight was perfect. And so was the dress, Joanna thought, staring at herself in the three-way dressing room mirror.

The color was wonderful, almost the same shade as her eyes and a perfect foil for her creamy skin and dark hair.

The neckline certainly was low and the skirt certainly was short...not that Fifth Avenue wasn't crowded with stylish women wearing their necklines just as deeply cut and the hems just as high. Still...

"Madam looks..." The salesclerk's stunned eyes met Joanna's in the mirror. "She looks beautiful!"

Joanna turned, frowned, and peered at herself over her shoulder. She had a sudden vision of David, seeing her in something so outrageous.

"I don't know," she said slowly. "Maybe you were right. This dress is—"

"Stunning," the girl said. "With your hair done differently and the right shoes..."

The women's eyes met in the mirror. Joanna could feel her courage slipping.

What are you doing, Joanna? What would David think?

There was no way of knowing. But I know what I think, she thought suddenly. I think I look—I think I look...

She reached behind her and gave the zipper a determined tug.

"I'll take it," she said, before she lost her courage completely.

The rest was easy.

The right shoes turned out to be conveniently waiting one department over, a pair of silver sandals with slender high heels and narrow straps, and there was a tiny purse on a silver shoulder chain to match. The right underthings—an ivory silk teddy with lacy garters and a pair of gossamer-sheer stockings—were just a couple of blocks away, almost calling out Joanna's name from the window of a stylish boutique.

There was only one last step to take.

Joanna stood before the mirrored door of a beauty salon. Her appointment book had confirmed that she had standing appointments at this trendy place three times a week.

The door swung open and the scent of hair spray and expensive perfume came wafting out, born on a cloud of lushly romantic music.

Joanna squared her shoulders and marched inside.

The girl at the reception desk did a double take. "Oh, Mrs. Adams," she squealed, "how lovely to see you again. We'd heard you were in an accident!"

Joanna admitted that she had been, assured the receptionist that she was well on the road to recovery and said she was here to have her hair done.

"I know it's not my day but I was hoping you could fit me in."

The girl smiled. "Of course." She motioned to the glittering mirrors beyond them. "Arturo's just finishing up with a client so if you wouldn't mind waiting just a couple of secs . . . ?''

Joanna followed the girl's pointing finger. Arturo confirmed he was her usual hairdresser by waving his hand and smiling. He was a gray-haired man in late middle age, as was his client whose hair was being pinned and sprayed into a style that was the duplicate of Joanna's.

"That's OK," she said quickly, "someone else can do my hair today."

"We wouldn't dream of letting that happen, Mrs. Adams. I promise, Arturo will only be—"

"How about him?"

The girl's eyes widened. The man Joanna had indicated was young, with shoulder-length hair and a tiny gold stud in one earlobe. He was cutting the hair of a woman in her mid-twenties—just about my age, Joanna thought with a surprised start—and shaping it into a style that was swingy, sexy and feminine.

"Oh, but, Mrs. Adams," the receptionist said nervously, "I don't think Mick's the right guy for—"

"I think he's perfect," Joanna said, ignoring the butterflies swarming in her stomach. She smiled, sat down in an empty chair and piled her gaily wrapped packages beside her.

"And I'll be happy to wait until he's free. Oh, by the way... the sign outside says you do cosmetic makeovers, too. Is that right?"

The girl's throat worked. "Uh—uh, yes. Yes, we do. In fact, Mick is the one who—"

"Great." Joanna plucked a magazine from a lamp table, opened it and buried her face inside. After a moment, the receptionist took her cue and fled.

Joanna let out a shuddering breath and thought how perfect it would be if only the butterflies would do the same.

She taxied home, locked herself into her bedroom. Then, like a cygnet exchanging its dull feathers for the glorious plumage of a swan, she took off her old clothes and replaced them with the new.

The teddy first, and the sheer stockings followed by the violet dress, which floated down around her like the petals of a flower. She slipped on the silver shoes. Thanks to Mick, her hair was now loose on her shoulders, layered just lightly around her face. It needed only a fluff of the brush, and her new makeup—eyeliner, mascara and a touch of pale lip gloss—was easy enough to touch up, even with trembling hands.

Because her hands were trembling now, and her teeth were tapping together like castanets.

What in the hell had prompted her to do this?

She swung toward the mirrored wall against which the vanity table stood and stared at herself. She had awakened in a hospital room weeks ago, a stranger to herself.

Now, she'd replaced that stranger with another, one David had never seen before.

The enormity of what she was doing almost buckled her knees. But there was no going back now.

Joanna gave her reflection a shaky smile.

"*Carpe diem*, kid," she whispered, and gave herself a thumbs-up.

She hadn't only seized the day, she was about to wring it dry.

David was sitting behind his oak desk in his spacious office in lower Manhattan, his chair turned to the window and his back to the door, staring sightlessly over the gray waters of the Hudson River while he mentally cursed his own stupidity.

What other word could you use to describe the way he'd trapped himself into the upcoming evening of unrelieved boredom?

He'd attended parties like tonight's in the past. Joanna belonged to virtually every committee around; she'd dragged him from one mind-numbing gala to another, all in the name of what she considered to be "Good Causes," where the same dull people stood in little clusters talking about the same dull things while they chomped on soggy hors d'oeuvres and sipped flat champagne.

Finally, he'd put his foot down and said he'd write checks to Save the Somalian Snail and the Androgynous Artists of America but he'd be damned if he'd go to one more inane benefit on their behalf.

In a way, that had been the beginning of the end. He'd taken a good, hard look at the four years of his marriage and admitted the truth, that the Joanna he'd married had metamorphosed into a woman he didn't understand, a woman who was interested in knowing the right people and buying the right labels, whose only goal was to be accepted in the upper echelons of New York society...

...Who had loved his money and his position but not him. Never him.

He had to admit, she'd done a fine job of pulling the wool over his eyes. She'd been so young, so seemingly innocent, and he'd been so crazy about her that he'd even worried, at the beginning, that he might overwhelm her with the intensity of his love.

He'd admitted as much to Morgana, who knew him better than anyone after working beside him for five years, and she'd generously offered him the benefit of her insight into the members of her own sex.

"I understand, David," she'd said. "Joanna's a child, only twenty-two to your thirty, and a free spirit, at that. You must be careful that you don't make her feel trapped."

His mouth twisted. He needn't have worried. While he'd been busy trying to keep his wife from feeling trapped, she'd been busy re-arranging his life until the night they'd been at some stupid charity ball and he'd suddenly realized that *he* was the one who was trapped, in a loveless marriage to a woman with whom he had absolutely nothing in common and never would have.

Until the accident. Until a bump on the head had wiped away Joanna's memory and turned her into...

"Dammit," he said.

It was dangerous to think that way. The accident hadn't "turned" her into anything but a woman struggling to recover her memory. Once she did, life would return to normal and so would Joanna.

And then they'd be back where they'd been a couple of months ago, with their divorce only days away, and that was just fine. It was better than fine, it was freedom. It was—

"David?"

He swung his chair around. Morgana had inched open the door to his office, just enough so she could peer around the edge.

"I'm sorry to bother you, David. I knocked, but..."

"Morgana." He straightened in his chair, feeling strangely guilty for having been caught with his thoughts anywhere but on the papers strewn across his desk, and smiled at his assistant. "Come in."

"Are you sure?" she said, as she stepped inside the office. "If you're busy..."

"Don't be foolish. I'm never too busy to talk to you and anyway, I really wasn't working. I was thinking about—about this party I'm supposed to go to tonight. Did you phone and say I'd changed my mind about not attending?"

"I did. And Mrs. Capshaw herself told me to assure you it wasn't too late. She wanted you to know that the entire Planning Committee would be delighted to know you'd decided to come."

David smiled thinly. "How nice."

"She asked if Joanna would be with you." Morgana's perfect features settled into serious lines. "I told her it was far too soon for Joanna to be up and about. Which reminds me, David, I haven't asked in days...I do so want to stop by for a visit. Do you think she's up to seeing anyone yet?''

''That's kind of you, Morgana, but—''

''It isn't kind at all. I've always liked Joanna, you know that. And I know how difficult this must be for her and for you both.'' She hesitated, the tip of her pink tongue just moistening the fullness of her bottom lip. ''She hasn't shown any signs of recovery yet, I suppose?''

The muscle in David's cheek knotted. ''No.''

''It will be good for her, knowing you've gone to a party she helped plan.''

''She doesn't know she helped plan it.''

''Oh? But I thought—I assumed that was why you decided to attend.''

David frowned. Morgana was his assistant and his friend, and from the time of his marriage, she'd been Joanna's friend, too. But he wasn't about to tell her that he'd decided to go to tonight's gala only to make it clear to his wife that their lives went in separate directions...

...And what a stupid thing that had been to do, when he could make the same point just as easily and far more comfortably by going home and asking Mrs. Timmons to serve him his supper on a tray in his study.

"Actually," he said with a little smile, "now that I think about it, I'm not sure why I decided to attend. Eating soggy hors d'oeuvres and drinking flat champagne while I stare at the paintings of some artist who probably needs a bath more than he needs a paintbrush—"

"It's Tico the Chimp."

"What's Tico the Chimp?"

"The artist. You know, they profiled him in the *Times* a couple of weeks ago. The party's in his honor."

"That's just great." David began to laugh. "Soggy hors d'oeuvres, flat champagne . . . and for the guest of honor, a bunch of bananas."

"The art critic for the *Times* called him a great talent."

"Why doesn't that surprise me? Morgana, do me a favor. Phone Mrs. Capshaw, offer my regrets—"

"The mayor's going to be there, and Senator Williamson, and the Secretary-General of the UN. I know they're all friends of yours, but—"

"Acquaintances."

"Either way, it can't hurt to touch bases with all three of them with this new project in our laps." A sympathetic smile softened his assistant's patrician features. "Besides, it will be good for you to get out a bit. I know it's not my place to say so, but these last weeks surely must have been a strain."

David nodded. Morgana was the only person, aside from his attorney and Joanna's, who knew he and his wife had been about to divorce when the accident had occurred. Of course, she didn't know any of the details. Still, it helped that he didn't have to pretend with her.

"Yes," he said quietly, "it has been." He drew a deep breath, then let it out slowly. "For Joanna, too."

"Oh, certainly."

Morgana sat down on the edge of his desk, as she often did, and the skirt of her pale yellow suit hitched a couple of inches above her knees.

He almost smiled. When she became engrossed in something, her skirt would often hitch up, or she'd forget that her neckline might delicately gape open as she leaned forward to draw his attention to an item in her hand.

He'd have thought such things were deliberate if any other woman had done them but Morgana, though beautiful, was incapable of playing such games. She was the complete professional, a quality he'd come to appreciate more and more during the years she'd been working for him.

She'd started in his office as his secretary.

"But I don't intend to stay in that position," she'd told him bluntly when he'd hired her.

David had admired her drive. And the company had benefitted from it. Morgana was single-minded in her pursuit of success; she was nothing like the girls who'd preceded her, who'd batted their lashes a lot better than they took dictation or kept his files.

Not that she didn't have a heart. When he'd come to work one morning and announced he'd married the girl he'd met not ten days before, Morgana had probably been as stunned as his colleagues. But she hadn't shown it. If anything, she'd gone out of her way to befriend his young wife and ease her into his sophisticated world.

Little had he or Morgana known that Joanna had been more than ready to do that by herself.

Ever since the accident, Morgana had put her private life on hold, pitching in to take up the slack when he'd been out of the office the first couple of days, then staying late to help him play catch-up while Joanna was at Bright Meadows. He knew she was right, that there'd be networking opportunities at tonight's party...

...Opportunities she could take advantage of all on her own.

David felt a load lift from his shoulders. Why hadn't it occurred to him before? Morgana would get the chance to enjoy herself—she was far better than he at putting on a polite, social mask. And he'd be off the hook.

"You know," he said, "you could use some time off, too."

"That's kind of you to say, David, but—"

"Would you like to go to that party tonight?"

Her lovely face lit. "Why...I would, yes."

He smiled. "Well, then, why not go?"

"Oh." She gave an uncharacteristically breathless laugh. "How generous. Thank you, David. I'd enjoy that very much."

"Here," he said, opening his desk drawer and digging out his tickets for the event. "You take these and—"

"No, you'd better hang on to them." Morgana got to her feet. "I'll have to go home and change first, but I promise, I won't take very long. I can meet you at the gallery. Will that be OK?"

"Morgana," he said quickly, "you don't—"

"Oh, it's lovely of you to say that, David." She laughed again, that same soft, breathless sound. "But I can't possibly go to a party dressed like this. I promise, I'll be there by eight and not a moment later."

A dull pain began to throb behind David's eyes.

"Don't worry about it," he said wearily. "We'll take a taxi to your place. I'll wait while you change."

Morgana's smile flashed like a thousand-watt bulb.

"Oh, David, you're so kind! I just know we'll have a wonderful time."

"Yeah." He smiled, too, and the pain in his head intensified. "I just know it, too."

The hors d'oeuvres weren't soggy. They were stale.

The champagne wasn't flat. It was awful.

As for Tico the Chimp...the animal loped around the gallery, hand in hand with his owner, both of them decked out in tuxedos complete with top hats and bow ties. Every now and then, Tico rolled back his lips and let loose with a cackling shriek.

It was, David thought, the most honest comment anybody in the packed room made all night.

The whole thing was ludicrous, right down to the wild blobs of color that hung on the wall, each of them bearing the chimp's official handprint. Or was it footprint? David fought back the wild desire to ask. Everybody in the place was taking things so seriously, even Morgana.

Well, no. She couldn't be, she was too intelligent to swallow garbage like this but she was certainly putting on an amazing face, peering intently at the paintings, nodding over the notes in the program. Now, as he waited patiently, she'd lined up to shake Tico's hand. Or his paw. Or whatever in hell you called it.

It was hard to imagine Joanna as part of the committee that had planned this event even knowing, as he did, the penchant his wife had shown for fitting readily into the time-wasting habits of the idle rich. It was especially difficult because, for some crazy reason, he kept thinking back to the first one of these things they'd attended together.

They'd only been married a couple of months then and half the reason he'd decided to go to the party was because he could hardly wait to show off his gorgeous bride.

"Are we supposed to dress up?" she'd asked him and he'd kissed away the worried frown between her eyebrows and assured her that whatever she wore, she'd be the most beautiful woman in the room.

And she had been. She'd worn a hot pink dress, very demure and proper except that beneath it there'd been the hint of her lush, lovely body; her hair had streamed down over her shoulders like a midnight cloud. She'd clung to his arm, trying to look suitably impressed by— what had been on exhibit that night?

A display of cardboard boxes, that was it, some arranged on the walls, some grouped on the floor, all of them with price tags attached that made them Art instead of cardboard. They'd strolled from one end of the room to the other and then he'd bent his head to Joanna's and whispered that when they got back to Connecticut, he was going to go through the entire house, sign every box he found and then donate them all to the museum.

Joanna had looked up at him, her eyes wide and her lovely mouth trembling, and then she'd burst into laughter so hard that she'd had to bury her face against his chest.

An ache, sharper than the pain behind his eyes, crushed David's heart. Why was he thinking such dumb thoughts? That had been a million years ago. And it hadn't been real, it had all been illusion, just like Joanna herself.

If only he could forget the look of her, the sound of her voice...

"Hello, David."

The words were soft but their power stopped his breath. He turned slowly and there she was, as he remembered her. No artifice. No cool, matronly elegance. She wore little makeup, her hair was a glorious tide of midnight waves that tumbled down her back. Her dress was almost the color of her eyes; it clung to her breasts and narrow waist before flaring into a short, full skirt that stopped above her knees and made the most of her long legs.

Had he gone completely around the bend? Had he conjured up this image? For a minute he thought that maybe he had...but then she gave him a tremulous smile and he knew that she was real, this was Joanna, this was his beautiful, once-upon-a-time wife standing before him like a remembered vision come to life.

"I know I should have phoned and told you I was coming but..."

Say something, he told himself fiercely. But what?

"I hope you're not angry. It's just that I looked in my appointment book and saw that I was supposed to be here tonight and I thought, well, perhaps it's time I began to pick up the pieces of my life, and so—and so..."

Damn! Joanna bit down on her bottom lip. She'd spent the ride to the gallery promising herself she wouldn't lose her nerve the minute she came face-to-face with David, but after one shocked look from his green eyes, she was stammering.

Stop that, she told herself sternly, and despite the way her heart was hammering in her throat, she forced a smile to her lips.

"And so," she said, "here I am. You don't mind, do you?"

Mind? *Mind*? David stared at his wife. He wanted to grab her by the shoulders, spin her around and point her toward the door. He wanted to pull her into his arms and kiss her until night faded into dawn. He wanted to corner Corbett and every other arrogant, insufferable M.D. in New York who pretended to know what in hell was happening inside Joanna's head but who obviously didn't know a damned thing more than he did...

"No," he said, very calmly, "I don't mind, Joanna, but are you sure you're up to this?"

Up to having her husband look at her as if he were hoping she'd vanish in a puff of smoke? To seeing the stunned expressions on people's faces as she'd entered the room? To have people say, "Hello, it's wonderful you're up and around, Joanna" as she went by and not to have the foggiest notion who they were?

Joanna tried her best not to laugh. Or to cry. Or to do an impossible imitation of both at the same time.

"I'm absolutely up to it," she said with a hundred times more assurance than she felt. "In fact, I think a night out will do me—"

"Joanna? Joanna, is it really you?"

The voice came from a woman who'd stepped out from behind David. She was tall and slender, with pale blond hair cut in a feathered cap that emphasized the perfect structure of her face. Her eyes were pale blue, her lashes dark as soot; her mouth was full and pink. She wore a white silk suit, severely cut yet designed so that it was clear it depended for the beauty of its line not on cut or fabric but on the flawless body beneath.

Joanna smiled hesitantly. She looked at David for help but his face was like stone.

"I'm sorry," she said to the woman, "but I'm afraid I don't..."

"I'm Morgana."

Morgana. David's P.A. This—this Nordic goddess with the flawless face and the marvelous body was Morgana?

Joanna felt a flutter of panic deep in her stomach.

"Morgana," she said, and held out her hand, "how...how nice to see you again."

Morgana seemed to hesitate. Then she took the outstretched hand, leaned forward and pressed her cheek lightly to Joanna's.

"What a lovely surprise." She drew back, looked at David and smiled, and it struck Joanna that the smile seemed strained. "You never said Joanna would be joining us, David."

"No." His eyes held Joanna's. "But then, it's a surprise to me, too."

Joanna flushed and disentangled her fingers from Morgana's. "I only decided to come at the last minute," she lied. "I was just telling David, I...I suppose I should have let him know..."

"Ah-ha! Here we are. Tico, I do believe that this is the lovely lady we have to thank for tonight's marvelous party!"

Joanna swung around and blinked in astonishment. A man and a chimpanzee, dressed in identical tuxedos and trailed by a crowd of onlookers, had appeared at her side.

"You are Mrs. Adams," the man said, "are you not?"

"Why...why yes, I—"

"Joanna," someone called, "yoo-hoo, over here!"

Joanna looked past the man in the tux. A woman with diamonds blazing at her ears and throat was waving at her.

"I'm sorry," Joanna said, "I'm afraid I don't—"

"Tico insisted you weren't Mrs. Adams," the man in the tux said. Joanna turned toward him again and he shot her a blazing smile. "But I said, yes, of course you were, and I was right." He sighed dramatically. "Tico can be so stubborn."

"Jo? Over here. It's so great to see you again. You remember me, don't you?"

Joanna's gaze flew from face to face. "No," she said, "actually, I'm afraid that I—"

"Anyway, Tico was determined to meet you."

"Are you talking about, ah, about the chimp?" Joanna said, looking at the man in the tux again.

"We don't call him that. Not to his face, anyway. It tends to upset him, but then, you know how *artistes* are, they have such delicate..."

"Oh, Joanna," a voice squealed, "I didn't know they'd let you out. How lovely!"

"No one 'let me out'," Joanna said, staring at the blur of faces. "I mean, I'm not sick. Or crazy. I'm just—"

"...egos."

She swung back to the man with the chimp. "Egos?"

"Egos," he said, and nodded. "Delicate ones. All artists are like that, don't you agree?" He stepped closer and breathed into Joanna's face. She pulled back from the scent of... bananas? "Tico, particularly. It truly upsets him to be referred to as a primate."

"As a primate," Joanna repeated stupidly. She looked down at the chimp and it looked back at her.

"Exactly. Oh, do forgive me for not introducing myself. My name is Chico."

"Chico," Joanna repeated. A nervous giggle rose in her throat. "He's Tico? And you're...?"

"Mrs. Adams." A youngish man with his hair sprayed firmly into place shoved forward and stabbed a microphone into her face. "Tom Jeffers, WBQ-TV news," he said with a self-important smile. "Would you care to tell our viewers how you're feeling?"

"Well..." Joanna blinked as the hot lights of a video camera suddenly glared into her eyes. "Well, I'm feeling—"

"Is it true you lost your memory and that you were in a coma for two weeks?"

"No. I mean, yes, but—"

A lush, bleached blonde in a miniskirt jammed a tape recorder under her nose.

"Mona Washbourne, from the *Sun*. Mrs. Adams, what about the rumors that you'd broken all the bones in your body?"

"That's not true. I didn't—"

"How about the plastic surgery they had to do on your face. Any comment?"

"Actually, I—"

"Mrs. Adams." Chico and his tuxedo were all but bristling. "Tico is not accustomed to being kept waiting. If you wish to meet him, you'll have to—"

"All right," David said brusquely, "that's enough."

His arm, hard and warm and comforting, swept around Joanna's waist. She sagged against him, her knees weak.

"My wife has no comment."

"Of course she does," the blonde snapped. "Women are perfectly capable of speaking for themselves. Isn't that right, Mrs. Adams?"

Joanna shook her head in bewilderment. "Please," she whispered, "I don't...I can't..."

A flashbulb went off. Joanna cried out, turned and buried her face in David's chest.

"That's it," he said grimly, and he swung her into his arms. She made a strangled sound and wound her arms around his neck. Another flashbulb went off in her face. "Bastards,"

David snarled, and without any apologies he shouldered his way through the mob.

Joanna didn't lift her head until she felt the sudden coolness of the night air on her skin. Carefully, she looked up and peered behind her.

"Oh, God," she moaned.

The crowd had followed them with Chico and Tico, in their matching tuxedos, leading the parade.

"Mrs. Adams!" Chico's high-pitched voice trembled with indignation. "If you don't speak with Tico this instant, he's going to be dreadfully upset!"

"Give him the banana you were saving for yourself," David muttered. "How did you get here, Joanna? Did Hollister bring you?"

She nodded. "He said he'd wait around the corner."

"At least you did something right," he snapped.

A moment later, they were safely inside the Bentley, with the privacy partition up, racing through the darkened streets toward home. Joanna was still in David's arms, held firmly in his lap.

Her heart thumped. He was angry. He was furious! She could feel it in the rigidity of his body, in the way he held her, so hard and close that it was almost difficult to breathe.

"David?" She swallowed dryly. "David, I'm sorry."

In the shadowed darkness, she could just make out the steely glimmer of his eyes as he looked down at her.

"Really," she said unhappily, "I'm terribly, terribly sorry. I never dreamed...I mean, I never thought..."

"No," he growled, "hell, no. You never dreamed. You never thought. Not for one damned minute, not about anybody but yourself."

"That isn't true! I didn't mean to make a scene. It never occurred to me that—"

"What did you think would happen, once the sharks smelled blood in the water?"

"I'm trying to tell you, I never imagined they'd—"

"What in bloody hell was the point in my working my tail off to keep them away from you in the hospital?"

"David, if you'd just listen—"

"And what were you thinking, showing up looking like this?"

Joanna's cheeks flushed. "OK, I suppose I deserve that. I know you prefer me to dress more demurely. It's just that the other night...I thought you said...I realize now, I must have imagined it, but I thought you said you didn't like my hair in a chignon and the kind of dress I was wearing, and...and..."

"Dammit, Joanna, you should never have showed up tonight!"

A rush of angry tears rose in her eyes. She put her hands against David's chest and tried to push free.

"You've made that abundantly clear," she said, "and I promise you, I won't bother you and your little playmate again."

"Playmate? What playmate?"

"Morgana," she said stiffly, "that's what playmate. Damn you, David, if you don't let me go I'll...I'll..."

"What?" he said, and suddenly his voice was low and soft and almost unbearably sexy. "What will you do, Gypsy?"

She tried to tell him, but she couldn't think of an answer. It wouldn't have mattered if she had because his arms tightened around her, his mouth closed on hers, and suddenly he was kissing her as if the world might end at any second.

Joanna hesitated. Then, trembling with pleasure, she buried her fingers in her husband's thick, silky hair and kissed him back.

CHAPTER EIGHT

His mouth was hot, and so were his hands.

And she was burning, burning under his touch.

This is wrong, Joanna's brain shrieked, *it's wrong...*

How could it be wrong, when the searing flame of David's kiss felt so wonderful?

She whispered his name and he drew her even closer, until she was lying across his lap, her hair spilling over his arm, her hands clutching his shoulders desperately as his mouth sought and found the tenderness of hers.

"Open to me, Gypsy," he breathed and she did, parting her lips under the heat of his, moaning softly as he nipped her bottom lip, then stroked the sweet wound with the tip of his tongue.

He groaned and she felt his fingers at the nape of her neck, undoing her zipper, sliding it down until the bodice of her dress fell from her shoulders.

"No," she said, clutching at the silky fabric, "no, David, we can't..."

He cupped the back of her hand, his fingers tangling almost cruelly in her hair as he tilted her head back.

"The hell we can't."

"Hollister..."

"The partition's up. Hollister can't see or hear us." In the dark, his eyes gleamed with an almost predatory brilliance. He bent to her and kissed her until she was trembling in his arms. "This is our own little world, Gypsy. No one can see us. No one even knows we're here." He kissed her again. "And you are my wife."

His wife.

Joanna's breath caught. The simple words were as erotic as any a man had ever whispered to a woman.

And he was right. In the night, surrounded by the anonymity of the city, she felt as if they were alone in the universe.

She sighed with pleasure as he kissed her throat, and then the delicate flesh behind her ear.

"I never forgot the taste of you," he whispered thickly. His kisses were soft as rain, warm as sunlight against her skin. "Like honey. Like cream. Like..."

His lips closed over her silk-encased nipple and she cried out softly and her body arched toward him, a tautly strung bow of consummate sensation.

"Yes," he said, as she whispered his name and wound her arms tightly around his neck.

He groaned softly and shifted her, positioning her over him so that she was kneeling on the leather seat, her short, full skirt draping over his legs like the downturned petals of a flower.

His hand slid under the skirt, cupping her, feeling her wetness, teasing it until finally he hooked his fingers into the fragile crotch of her silk teddy and tore it aside.

Joanna gasped and jerked her head back.

"We're alone, Gypsy," David whispered against her mouth. "There's no one here but you and me. And I want you more than I've ever wanted a woman in my life."

He kissed her, hard, and she responded with an ardor that equaled his. It was what she wanted, too. No preliminaries. No sweet words. Just this, the blinding passion, the urgent need, the coupling that their flesh demanded.

That her heart desired.

Joanna's breath caught.

How could she have been so blind? She loved him. She had always loved him, this stranger who was her husband.

Her injury might have made her head forget him but her soul and her flesh remembered. He was a part of her, he always had been, and now her blood was throbbing his name with each beat of her heart.

"Gypsy?"

He was waiting, waiting for her to give him her answer. And she gave it, blindly, gladly, lifting her mouth to his for the sweet, possessive thrust of his tongue, clasping his face in her hands and dragging it down to hers.

He groaned softly, a primitive sound of triumph and need.

"Unzip me," he said, and she hurried to obey, her hands shaking with the force of her desire.

Her fingertips brushed over the straining fabric of his trousers. She felt the pulsing hardness of his erection.

"Joanna," he said urgently, and his hand moved, his fingers seeking, finding, caressing her secret, weeping flesh.

She was sobbing now, aching for him, empty without him; she had been empty for a long, long time.

"David," she whispered, and her fingers closed on the tab of his zipper...

The Bentley lurched. A horn blared, and the big car lurched again.

Joanna blinked. She pulled back in David's arms. "What was that?"

David cursed softly. "I don't know." His arms tightened around her. "And I don't care."

"No. No, wait..." She lay her palms against his chest. "David, stop."

"Come back here!" His voice was rough with desire; he cupped her face in one hand and kissed her. "I'm crazy with the need to be inside you, Gypsy. I want to feel your heat around me, to hear you cry out my name as you come."

Joanna felt as if she were awakening from a deep, drugged sleep. The Bentley had slowed to a crawl. She turned her head to the window, peered out the dark glass. They were moving through a construction zone; yellow caution lights blinked in the road.

She felt her face grow hot. No one could see in, she knew that. The tinted glass made it impossible. But that didn't keep her from suddenly feeling as if she and David were on display.

His hand stroked over her naked shoulders.

"David," she said, "please..."

His mouth burned at her breast.

"No. Stop it." She began to struggle. "David," she said sharply, "stop!"

He lifted his head. His eyes were dark, almost unfocused; his breathing was ragged. A *frisson* of fear tiptoed down her spine. All at once, her husband seemed more a stranger than ever.

"David." She shoved harder against his chest and shoulders. "Let me go, please."

"Don't be a fool! You know you want this— need this—as badly as I do. Come back here and—"

"No!" She tried to twist away from him but he wouldn't let her. "You don't know the first thing about what I want."

"I know exactly what you want. And you damned well almost got it."

Her hand cracked against his jaw. They stared at each other and then David let go of her and she scrambled off his lap. He turned away and lay his forehead against the cool window glass.

What in hell was the matter with him?

Here he was, a grown man, sitting in the back seat of a limousine with his wife straddling his lap, the bodice of her dress down at her waist and her skirt hiked up to her hips, and if she hadn't stopped him he'd have taken her here, on the cold leather seat, with no more finesse than a boy out on his first date.

And he was angry at Joanna?

God, what a pathetic excuse for a man he was.

She hadn't done a thing. Not one damned thing. She'd simply appeared from out of the blue, looking the way he'd never stopped remembering her, sounding the way she'd once sounded, and against all the rules of logic and reason he'd gone crazy, first with rage and then with lust and all because the terrible truth was that he'd never stopped loving the woman he'd thought he'd married.

For all he knew he might never, ever stop loving her.

What a joke.

He'd called Joanna a fool but if she was a fool, what did you call a man who was in love with a woman who'd never really existed?

Whoever this Joanna was, once her memory returned, she'd vanish as quickly as she had the first time. And then they'd be right back where they'd been before the accident, two people with nothing in common but his status and their impending divorce.

It would have made things easier if she understood. But what could he tell her? That the loss of her memory had made her a better person? That while she prayed for the return of her memory, he dreaded it?

David drew a shuddering breath. Making love to Joanna would have been like making love to a dream.

It was a good thing she'd stopped him. A damned good thing.

It had probably taken all her courage to show up at the party and he'd repaid that courage by being a selfish bastard.

"Joanna?" He reached out his hand and she slapped it away. "Jo, listen, I know how you feel—"

She turned toward him. He'd expected to see anguish in her eyes, that her mouth—that soft, sweet mouth—would be trembling, but he was wrong.

What he saw wasn't anguish but rage.

"You're truly remarkable," she said bitterly. "First you know what I want, now you know what I feel."

"Jo, I'm trying to apologize. I should never have . . ."

The limousine pulled to the curb. The engine shut off and the silence of the night settled around them. Joanna glared at him in the darkness.

"If you ever touch me again," she said, "so help me, David, I'll—I'll . . ."

Her voice broke. The door swung open. He caught a quick glimpse of Hollister's startled face as Joanna shoved past him, ran up the steps and disappeared inside the house.

*   *   *

At five in the morning, David was still sitting in the darkened living room.

He'd been there for hours, ever since they'd come in. His jacket was off, his tie was gone and the top few buttons of his shirt were undone. His shoes lay beside his chair. There was an open decanter of cognac on the table beside him and a glass in his hand. He wasn't drunk though, God knew, he'd done his best.

Footsteps sounded softly on the stairs.

He rose to his feet and ran his hand through his hair. Then he walked quietly to the door and into the pool of pale yellow light cast by the lamp in the foyer.

"Joanna?" he said softly.

She paused, midway down the stairs. She was wearing a long yellow robe, her hair was caught back in a loose braid, and if she was surprised to see him, it didn't show on her face.

"Hello, David," she said tonelessly.

"Are you all right?"

"I'm fine."

She wasn't. Shadows lay like bruises below her eyes.

"I was just . . ." He raised his cognac snifter. "Would you like some?"

"No. No, thank you." She lifted both hands to her face and lightly touched her fingertips to her temples. "Actually, I came down for some aspirin. I couldn't seem to find any in my bathroom.''

''I'll get you some.''

''I'll get it myself, thank you.''

Her voice was cool. Don't argue with me, it said, and he decided it might be best to take the hint.

He sighed, went back into the living room and sat down, nursing his cognac, anticipating her return, trying to figure out what to say, hell, trying to figure out what he could possibly do, to convince her he was sorry.

The seconds passed, and the minutes, and finally he put down his glass, stood up and walked back out to the hallway.

''Joanna?''

There was a light at the end of the hall. He followed it, to the kitchen. Joanna was standing in front of the open refrigerator, in profile to him. Her body was outlined in graceful brush strokes of light: the lush curve of her breast, the gentle fullness of her bottom, the long length of her legs.

His throat went dry. His hands fisted at his sides as he fought against the almost over-whelming urge to go to her, to take her in his arms and hold her close and say, Don't worry, love, everything's going to be fine.

He cleared his throat.

"Did you find the aspirin?"

She nodded and shut the refrigerator door.

"Yes, thank you. I was just making myself some cocoa."

"Cocoa?" he said, and frowned.

She went to the stove. There was a pot on one of the burners. She took a wooden spoon from a drawer and stirred its contents.

"Yes. Would you like some?"

He shut his eyes against a sudden memory, Joanna at the stove in Connecticut, laughing as she stirred a saucepan of hot milk.

Of course it's cocoa, David. What else would anybody drink when there's a foot of snow outside?

"David?"

He swallowed, looked at her, shook his head.

"Thanks, but I don't think it would go so well with cognac."

She smiled faintly. Then she shut off the stove, took a white porcelain mug from the cabinet and filled it with steaming cocoa.

"Well," she said, "good night."

"Wait." He stepped forward, into the center of the room. "Don't go, not just yet."

"I'm tired," she said in a flat voice. "And it's late. And I don't see any point in—"

"I'm sorry."

Her head came up and their eyes met. Joanna's throat constricted. He looked exhausted and unhappy, and she imagined herself going to him, taking him in her arms and offering him comfort. But there was no reason for her to comfort him, dammit, there was no reason at all!

It was he who'd hurt her, who'd been hurting her, from the minute she'd awakened in the hospital.

Tears stung in her eyes. She blinked hard and forced a smile to her lips.

"Apology accepted," she said. "We've both been under a lot of pressure. Now, if you'll excuse me——"

"Joanna."

His hands closed on her shoulders as she walked past him.

She stood absolutely still, her back to him.

She'd been awake all the night, staring at the ceiling and telling herself that what she felt for her husband—what she'd thought she'd felt—had been a lie, that in her confusion and the loneliness that came of her loss of memory, she'd fooled herself into thinking he meant something to her.

And she'd believed it.

Then, why was his touch making her tremble? Why was she fighting the urge to turn and go into his arms?

Stop being a fool, she told herself angrily, and she slipped out from beneath his hands and swung toward him.

"What do you want now, David? I've already accepted your apology." She took a ragged breath. "In a way, I guess some of what happened was my fault."

"No. You didn't—"

"But I did. I showed up uninvited, as you so clearly pointed out. And . . . and I suppose I should have worn something more in keeping with . . . with my status as your wife."

"Dammit, Jo—"

"As for what happened in the limousine . . ." Her cheeks colored but her gaze was unwavering. "I'm not a child, David. I'm as responsible for it as you. I shouldn't have let you—I shouldn't have . . ."

"Will you listen to me?"

"Why? We have nothing to discuss . . . unless you want to talk about a separation."

He recoiled, as if she'd hit him again. She couldn't blame him. What she'd said had shocked her, too. She hadn't expected to say anything about a separation, even though that was all she'd thought about for the last few hours.

"What in hell are you talking about?"

"It would be best," she said quietly. "You know we can't go on the way we are."

"You're talking nonsense!"

"Just give me a couple of days to—to find a place to live and—"

His hands clamped down on her shoulders.

"Are you crazy? Where in hell would you go?"

"I don't know." Her chin lifted. "I'll find a place. All I need is a little time."

"You're ill, don't you understand that?"

"I'm not ill. I just—"

"Yeah, I know. You just can't remember." David's eyes darkened. "Forget it, Joanna. It's out of the question."

"What do you mean, it's out of the question?" She wrenched free of his grasp. "I don't need your permission to leave. I'm not a child."

"You're behaving like one."

They glared at each other. Then Joanna slammed the mug of cocoa down on the table, turned on her heel and marched out of the room.

"Joanna?" David stalked after her. She was halfway up the stairs. "Where in hell do you think you're going?"

"Stop using that tone of voice with me." She spun toward him, her eyes flashing with anger. "I'm going to my room. Or do I need your approval first?"

"Just get this through your head," he snapped. "There won't be any separation."

"Give me one good reason why not!"

"Because I say so."

Joanna's mouth trembled. "That's great. If you can't win a fight, resort to typical male tyranny..." Her words tumbled to a halt and a puzzled look came over her face. "Typical male tyranny," she whispered. Her gaze flew to his. "David? Haven't I... haven't I said that before?"

He came slowly up the stairs until he was standing a step below her. "Yes," he said softly, "you have."

"I thought so." She hesitated. "For a minute, I almost remembered... I mean, I had one of those flashes... Did we... when I said that to you, had we been quarreling over the same thing? About—about me leaving you?"

A smile curved across his mouth. He reached out his hand and stroked his forefinger along the curve of her jaw.

"We hadn't been quarreling at all," he said in a quiet voice. "We'd been horsing around beside the pond——"

"In Connecticut?"

He nodded. "I'd been threatening to toss you in and you said I wouldn't dare——"

"And—and you made a feint at me and I laughed and stepped aside and you fell into the water."

He was almost afraid to breathe. "You remember that?"

Joanna's eyes clouded with tears. "Only that," she whispered, "nothing else. It's—it's as if I suddenly saw a couple of quick frames from a movie."

He cupped her cheek with his hand. "I came up sputtering and you were standing there laughing so hard you were crying. I went after you, and when I caught you and carried you down to the pond to give you the same treatment, you said I was a bully and that I was resorting to——"

"Typical male tyranny?"

"Uh-huh." His voice grew husky. "And I retaliated."

Joanna stared at him. There was something in the way he was looking at her that sent a lick of flame through her blood.

"How?"

His smile was slow and sexy.

"I didn't dump you into the pond. I carried you to the meadow instead."

"A...a green meadow," Joanna said. "Filled with flowers."

"...and I undressed you, and I made love to you there, with the sweet scent of the flowers all around us and the sun hot on our skin, until you were sobbing in my arms." He cupped her face with his hands. "Do you remember that, Gypsy?"

She shook her head. "No," she whispered, "but I wish... I wish I did..."

Silence settled around them. Then David drew a labored breath.

"Go to your room," he said quietly.

Joanna swallowed hard. "That's where I was going, before you—"

"Get dressed, and pack whatever you'll need for the weekend."

Her brow furrowed. "What for?"

"On second thought, don't bother." He smiled tightly. "It seems to me you left the skin you shed in the bedroom closet in Connecticut."

"What on earth are you talking about?"

"We're going away for the weekend. Trust me," he said brusquely, when she opened her mouth to protest, "it's a very civilized thing to do, in our circle."

"I don't care if it's the height of fashion! I'm not going anywhere with you. I absolutely refuse."

"Even if going with me means you might begin to remember?"

She stared at him, her eyes wide. "Do you really think I will?"

Did he? he thought. And if she did...heaven help him, was that what he really wanted?

"David?"

"I don't know," he admitted.

"But you think I might...?"

"Get going." His tone was brisk and no-nonsense as he clasped her elbow and hurried her to her room. "I'll give you ten minutes and not a second more."

"David?"

He sighed, stopped in his tracks halfway down the hall, and turned toward her.

"What now?"

Joanna moistened her lips. "Why do you call me that?"

"Why do I call you what?" he said impatiently.

"Gypsy."

He stared at her and the moment seemed to last forever. Then, slowly, he walked back to where she stood, put his hand under her chin and gently lifted her face to his.

"Maybe I'll tell you while we're away."

He bent his head to her. She knew he was going to kiss her, knew that she should turn her face away...

His lips brushed softly over hers in the lightest, sweetest of caresses.

The gentleness of the kiss was the last thing she'd expected. Her lashes drooped to her cheeks. She sighed and swayed toward him. They stood that way for a long moment, linked by the kiss, and then David drew back. Joanna opened her eyes and saw a look on his face she had not seen before.

"David?" she said unsteadily.

He smiled, lifted his hand and stroked her hair.

"Go on," he said. "See if you can't find some old clothes and comfortable shoes buried in that closet of yours and then meet me downstairs in ten minutes."

Joanna laughed. It was silly, but she felt giddy and girlish and free.

"Make it fifteen," she said.

Impetuously, she leaned forward and gave him a quick kiss. Then she flew into her room and shut the door behind her.

CHAPTER NINE

THERE'D been a time David would have said he could have made the drive to Fenton Mills blindfolded.

He hadn't needed to check the exit signs to find the one that led off the highway, nor the turnoffs after that onto roads that grew narrower and rougher as they wound deeper into the countryside.

It surprised him a little to find all that was still true.

Even after all this time, the Jag seemed to know the way home.

Except that it wasn't exactly "home" and hadn't been for almost three years.

A young couple who farmed some land up the road from the house were happy to augment their income by being occasional caretakers. They kept an eye on things, plowed the long driveway when it snowed and mowed the grass when summer came, even though David never bothered coming up here anymore.

Sometimes, he'd wondered why he bothered hanging on to the property at all.

His accountant had asked him that just a few months before.

"You get no financial benefit from ownership," Carl had said, "and you just told me you never use the house. Why not get rid of it?"

David's reply had dealt with market conditions, real estate appreciation and half a dozen other things, all of which had made Carl throw up his hands in surrender.

"I should have known better than to offer financial advice to David Adams," he'd said, and both men had laughed and gone on to other topics.

Remembering that now made David grimace.

He'd done such a good snow job on Carl that he'd damned near convinced himself that he was holding on to the Connecticut property for the most logical of reasons.

But it wasn't true.

He'd hung on to the house for one painfully simple, incredibly stupid reason.

It reminded him of a life he'd once dreamed of living with a woman he'd thought he'd loved.

With Joanna.

He'd bought the place years ago, with his first chunk of real money. He had no idea why. This was not the fashionably gentrified part of Connecticut, though the area was handsome.

As for the house...it was more than two hundred years old, and tired. Even the real estate agent had seemed shocked that someone would be interested in such a place.

But David, taking the long, leisurely way home from a skiing weekend, had spotted the For Sale sign and known instantly that this house was meant for him. And so he'd written a check, signed the necessary papers, and just that easily, the house had become his.

He'd driven up weekends, with a sleeping bag in the back of his car, and camped out in the dilapidated living room, sharing it from time to time with a couple of field mice, a bat and on one particularly eventful occasion, a long black snake that had turned out to be harmless.

Carpenters came, looked at the floors and the ceiling, stroked their chins and told him there was a lot of work to be done. Painters came, too, and glaziers, and men with specialties he'd never even heard of.

But the more time David spent in the old house, the more he began to wonder what it would be like to work on it himself. He found himself buying books on woodworking and poring over them nights in the study of the Manhattan town house he'd bought for its investment value and its location and never once thought of as home.

He started slowly, working first on the simpler jobs, asking for help when he needed it. Had he undertaken such a restoration in the city, people would have thought him crazy but here, in these quiet hills, no one paid much attention. New Englanders had a long tradition of thrift and hard work; that a man who could afford to let others do the job for him would prefer to do it himself wasn't strange at all.

He found an unexpected pleasure in working with his hands. There was a quiet satisfaction in beginning a job and seeing it through. He learned to plane wood and join floor boards, and the day he broke through a false wall and uncovered a brick fireplace large enough to roast an ox ranked right up there with the day years before when he'd opened the *Wall Street Journal* and realized he'd just made his first million on the stock exchange.

Local people, the ones who delivered the oak boards for the floors or the maple he'd needed to build the kitchen worktable, looked at the house as it evolved under his hands and whistled in admiration. The editor of the county newspaper got wind of what he was doing and politely phoned, asking to do what she called a "pictorial essay."

David just as politely turned her down. Dumped on a church doorstep as a baby, he'd grown up the product of an efficient, bloodless state system of foster child care.

This house, that he was restoring with his own hands, was his first real home. He didn't want to share it with anyone.

Until he met Joanna.

He brought her to the house for a weekend after their second date. The old plumbing chose just then to give out and he ended up lying on his back, his head buried under the kitchen sink. Joanna got down on the floor with him, handing him tools and holding things in place and getting every bit as dirty as he got.

"You don't have to do this stuff, Gypsy," David kept saying, and she laughed and said she was having the time of her life.

By the end of that weekend, he'd known he wanted Joanna not just in his bed but in his heart and in his life, forever. Days later, they were married.

At first, he was wild with happiness. The usual long hours he spent at his office became less important than being with his wife.

Morgana came as close to panic as he'd ever seen her.

"I don't know what to tell people when they phone, David," she said. "And there are conferences, and details that need your attention ..."

He pondered the problem, then flew to the coast for three intensive days with the latest Silicone Valley *wunderkind*. By the time he returned home, the problem was solved.

After a squad of electricians spent a week rewiring the house, a battery of machines came to beeping, blinking life in the attic. Faxes, computers, modems, laser printers, even a high-tech setup that linked David to his New York office by video...

There was nothing he could not do from home that he had not once done in Manhattan, though he still flew down for meetings on Thursdays and Fridays, and always with his beautiful, beloved wife at his side. Sometimes the meetings ran late. Joanna never complained but David was grateful to Morgana, who kept her occupied the few times it happened.

And then, things began to change.

It started so slowly that he hardly noticed.

Joanna suggested they spend an extra day in the city. "I'd really love to see that new play," she said.

An invitation to the opera came in the mail. He started to toss it away but Joanna caught his hand, smiled, and said she'd never been to the opera in her life.

Before he knew it, they were spending five days a week in New York, then the entire week. Joanna met people, made friends, joined committees.

Connecticut, and the simple life they'd enjoyed there, got further and further away.

Morgana, who knew him as well as anyone except his wife, sensed his unhappiness and tried to help.

"You mustn't be so possessive," she told him gently. "A woman needs room to grow, especially one as young as Joanna."

So he backed off, gave her room. But it didn't help. The gap between them became a chasm. Joanna gave up pretending she liked the country at all. She begged off lazy weekend drives and quiet evenings by the fire. She hinted, then straight out told him she preferred the luxury of their Manhattan town house, and before David knew what was happening, the town house was crammed with ugly furniture and his life was governed by the entries in his wife's calendar.

The girl he'd fallen in love with had changed into a woman he didn't like.

Joanna traded denim and flannel for cashmere and silk. She scorned hamburgers grilled over an open fire in favor of *filet mignon* served on bone china in chic restaurants.

And she'd made it clear she preferred her morning coffee brought to her bedside by a properly garbed servant, not by a husband wearing a towel around his middle, especially if that husband was liable to want to sweeten the coffee with kisses instead of sugar.

David's hands tightened on the steering wheel of the Jaguar. That had been the most painful realization of all, that his passionate bride had turned into a woman who lay cold in his arms, suffering his kisses and caresses with all the stoicism of a Victorian martyr.

Had she worn a mask all along, just to win him? Or had his status and his money changed her into a different person?

After a while, he'd stopped touching her. Or wanting her. He'd made a mistake, and he'd fix it.

Divorce seemed the only solution...

Until last night, when his kisses had rekindled the fire they'd once known and she'd burned like a flame in his arms.

Was that why he'd suddenly decided on coming here this weekend? Not in hopes of jarring her memory, as he'd claimed, but because...

No. Hell, no. He wasn't going to make love to Joanna, not this weekend or any other. He'd brought her to Connecticut because she'd had another of those all-too-swift flashes of memory, and they'd all been connected to this house.

The sooner she remembered, the better. The sooner he could give up his sham of a marriage and get on with his life—

"We'll be there soon, won't we?"

Joanna's voice was soft and hesitant. David looked at her. She was staring straight ahead. The sun was shining on her hair, making it gleam with iridescence.

"Just another few miles," he said. "Why? Do things seem familiar?"

She shook her head. "No. I just had the feeling that we were coming close... What a pretty road this is."

"Yes, it is."

"I like the stone walls we keep passing. Are they very old?"

"Most of them date back to Colonial times. Farmers built them with the stones they cleared from the land as they plowed."

"So many stones... It must have been hard land to cultivate."

"They still say that stone's the only crop that grows well in New England."

She smiled. "I can believe it."

I can't, David thought. We're talking like two characters in a travelog.

"What kind of house is it?"

So much for travelogs. That was the same question she'd asked the first time he'd brought her here, and in that same soft, eager voice. He remembered how he'd smiled and reached for her hand.

"A house I hope you'll love as much as I do," he'd said.

This time, he knew enough not to smile or to touch her, and the only thing he hoped was that this weekend would end her amnesia and his charade.

"It's an old house," he said, and launched into the safety of the travelog script again. "The main section was built in the 1760's by a fairly prosperous farmer named Uriah Scott. His son, Joseph, added another wing when he inherited the house in the 1790's and each succeeding generation of Scotts added on and modernized the place."

"The house stayed in the Scott family, then?" Joanna sighed. "How nice. All those generations, sharing the same dreams...that must be wonderful."

David looked sharply at his wife. She had said that the first time, too, and just as wistfully. The remark had seemed poignant then, coming from a girl who'd been raised by a widowed father who'd cared more for his whiskey than he had for her; it had made him want to give her all the love she'd ever missed...

What a damned fool he'd been!

"Don't romanticize the story, Joanna," he said with a hollow smile. He glanced into his mirror, then made a turn onto the winding dirt road that led to the house. "Old houses are a pain in the ass. The floors sag, the heating systems never work right no matter what you do to them, there are spiders in the attic and mice in the cellar—"

"Is that it?"

He looked at the white clapboard house with the black shutters, standing on the gentle rise at the top of the hill. It was a small house, compared to the newer ones they'd passed along the way; it looked lonely and a bit weary against the pale Spring sky. The winter had been harsher than usual; the trim would need to be painted as soon as it got a bit warmer and he could see that the winter storms had worked a couple of the slate roof tiles loose.

A bitter taste rose in his mouth.

What had he ever thought he'd seen in this place to have made it magical?

"Yes," he said, "that's it. I'm sorry if you expected something more but—"

"Something more? Oh, David, what more could there be? It's beautiful!"

What in hell was this, a game of *déjà vu*? That was another thing she'd said the first time they'd come here. Later on, he'd realized that it had all been said to please him.

He prided himself on being a man you could only fool once. He swung toward her, a curt retort on his lips, but it died, unspoken, when he saw the enraptured expression on her face.

"Do you really like it?" he heard himself say.

Joanna nodded. "Oh, yes," she whispered, "I do. It's perfect."

And familiar.

She didn't say that, though she thought it. It was far too soon to know if this weekend would jog her memory and there was no point in getting David's hopes up, nor even her own. And she sensed that he was having second thoughts about having brought her here. She was having second thoughts, herself. If she didn't begin to remember after this weekend the disappointment would be almost too much to bear.

"Jo?"

She blinked and looked up. David had parked the car and gotten out. Now, he was standing in the open door, holding out his hand.

"Shall we go inside?"

She looked into his eyes. They were cool and guarded. She had the feeling that he was hoping she'd say no and ask him to turn around and go back to the city. But she'd come too far to lose her courage now.

"Yes," she said quickly, "yes, please, let's go inside."

David wasn't sure what he expected once Joanna stepped inside the door.

Would she clap her hand to her forehead and say, "I remember"? Or would she take one look at the small rooms and the old-fashioned amenities and say that she didn't remember and now could they please go home?

She did neither.

Instead, just as she had all those years ago, she almost danced through the rooms, exclaiming with delight over the wide-planked floors and the windows with their original, hand-blown glass; she sighed over the banister he'd once spent a weekend sanding and varnishing to satin smoothness.

He'd made an early morning phone call to the couple who were his caretakers and he could see that they'd stopped by. The furniture was dusted, the windows opened. There was a pot of coffee waiting to be brewed on the stove and a basket of home-baked bread on the maple table he'd built. A jar of homemade strawberry jam stood alongside and there was a bowl of fresh eggs, butter and a small pitcher of thick cream in the refrigerator.

Joanna said it was all wonderful, especially the fireplaces and the hand pump on the back porch. But she added, with a happy laugh, that she was glad to see there was a modern gas range and real running water and a fully stocked freezer because she wasn't that much of a stickler for the good old days.

And suddenly David thought, but these *were* the good old days. This woman bent over the pump, inelegantly and incongruously attired in a pale gray cashmere sweater, trendy black nylon exercise pants and running shoes... "It's the only comfortable stuff I could find," she'd explained with a little laugh, when she'd reappeared that morning... this woman, with her hair hanging down her back and her face free of makeup, was everything he'd ever wanted, everything he'd thought he'd found when he'd found Joanna.

Dammit, what was wrong with him?

He muttered a short, sharp epithet and Joanna swung toward him.

"What's the matter, David?"

"Nothing."

"But you just said—"

"I, ah, I saw a mouse, that's all."

"A mouse? Where?"

"It ran out from under the sink. Don't worry about it. There are probably some traps in the barn out back. I'll set some out later."

"You don't have to do that. I'm not—"

"I'll show you upstairs," he said brusquely. "You didn't get much sleep last night, Joanna, and this trip has probably been tiring. I think it might be a good idea for you to take a nap."

"Oh, but..." But I'm not tired, she'd almost said.

But being tired had nothing to do with it. He wanted her out of the way for a while; she could hear it in his voice. They'd only just arrived and already he was sorry he'd brought her.

Joanna nodded. "Good idea," she said with a false smile. "You lead the way."

There were three closed doors upstairs. One opened onto a bathroom, one onto a steep flight of steps that led to the attic. The third gave way on a spacious bedroom with exposed beams and a fireplace, dominated by a massive canopied bed...

One bedroom? Only one?

Joanna stopped just inside the doorway. "Oh," she said. "I never thought..."

David understood. "It's not a problem," he said quickly. "There's another bedroom downstairs. I'll be perfectly comfortable there. You go on, Jo. Take a nap. When you get up, we'll go for a drive. I'll show you a little bit of New England. Who knows? Maybe something you see will jog your memory.''

''Sure,'' she said brightly, ''that'll be fun.''

She shut the door after him. Then she walked to the window, curled onto the wide sill, and stared out at the rolling hills dressed in the tender green of late Spring and wondered why in heaven's name she couldn't just bring herself to ask him, straight out, why they didn't share a bed or even a room.

And if, in fact, they ever had.

Joanna did nap, after a while, and when she awoke, she was amazed to see that there were long shadows striping the room.

She got up, padded across the narrow hall to the bathroom, washed her hands and her face. In the process, she caught a glimpse of herself in the mirror.

Ugh, what a mess! Her hair needed combing, and a touch of lipstick wouldn't hurt. And this silly outfit... There was a wall-length closet in the bedroom, and David had said something cryptic about her not needing to bring anything with her. Maybe there was something in the closet that would look and feel better than this.

She made a soft exclamation of surprise when she looked into the closet. It was filled with clothing, all things she must have bought and all very different from what hung in her closet back in New York. There were jeans and corduroy pants, worn soft and fine with age and washing. Cotton shirts, and sweaters. Sneakers and walking shoes, hiking boots and a pair of rubber things that were as ungraceful as anything she'd ever seen but would surely keep your feet dry and warm in snow.

And there were David's clothes, too. Jeans, as worn as hers. Boots and shoes, sweaters and flannel shirts...

Joanna's throat constricted. They had shared this room, then.

This room. And this bed...

"Jo? Are you awake?"

She spun toward the door, and toward his voice just beyond it. "Yes," she called, and cleared her throat, "yes, David, I am. Just give me a minute and I'll be down."

"Take your time."

Her fingers flew as she pulled off her clothes. She put on jeans, a pale pink cotton shirt and a pair of gently beat-up leather hiking boots that felt like old friends as soon as she got them on. Then she tied a navy blue pullover sweater around her shoulders and brushed her hair back from her face. She found a tube of pale pink lipstick in a tray on the maple dresser, put some on her mouth, and went downstairs.

"Hi," she said brightly, as she came into the living room.

David turned around. "Hi, yourself." His smile tilted as he looked at her. "Well," he said, "I see you found your clothes."

"Uh-huh." She caught her lip between her teeth. "David? What did you mean about me shedding my skin in Connecticut?"

His face closed. "It was a stupid thing to have said."

"But what did you mean?"

"Only that I knew you had a closet filled with stuff to wear."

"Yes, but—"

"What do you feel like having for dinner?"

"Dinner? I don't know. I haven't even thought about—"

"There's a place half an hour or so away that's supposed to have excellent French cuisine."

She laughed. "French cuisine? Here?"

David smiled. "We're not exactly on the moon, Jo."

"Oh, I know. I just meant... I know you're going to think I'm crazy..."

"What?"

"No. Never mind. French is fine." She smiled and gave a delicate shudder. "Just so long as they don't serve—what was that stuff? Goat cheese?"

He laughed, leaned back against the wall, and tucked his hands into the rear pockets of his jeans.

"Goat cheese will be the least of your worries," he said. "Go on, tell me what you were going to say."

She took a deep breath and somehow, even before she spoke, he knew what was going to come out of her mouth.

"You'll laugh, I know, but when I looked in the freezer before... David, what I'd really love for dinner is a hamburger."

It was a mistake.

The whole damned thing was a mistake, starting with the minute they'd left Manhattan straight through to now, sitting here on the rug beside the fireplace in the living room with his wife, his beautiful wife, watching her attack an oversize burger with total pleasure while smoky music poured like soft rain from the radio.

What in hell was he doing? Why was he pretending to listen to what she was saying when he couldn't hear a word because he was too busy thinking how the light of the fire danced on her lovely face?

He forced himself to concentrate. She was telling him a story about one of the woman at Bright Meadows who'd been convinced she'd been born on the planet Pluto.

"...know I shouldn't laugh," she said, licking a drop of ketchup from her finger, "but, oh, David, if you could have heard how serious she was..."

He laughed, because he knew she expected it. But he wasn't laughing inside, where it counted, because he was too busy admitting that the best thing that could come out of this weekend was that Joanna would remember nothing.

Heaven help him, he was falling head over heels in love with her all over again.

"...asked me where I was born and when I said, well, I couldn't really say because... David? What's the matter?"

David rose to his feet.

"Listen, Joanna..."

Listen, Joanna, we're leaving. That was what he'd intended to say. We're gonna get out of here while the getting's good.

But that wasn't what he said at all.

"Jo," he said, and held out his hand, "will you dance with me?"

Her eyes met his. Color, soft as the pink of a June sunrise, swept into her cheeks. She smiled tremulously, put her hand in his and got gracefully to her feet.

He led her to the center of the room and put his arms around her. There was no pretense, no attempt to pretend that dancing was really what this was all about. Instead, he drew her close against his hard body, his hands linked at the base of her spine. She stiffened and he thought she was going to resist. But then she gave a soft, sweet sigh, looped her arms around his neck and let herself melt into the music and his embrace.

It was wonderful, holding her like this. Feeling the sweet softness of her breasts against his chest, the warmth of her thighs against his. His hand dropped from the small of her back and curved over her bottom. He lifted her against his growing hardness so that she could know what was happening to him.

Joanna made a little sound as she felt him pulse against her. The knowledge that he wanted her was like a song drumming in her blood. He'd wanted her last night, too, but not like this. What had happened in the car had been about lust but this...

This was about love.

She was sure of it, as sure as she could ever be about anything. She loved David, she knew that with all her heart. And he loved her. She could feel it in his every caress.

She drew back in his arms and looked deep into her husband's eyes.

"David?" she whispered.

"Gypsy," he said softly, "my Gypsy," and then his mouth was on hers and his hands were on her breasts and he was drawing her down to the rug in front of the fireplace and into a drowning whirlpool of passion.

CHAPTER TEN

THE wind sighing through the trees and the rain pattering gently against the roof woke David from sleep.

He lay unmoving, struggling to get his bearings in a darkness broken only by the flickering light of the fire on the hearth. Then he felt the sweet warmth of Joanna's body curled into his, smelled the fragrance of her hair spilled across his shoulder, and joy filled his heart.

His wife lay in the curve of his arm, snuggled tightly against him. Her head was nestled on his biceps, her hand lay open and relaxed on his chest. Her leg was a welcome weight thrown over his.

It was the way they'd always fallen asleep after they'd made love, the way it had been in those days so long gone by, days he'd never dreamed of recapturing.

But they had.

Was it a miracle? Or was it some cruel trick of fate? Would his wife stay as she was, even after she recovered her memory...or would she go back to being the cool, acquisitive stranger he'd been about to divorce?

There were so many questions, but there were no answers.

David eased onto his side, slid his other arm around Joanna and drew her close. The last, faint light of the dying fire played across her face, highlighting the elegant bones. She was so beautiful, and never more so than after they'd made love, and he knew that the questions didn't matter, not tonight.

All that mattered was this.

He buried his face in her hair, nuzzling it back from her shoulder, and pressed his mouth gently to the curving flesh. Still asleep, she sighed and snuggled closer.

The scent of her rose to his nostrils, a blend of flowers and sunshine and the exciting muskiness of sex. He kissed her again, his lips moving up her throat and to her mouth.

"Mmm," she said, and stirred lazily in his arms.

His hand cupped her breast.

"David," she sighed, and linked her hands behind his neck.

He smiled against her mouth. "Hello, sweetheart."

"Was I asleep?"

"We both were." He bent his head and kissed her with a slow, lazy thoroughness. "It's late."

"Mmm."

"The fire's almost out, and it's pitch black outside."

"Mmm."

"We should go to bed."

Joanna's laugh was soft and wicked. "What do we need a bed for? I thought we managed just fine."

His hand slid down her body and slipped between her thighs. She made a small sound of pleasure as he cupped her warm flesh.

"Better than fine," he murmured. "But now I want to make love to my wife on soft pillows and under a down comforter."

"That sounds wonderful." Joanna's smile tilted. "David? We . . . we shared a bedroom, didn't we? Before my accident, I mean."

She felt him stiffen in her arms and she cursed herself for ruining this perfect night. But instead of rolling away from her, as she'd half expected, he sighed and lay back with her still in his arms.

"Yes," he said, after a long silence. They had shared a bedroom, they'd shared every-thing . . . a long time ago. But he couldn't tell her that, not without telling her all the rest, about the divorce, about how different she was now... "Yes," he said again, "we did."

Joanna rolled onto her stomach, propped her elbows on the rug and her chin in her hands and looked down into her husband's face.

"Even back in the city?"

"Yes, even there." He reached up his hand and gently stroked her tangled curls back from her face. "We used to share my bedroom until..."

"Until what? Why did we... why did we decide on separate rooms? And when? Have we been sleeping separately for a long time?"

He sighed. Trust this new Joanna to come up with some damned good questions. And trust him not to have any good answers.

The truth was that they'd never "decided" on separate rooms; it had just happened. He'd started spending occasional nights in his study, stretching out on the leather sofa after working late. The excuse he'd offered himself, and Joanna, was that he hadn't wanted to wake her by coming to bed after she was asleep.

And Joanna had said there was no reason for him to spend the night on a sofa when they had a perfectly usable extra bedroom available. She'd been thinking of converting it into something more to her tastes, she'd added with a brittle smile. Would that be all right?

Of course, he'd told her, and not long after that he'd come home and found Joanna's clothes gone from the closet in the master suite and what had been the guest room remade into something that looked like a bad layout from a trendy magazine...

"David?"

He looked at his wife. She was still waiting for an answer and he decided to give her the only one he could. An honest one, as far as it went.

"I can't really tell you, Jo." Gently, he clasped her shoulders and rolled her onto her back. "It just happened. I'm not even sure exactly when."

"I asked you once if we'd been unhappy," Joanna said, "and you gave me the same kind of answer. But we weren't happy, David, I know we weren't."

In the shadowy darkness, he could see the tears welling in her eyes. For one wild moment, he thought of telling her the truth. No, he'd say, hell, no, we weren't happy...

But they had been, once. And they could be again. The thought surged through him, pushing aside everything else.

"I mean," she said, her voice trembling, "if we were sleeping in separate beds, leading separate lives..."

David didn't hesitate. He crushed his mouth to hers, silencing her with a deeply passionate kiss.

"That's over," he said fiercely. "No more sleeping apart, Gypsy. And no more separate existences. You're going to be my wife again."

"Oh, yes, that's what I want. I..." She caught herself just in time. I love you, she'd almost said, I love you with all my heart.

But the idea of being the first to say the words frightened her. It was silly, she knew; there was nothing frightening about telling your husband you loved him—unless you couldn't recall him ever saying those three simple words to you.

"I want to be your wife," she whispered instead, and she smiled. "And I want to know why you call me Gypsy. You said you'd..." Joanna's breath caught. "David! What are you...?"

"I'm getting reacquainted with my wife," he murmured, his breath warm against her breasts and then against her belly. "Your skin is like silk, do you know that? Hot silk, especially here."

She cried out as he buried his face between her thighs and kissed her, again and again, until she was sobbing with the pleasure of it. And after she'd shattered against his mouth he rose over her and buried himself deep inside her, riding her with deep, powerful thrusts until she climbed that impossible mountain of sensation once again, then tumbled from its peak as he exploded within her.

There were tears on Joanna's cheeks when David at last withdrew from her. He tasted their salinity as he kissed her.

"Don't cry, sweetheart," he whispered.

"I'm not," she said, and cried even harder, "I'm just so happy."

He kissed her again as he gathered her into his arms.

"Joanna," he said, "I..."

He bit back the words just in time. Joanna, he'd almost said, I love you.

But how could he tell her that? It was too soon. He couldn't even let himself think it, not so long as he both knew and didn't know the woman he held in his arms.

"I'm glad," he said softly, and then he rose to his feet and carried her up the stairs to their bedroom, where he held her tightly in his arms all through the rest of the long night.

When he awoke again, it was morning.

The rain had stopped, the sun was shining, a warm breeze was blowing through the open window.

And the wonderful scent of fresh coffee drifted on the air.

David rose, dragged on a pair of jeans and a white T-shirt. He made a quick stop in the bathroom. The shower curtain was pulled back and there was a damp towel hanging over the rod.

Barefoot, thrusting his fingers into his hair to push it back from his forehead, he made his way down to the kitchen.

Joanna was turned away from him, standing in the open back door so that the morning sunlight fell around her like a golden halo. Her hair was still damp and fell over her shoulders in a wild tumble. She was barefoot and wearing a pair of incredibly baggy shorts that sagged to her knees and an old cotton shirt of his that still bore traces of the buttercup yellow paint they'd used to paint the pantry years before.

My wife, he thought, my beautiful wife.

His heart felt as if it were expanding within his chest. Back in his college days, during one of the all-night bull sessions that had been, in their way, as valuable as any class time, a guy who'd had one beer too many had said something about there being a moment in a man's life when everything that was important came together in a perfect blend.

David knew that this was that moment. No matter what the future held, there would never be an instant more right than this one, with Joanna standing before him, limned in golden sunlight, after a night spent in his arms.

"Good morning," he said, when he could trust his voice.

She spun toward him. He saw the swift race of changing emotions on her face, the joy at seeing him warring with the morning-after fluster of a woman new to a man's bed, and he smiled and held out his arms. She hesitated for a heartbeat, and then she flew into his embrace.

"Good morning," she whispered, tilting her face up to his. He accepted the invitation gladly and kissed her. She sighed and leaned back in his arms. "I didn't wake you, did I?"

He shook his head and put on a mock ferocious scowl. "No. And I want to talk to you about that."

Joanna's brows rose. "What do you mean?"

"I like it when you wake me." The scowl gave way to a sexy grin. "Very much, as a matter of fact. There I was, all ready to greet the day with a special pagan ritual—"

"A special pagan . . . ?"

"Uh-huh. And I had all the ingredients, too. The sun, the bed, my ever-ready male anatomy . . ."

"David!" Joanna blushed. "That's awful."

His arms tightened around her. "You didn't think so last night."

"Well, no. I mean, *that's* not terrible. I mean..." She giggled, then dissolved in laughter. "Sorry. I never thought about your 'ever-ready male anatomy.' I just thought about being desperate for coffee."

"I'm desperate, too." He lifted her face to his. "For a kiss."

Joanna sighed. "I thought you'd never ask."

Their kiss was long and sweet. When it ended, David kept his arm looped around Joanna's shoulders while he poured himself a cup of coffee.

"What do you want to do today?"

She smiled up at him. "You pick it."

"If it's left to me to choose," he said, bending his head to hers and giving her another kiss, "we'll go back to bed and spend the day there."

She blushed again, in a way he'd all but forgotten women could.

"That doesn't sound so terrible to me," she whispered.

David put down his cup, took Joanna's and put it beside his.

"I don't want to tire you out, Jo," he said softly. "I know, I know, you haven't been ill. But you've been under a lot of stress."

Joanna put her arms around his neck. "Making love with you could never tire me out. But I have to admit, I'd love to see more of the countryside. It's so beautiful here."

"Beautiful," he agreed solemnly, and kissed her again. When the kiss ended, he knew he had to do something or he'd end up carrying her back to bed and keeping her there until neither of them had the strength to move. So he took a deep breath, unlinked her hands from around his neck, and took a step back. "OK," he said briskly, "here's the deal. I'll shower, then we'll go get some breakfast."

"I can make breakfast. We've got those lovely eggs in the fridge, and that fresh butter and cream..."

"Lovely eggs, huh?" David grinned. "OK. Just give me ten minutes to shower... Come to think of it, that was another thing I'd planned."

"What?"

"Well, first the pagan ritual to greet the day, then a shower together." A wicked gleam lit his green eyes. "What the heck. I had to do without the pagan bit but there's no reason to ditch both ideas."

"David?" Joanna danced away as he reached for her. "David, no! I already took a shower. See? My hair is...David? David!" Laughing, she pounded on his shoulders as he caught her in his arms, tossed her over his shoulder, and headed for the stairs. "You're crazy. You're impossible. You're..."

But by then, they were already in the shower, clothes and all, and she shrieked as he turned on the water and it cascaded over them. And somehow, in the process of stripping off each other's soaked clothing, somehow, they ended up worshiping the sun and each other, after all.

"Tell me again," Joanna said, wiping a ribbon of sweat from her forehead with the back of her hand, "we really used to do this?"

David nodded. They were standing in the midst of what looked like an automotive graveyard.

"All the time," he said absently. "Hey, is that what I think it is?"

"Is what what you think it is?" Joanna followed after him as he wove his way through the rusting hulks of what had once been cars.

"It is," he said triumphantly. He plucked something from the nearest pile of rubble and held it out. "Ta-da!"

"Ta-da, what?" She poked a finger at the thing. It looked like a metal box with pipes attached. "What is that?"

"A heat exchanger. If you knew how long I've been looking for one..."

Joanna laughed. "Yeah, well, to each his own, I guess. This place is amazing. To think anybody would save all this junk..."

"It's not junk," David said firmly, "it's a collection of what may be the best used sports car parts in the northeast."

"Uh-huh."

"And this heat exchanger, woman, is the catch of the day."

"Will it fit the Jag?"

"Of course."

"Do you need it?"

David shot her a pitying look. "I don't. But you thin-blooded types do. Come on, give me your hand and we'll go pay the man for..." He turned toward her. "That's just what you used to ask me," he said softly.

"What?"

"Do you need it?" He lay his hand along the curve of her cheek. "We bought the Jaguar together. And we worked on it together. And we had a great time, but you used to tease me, you'd say that you didn't know buying the car meant we'd have to poke through—"

"—through every junkyard in the lower forty-eight," Joanna said, "with long-term plans for Hawaii and Alaska." Her eyes flew to his. "That's what I used to say, wasn't it?"

David nodded. "Yes."

"I can hear myself saying it." Her throat worked dryly. "David? What if . . . what if my memory comes back and—and spoils things?"

Her fear mirrored his, but he'd be damned if he'd admit it.

"Why does it have to?" he said, almost angrily.

"I don't . . . I don't know. I just thought—"

"Then don't think," he said, and kissed her.

They stopped for lunch at a tiny diner tucked away on a narrow dirt road.

"No menus," David said, waving away the typed pages the waitress offered. "We'll have the chili. And two bottles of—"

"—Pete's Wicked Ale," Joanna said, and smiled. She waited until the woman had gone to the kitchen before she leaned toward David.

"Do I like chili?" she whispered.

He grinned. "Does the woman like chili? I used to say you must have been born south of the border to love chili as much as you did."

"Is that why you call me Gypsy? Because you teased me about being born in Mexico?"

His grin faded. "Gypsies don't come from Mexico. You've got your continents mixed."

"I know. But every time I try to get you to tell me why you call me that name, you change the subject." She reached across the scarred tabletop and took hold of his hand. "So I figured I'd back into the topic."

"Cagey broad," David said, with a little laugh. He sighed and linked his fingers through hers. "There's no mystery, Jo. It just..." It hurts me to remember, he wanted to say, but he didn't. "It just happened, that's all."

"How?"

"Because that's how I thought of you." He looked at her and smiled. "As my wild, wonderful Gypsy."

"Was I wild?"

"Not in the usual sense. You just had a love for life that..."

"Ale," the waitress said, putting two frosted bottles in front of them. When she'd left, David leaned forward.

"You were nothing like the women I knew," he said softly. "You didn't given a damn for convention or for the rules."

"Me?" Joanna said, her voice rising in a disbelieving squeak as she thought of her conventionally furnished town house, her chauffeured car, her clothing, her life as it was mirrored in her appointment book.

"The first time I saw you, you were wearing hiking boots, wool socks, a long wool skirt and a lace blouse with big, puffy sleeves that narrowed at your wrists."

"Leg-o'-mutton," she said, frowning. "Where was I? At a costume party?"

He laughed. "You were sitting at the reception desk at Adams Investments."

Joanna's eyes rounded. "I was what?"

"Our regular receptionist had called in sick. She said she had the flu and she'd be out for the week. So Morgana phoned a temp agency and they sent you over."

"Morgana," Joanna said, frowning.

"Yeah." David chuckled. "She didn't want to hire you, she said you didn't fit our image."

He paused as the waitress served their chili.

"And I agreed with her," he continued, after they were alone again. "But we were desperate. There were six people in the waiting room, the telephones were ringing off the walls, and who else could we have come up with on such short notice?"

Joanna smiled. "It's so lovely to be hired because you're wanted," she said sweetly. "Thank you, David." She spooned some chili into her mouth and rolled her eyes in appreciation.

"Good?"

"Wonderful. So, go on. I looked like a refugee from a thrift shop but you hired me anyway, and—"

"And I offered to drive you home that night, because we worked late."

"I'll bet that didn't thrill Morgana."

He frowned. "You don't like her very much, do you?"

"Don't be silly," she said quickly. "How could I not like her when I hardly know her?"

David reached across the table and took Joanna's hand. "She was a good friend to you, Jo. After you and I married, you felt a little, well, lost, I guess. And Morgana did everything she could to help you settle in."

"Settle in?"

"Yeah." He cleared his throat. "It was all new to you. Living in Manhattan, entertaining..."

"You mean, I was the poor little match girl who married the handsome prince and went to live in his luxurious castle," she said softly.

"No. Hell, no." His fingers tightened on hers. "You weren't accustomed to..." *To money. To status. But, by God, she'd grown accustomed quickly enough...*

"I understand." Joanna sighed. "And I'm sure Morgana was terrific. I don't know why..." She sighed again and gave him a little smile. "Actually, I do know. It's because she's so gorgeous and she gets to spend so much time with you. For a while there, I even thought—I imagined..."

"Morgana is my right-hand man," David said, dragging his thoughts from where he wished they hadn't gone. "She's efficient, and very bright, and I trust her implicitly. But that's all she is and all she ever has been."

"I'm glad to hear it," Joanna said, and smiled. "Go on. Tell me what happened when you drove me home."

He felt some of the sudden tension ease from his muscles. He grinned, let go of her hand and picked up his spoon.

"What do you think happened?"

"What?"

"Nothing."

"Nothing?"

"Cross my heart. You were the soul of propriety, and so was I."

"Good." She laughed. "For a minute there, you had me thinking that—"

"I wanted you so badly that I ached."

Color swept into her face. "Right away?"

"Oh, yeah." He spooned up some chili. "The minute I saw you. But I did the right thing," he said, deadpan. "I waited until our second date."

"Our second..." Joanna's color deepened. "Tell me you're joking!"

"We made love," he said, smiling into her eyes, "and it was incredible."

"Incredible," she whispered, as fascinated as she was shocked.

"Uh-huh. And a few days after that, we got married."

Joanna's spoon clattered against the tabletop.

"Got married? So fast? After knowing each other, what, two weeks?"

"Ten days," he said, making light of it, wishing he could tell her how he'd proposed with his heart in his mouth for fear she'd turn him down and walk out of his life... and how, not even a year later, he'd wished she had.

Ten days, Joanna thought. Well, why not? It couldn't have taken her more than ten minutes to have fallen in love with David.

But what about him? She'd been the soul of propriety, he'd said. What had happened? Had he wanted her to sleep with him—the ever-ready male anatomy at work—and when she'd refused, had he made an impulsive offer of marriage and ended up regretting it?

Was that what had gone wrong between them? Had he simply looked at her across the breakfast table one morning and asked himself what in hell she was doing there?

When the sexual excitement of this weekend was over, would he look at her and think that same thought again?

"Jo?" David reached for her hand. "What is it? You're so pale."

Joanna forced a sickly smile to her lips. "I think...I think you were right when you said I shouldn't overdo." Carefully, she pushed her bowl of chili away. "Would you mind very much if we went back to the house now?"

He was on his feet before she'd finished speaking. "Let's go," he said, tossing a handful of bills on the table. She stood up, he put his arm around her and the next thing she knew, he was carrying her from the diner.

"David, put me down. This is silly. You don't have to pick me up every time I—"

He kissed her, silencing the quick flow of words in a way that made her heartbeat stutter.

"I love holding you," he whispered fiercely. "I'd hold you in my arms forever, if I could."

He tucked her gently into the car, buckled her seat belt, then got behind the wheel and drove slowly home. And all the time, she wondered if he'd meant what he'd said, if it would last or if everything that had happened between them would end when the weekend did.

He insisted on lifting her from the car and carrying her into the house.

"I'm going to take you upstairs and put you to bed," he said. "And when you're feeling better, I'll make us some supper."

"Don't be silly. I feel better already. I'll cook."

"What's the matter? Afraid of trying my extra-special canned chicken soup?"

Joanna laughed. "At least let me lie down in the living room so I don't feel like a complete invalid."

"Deal." He lowered her gently to the couch and smiled at her. "And since you're feeling better, I'll let you have a vote."

"A vote on what?"

David grinned. "Raise your hand if you want us to stay right where we are for the rest of the week."

Her eyes widened. "Do you mean it?"

"Scout's honor."

"Oh, that would be wonderful. But your office…"

"They'll manage." He leaned down, brushed his mouth lightly over hers. "Lie right there and don't you dare move an inch. I'll put up the kettle for some tea and phone Morgana." He smiled. "She'll probably be delighted at the chance to run things without me for a while."

Joanna smiled and lay her head back as David made his way to the kitchen.

Had she ever been so happy in her life?

Even the fears she'd had just a little while ago didn't seem quite so awful now. There was more to her relationship with David than sex. There had to be. That he wanted to stay here with her, away from the rest of the world, was wonderful.

Regaining her memory no longer seemed as quite as important as it had. What mattered now was getting her husband to admit that he loved her.

"Jo?"

She looked up. David was coming slowly toward her, his smile gone.

"David, what's wrong?"

"Nothing, really." He squatted down beside her and took her hand in his. "I mean, it's not like it's the end of the world or anything..."

"But?"

He sighed. "But Morgana said she'd been just about to phone me. I've been working on this project for the Secretary of Commerce... Hell," he said with an impatient gesture, "the point is, the White House has become interested."

Joanna gave a little laugh. "The White House? Are you serious?"

David nodded. "The Secretary wants a meeting. Gypsy, there's no way I can put him off."

"Of course not."

"If it was anything else . . ."

"David, you don't have to explain. I understand."

"Look, we'll go back to New York tomorrow, I'll meet with the Secretary and his advisors and next weekend, we'll drive up again and stay for the week. OK?"

Joanna nodded. "Sure."

She hoped she sounded as if she meant it but as she went into David's arms and lifted her face for his kiss, there was a hollow feeling in the pit of her belly, as if she knew in her heart that they would not be returning to this house again.

CHAPTER ELEVEN

THE servants in the Adams town house were in the habit of taking their mid-morning coffee together.

It was Mrs. Timmons's idea and though it made for a pleasant start to the day, it was a ritual that had less to do with congeniality than with efficiency. The housekeeper had found she could best organize the day with Ellen and Hollister seated opposite her at the kitchen table.

But she could see instantly that that wasn't going to work this morning.

Nothing was going according to schedule. And she had the feeling that nothing would.

The Adamses had returned from their weekend outing late last night. Mrs. Timmons had been watching the late news on the TV when she'd heard them come in and she'd risen from the rocking chair in her bedroom cum sitting room off the kitchen, hastily checked her appearance in the mirror, and gone out to see if she were needed.

What she'd seen had made her fall back into the shadows in amazement.

There was Mr. David, carrying his wife up the stairs. He'd done that the day he'd brought her home from the rehabilitation center, but this...oh, this was very different.

Mrs. Adams's arms were tightly clasped around her husband's neck. They were whispering to each other, and laughing softly, and halfway up the stairs Mr. David had stopped and kissed his wife in a way that had made Mrs. Timmons turn her face away. When she'd dared look again, the Adamses were gone and the door to Mr. David's bedroom was quietly clicking shut.

Now, at almost ten in the morning, the door to that room had yet to open. Neither of the Adamses had come down for breakfast and Mr. David had even foregone his daily run.

"Never happened before," Hollister said, dipping half a donut into his coffee.

"Of course it has," Mrs. Timmons said briskly, "it's just that you weren't here at the beginning."

"The beginning of what?"

"I'll bet she means when they were first married," Ellen said with a giggle, "when they were still newlyweds. Isn't that right, Mrs. Timmons?"

Ellen blanched when the housekeeper fixed her with a cold eye. "Isn't this your day for organizing the clothing for the dry cleaner?"

Hollister came to Ellen's defense.

"She was only picking up on what you'd just said," he began, then fell silent under that same stern gaze.

"And you," Mrs. Timmons said, "are supposed to be polishing the silver."

Hollister and Ellen looked at each other, shrugged their shoulders and pushed back their chairs.

"We can take a hint," Hollister said with quiet dignity.

Mrs. Timmons began clearing the dishes. "Good," she said grumpily. But after the door had swung shut and she was alone in the kitchen, she stood still.

She had worked for David Adams for many years and she'd come to respect him. She supposed, if pressed, she might even admit she'd developed a certain liking for him.

"Damnation," she muttered.

The truth was that she'd come to think of him as if he were a kind of son. Not that she'd ever let him or anyone else know it. That would not have been proper.

But if Joanna Adams, who had broken his heart once, had somehow got it into her head to break it twice...

The coffee cups clattered against each other as Mrs. Timmons all but jammed them into the sink.

No. It was just too impossible to contemplate.

Not even fate could be that cruel.

Upstairs, in the master bedroom suite, David stood gazing down at Joanna, who lay fast asleep in his bed.

The weekend, and the night they'd just spent together, had been wonderful.

His gaze moved slowly over his wife. She was lying on her belly, her head turned to the side so that he could see her dark lashes fanned down over her cheek. The blanket was at her hips, exposing the long, graceful curve of her back. Her hair, black as night against the white linens, streamed over her shoulders.

He loved her, he thought. Lord, he loved her with all his heart.

If only he dared tell her so.

Joanna sighed. She stretched lazily, rolled onto her back and opened her eyes. Her face lit when she saw her husband, standing beside the bed.

"David," she whispered, and without any false modesty or hesitation, she raised her arms to him.

He came down to her at once, his freshly pressed suit, crisp white cotton shirt and perfectly knotted silk tie be damned, and folded her tightly into his embrace.

"Good morning," he said softly, and when she smiled, he kissed her.

It was a slow, gentle kiss but almost instantly he felt his body begin to react to the warmth and sweetness of hers.

"Mmm," he whispered against her mouth, and he moved his hand to the silken weight of her breast. His fingers stroked across her flesh and then he bent his head and drew her nipple into his mouth.

Her response was swift and exciting. She made a soft little sound that was enough to drive him crazy all by itself but when she arched toward him, murmuring his name, her hand cupping the back of his head to bring his mouth even harder against her, it was almost his undoing.

With a groan, he lifted his head, kissed her lips, and drew back.

"I can't, darling," he said softly. "My meeting is in less than an hour."

Joanna smiled and smoothed his hair back from his forehead.

"I understand."

"I should have told Morgana to say I couldn't make it."

"No, you shouldn't. It's OK, David. Really. I do understand."

David took her hand and brought it to his lips. "I'll be back as soon as I can."

She sat up, put her arms around his neck, and kissed him.

"I'll be waiting," she whispered.

He stroked his hand down her cheek. Then he stood, straightened his clothes and headed for the door while he could still force himself to leave.

This Joanna, this woman he'd fallen in love with all over again, couldn't be a temporary aberration. She had to be real, and lasting.

He could not suffer her loss again.

Not even fate could be that cruel.

Morgana picked up the papers on David's desk and squared them against the blotter though she'd done the same thing only moments before. She looked at the onyx desk clock.

David was late. Twenty minutes late. That wasn't good.

He was never late. Not for the past couple of years, at any rate; not since he'd stopped being cutesy-cozy with his adoring little minx of a wife.

Morgana's sculpted lips pressed together with distaste. David's marriage had almost marked the end of all her plans. Until then, it had only been a matter of time before he'd have realized what she, herself, had known from the first day she'd come to work for him.

She and David were meant for each other.

One look, and she'd fallen deeply in love. David...well, he was a man. It took men longer to realize such things. For a long while, it had been enough that he'd found her the best P.A. he'd ever had. Morgana had taken each compliment on her efficiency, her dedication, and clutched them to her heart.

Soon, she had told herself, soon he'd know.

Instead, he'd been captivated—seduced—by a common piece of baggage from out of nowhere.

Morgana shot a look of pure venom at the photo of Joanna that stood on the corner of David's desk.

"Just look at her," she muttered under her breath.

The hair, blowing in the wind; the oversized denim shirt tucked into torn jeans. And that smile, that oh-so-innocent smile.

Morgana smiled, too, but her smile was as frigid as a January night.

At first, it had seemed an insurmountable problem. It had been bad enough that David had gotten married. But when he'd begun spending less and less time at the office, Morgana had suffered in silence, watching as her plans for a future with him began to fall apart.

Until one day, she'd seen her chance.

David had made a comment, a light one, really, something about not wanting to overwhelm his bride with the pressures of her new life. But Morgana had sensed real concern behind his words.

All smiles, she'd offered to befriend Joanna.

The girl had been so young. Stupid, really. She'd swallowed everything Morgana fed her, hook, line and sinker.

"I'm so happy for you," Morgana had purred. "It must be so wonderful, up there in Connecticut. Why, David's missed several important meetings because he didn't want to leave. He didn't tell you? No? Oh, dear, I suppose I shouldn't have said anything."

"No," Joanna had replied, "no, I'm glad you did. I surely don't want to interfere in David's life."

After that, it had been easy. A few woman-to-woman chats about things like David's status. His position. His importance on the national and international scenes. His need to entertain, to network with his peers.

"But why hasn't he told me these things?" Joanna had said pleadingly, each time Morgana worked around to the topic, and Morgana sighed and said, well, because he loved her and he was afraid of making too many demands on her too soon.

"Perhaps if you were the one to suggest that you'd like to make some changes," Morgana had said in her most kindly way. "I mean, if David thought you wanted to move back to the city, mingle with his old crowd, if he saw you beginning to adapt yourself to his sort of life...that would please him so, Joanna, and he wouldn't have to feel guilty about asking *you* to change for *him*, do you see?"

Morgana's heels tapped briskly across the Italian tile floor of David's office as she headed out the door to her own desk. It had been as simple as striking a match to start a fire. Joanna made changes, David reacted with disappointment, Joanna—the stupid girl—reacted by making even more changes, and the fire grew larger.

It had been difficult, watching David's growing distress, but it was for the best. His marriage was an error; it was up to Morgana to make him see that.

Finally, he had.

He'd come in one day, called Morgana into his office. Grim-faced, he'd told her that he and Joanna would be getting a divorce.

Morgana had made all the right sounds of distress and concern, even though she'd wanted to throw her arms around him and shout for joy. But she'd told herself she had only to bide her time, that once the divorce was over, she could carefully offer consolation.

Her jaw clenched as she sat down at her desk.

And then Joanna had her accident. If only that taxi hadn't just hit her a glancing blow, if only it had done a proper job...

Morgana took a trembling breath. She put her hands to her hair and smoothed the pale strands.

This had been a long, and terrible, weekend. When she'd gotten the call from David, telling her he was in Connecticut, she'd known immediately that the little slut had seduced him again. It was there in his voice, that soft hint of a male who had been pleasured.

And in that instant, Morgana had known she could no longer wait to see if Joanna's memory would come back, that she'd have to take action if she wanted the fire that she'd started to consume that interfering little bitch.

She would not lose David again. She'd worked too hard to let that happen.

"Good morning."

She looked up. David was coming through the smoked-glass doors toward her. A smile curved across her mouth. How handsome he was. How much she adored him.

"Good morning," she said in her usual, businesslike manner. "There have been some calls for you. I put the memos on your desk." She rose and hurried after him as he went into his office. "A couple of faxes came in from Japan during the night, nothing terribly urgent. Let's see, what else? John Fairbanks phoned to see if you could make lunch today. I said you'd call him when you came in. Oh, and the Mayor's office wanted you to—"

"What time are they coming in?"

Morgana looked blank. "Who?"

"The Secretary and his people." He yanked out his chair, sat down, and began to leaf through the stack of memos and faxes. "Didn't you say something about noon?"

Morgana frowned. What was the matter with her? Yesterday, all she'd thought of was that she had to get David back into his real life and away from his wife.

Now, suddenly remembering how she'd accomplished that, she scrambled for words.

"Oh," she said, "oh, that..."

David looked up at her. His hair was neatly combed, he was clean-shaven, his shirt and tie and suit were impeccable...but she could see beyond all that, she could see the satiation in his face, she could almost smell the damnable stink of that woman.

"Yes," he said impatiently, his voice politely echoing hers, "that. When are these guys supposed to put in an appearance? I don't much feel like cooling my heels today, Morgana."

"They called a few minutes ago," Morgana said quickly, "and changed the time to one o'clock."

That would do it. By one, she'd have David up to his eyeballs in work. Thoughts of his little wife would be relegated to the back burner, where they belonged. And by six or seven, when Morgana suggested she phone out for supper...

"Hell," David muttered, looking at the onyx clock. He ran his hand through his hair. "All right, then, let's not sit around and watch dust settle. Get your notebook and we'll deal with these faxes."

Morgana smiled happily. "Yes, David."

By noon, David had his jacket off and was deep in work.

Morgana sent out for sandwiches. He nodded his thanks and ate what she'd ordered without comment.

At ten of one, she excused herself, and went out to her desk, dialed the phone company and said she thought her telephone might be out of order and would they please ring her right back?

When her phone rang, she picked it up, said thank you, then hung up. She waited a couple of minutes before going into David's office.

He looked up from his desk. He was scowling. A good sign. It surely meant that he was engrossed in his work.

"David, that was a call from Washington. The Secretary sends regrets but he can't make it today."

"Damn!" David tossed down his pen. "You'd think they'd have called sooner."

"Well," Morgana said apologetically, "you know how these people are."

"To think I rushed all the way back to the city for this..."

"But it's a good thing you did," Morgana said quickly. "Just look at all the work you've done."

"Yeah." He pushed back from his desk. "Terrific."

Something in his voice made her scalp prickle. "You know, you never did answer that letter that came in last week from——"

"I suppose, as long as I'm here, I might as well put the rest of the day to good use."

Morgana smiled. "Exactly. That letter..."

David wasn't listening. He'd pulled his telephone toward him and he was dialing a number.

"This is David Adams," he said. "I'd like to speak with Doctor Corbett."

"David," Morgana said urgently, "there's work to do."

David held up his hand. "Corbett? I'm fine, thank you. Look, I've been thinking... Do you have some time free this afternoon, Doctor? I really need to talk to you."

"David," Morgana hissed, "listen——"

"Half an hour from now, in your office? Yes, that's fine. Thanks. I'll be there."

David hung up the phone and got to his feet. He grabbed his suit jacket from the back of his chair and put it on as he walked to the door.

"Where are you going?" Morgana demanded. "Really, David..."

"Joanna's just the way she used to be," he said, and smiled at her. "She's...hell, she's wonderful! Do you remember what she was like, Morgana?"

Morgana's mouth whitened. "Yes," she said, "I do."

"What occurred to me was...I know it sounds crazy, but maybe that blow to the head changed her personality."

"Honestly, you can't believe that."

"Why not? Something's happened to change her." He smiled again, even more broadly. "I've got to talk to Corbett about it. Maybe he can shed some light on things."

"David, no! I mean, that's crazy..."

He laughed. "No crazier than me falling in love with my wife all over again. I'll see you tomorrow." He grinned. "Or maybe I won't. Maybe I'll whisk Joanna off to Paris. Hell, who knows what will happen? I'm beginning to think that anything is possible."

Morgana stared at the door for long minutes after he was gone. Then, her mouth set in a thin, hard line, she collected her jacket and her purse and left the office on the run.

Joanna sat on the delicate, silk-covered sofa in her own living room and wondered if it was possible to feel more out of place than she felt at this moment.

Morgana, an unexpected visitor, sat in an equally delicate chair across from her. In her ice blue, raw silk suit, with her blonde hair perfectly arranged and her hands folded in her lap, she looked completely at home.

Joanna, caught in the midst of trying to bundle most of the contents of her clothing closet for the Goodwill box, knew she looked just the opposite. She glanced down at her jeans, dusty from her efforts, and her sneakers, still bearing grass and mud stains from the weekend in the country. Her hair was a mess, with some of the strands hanging in her eyes. Her hands were grungy and she saw now that she'd broken a nail...

Quickly, she laced her fingers together but it was too late. Morgana was looking at the broken nail as if it were something unpleasant she'd found on her dinner plate.

"You really need to see Rita," she said.

Joanna cleared her throat. "Rita?"

"Yes. The girl who does your nails. You have a standing appointment, hasn't anyone told you?"

"No. I mean, yes, I know I do but I haven't... I mean, the thought of going to a nail salon seems so weird."

Joanna took a breath. This was ridiculous. This was her house. Morgana was her guest. An uninvited one, at that. There was no reason to feel so...so disoriented.

"Morgana," she said, and smiled politely, "would you care for some tea?"

"Thank you, no."

"Coffee, then? It's Mrs. Timmons's afternoon off, and Ellen's out running errands, but I'm perfectly capable of—"

"No."

"A cool drink, then?"

"Joanna." Morgana rose in one graceful movement and dropped to her knees before Joanna. "My dear," she said, and clasped Joanna's hands in hers.

"Morgana," Joanna said with a nervous laugh, "what is this? Please, get up."

"Joanna, my dear Joanna." Morgana's sympathetic blue eyes met Joanna's wary violet ones. "I've felt so badly for you, ever since that dreadful accident."

"I don't want to talk about the ac—"

"And for David, too."

"Morgana, really, get up. You're making me uncomfort—"

"He told me today why you went away for the weekend. That you'd both hoped the time in the country might help you recover your memory.''

It was a shot in the dark, but an accurate one. Joanna flushed. ''He told you that?''

''Oh, yes. David and I are very close, Joanna. Surely you remember...well, no, I suppose you don't.''

''I know that he thinks very highly of you,'' Joanna said cautiously.

''Of course he does.'' Morgana squeezed her hand. ''But it's you I'm thinking of now, my dear.''

''I don't...I don't follow you.''

Morgana sighed and got to her feet. ''You were intimate with David this weekend, Joanna.''

Joanna blanched. ''How did you...''

''He told me.''

''David told you...?'' Joanna shot to her feet. ''Why? Why would he tell you something so...so personal about us?''

''We're very close, I've told you that. And perhaps he was feeling guilty.''

''Guilty?'' A chill moved over Joanna's skin. ''Guilty about what?''

''Are you sure you're up to this? Perhaps I've made a mistake, coming here. I wrestled with my conscience all day but—''

"I feel strong as an ox. Why should my husband have told you that he and I . . . that we were together this weekend? And why should he have felt guilty about it?"

Morgana's teeth, very tiny and very white, closed on her bottom lip. "Because he's done a cruel thing to you, and he knows it." She took a deep breath. "I can't stand by and see him do it. You see, Joanna, David intends to divorce you."

Joanna felt the blood drain from her face. "What?"

"He should have told you the truth weeks ago. I tried to convince him. So did his attorney, but—"

"His attorney?"

"Yes." Morgana clasped Joanna's hands. "You must be strong, dear, when I tell you this."

"Just tell me," Joanna said frantically, "and get it over with!"

"The day of your accident," Morgana said slowly, "you were on your way to the airport. You were flying to the Caribbean, to get a divorce."

Joanna pulled her hands from Morgana's. "No! I don't believe you. I asked David about our marriage, he never said—"

"He listened to the doctors, who said it was vital you have no shocks to your system."

"I don't believe you. It isn't true..."

Joanna's desperate words halted. She looked at Morgana and then she gave a sharp cry of despair, and spun toward the window and the sad little garden beyond.

It *was* true. Every word. What Morgana had just told her made a terrible kind of sense.

David's unwillingness to bring her home from the hospital. His coldness. His silence. His removal.

Their separate rooms...

But their rooms hadn't been separate this weekend.

"I suppose," Morgana said kindly, as if she'd read Joanna's thoughts, "that it's difficult to accept, especially after the intimacy of the past weekend." She sighed. "But if you could only remember the past, you'd know that...well, that sex was all you and David ever had together. It's what led up to your marriage in the first place."

Joanna looked at her. "What do you mean?"

"Surely you know that David is a man with strong appetites. There have been so many women... They're in his life for a while and then, poof, they're gone. And then he met you.

You were so young..." Morgana struggled to keep the anger and hatred from her voice. "He's a moral man, in his own way. I suppose, afterward, he felt an obligation." Morgana smiled pityingly. "Unfortunately, it wasn't love. Not for David."

Joanna's legs felt as if they were going to give out. She made her way to the couch and sat down.

"He said things this weekend," she whispered while the tears streamed down her face, "we planned things..."

"Yes, I'm sure. He was full of regrets for what had happened in Connecticut. I was blunt, I said, 'David, it's your own fault, you shouldn't have listened to the doctors, you should have told Joanna the truth, that your marriage had been an impetuous mistake and you were in the process of ending it...'"

And, with dizzying swiftness, Joanna's memory returned.

"Oh, God," she whispered, "I remember!"

Pictures kaleidoscoped through her head. She saw herself coming to New York from the Midwest, looking for a new life and finding, instead, the only man she would ever love.

David.

He was almost ten years older and he moved in such exalted circles... It was hard to imagine him taking notice of someone like her.

But he had, and on their very first date, Joanna had fallen head over heels in love.

She remembered the passion that had flamed between them, how she, the girl her friends had teasingly called the eternal virgin, had gone eagerly to his bed soon after they'd met.

Oh, the joy of his proposal. The excitement of flying to Mexico to get married, the honeymoon in Puerto Vallarta, the weeks of happiness and ecstasy...

And then the slow, awful realization that she wasn't what David had wanted at all.

He'd never said so. He was too decent. But it was a dream that could not last and the signs of its ending had been easy to read.

David had given up his everything. His friends. His charities. He stopped going to the office, saying he preferred living in Connecticut but Joanna knew that everything he'd done was based on his conviction that she wouldn't fit into the sophisticated life he led in the city.

When Morgana offered her help, Joanna leaped at the chance to salvage her marriage.

What she needed, Morgana told her, was a life of her own, a life that would make David see her as more than just a woman he was responsible for but as someone as proficient in her sphere as he was in his.

"A man of his energies needs challenge to perform at his best, my dear," Morgana said. "By devoting so much time to you, he cheats himself. You must develop interests of your own. Show him you're equal to the position he holds in the world. Perhaps if you joined some clubs, or sat on some charity committees, you'd learn how to organize this house, how to look..."

Morgana clamped her lips together but it was too late.

"You mean," Joanna asked in a choked voice, "he's embarrassed by the way I look?"

"No, not at all," Morgana quickly replied.

Too quickly. Joanna understood that "embarrassed" was exactly what she'd meant.

But nothing she'd tried had been enough to halt the collapse of the marriage. David had grown more distant. The bed that had once been a place of intimacy and joy became the cold setting in which they ended each day by lying far apart until finally, Joanna had salvaged what little remained of her pride by moving into a separate room. Eventually, David had suggested divorce. Joanna had agreed. It had all been very civilized, though the day she'd set out for the airport and the legal dissolution of her marriage she'd been so blinded by tears that she hadn't seen the oncoming taxi until it was too late...

The memories were almost too painful to bear. Joanna buried her face in her hands while Morgana stood over her.

"Poor Joanna," she crooned. "I'm so sorry."

Joanna lifted her tear-stained face. "I can't...I can't face him," she whispered, "not after..."

It was difficult for Morgana to hide a smile of triumph.

"I understand," she said soothingly.

"I don't want to be here when David gets back. I don't want to see him ever again." Joanna grasped Morgana's hands. "Please, you must help me."

"Help you?"

"I have nowhere to go. I don't really know anyone in this city...except you."

Morgana frowned. Time was of the essence. She had to get Joanna out of here before someone showed up. Luck had been with her, so far. The maid and the housekeeper were out; the chauffeur was among the missing, too.

But David...David could come home at any minute.

She made a quick decision. "You can sleep on the pull-out sofa in my living room until we work out the details."

"Oh, no, I couldn't impose."

"Nonsense. Go on, now. And I suppose you'd best leave a note."

"A note?"

"Yes. Something clear and concise, so David understands why you've gone." *So he knows you've left him deliberately, so that he doesn't scour the streets, trying to find you...*

"But what shall I say?"

"Just the truth, Joanna, that you've recovered your memory and you wish to proceed with the divorce."

Joanna nodded. Still, she hesitated.

"Morgana? I'm almost ashamed to admit it but when I first heard David talk about you, I was...I was jealous."

"Of me?" Morgana's smile felt stiff. "What nonsense, Joanna. David's never even noticed that I'm a woman."

But he would notice it, at long last, she thought as Joanna left the room.

Finally, *finally*, she was about to take her rightful place in David Adams's life.

CHAPTER TWELVE

"DAVID," Morgana said, "you must calm down."

"How the hell can I calm down?" David, who had been pacing the floor of his office for the past ten minutes, swung toward Morgana. "It's a week since Joanna disappeared. A week, dammit! And all these damned private investigators are no closer to finding her than they were when I first hired them!"

"Getting yourself all upset won't help."

"I am not getting myself all upset," he snarled, "hell, I'm already upset!" He strode to the triple window and looked out. "Look at the size of that city! Jo could be out there anywhere, alone and hurt and in God only knows what sort of trouble."

"She's not in trouble, and she didn't disappear. She simply left you, David. I mean," she added quickly, when he swung toward her, "that's what you told me. You said she wrote a note."

"Yeah, but what does that prove? She'd been ill. She'd been in an accident. She'd hurt her head..." His face, already pale beneath its usual tan, seemed to get even whiter. He kicked the chair out from behind his desk, sighed and sank down into it. "If only I knew she was OK."

"She is."

"You don't know that."

But I do, Morgana thought smugly, *I surely do*. Joanna Adams was as well as could be expected for a woman who moped around Morgana's apartment all day, looking as if she'd lost her best friend.

It was definitely time to get her out from underfoot. Joanna thought so, too; Morgana had come home two days ago and found her unwelcome boarder with her suitcase packed. She was moving into a hotel, Joanna had said, and though Morgana's first instinct had been to applaud, common sense had prevailed.

If Joanna were on her own, there was no telling what might happen. Suppose she changed her mind and decided to confront David? Or suppose she and David simply bumped into each other? Manhattan was a big island, jammed with millions of people and the odds on that happening were small but still...

Morgana's brain had recoiled from the possibilities. She had to keep Joanna on ice just a little longer. So she'd thought fast and come up with a story about David cutting off Joanna's credit cards and bank accounts.

"The bottom line," she'd said with a gentle smile, "is that you'll just have to stay here a little while longer, dear."

What could Joanna have done but agree?

The only problem was that things weren't going quite as Morgana had expected. She'd assumed David would be distraught, yes, but not...what was the word to describe his behaviour the last several days? Disturbed? Upset?

Frantic, was more like it. He'd gone half crazy when he learned his wife had left him, calling the police, hiring private detectives...

And brushing off all Morgana's attempts to offer comfort.

She looked at him now, sitting behind his desk with his head buried in his hands. It was ridiculous, that he should mourn the loss of a girl as common as Joanna.

"Ridiculous," she muttered.

David's head came up. "What's ridiculous?"

Morgana flushed. "That—that the police haven't found her yet."

David sighed wearily and scrubbed his hands over his face. He hadn't slept more than an hour at a time since he'd come home to find

Joanna gone and exhaustion was catching up with him.

"Jo left a note...it means she's not technically a missing person. If it wasn't for her having amnesia, they wouldn't bother looking at all."

"She doesn't have amnesia, not anymore. She remembered everything."

David's eyes narrowed. "How do you know that, Morgana?"

"Well..." She swallowed dryly as she searched for the right words. "Well, you said that was in the note. That she'd gotten her memory back."

"Yeah, but what does that mean? What does she remember?" He put his hands flat on his desk and wearily shoved back his chair. "Corbett says memory sometimes returns in bits and pieces. For all I know, she doesn't remember the things that matter."

A look came over his face that made Morgana's stomach curdle.

"Honestly, David," she snapped, "one would think *you'd* remember the things that matter, too."

The look he gave her all but stopped her breath.

"Maybe you'd like to explain that," he said with sudden coldness.

Morgana hesitated. Well, why not? It might be time for a little straight talking, if she could do it with care.

"I mean," she said, "that you seem to have forgotten that your marriage to Joanna was always doomed."

"Doomed?" David rose to his feet. "What in hell gives you that idea?"

"David, don't let your irritation out on me!"

"I just want a simple answer to a simple question, Morgana. Why would you think my marriage had been doomed?"

Morgana's lips pursued. "Honestly, you act as if I weren't privy to the divorce proceedings. And to the years that led up to them. I know, better than anyone, how badly things had gone for you and Joanna."

David's mouth thinned. "You weren't privy to how much I loved her," he said coldly. "As for the divorce proceedings . . . that was behind us."

"After she'd lost her memory, of course, but—"

"Memory be damned!" He slammed his fist on the desk. Morgana jumped, and papers went flying in all directions. "I love her, do you understand? Even if she'd recovered her memory, there was no reason to think we couldn't have worked things out. Corbett made me see that. I'd loved the woman Joanna had once been, I loved the woman she'd become . . . Hell, there had to have been a reason she'd changed during our marriage. And I came home that day, knowing it was time to tell her the truth and to tell her that, together, we could find the answers . . ."

He turned away sharply and his voice broke. Morgana hesitated. Then she went slowly to where he stood and put her hand on his back.

"David," she said softly, "you've got to accept what's happened."

"I don't know what's happened, don't you understand?"

"Joanna remembered. And when she did, she knew she wanted just what she'd wanted before the accident, to be free of you—"

She cried out as he swung around and grabbed hold of her wrist.

"How do you know that?"

Morgana stared at him. "Because . . . because that's the way it was," she stammered. "You told me—"

"Never."

"You did! You said she wanted a divorce."

"I said we'd agreed on a divorce." David's eyes were cold as the onyx clock on his desk as they searched Morgana's face. "I never said Jo wanted to be free of me."

"Well, I suppose I just assumed..." Morgana looked at his hand, coiled around hers. "David, you're hurting me."

"Hell," he muttered. He let go of her wrist and drew a ragged breath. "I'm sorry. I don't know what I was thinking."

"It's all right. I understand."

"If only I'd gotten home earlier."

"You mustn't blame yourself."

"If only the maid or the housekeeper had been there."

"David, please. Try and relax."

"Even Hollister was gone. He had to pick that damned afternoon to get the oil changed in that miserable car."

"Oh, David, my heart breaks for you. If there were only something I could... What are you doing?"

David shrugged on his jacket. "I'm going home. It's better than pacing a hole in the floor."

"Oh, don't! Let me make us some tea."

"I need an hour's sleep more than I need tea. You might as well take the rest of the day off, too."

"But it's only midafternoon. We can't just abandon the office!"

He smiled. "Trust me, Morgana. We can."

"But..."

It was useless to protest. He was gone.

Morgana walked around David's desk and sat down in his chair. Her mouth twisted.

Damn Joanna! She might have been gone but she wasn't forgotten. And she was an ever-present threat, so long as she remained in New York. She didn't belong here. She never had. She wasn't sophisticated enough, or clever enough, or beautiful enough. Not for the city and not for David.

Joanna belonged back in whatever hick town she'd come from.

Morgana's grimace became a smile. She shoved back the chair and marched to the door.

And the sooner, the better.

Morgana's apartment held the deep silence of midafternoon.

"Joanna?" She slammed the door and tossed her purse and briefcase on a chair. "Joanna, where are you? We have to talk."

Not that she'd give the little slut the chance to talk. She'd simply hand the girl a check, tell her to buy herself a one-way bus ticket, and that would be that.

Life would return to normal. To better than normal, because now David would need solace.

And Morgana would be there to offer it.

What was that?

Her heart began to hammer as soon as she saw the note propped against the toaster in the kitchen. The quiet and that folded piece of white paper filled her with foreboding.

She opened the note, smoothed it carefully with her fingers.

Dear Morgana,
You've been so kind but I can't go on imposing. This morning, I remembered a small cache of money I'd tucked away. I'm going home to get it and then ...

"No," Morgana whispered. She crumpled the note in her hand. "No," she said, her voice rising to a wail, and she raced from the apartment.

It didn't take Joanna very long to find what she was looking for.

The couple of hundred dollars she'd squirreled away more than a year ago was in her night table, right where she'd left it. She'd put the money aside last year, to buy David a special birthday gift ...

As if that would have changed anything.

Her eyes misted and she rubbed them hard with the heel of her hand. It was stupid, thinking about that. Those days were over and gone. Now, what she had to do was concentrate on the future.

And on slipping out of the house as quietly as she'd slipped in.

It was foolish, she knew, but she didn't want to see anybody. Her timing was right. At this hour on a Friday, Mrs. Timmons would be out marketing. Ellen and Hollister would be in the kitchen, eyes glued to their favorite soap operas.

Joanna made her way quietly down the stairs. The house lay in midafternoon shadow, adding to its natural gloom. She shuddered and thought that she would not miss these over-furnished, cold rooms.

The only thing she'd miss was David, and that was just plain stupid. Songs by the truckload had been written about the pain of unrequited love but in the real world, how could you go on loving someone who didn't love you?

Before the accident, she'd come to terms with that fact. She'd accepted the truth of their impending divorce, and she would again. Her weepiness this past week, her anguish at the thought of losing her husband...it was just a setback, and perfectly understandable in light of all that had happened to her, first the amnesia and then the shock of her recovery, and in between that long, wonderful weekend...

No. It hadn't been that at all. The weekend had been a lie. And she could never forgive David for that, for what he'd stirred in her heart while she'd lain in the warmth of his arms...

The front door swung open just as she reached it. Startled, Joanna jumped back, expecting to see Mrs. Timmons's dour face.

But it wasn't the housekeeper who stood framed in the doorway, it was David.

They stared at each other, the both of them speechless. Joanna recovered first.

"Hello, David," she said. He didn't answer but he didn't have to. The look on his face was far more eloquent than words. He was glaring at her, his amazement giving way to repressed rage. "I—I suppose you're surprised to see me."

Surprised? He was stunned. He was a man who'd never been at a loss for words in his life but at this moment, he was damned near speechless and torn by half a dozen conflicting emotions, all of them warring to get out.

Anger, born of a week's worth of pain and fueled by the way Joanna was looking at him, as if he was the last man on earth she'd ever wanted to see, won out.

"Where in hell have you been?"

Joanna winced. "You don't have to yell, David, I'm not deaf."

"Thank you for the information." A muscle jumped in his cheek. "Now answer the question. Where have you been?"

"I didn't come here to quarrel," she said carefully.

"No?"

"No."

David slammed the door behind him. He took a step toward her and she held her ground through sheer determination.

"Why did you come here, then? To see if I'd torn the wallpaper as I climbed the walls while I tried to figure out if you were dead or alive or maybe just sitting in an alley someplace, singing *Hey Nonny Nonny* while you wove flowers into your hair?"

Color swept into her cheeks. "I am perfectly sane. I've told you that before."

"Yeah?"

"Yeah," she said, and this time when he moved toward her she couldn't keep from taking a quick step back because if she hadn't, they'd have been nose to nose. Or nose to chest, considering the size of him . . .

"Well, lady, you sure could have fooled me."

Joanna's chin lifted. "I didn't come here to be insulted."

"Fascinating." He unbuttoned his jacket and slapped his hands on his hips. "You didn't come here to quarrel. You didn't come to be insulted. Near as I can figure, that only leaves us with a couple of thousand other possibilities. Are we going to go through them one by one or are you going to tell me how come you decided to honor me with your presence?''

It took a few seconds to get enough moisture into her mouth so she could swallow.

''I came to get something.''

''Something?''

''Yes.''

David folded his arms over his chest. ''I never much cared for Twenty Questions to start with, Joanna, and I find I'm liking it less and less as this conversation goes on.''

''It isn't a conversation, it's an inquisition!''

His smile was quick and chill. ''No, it's not. Not yet, anyway, but if I don't start getting some straight answers it's sure as hell going to become one.''

Joanna folded her arms over her chest, too.

''I came to get some money I'd put...''

She bit her lip. Hollister and Ellen had materialized in the hallway and were staring at them both with wide eyes. David frowned and swung around, following her gaze.

''Well?'' he barked. ''What do you want?''

''Nothing, sir,'' Hollister said quickly. ''We simply heard the door slam, and then voices . . ." He looked at Ellen. "Well, uh, we'll just go be getting back to the kitchen."

"You do that," David said coldly. "Better still, go for a walk. Or a drive. Just leave us alone."

Hollister nodded, grabbed Ellen's arm and hustled her away. Joanna, trying to take advantage of the interruption, headed for the door. David reached out and clamped his hand around her wrist.

"Let go," she demanded.

"The hell I will. You were about to explain why you came here."

"I told you, I'd put away some money. I came to get it." Her chin lifted. "I admit, it was yours to begin with but I—"

David cursed, with an eloquence that made her blush.

"Your money? My money? What kind of garbage is that? Money is money, that's all. It always belonged to the both of us."

"I only meant that I'd saved this on my own."

"And what, pray tell, do you need this little 'nest egg' for?"

Joanna licked her lips. "To leave town,"

"Leave town," David repeated. His voice was flat but the muscle was jumping in his cheek again. "As in, cut and run without having the decency to face me and tell me you were leaving me?''

''I *did* tell you,'' Joanna said, wrenching out of his grasp. ''I left you a note.''

''Oh, yeah, you certainly did. 'Dear David, My memory came back and I want the divorce.' Yours Very Truly...''

''I didn't say that,'' she snapped, her cheeks flaming.

''No,'' he said coldly, ''not the 'Yours Very Truly' part but you might as well have.''

''David, this is senseless. I told you, I didn't come to argue.''

''Right. You came for money you'd squirreled away, I suppose for just such an occasion, so you could do a disappearing act if the going got tough.''

She moved so fast that her fist, slamming into his shoulder, was a blur.

''Hey...''

''You...you rat!'' Her eyes, black with fury, locked on his. ''I saved that money so I could buy you a carburetor for your last birthday!''

David's face went blank. ''A what?''

''A carburetor. That—that thing you kept drooling over in that stupid car parts catalog, the Foley or the Holy...''

''Holley,'' he said in a choked whisper. ''A Holley carb.''

"Whatever. You had this dumb thing about just ordering it from the catalog, all this crazy male macho about it being better to stumble across it yourself in some stupid, dirty junkyard..."

"It isn't male macho, it's simple logic," David said with dignity, "and what were you doing, buying me a Holley carb in the first place? It sure as hell didn't go with your image."

"No," Joanna said, and all at once he could see the anger drain from her face. "It didn't. But then, just before your last birthday I was still fool enough to think—to hope—that maybe buying you a gift would remind you of how things had once been for us..."

She stared at him, her mouth trembling, despising herself for what she'd almost blurted out, that she loved him, that she would always love him...

A choked sob burst from her throat. Eyes blinded with tears, she turned away. "Goodbye, David. I'll let you know where to send my things. On second thought, you can give them away. Maybe the Goodwill people want—"

She cried out as he hoisted her unceremoniously into his arms and stalked into his study.

"David, are you crazy? Put me..."

He dumped her on her feet, slammed the door shut behind them, and glared at her.

"You're not going anywhere until we've had this out," he said grimly.

"We have nothing to talk about."

"No?"

"No."

"What was all that, about you caring how things once were between us?"

Joanna's shoulders slumped. "I was just babbling. Besides, it doesn't matter anymore."

"The hell it doesn't!" He caught her face in his hand and forced her eyes to meet his. "Does it really matter to you, how things used to be?"

She stared at him, warning herself not to let go, to hang on to what little remained of her self-respect...but it was too late. The words were there, bursting from her heart and her lips.

"Damn you, David," she cried, "I'll always care!" Color stained her cheeks, giving her a wild, proud look. "Do you feel better, now? Wasn't it enough that I couldn't live up to your standards?"

"What the hell are you talking about? What standards?"

"Your wealth. Your status. Your friends. You married me without really thinking about whether or not I'd fit into your life, and then you woke up one morning and realized that I didn't."

"You mean, I woke up one morning and discovered that my beautiful Gypsy had changed into a...a..." David let go of her, flung up his arms and paced across the room. "I don't know how to describe what you'd become! A woman who cared more about other people than about me, who was determined to turn this damned house into a mausoleum, who didn't want me to touch her—"

His words faded way. He looked at her, and suddenly Joanna could see the anguish in his eyes.

"Why, Jo? Why did you turn to ice whenever I tried to make love to you? More than anything else, that damn near killed me."

"Because...because..." Joanna took a deep breath. It was a moment for truth, and she would see it through. "Because I was ashamed of...of how I was, whenever we...we made love."

David stared at her in disbelief. "Ashamed? My God, why?"

Joanna's head drooped. Her voice came out a whisper. "She never said anything, not about that. I'd never mentioned—I would never talk about something so intimate." She laced her hands together to stop their trembling.

"But...but she'd hinted. About certain things that I might do or say that would seem coarse..."

David crossed the room with quick strides. "Who?" he said through his teeth. "Who hinted?"

"I did try, David. To do what she said. To be the right wife for you."

"Who told you these things, Joanna?" But with gut-wrenching swiftness, he knew, and he could feel the blood heating in his veins. "Who told you that you weren't what I wanted in a wife?"

"Morgana," Joanna whispered. "She tried so hard to help me make myself over, but it was useless."

David's arms swept around her. "Listen to me," he said. "And look at me, so you'll know that what I'm about to tell you is the truth." He waited until she raised her head and then he took a deep breath. "I never wanted you to change, Gypsy. I loved you, just as you were."

"But Morgana said..."

"She lied."

"Why? Why would she have lied, David? She was so kind to me. Even this week, when I had nowhere to go, she took me into her apartment..."

David's eyes darkened with rage. "You spent this week with Morgana? I was tearing this miserable city upside down to find you and she had you tucked away all the time?"

His voice was cold as stone, and just as hard. It sent a shudder down Joanna's spine.

"Yes. After she told me about the divorce, after I remembered everything..." Joanna caught her breath. "Did you say you'd tried to find me?"

David drew her closer. "I went crazy this past week," he said gruffly. "Don't you know how much I love you?"

Joanna sighed. She lifted her arms and looped them around his neck.

"No," she said, with a little smile. "You're just going to have to tell me."

"For the rest of our lives," David said, and just then the door burst open.

"Mr. David?" Mrs. Timmons said, "are you...?" Her eyes widened. "Mrs. Adams. I didn't know you'd come back, ma'am. I'm terribly sorry to disturb you, but—"

Morgana pushed the housekeeper aside and came sweeping into the room.

"David," she said importantly, "I've seen Joanna, and I think you should know..." Her face turned white with shock but she recovered quickly. "She's here already, I see. David, I don't know what she's told you but I assure you, it's all lies!"

David put his arm around Joanna's shoulders. The green chips of sea ice that were his eyes told the whole story.

"If you were a man," he said softly, "I'd beat the crap out of you and smile while I did it."

"Please, David, I can explain—"

"Get out!"

"This snip of a girl isn't for you. She's... she's..."

David let go of Joanna and took a step forward. "You lying bitch! If I ever see your face again, I won't be responsible for my actions. Now, get out of this house and out of our lives or so help me, I'll throw you out!"

Morgana drew herself stiffly erect. "You'll regret losing me some day, but it will be too late then. I'm giving you one last chance to come to your senses—"

She cried out as Mrs. Timmons grasped the back of her collar and hustled her out of the room. The door slammed shut. There was a cry of outrage, then the sound of the front door opening and closing, and then there was silence.

"David?" Joanna looked up at her husband. "Do you think she's all right?"

David drew his wife into his arms. "I don't really care," he said. His mouth twitched. "Yes, I'm sure she's fine. But after this I'll think twice about ever crossing Mrs. Timmons."

Joanna laughed softly and linked her hands behind his neck.

"Have I told you lately that I love you, Mr. Adams?"

David smiled. "Welcome home, Mrs. Adams," he said softly and then, for long, long moments, there was no need for either of them to say anything at all.

EPILOGUE

Five years later

"KATE? Benjamin? Where are you?"

Joanna sighed as the sound of childish giggles spilled from the old-fashioned country kitchen behind her.

"Your daddy's car is going to be coming up that road any minute and if you want to be ready to go outside and greet him, you'd better show yourselves and let me get your boots on." She waited. "OK," she said, "I'm going to count to three and then whoever's not standing right in front of me is going to have to wait in the house. One. Two. Th—"

"Here I am, Mommy."

A little girl with dark hair and eyes the color of violets raced like a whirlwind into the living room.

"That's my girl," Joanna said. She hugged her daughter close and gave her a big kiss. "Now, where's that brother of yours?"

"Here, Mommy," her son sang out, and hurled his chubby, three-year-old self into her outstretched arms. "Daddy's gonna be here soon."

"That's right, darling. Sit down and let me get these boots on."

Benjamin collapsed on the carpet next to his twin sister.

"He's gonna bring me a truck," he said importantly, "with big wheels and a horn that goes beep."

Joanna laughed. Her son was the image of his father, with his dark hair and his green eyes. He had his father's passion, too, for anything on wheels.

"There we go," she said. "Almost ready. Just let's button you guys up..."

"Ugh," Kate said.

"Ugh," Benjamin echoed.

"Yes, I know, but it's cold out and there's lots and lots of snow..."

A horn sounded outside the snug Connecticut farmhouse. The children screeched happily and flew out the front door, trundling down the steps clumsily in their boots and snowsuits just as a black Land Rover pulled up. The door opened and David stepped out.

"Hey," he said, grinning as he squatted down and opened his arms. The children raced into them and he kissed them both, then scooped them up, one in each arm. "Did you miss me?"

Kate laughed. "Silly Daddy. You were only gone one day." Then she leaned forward and planted a wet kiss on his cheek. "I missed you every minute," she whispered.

"Me, too," Benjamin said, and delivered an equally sloppy kiss on the other side of his father's face. Then he craned his neck and peered over David's shoulder. "Did you bring my truck, Daddy?"

"Let's see," David said thoughtfully, as he set his children on the ground. "Did I bring Benjamin a truck? Well...I think maybe I did." He pulled a gaily wrapped package from the Land Rover and handed it to his son, who promptly sat down in the snow and began ripping it open. "There might even be something in here for Kate...yup, by golly, there is." Wide-eyed, his daughter accepted a box almost as big as she was. She plopped herself down beside her brother and set to work. "And there might even be one more thing in here someplace..."

For the first time, David looked up at the porch where Joanna stood framed in the doorway. After nine years of marriage and two babies, she was more beautiful than ever and his heart did what it always did at the sight of her, rose straight up inside his chest until he felt as if he could float.

"Hello, wife," he said softly.

Joanna smiled. "Hello, husband."

He mounted the steps slowly, his eyes never leaving hers, and when he reached the porch she went into his arms and kissed him.

"A year," she whispered, her lips warm against his cold cheek. "That's how long it seems since you left yesterday morning. A year or maybe a month or—"

David kissed her again. "I know. The next time I have to go into the city, you and the kids are coming with me."

"That sounds like a wonderful idea. How's the apartment?"

"Fine. Mrs. Timmons sends her best." David drew back, then held out the package. "I brought you something."

Joanna looked at the box and smiled. "Do I get to guess what it is?"

"Sure. Three guesses, then you pay a penalty."

She pursed her lips. The box was blue. It was small and square. It came from Tiffany's...

"A bread board?" she asked innocently.

David's lips twitched. "Try again."

"Um...a vacuum cleaner?"

"Last shot, coming up."

"Let's see...a new washing machine?"

He sighed. "Not again."

"Well, that's what happens when you have twins. The washing machine just works itself to death."

"Yeah." He smiled. "And you've used up all three guesses, Mrs. Adams. So I guess you'll just have to pay the penalty."

Joanna laughed softly. "Oh, my."

His grin turned wickedly sexy. "Oh, my, indeed."

"At least let me see what's in that box..."

"Uh-uh," he said, taking it out of her reach. "Not until you pay up."

Joanna batted her snow-tipped lashes at him. "Why, Mr. Adams, sir, whatever do you have in mind?"

David put his lips to his wife's ear and whispered exactly what he had in mind. She turned pink, laughed softly, and buried her face in his neck.

"That sounds wonderful. When?"

"Tonight, right after the kids are in bed. I'll build a fire, we'll open some champagne..."

Joanna's smile faded. She leaned back in her husband's arms and looked into his eyes. "I love you," she said softly.

David brushed his lips over hers. "My Gypsy," he whispered.

Then, together with their son and daughter, Joanna and David Adams went inside their home and closed the door.